I0772329

RIVER OF LAVENDER

ALLIUM SERIES BOOK THREE

MALLORY BENJAMIN

RIVER OF LAVENDER

To Anthony—I will choose you in every lifetime.

NARWAY
KITLARN
THE DARK KINGDOM OF TENNEBRIS

BACKERLY
PALM
ADDLER
LAKEWOOD

The Light Kingdom of Lux
Sunindaya River
Luxian City
Bay
Public Beaches

GODDESS TEMPLES
WATERFALL
LUXIAN JUNGLE
THE HUT

BRIGHTA
TENTS
MORTAL TERRITORY

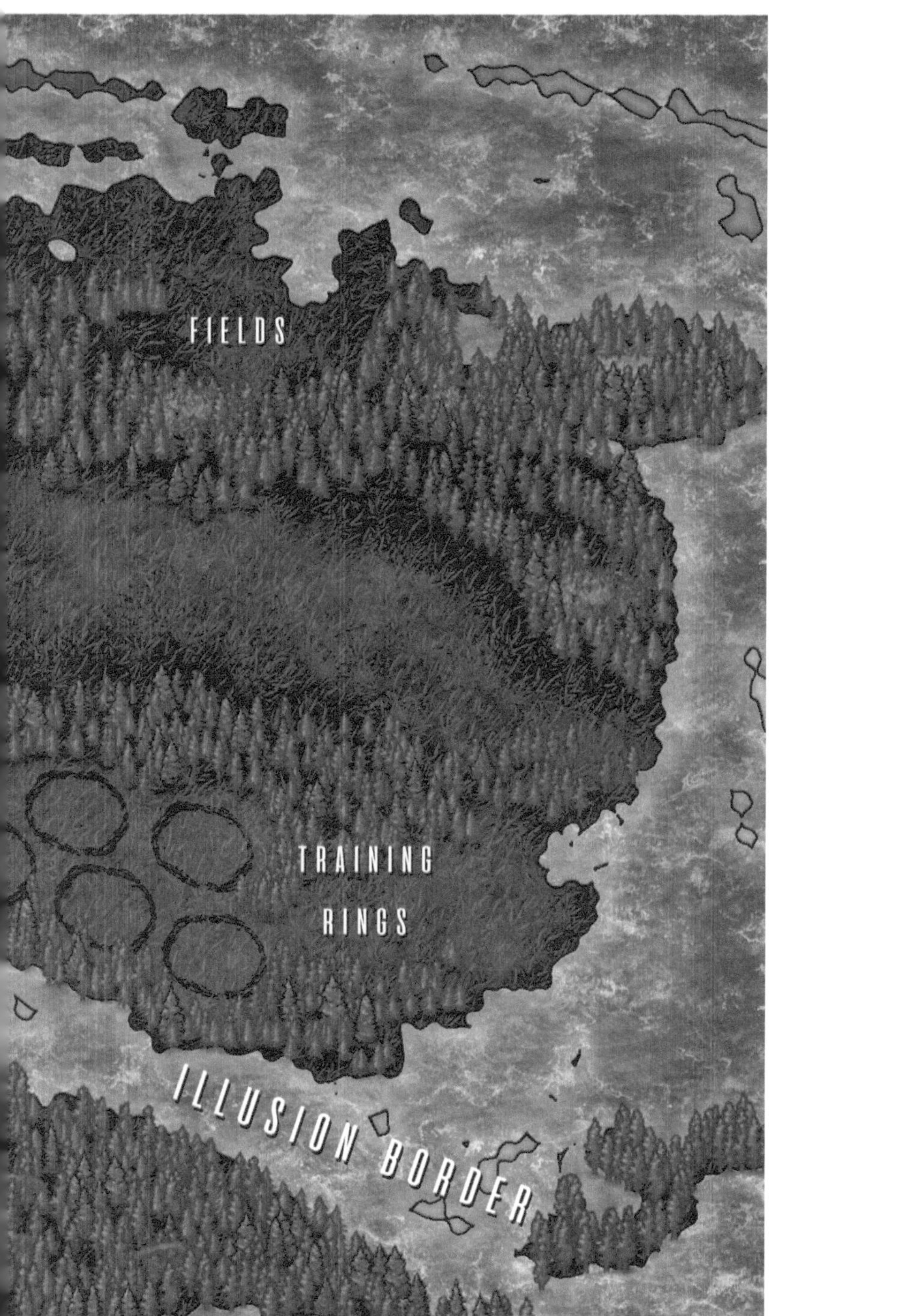

FIELDS
TRAINING
RINGS
ILLUSION BORDER

———

Please note this book is dark—darker than the first two in the series. This is the conclusion to Scotlind Rumor's story, and in order to get there, the characters face a lot of hardships. If you're ready, prepare to enter Allium through Scottie's eyes for the final time.

Visit malwrites.com for a full list of content warnings.

———

PROLOGUE

SAVANNAH

"You're needed in the war tent."

"War tent?" I whipped my head toward the soldier who approached me. It was the only tent that held detailed maps of each territory. My father often went there alone to think, but he never requested anyone to join him unless he was holding council. "What's being discussed? What happened?"

"I wasn't privy to that information. I only know it's where your father is, and that he requested your presence immediately."

"The meeting is now? I'm nowhere close to there."

He cocked a grin like he knew I was screwed. "Better get running, *Lavender*."

I bristled. I hated the nickname my father's men gave me ever since I started dyeing my hair purple. Not that I was going to change it back to my natural blonde just because they didn't like it. I loved my hair, and I knew I looked good. I was about to lay into him and tell him just that, but he was right. I had to run if I wanted to even remotely make it on time, and my dad wouldn't wait for me to start a meeting. It was a lesson I learned one too many times, and there was no way I was missing this. I started sprinting across the stretch of flat land, not caring who I blew past in the process or how crazy I looked.

When I pushed the flaps open, I found my father and brother already sitting at the table. Wheezing, I rested my hands on my knees while scanning the rest of the tent, but no one else was here. "I thought there was a meeting?"

I could feel my father's gaze assessing me. He eyed my newest tattoo across my forearm before his gaze strayed to the large hoop ring through my nose. He hated all my piercings and tattoos, though I had way more of the latter. But I was old enough now that he couldn't stop me.

"There will be an official meeting soon," he said carefully. "I wanted to talk to you both before it happens."

I sank down into the chair next to my brother, still trying to catch my breath. My father folded his arms as he sat across from us. There was an Advenian map stretched in front of him with a half-drunk glass of ale sitting on top it.

I picked up the ale before my father could protest and finished it in one long gulp. He glared at me, but I only smiled. "It was ruining the map," I commented, cringing that the condensation had already seeped through the paper.

I loved the war tent. It was my favorite place in our home. It was the only place I liked here. I tried to leave the horrid tents whenever I could. But this tent... it held the wonders I sought. I often snuck in here to rummage through his files, snooping whenever I could. I stared at the maps, trying to memorize every place until my head throbbed, wishing I could see everything in person instead of just on paper.

My brother was tapping his foot against the grass beside me. He was anxious, and his nervous tics often drove me insane, though I tried not to let it show. He hated the tents too, or anywhere else for that matter, besides his lab.

"They're coming here."

"That's good news," I said slowly as I set the empty glass back down on the table away from the map. "I miss everyone. It's been a while since we had a visit—"

He cut me off. "It's not a visit. They're coming because they fled their city. You don't understand, Sav, they started a war, and they're bringing it right to us."

"Holy Goddess of shit balls." I blew out a breath.

No one said anything as the silence stretched out between us. I waited for my father to elaborate, but he didn't. My brother's leg shook to the point where he started rattling the table.

"Who is *everyone* exactly?" I finally asked because I knew it was eating my brother up inside, wondering if Arcane was included.

Wells tensed, and I gently placed my hand over his knee under the table so our father wouldn't see. I was hoping it would calm him, but I selfishly needed to stop his incessant shaking. It wasn't exactly a surprise Arcane and Wells had a history, but no one admitted it in front of our father.

"I'm not sure yet. Tezya only sent a brief message about coming and bringing *guests* along." His jaw worked as he pinched the bridge of his nose. The youngest prince often withheld important details that made my father furious, and this was just the cherry on top. And the fact that he was drinking—or had been prior to me finishing his ale— yeah, he was pissed off.

I shrugged. "So we'll fight. We all knew this was coming eventually. Their father is a dickwad."

"Absolutely not," he seethed, knocking over the empty glass, which was exactly why I downed it in the first place. "I didn't call you in here so you could join their cause."

I bristled. "Then why am I here? Why are you telling us any of this if you expect us to do nothing?"

He sighed heavily. "Because that's exactly what I'm begging you to do—nothing. I know you like running off. I know you don't like it here, Savannah, but you can't leave, not right now. Not when it's not safe."

"I'll be fine."

"No, you won't. You're a—"

"Yeah, yeah. I get it. I'm a human. I'm weak. You don't want me doing anything stupid. Can I go now?"

His thick brows furrowed as he assessed me, probably trying to gauge if I would listen to his warning. I leaned forward on the table, waiting for his reply. My fingers grazed over something thick that was definitely not a map. I leaned further into the wood, meeting his gaze so he didn't look down to see what my hands were doing.

My father didn't reply. He knew there was nothing he could say to get me to change my mind. If I wanted to leave, I could easily slip past the defenses without anyone knowing. I'd been doing it ever since I was sixteen, and now, seven years later, no one could stop me.

"Right. Well, this has been fun," I said as I rose from the table.

I didn't stop walking until I made it to my own tent. My hands were surprisingly steady as I looked down at the file I just stole from him.

It had one word on it. A name seemed more likely: *MaryLynn*. The woman whose picture marked the thick file was absolutely breathtaking. Her brown spiral curls curtained her oval face. She was abnormally pale, to the point where it would have looked sickly on anyone else, but it somehow added to her appeal. Her eyes kept drawing my attention. They were the lightest shade of blue, so translucent they were almost devoid of color, and despite her cool undertones, she seemed warm, and I knew she was important.

Letting out a breath, I opened the file and was not prepared for *who* I just discovered.

ONE
TEZYA

THIS WAS A SUICIDE MISSION. I was all too aware it was downright stupid to let Scotlind talk me into rescuing Sie, not that it took much convincing. I didn't give a shit what her annoying blonde friend wanted, but the moment *she* wanted it... I knew I'd do anything she asked.

I was terrified of what would happen next—terrified if we would even make it out alive. I knew our chances of getting caught were just as likely as getting killed.

My brain kept playing out different scenarios. I wasn't sure what would be worse—having them throw us into the prison or hand us over to the Lux King. I'd heard horror stories of the prison, but there was no way the King was getting his hands on Rumor ever again...

She hadn't spoken to me since the first day on the balcony when we arrived in Florida, and even then, her words were few and far between and every last one laced with anger. It was torment. I was terrified she wouldn't forgive all my lies. Not that she should. I didn't deserve it.

I rubbed the scab over my palm, which I found myself doing more times than I could count. I knew we had to rescue Sie. My feelings aside, it was what Scottie wanted, what she *needed*. She felt guilty about his imprisonment. I could see it in her eyes. She was determined to get him back, and she'd do it with or without my help.

But what ate at me the most was if by some miracle we did succeed... What would happen then? What if she wanted him? If she chose him over me—

I gritted my teeth as I closed my palm over my scar. I'd accept it if she wanted Sie back in more ways than one.

"What's your plan?" I asked Peter. "You said you can scope out the prison without getting caught, so how do you plan on doing it?" The male had fully recovered, and I found I liked him unconscious better. He never stopped talking and was enjoying the tension between Scotlind and me too much.

"Go in the trench as a fish, turn into a fly or a spider or whatever small creature I fancy once I get down there, scope it out, then come back up. Easy-peasy."

He made a motion of a spider crawling with his fingers, and I had to stifle a laugh to even take him seriously.

"You are talking about breaking into the most heavily guarded place of our kind. I wouldn't call it *easy-peasy*," Dovelyn snapped.

Dove and Kallon came to the Florida condo yesterday. I was thankful they were willing to help, no questions asked, even if neither of them agreed with it. Dove told us the King hadn't noticed our disappearances yet. Thanks to her cover story and her threats to Arcane, we had a week, maybe two, before he would figure it out.

Peter turned to my sister and smiled, two dimples indenting his silken cheeks. "I'm just having a look. People only notice things when they suspect something. Besides, I've snuck into council meetings you had with your father-king, and *you* never noticed."

Dovelyn glared at Peter. She'd been lying on the sofa, the perfect image of cool indifference, but I knew she was anything but. "If you ever spy on me again," her gaze narrowed, "I will remove your eyes from your skull and your tongue from your throat so you can never—"

"Enough bickering," Kallon interrupted. "If Peter wants to scope out the prison and put his life at risk, then let him. Rescuing Sie is already near impossible, so if he can gather any intel, it will only help us."

Peter just nodded, having complete dumb faith in himself.

"How long can you stay shifted?" I asked, not sharing any confidence in his skills.

"About twenty to twenty-four hours. It depends on what I shift into and how many shifts I make."

"Shift as little as possible then. The prison is located at the bottom of what the mortals call the Mariana Trench. It leads to the deepest part of the ocean. The passage is shielded from portal and teleport users, so the only way in or out is to swim. Kallon can portal you to the surface where the opening of the trench is, but from there, you'll have to go down on your own."

I could tell he wasn't taking this seriously. He wasn't even looking at me as I talked. "Don't do anything stupid," I warned. I didn't particularly care what happened to him, but I knew Scottie did, and it would break her if he didn't come back. "I don't care what you see down there," I added. "You scope out the prison, learn the guard rotation for as long as you can, and then you get out. Don't rescue Sie on your own, even if you find him."

Peter glared at me, and I knew it was something that crossed his mind. It would kill him to see Sie and not be able to save him right away. Not that Peter was even capable of rescuing him. He didn't possess air or water elemental abilities. An Advenian without those powers wouldn't survive the swim without an air shield over their face. But I didn't put it past him to convince Sie to compel an air guard and still attempt the rescue himself. "I mean it, Peter. You'll only get yourself killed if you try to do this on your own."

"Alright," he finally agreed before turning toward Scottie. She had been surprisingly silent throughout the whole conversation, taking everything in.

"Please be safe," she said softly to him. Then even softer she whispered, "I can't lose you too."

He pulled her into a hug, tucking his head into her neck, before he smirked. "Well, now I guess I have to come back since I'm so important to you and all." She laughed, the sound more of a sob being muffled through tears. "I'll see you in about twenty hours," he said as he stepped out of her grip.

Peter turned toward where Kallon was lurking in the corner. Her hair was braided out of her face. Today it was black and saffron, the two colors mixing in intricate twists behind her back. She was armed with hidden daggers in case anything went awry. Peter had just as many, and I prayed he knew how to use them. Not that it would do much against all the guards in the prison. They were the most lethal and powerful Advenians from both the Tennebrisian guard and the Luxian army. Only the top of each took shifts watching over the prisoners.

Before Brock became second in command, he used to get rotated down there, which was the only reason I knew anything about it, but he barely went into details. He hated it, claimed over and over it was the most horrid, fucked up place imaginable. A pang of guilt rang through me.

I prayed Rainer was able to find him—not because he knew the prison layout better than anyone, and we wouldn't have to go in blindly if he were here—I honestly didn't give a shit if Brock wanted to sit this one out or not. I just needed him to be okay.

I shook my head, knowing Brock, he'd offer to help even if he could barely stand up straight.

I tried not to think about the constant torture he was most likely enduring just because of his association to us. He didn't deserve whatever he was going through. Everything that's happened in his life has been from taking on punishments for things he didn't do, and I fucking hated that I was now adding to the list.

"You ready?" Kallon asked Peter as she came up behind him.

They disappeared before he could nod, leaving a trail of black and purple smoke in their wake.

———

I DIDN'T THINK things could get any more tense as Rumor, Dovelyn, and I ate breakfast the next morning. Twenty-six hours had passed, and they should have been back by now.

"You know we have to leave today. Whether they come back or not. We can't stay and wait for them," Dove said as she took a sip from her glass.

Scottie's plate was untouched. She hadn't eaten anything since Kallon and Peter left yesterday. She set her fork down—which she was only using to move food around her plate—and glared at Dovelyn. "You can leave whenever you want. The door is there, but I'm staying and waiting for them."

Dovelyn's icy eyes turned to her. "Don't you dare order me around in *my* house."

"This isn't your house. It's Tezya's, and I'm not ordering you. I'm informing you where the door is. Unless you want to use the balcony again. Feel free to fly away. Whichever you prefer."

"Well, you're a bitch this morning. All I was saying is that the King is bound to notice you and the blonde's disappearances, and if he realizes it earlier than anticipated, and you're still here, you'll regret it when he finds you. We already agreed before Kal and your friend left that we're leaving the condo tonight. This is the first place he's going to look for you, and it's foolish to wait here any longer."

"Don't pretend to care about me," Scottie snapped. I was surprised to see so much loathing in her voice. I knew the two of them never got along, but this was different.

"I don't," Dovelyn said casually, "but my brother does, and I care for him."

"Is that really all you're worried about? That your brother would be sad if I was gone?" Scottie nodded her head toward me but didn't turn her gaze away from Dovelyn. "Or are you worried that if I'm captured, I'd join your father? I overheard the conversation you had with Tezya. I think you used the phrase *I will turn against him.*"

Holy shit. Everything stilled. Dovelyn actually stopped eating to glare at Scotlind.

"No? You don't want to talk about that?" Scottie sneered into the silence with a surprising amount of coolness in her voice. Dove and I were still speechless. "How about we talk about the fact that you were the reason I was sent to Tennebris. Did you murder my parents?"

Fuck. That confirmed she overheard *everything*. My mind whirled. How long had that been stirring inside her?

"What? No, of course I didn't kill them. I wouldn't do that," Dove deadpanned.

"I don't believe you."

"You don't know what you're talking about. I didn't kill your parents."

"Then why don't you enlighten me?"

Dovelyn said nothing.

"No? You don't want to talk about that either?" Scottie huffed. "Tell me, what other secrets are the two of you hiding?"

I felt gutted, finally understanding the full extent of her anger. I promised I wouldn't keep anything else from her, but I lied. Again.

I was about to explain when Kallon and Peter portaled back. They were both drenched in water with a puddle already collecting under their feet.

Scottie jumped to her feet and rushed over to them. "Are you okay? What happened?"

"Let them breathe," Dove panned dryly. She continued to eat her breakfast unfazed by their return or the glimpse of the conversation we just had. But I couldn't let go of Scottie's words, of what she'd overheard.

"We can get into the prison," Peter panted. His emotions were flickering so fast between relief and worry, it was giving my ability whiplash. "I found a way to get Sie out, but we have to go right now."

TWO

SCOTLIND

"WE'RE NOT RESCUING Sie right now," Dovelyn said, wiping the crazed smile off Peter's face. "I agreed to make a plan today, and then help move you to a new location."

"We can't wait. We have to get him out *now*—" Peter started to cut in.

"You aren't in any position to make demands," Dovelyn snapped. "You can barely breathe, and your body needs time to refill your reserves."

"My reserves are fine."

"Breaking into the prison isn't a last minute thing with half-ass plans. I'll come back in a week, and we'll get him out then. That's final." Dovelyn crossed her arms over her chest, still refusing to get up from her chair. "It gives you time to finalize a plan and—"

"Sie doesn't have a week." Everyone stilled at Peter's words. "He's dying. I don't even know if he has a day."

"What makes you say that?" Tezya asked.

"Because I saw it. I saw him while I was down there."

"Bullshit," Dovelyn drawled. "You just don't want to wait."

"You're right. I don't want to wait," Peter said. "But I'm also not lying. Sie *is* dying. His arm's broken, and—"

"You want to prioritize him because of a broken arm?" Dovelyn scoffed.

"No." Peter ground his jaw. "I want to prioritize him because he has a fever. His body broke out in a sweat, and he's half convulsing. They left the bone sticking out of him. They aren't healing him."

"Shit," Tezya swore as his gaze flicked to his sister's.

"Why do we have to wait a week?" I asked, not understanding why they were so hesitant.

"Your friend will still be fine in a week," was all Dovelyn said, completely ignoring my question.

"No, he won't," Peter retorted. "Besides, wouldn't it be better to act right away? Waiting will only risk the Lux King finding out we're all gone, and everything I did to scope out the prison will be for nothing if he ups the security down there."

"He won't realize you're missing in a week. We have time," Dovelyn said before leaning back into her seat, her expression set.

"And how exactly is he not going to realize we're all missing yet? It's been, what, three days, hasn't it?" Peter asked, holding up three fingers for emphasis.

"Dove told her father we're taking a trip to the hut," Kallon answered as she gestured to Tezya and Dovelyn. "She said that Tezya needed a distraction from Scotlind. We take trips there often to get away from the castle, so he didn't think twice about it."

"And me? I was chained in Arcane's room. Won't he notice I'm not there?" I asked.

"She threatened Arcane with the only thing he cares about, so he's putting up the facade that he's still running tests on you, and you can't leave his lab. The King wants to make your blood into serums, so he won't bother Arcane if he believes he's getting close to succeeding."

"Okay, fine," Peter countered. "The bitchy silver one came up with good excuses." Dovelyn's eyes narrowed at Peter's nickname for her, but he was either oblivious to it or didn't care. "But it still doesn't fix the issue that Sie isn't going to make it a week," he continued. "I'm not risking him by waiting."

"The King still has Brock," Tezya said. "Rainer is searching for him right now, but he can't find him. That's why we need another week. It's not just about Sie."

"What do you mean he can't find him?" I asked. Guilt washed over me—I completely forgot about Tezya's two other friends. I knew Tezya told me Brock was missing, but that was back in Tennebris. I assumed Rainer already found him, but now, knowing he hadn't...

Dove turned to me. "Ever since you blinded him, no one's seen him."

"It's not her fault," Tezya warned.

Dovelyn blew out a breath, turning the other way.

"We were going to go back to help Rainer find him," Kallon said, lowering her voice. "We need to get Brock out of the castle before we go after Sie."

I swallowed. A lot was at stake because Tezya freed us. I was still furious at him for lying to me and confused on his part for why I was sent to Tennebris, but I was also grateful. He risked everything to get me and Peter out of there, and now he was putting his friends at risk because of it.

"I'm sorry about Brock," I said into the silence. I felt horrible that I hadn't thought about him again. I just assumed he recovered, but if he was still blind...

"We'll find him," Tezya said, looking right at me.

"Is this Brock person dying?" Peter asked. "Because my friend is."

No one answered. I could tell Tezya was working through both options—getting Sie or Brock first.

It was Kallon who finally broke the silence, "Brock isn't dying. The King won't kill him, but there's a good chance he's being tortured."

"Then please, *please*," Peter's voice broke, "can we save Sie first?"

"You said you have a plan to get him out? Can it be done without anyone realizing he's gone?" Tezya asked.

Peter grinned, and it looked like it belonged to a madman. "I can make it look like Sie died in the prison. No one will even know he's missing."

———

AFTER we finally convinced Dovelyn to get Sie out before Brock, we'd been discussing what Peter observed for the past four hours—detailing the prison layout and the guards' rotation schedules. Peter planned to take out and transform into one with fuchsia colored eyes that had direct access to Sie.

"I'm going with," I said.

"No, you aren't," Dove quipped. "You won't be helpful. You're staying here with Tezya."

There was no way I was staying in this tiny room alone with Tezya while everyone else rescued Sie. We moved locations right after we fought over who to rescue first and have been staying in something called a *motel*. I wanted to be in Tezya's condo again. I took the luxury and extra space for granted. The new place only consisted of one small room where the bed took up the entirety of the space and it wasn't even a particularly large bed. All of us were crammed around it, leaning against the walls, talking—more like arguing—over a plan. Only Peter lounged on the mattress with his arms folded behind his head.

"I can breathe underwater, and it's an underwater prison. How can you say I won't be helpful?"

"Because you've barely practiced. You're a novice when it comes to your abilities. Your reserves were never tested, and you have no idea how long you can maintain your powers. The last thing we need is for you to stop breathing underwater and die." Dovelyn inspected her nails, not even bothering to look at me as she spoke.

"We only have to be submerged in water to go down through the trench," I countered, recalling every detail Peter told us about the prison. I withheld a shudder as I tried not to linger on the prison itself. I internally revolted when Peter was describing the two sections: the cages suspended above some sort of larger, communal one below. "Once we enter, it's just like breathing regular air. I can hold my breath for that long."

"You won't be useful once we're down there," Kallon said,

surprising me. "So it really doesn't matter if you can or can't hold your breath for a period of time."

I bristled at the harshness of Kallon's words as I scanned the room for anyone to side with me, but no one spoke up. I looked at Kallon. Her yellow eyes matched half her dyed hair today. Out of everyone, I thought she would've agreed with me.

She seemed to sense my disappointment. "I'm sorry, babes, but Dove kind of has a point. I'm not going down either. Besides, the more people that go, the more Dovelyn has to cast her invisibility over, and the more I have to portal. It gets too risky. If either of us diminishes our reserves, we're screwed. The less people the better."

"That's bullshit—" I started, knowing full well Kallon was strong enough. Her portals were only taxing when she created new ones or if she was transferring a lot of people. One more wasn't going to make a difference. And Dovelyn was known to be the strongest air user in Lux. It was just a pathetic excuse to leave me behind.

"It's final," Tezya interrupted, and I shot daggers his way, but he didn't flinch away from my glare. Instead, he ignored me and turned to Peter. "Go over your plan again."

Peter groaned. "We already went over it five times."

"You'll go over it a hundred more if that's what it takes until everyone knows exactly what's happening. You won't be able to talk once you enter so it's imperative every second is accounted for."

I could sense Tezya's military leadership shining through, and I half wondered why he wasn't arguing to join them. It didn't seem like him to stay behind, and no matter how good of a mask he donned, I could see through it. He didn't like the idea of not going either. He was nervous.

"Kallon will portal us to the entrance of the trench," Dovelyn answered. "From there, Peter and I go down. Kal will wait at the surface. I'll have my invisibility over the two of us, as well as one over Kallon."

Peter spoke next, "Once we're in, I'll find the guard that lingers by Sie's cell. We'll wait until he goes to the bathroom, which he does often because he sneaks drinks on the job, and I'll knock him out.

"Then I'll shift into him and unlock Sie's cell, pretending to take him to the torture room, but we won't make it there." He pointed to a spot on a piece of paper where he sketched a hand-drawn map of the prison. It looked more like a circular, spiraling maze than holding cells. I was impressed Peter was able to scope out so much of it, nonetheless, recall all the painstaking details. Even if the map looked like a five-year-old drew it, it held the information we needed for the plan to work. "There's a section here," Peter pointed, "where there aren't any prisoner cages. Once we get here, Dovelyn will cast her invisibility over us, and we'll bring Sie into the bathroom where the real guard is tied up. We'll swap their outfits, and then I'll shove the guard into Sie's cage."

"Won't people recognize he's not really Sie?" Kallon asked.

"Yeah." Peter shrugged. "But I'm gonna beat the crap out of him, so he won't be recognizable."

"He's eventually going to heal though. You can't beat him up that badly," Kallon said.

Peter just grinned. "I won't have to. After I re-lock Sie's cage, I'll shift into a bear, and then with her invisibility," he gestured toward Dovelyn, "I'll tear open the bottom of the cage, sending the fake Sie into the pit below, making it look like the crate gave out."

"That's barbaric," I gasped. Even if the reasoning made sense, we couldn't kill a guard just for working there, and the way Peter described the lower level... there was no way he was going to survive, and what they'd have to do to him to pull it off... "You said everyone dies that goes into the pit, how can you send a guard in there?"

"Scottie, if you met this guard, you'd want him dead. Trust me."

I crossed my arms, not bothering to reply. I trusted Peter's judgment, but it still felt wrong.

"That's risking that no one stops and questions you," Tezya said. "You could blow your cover. If someone stops you, you'll basically be exchanging Sie's spot in the prison for yourself. And," he added, "what happens if someone is at this location? Dove might not be able to put Sie under her invisibility, and you'd be forced to go through with the torture room." Tezya gestured toward the spot on the map Peter still had his finger on.

"I'll stall." Peter shrugged. "I'll tie my shoe or something."

"And if you can't?" Tezya asked. "What happens if you have to bring Sie into it? Are you prepared to torture him?"

Peter shifted on the bed. "I'll manage."

"And you're comfortable with that?" Tezya pressed. "Because this plan has *you* at risk more than anyone else. If you get caught, Dovelyn can't save you."

"I know the risk," Peter replied harshly. "The plan will work, but we'll have to time everything perfectly. The prison entrance only opens once a day. It's the reason it took me so long to come back. Once we enter, we'll be stuck there for exactly twenty-four hours. We'll have to plan to break Sie out in perfect timing with the prison opening for the change of shift."

No one commented on what that would mean. Dovelyn and Peter wouldn't be able to hold their abilities for another day. If they didn't make it out during the next change, they were never coming back. Their reserves would drain, and they'd be captured along with Sie.

I looked over at my friend lounging on the bed. He looked nowhere near ready to maintain his ability for an entire day, nonetheless, with multiple shifts this plan would require him to make.

He needed me. This plan needed me. I could use my enhancement to make sure their powers lasted long enough. I could do it.

"Are you sure you don't want me to go?" Tezya asked. "I could be useful if you get into trouble."

"No offense, Fire Boy, but your flames won't have any effect on the water, and if you burn the prison down, we're all dead. It's best if you sit this one out," Peter interjected.

I knew Tezya wasn't talking about his flames. He was talking about his Dark ability, his Tennebrisian power—his compulsion. But Peter was unconscious when he saved us, so he still had no idea what Tezya was capable of.

"No, Tez," Dove answered. "It's not worth the risk to bring you. One, I don't want you using your powers, and two, I can't cast that much of my own power to make you invisible too. My reserves wouldn't last with you there."

"Then bring me too," I said. I was planning on going whether or not they agreed with me, but it would be a lot easier if they'd just say yes. "I'll use my enhancement on you so you can use more of your air power to shield us."

"No," Tezya and Dove both said at the same time, before Dovelyn went on. "You haven't trained with your enhancement at all. What if you can only use it for fifteen minutes? There's no guarantee you'd be able to maintain that kind of power, and if you fail, you and Tezya will be seen, and we'll all be dead. You're too risky to bring along. You and Tezya will wait for us here. The plan is fine without you two."

"I used my enhancement for a week straight when your father had me—"

"One week," Dovelyn interrupted, her voice an icy rage. "You want to use that for your argument? That you trained for *one week*? I have a century over you."

I crossed my arms as I slumped back against the wall. I'd never been more pissed off about my lack of training than I was right now. If I'd grown up in Lux and got to use my powers during school, if I'd trained my entire life with my abilities like everyone else had, they wouldn't be questioning me. I knew I could do it. I knew I was capable. It'd be taxing and take everything out of me, but I could feel it in my bones that I would manage.

Peter looked between Tezya and me and smiled. "Oh, I would love to be a fly on the wall while you two are in here alone."

Kallon gave Peter a knowing look, and he threw his hands up as he corrected, "Yuck. Not like that *bumblebee*. They're fighting not sleeping with each other. I just meant this should be interesting."

"Bumblebee?" Kallon arched a thin brow.

He pointed to her hair. "Yeah cause black and yellow, get it? And I'm pretty confident you've got a stinger on you somewhere too."

Tezya looked like he was about ready to murder Peter, and I wasn't far off from doing it myself too.

Kallon looked him up and down before saying, "You're odd."

"Right back at—"

"Enough chit-chat," Dovelyn interrupted. "I think this is a horrible idea to begin with, and if I sit on it any longer, I won't go."

"Why are you helping us?" Peter asked, bringing his arms in front of him as he leaned forward on the bed.

"I'm not doing it for you or for Sie."

"Then why?" he pressed.

Kallon answered when Dovelyn didn't, "Because Tezya asked us to help. Actually he begged us to help…"

"That's enough," Tezya cut her off.

"How are you planning on keeping a shield over Kallon if you're down in the prison?" I asked Dovelyn, trying another tactic.

She turned to me, then shrugged. "I learned to separate my abilities."

"Is separating your abilities the same as our protective shields?"

"No, but the end result is similar."

"How?" I pressed.

"We don't have time for a history lesson," Dovelyn deadpanned.

Peter grinned as he cut in, "Actually, we do. We have to wait for the prison entrance to reopen for shift change, so we have about," he paused, pretending to look at his wrist, "ten minutes before we have to leave, and I'd *love* to hear your lesson."

Dovelyn pinched the bridge of her nose, but to my surprise, she answered, "Separating your powers allows you to leave your magic running even after you're gone. You have to initially be present to start your magic in a particular place, but if you have enough concentration and power, you can travel far distances while it's still working."

"Is that what keeps the balcony covered in Tezya's condo?" I asked, thinking back to how he'd told me it was always shielded.

"Almost. That's called partition of powers and it's even more rare than separation. I created the shield when I was at his condo, but in order to leave it up permanently without me having to concentrate, I had to give up a piece of my reserve." She sighed. "I guess there's no point in having it there now. In a couple of weeks, whenever my father realizes we've all left, he'll destroy the place." She shrugged. "It's why most Advenians don't create partitions, and they choose separation instead. You might realize one day you no longer need it, but you can never get that power back."

I was about to ask her to elaborate, but Kallon beat me to it. "Think of it like my portals," she said. "I have to be present to create each portal, but once it's up, my magic stays. The only difference is my portals don't permanently steal from my reserves. Partition is really advanced and not all ranks are capable of it. And you need a large reserve to even be able to manage it. Not all abilities have the potential for it so it's rarely taught.

"Then you have the protective shields surrounding Lux, Tennebris, and the prison. They're slightly different from partition," Kallon continued. "Partition of magic can remain in place for the duration of an Advenian's life, but it's technically still temporary. If the person who created it dies, their powers will fade with them. It's only permanent while the Advenian is alive. But the protective shields never go away. It took hundreds of air and illusion users to originally erect them, and they had to do it during the remaining effects of Lakimi. We don't have the time now to explain it all to you, but it involves reciting specific prayers to the Goddesses, and if it's done correctly, the shields become permanent. They will remain forever, even after the Advenians who made them die."

"What did Advenians do when they first came here?" Peter asked, seeming genuinely curious, and it made me wonder if this was something only taught in Lux. Our curriculum was supposed to be equivalent, but I was second guessing everything we'd ever been taught.

"They had air and illusion users stationed outside each perimeter and usually compulsion users in case a mortal did come across it," Kallon answered. "They constantly had to reinforce it and took turns in shifts. Think of it like tiers. Separation most Advenians are capable of, it just depends on how many and how far you can go with it. It drains your reserves, but with rest, it'll replenish. Partition permanently steals, but it will last as long as the Advenian who made it is alive, and our protective shields surpass the user as long as it was done under Lakimi."

"So you're willing to give up a piece of your reserves to rescue Sie?" Peter asked Dovelyn.

"No. I'm using separation."

"But separation will drain your reserves," I pressed. "You said you need to concentrate to be able to use it—"

"Don't," Dovelyn cut me off. "I know what you're trying to do, and it's not working. I don't need or want your help."

I went to open my mouth, but Dovelyn stopped me. "It's been ten minutes. Let's go before I change my mind." She walked over to Kallon and took her hand.

"Be safe," Tezya said, and I didn't miss the wariness in his voice.

"Always." Dovelyn smiled at her brother, and it was warm and sweet, the complete opposite of her usual cool arrogance. It was strange to see her soft side, despite knowing they were close.

Peter rose and grabbed Kallon's other hand.

I took a steadying breath, praying this would work. Tezya and I were on the opposite side of the room, the only ones not touching her.

As soon as Kallon opened the portal, I reached my enhancement toward her, stretching and opening the black and purple dome with my powers.

Kallon's yellow eyes widened once she felt what I was doing. Her portal expanded over the entire room, taking Tezya and I with her.

"Shit—" Tezya started to say as he leapt toward me, but we were already gone, swallowed whole in an endless vortex with nothing but a lingering trail of black and purple smoke.

THREE
SCOTLIND

I CURSED my stomach as nausea threatened to spill out of me. Even though only a few minutes had passed, it felt like hours stuck inside the portal. The trench was on the opposite side of the planet—we were lucky Kallon had already set up a portal close to the opening. She told us that decades ago, she traveled with Brock when he was stationed to guard and created one in case he needed a quick out. So the direct portal destination saved us precious time, but the long distance had my gut spinning.

It was made worse by Kallon not anchoring us. I learned the hard way that *not* holding onto her hand while we jumped had Tezya and I spinning in endless circles. She was the only one who could truly navigate through it, but when I connected my enhancement to hers, it was like I could glimpse a touch of her ability. It allowed me to keep us tethered to her so we wouldn't get permanently lost inside the portal. But the constant twirling had my body intertwining with Tezya's to the point where I couldn't tell where his started and mine ended.

My vision blurred with blue as a large wave tumbled over us. For a split second, the tumbling crest felt so similar to the spinning motion of the portal and the depths of the ocean looked almost as dark that it took me a second to process we were here. A rough hand grabbed onto my wrist and yanked me toward the surface, but it was just as dark above the water. Black clouds multiplied over us as rain started pouring in torrents from the sky. The water was so numbingly cold I couldn't feel any of my limbs.

I glanced over at Tezya. He was about to open his mouth to shout something at me, but I beat him to it. "I told you I can help," I said right before another wave tumbled over us, and we were pulled under again. I swam against the current, trying to break the surface, but the force of the wave kept pushing me down.

I forced myself to open my mouth under the water, breathing just as easily as I could above it, but Tezya—who refused to let go of my wrist—couldn't. If we stayed under too long he'd die, and the thought had me swimming harder and faster.

Tezya spit out sea water once we finally resurfaced. He didn't hesitate as he pushed my body against his, pulling me in close like he was scared of losing me. His chest was heaving deeply against mine, and I hated that I found it comforting.

"Can you add to Dovelyn's power from here?" Kallon shouted at me over the pounding rain. We were a mile off from the entrance of the trench. "If you stay with me, using your enhancement from the water, it won't risk Dovelyn having to use more of her invisibility inside the prison."

Tezya's grip tightened around me, adding warmth wherever his body met with mine. I was so frozen from the water that I convinced myself it was the only reason I wasn't pushing him off.

I spread my fingers and shook them out, embracing in the sensation of moving them. My power instantly gravitated toward his, and I realized he was using his fire, casting controlled amounts of it into the sea around us, warming the water.

The sky darkened even more, and the gray clouds above us turned fully black. Wind was ripping all around us, stirring the waves and making them more monstrous and powerful.

"I'd be more helpful below—" Another wave devoured us, halting our conversation. Tezya's grip on me tightened as we plummeted further into the sea. The warmth of the water vanished as he let go of his power and focused on swimming back up.

Dovelyn popped up from the water last. Her silver eyes met mine. "Scotlind needs to leave. I just had a vision. It'll be bad if she stays."

"That's bull—" I started to protest, calling Dovelyn's bluff, but she cut me off.

"No, it's not." Her silver eyes widened slightly as she took me in. I couldn't tell if it was from whatever vision she claimed she just had, or if she was still processing what I had done. I honestly was shocked it worked, that I could manipulate Kallon's power to my own will —*kind of*—by enhancing it. I got Tezya and I here, and I knew I could help, so I wasn't planning on backing down. Dovelyn's eyes narrowed like she knew it. "Get Scotlind out of here—"

Another wave pummeled over us before I thought to use my abilities. As I swam back up, I connected to the ocean, pushing the rough waves away from where we were treading water. Rain kept pouring from the sky and thunder roared from the distance.

Dovelyn caught on to what I was doing, and I felt the moment her air abilities flared as she created a shield over us, protecting us from the rain and lightning that was just about to strike.

"Portal her back now," Dovelyn said after everything calmed inside our protective bubble.

I twisted in Tezya's grip, but before I could say another word, Kallon grabbed onto Tezya and I, and we were swallowed up by her portal. The nausea took over in full force as we tumbled yet again through the purple and black mist.

I vomited on the floor as soon as she dumped us back into the cramped motel room. I went to look up at her, but she was already gone. She portaled back before I could attempt to connect my powers with hers again.

Crap.

The room felt infinitely smaller now that I was alone with Tezya. I turned toward him instead of the empty spot where Kallon just was. "Why didn't you do anything?" I spat as I started to push myself up to stand. He reached out his hand to help me, but I swatted it away. Then thought better of it and shoved him. "We could have helped. We could have done something!"

"No, we couldn't have."

"Why are you so adamant on *not* helping? Do you really think I'm so inexperienced that I'd mess everything up?" Tears pooled in my eyes, but I pushed them back. I was so sick of everyone doubting me. So sick of not having a say in what *I* wanted to do, in what I was capable of. I shoved him again and he let me, this time his back slammed into the wall.

Neither of us had anywhere to go. I was standing in front of him, the bed to my back.

I shoved him again.

Then again.

My hands were twisted in his shirt before his eyes softened. "Rumor, if Dove had a vision with you there that went south, we have to trust it."

"You and I both know she was just making that up because she didn't want me there."

"She wasn't," he said hoarsely. "I felt her emotions. She did have a vision, Scotlind, and all I could sense from her was fear." I didn't say anything. I just kept staring at him, not wanting to believe it. "I hated leaving them too," he added more softly. "I'm just as terrified as you are that they're alone right now, and we're stuck in here and can't help."

"Then why did you let Kallon bring us back?" I realized he might not have been able to stop her, that my anger was probably unwarranted, and I was projecting on him, but I was so frustrated. I wanted to help so badly—

"Because I trust my sister. I've been a fool in the past for not believing her visions, and I don't want to risk anything happening to you." His voice turned into a whisper. "I can't let anything happen to you."

I didn't respond for an embarrassingly long time. I just kept staring into his eyes, watching as water dripped over his face, completely mesmerized by it. We were both drenched from the ocean, water was collecting on the tiled floor around us.

I was in a stupor until a droplet landed on my forearm, and I realized my hands were still resting over his chest from when I shoved him. I took a step back, careful to avoid the bed, and started to pace instead.

I tried to distract myself from the task they would have to pull off, from the fact that they were all risking their lives because *I* demanded we rescue Sie. He didn't deserve to die in the prison. I knew that. I was riddled with guilt because of it, but now that it was actually happening, that we were really rescuing him, I couldn't stop thinking about the guilt I'd have if we failed. What if Peter, Dovelyn, and Kallon ended up in the prison with him? Or worse, what if they all ended up dead?

Everyone was risking themselves for this, for the mistake we both made the night of his coronation, and I was stuck in a small bedroom with Tezya, while we waited and waited and waited.

FOUR

DOVELYN

HOLDING hands with the Tennebrisian while swimming was just about the worst thing I'd done this past decade. He hadn't shifted yet. I wouldn't let him. I was supposed to fly above him, but with the storm I couldn't risk it. I wasn't as good with shields as Arcane was and there was no way I was risking damage to my wings. Which meant I had to swim, and I *hated* swimming.

There was no way I'd be able to maintain my invisibility over him in the vast ocean if we weren't close, and I refused to touch a fish. Their slimy scales disgusted me and were one of the many things I hated about the ocean. Water alone was my least favorite element, and the ocean was downright terrifying.

All the elements were their own living entity without an Advenian controlling it. It was why there was such an emphasis on users who could create versus manipulate. And water was always the most erratic and unpredictable to me.

Fire was confined to the ground, only expanding upward as it consumed trees and bushes through smoke. If the flames didn't have fuel or oxygen in the air, they'd be extinguished. But water... it engulfed everything in its path. It didn't have a weakness. You couldn't just take it away. If you added fire to it, it'd become a molten, scalding liquid. If you threw wind at it, you could only momentarily displace it before it would get angry and rush back in retaliation. The ground did nothing to it. If water was strong enough, it could erode mountains to carve out the space it needed.

I hated it. Not that I'd ever admit it to anyone, but whenever I willed my wings to emerge so I could fly in the sky, I opted to soar over the Luxian jungle rather than the ocean and bay surrounding the island. I often found myself by the Goddess Temples, and I wished more than anything I was in their presence now. I wanted to be high above the earth where the sun against my back felt blistering and the air was drier and hotter. I wanted the warmth on my wings as I beat them against the breeze and missed the sting of the wind on my face. But more than anything, I wanted to be alone with the Goddesses.

I imagined myself there as I tried not to use too much of my powers to block the waves tumbling over us, but each time we plummeted into the cold depths of the sea, I couldn't help it. I forced myself not to think of the monstrous things lurking below us, forced myself not to focus on the creatures that could swallow us whole. The fact that humans swam in the ocean for fun astounded me. Luxians had shields in place by the bay to keep sharks and other creatures out, but the mortal beaches were exposed, exactly as we were now, and they didn't possess any powers to protect themselves.

The storm didn't allow me much time to dwell on my fears as monstrous wave after wave constantly tumbled over us, trying to rip us apart. I was barely able to pray to Pylemo while we half swam, half drowned. I tried to keep my mind void and just focus on the task at hand—on staying alive and making it to the trench. On numerous occasions, I swore we weren't going to make it. And if we did succeed, I had no idea how we were going to swim back across the ocean with a half unconscious man. Because that's what I figured he'd be—*if Sie was even still alive*—he wouldn't be fit for what we needed from him.

Peter, at least, didn't seem bothered by the ocean. He was dragging me through the water, pulling me behind him. I kept my invisibility over us, so I couldn't see him, but I knew he was straining against the ocean's full power, and I was only making things harder for him.

Swimming and me did not mix, and I couldn't really pretend I was helping much. Even while pushing back against the waves with my air powers, we were still being dragged under.

My abilities were already draining too fast, and as much as Scotlind's enhancement would have helped me, I couldn't risk her staying here. I just prayed that Tezya got her away from this place before my vision had time to come to fruition.

The gift of sight was a curse. It often led me to make the wrong choices in the hopes of trying to avoid whatever I saw, but sometimes the future had a way of coming true anyway. It didn't matter how much I tried to prevent it, it usually found me. I prayed this time it wouldn't because I saw all of us captured—Scotlind and Tezya included. In my vision, they entered the trench with us, and no one left. Peter was killed on the spot, Scotlind was thrown into the dark pit below the cages, and my sight ended just as Tezya jumped down the hole after her.

But if Tezya got Scotlind away from this place, if he listened, maybe we still had a chance. I had managed to avoid some visions in the past, not many, but there was still a possibility this one might not happen. At least that's what I kept telling myself as my limbs grew weak and my body turned numb. I couldn't feel anything except for Peter's hand. He was clenching my wrist so tight I thought it'd fall off.

I sent prayers to all twelve of the lesser Goddesses, calling them each by name, before I sent my last plea to Pylemo, praying we could pull this off. We were swimming against the current, and I refused to believe it was their sign of answering me, urging us to turn around now before it was too late.

Peter stopped pulling me through the waves, and it took me a moment to realize we made it. I'd never been to the trench before. I completely avoided it every time I was offered the opportunity to visit.

The water stilled, and I realized air users must have erected a shield over the opening. It wasn't strong enough to be noticeable to humans, but it tampered down the storm surrounding us. The pouring rain still pounded against my face, not that it mattered, every single part of me was frozen and wet. But we weren't being pulled under the current anymore, and I was finally able to pause long enough to look around.

I wished I hadn't. We were hovering over the darkest part of the ocean, haunting me with its depths below. It looked like a circular hole within the water itself and somehow Scotlind's deep blue eyes came to my mind. I bristled. I hated her. I hated the spell she had over my brother, and I hated that I saw what was coming... what my visions portrayed of her...

She would destroy Tezya so thoroughly that it almost took away the guilt I felt about destroying her. I ruined her. Every horrible thing that happened to her was because of me. I guess it was Pylemo's sick way of revenge. Because the only two people I truly cared for in this world were going to get hurt by her. First Brock lost his vision, and now Tezya... I tried not to think about what would happen to him. What the Goddesses showed me...

I tried not to think about Brock either. It hurt too much. I had to fight off the urge to curl into a fetal position and cry every time I did. But no one would see me cry. *No one.* I'd only shed tears for him when I was alone. My father taught me that. It didn't matter that I knew Brock was suffering right now, that he was probably on the brink of death, going through unfathomable torture at the hands of my father —and now we were delaying getting him even more.

But being here, knowing Brock used to be forced to work shifts within the prison, that he used to make this trek alone, made it hard to not dwell on him. It was another one of my father's sick forms of torture. After he killed Brock's parents in front of him, he sentenced his entire extended family to the prison, then forced Brock to work there until every last one of them died.

It took two decades.

He had a younger brother, and I couldn't imagine what he went through not being able to save him, having to watch him die in this place. Brock was the last survivor of his family. It pained me how alone he was and always would be. He never forgave himself for what happened, even though none of it was his fault. His parents were in the rebellion and their entire family suffered because of it. My father made sure of it. I knew it was why he never fully opened up to anyone. I knew deep down he was terrified—terrified to hurt like that again, to lose everyone he ever loved.

Peter let go of my wrist, and the lack of contact brought me back to reality and the task at hand. He was transforming into whatever disgusting sea creature he had to in order to make it down the trench.

From the surface where we were treading water, the opening to the trench looked massive, like a black hole plopped in the middle of the sea. But it would narrow the moment we started swimming. My body repulsed thinking about how I had to swim lower and lower until I was at the deepest part of the ocean.

I tried not to shake profusely while I prayed, erecting an air shield over my face and taking in my last breath of fresh air before I slowly descended into the depths below... toward the entrance of the prison.

FIVE
PETER

I was one hundred percent certain that my entire body would be covered in bruises once I finally shifted back into my Advenian form. It took us three hours to make it down the narrowed opening of the trench.

I thought the Luxian Princess was supposed to be strong, but she was slowing me down to the point of concern. We almost missed the change of shift, which would have made swimming across the ocean for nothing. She flat out stopped moving all together for about five minutes, and I thought I'd have to shift into a larger fish just so I could push her the rest of the way down. It was at a spot in the trench where it narrowed to the verge of having to shimmy down, but she was abnormally tiny for an Advenian, and I knew for a fact she could fit.

The most annoying part was every time I—*gently* might I add—brushed my scales against her skin, the freaking pampered-know-it-all princess swatted me into the rock and coral so hard that my entire body was throbbing. I had to pay attention to the movement of water to make sure we were going at the same pace so she'd stop pummeling me into the walls of the trench.

By the time we finally made it to the entrance, I felt like I was one big swimming bruise. But regardless of how much I didn't care for her, she was still helping me save my best friend.

Since it took us longer than anticipated to get here—for reasons that were entirely because of the princess—we didn't have to wait long for the switch to happen. Dovelyn and I were pressed against the rock at the bottom, trying to make ourselves as flat as possible.

The end of the trench was met with black rock. It was so dark that even if we weren't invisible, no one would have been able to see us. The only reason I could just barely make out the small details in our surroundings was because I shifted into a deep-sea fish—one who's eyes could see in the dark. Even without a mirror, I knew I looked freaking hideous, and I was happy I couldn't see myself.

The dark rock opened into an antechamber during the shift change. An air shield was the only thing separating the seafloor from the prison during it. The water bounced against the shield, begging to wash out the prison below, but it was the strongest shield in Advenian existence. It freaking had to be from all the water pressure. This deep, the water felt like it was crushing my scales. I had no idea how the princess was holding up her own shield, and I didn't want to think about how much power she wasted during the swim down here.

We watched silently through the shimmer as the guards entered a cylindrical boat. Since their rotations were on a revolving schedule, and most of their shifts lasted weeks, only a few were leaving now.

Once the door slammed shut, ground users stretched the rock and coral, widening the trench to allow for the passage. It resembled a miniature version of the monorail in Tennebris, except this one was only a single compartment and had no tracks.

In a split second, the boat-monorail-thing catapulted toward the surface. We had exactly thirty seconds for the boat to break the surface, another thirty seconds for the old guards to exit and the new ones to enter, and a final thirty before the boat descended back down and the rock narrowed again. Then we'd have to wait twenty-four hours to do it all again.

A minute and a half was all we got.

I started to count as we pushed through the air shield separating the ocean from the prison, and it felt like walking through jello—not that I'd ever done that before, but a guy could imagine.

My pulse was jackhammering against my tiny body as I shifted into my spider form. I wasn't under Dovelyn's invisibility anymore, and I had to trust she could follow me through the passageways.

I also had to be really freaking careful because if I fell through one of the cages, I'd be done for. The floors that made up the hallways were solid concrete, but each cage was a floating crate that lined the walls. And below the crate-cages was a second prison.

I was freaking relieved spiders didn't have ears, and I couldn't hear the sounds coming from below us. The vibrations alone had my head spinning.

I attempted to focus my eyes directly above me and not look down into the prison-pit-from-hell, but I had so many freaking eyeballs in this form that it gave me an unwanted three-sixty field of vision.

It added to my paranoia of the place because there was no way I was going to get caught and end up down there. Nope. I'd been spinning so much web out of my butt to anchor myself—which was absolutely disgusting and felt like something I shouldn't be doing in front of people—but the gross sticky stuff became my security blanket. Because there was no way I was ending up down there.

I rounded a corner and halted abruptly, stopping before the entrance of the pit. It was a circular hatch centered directly in the middle of the concrete walkway. I knew the only way down was for one of the guards to open it—or if my spider body fell through the cracks in the grates—but I wasn't taking any chances.

I was so relieved we were finally getting Sie out of here. This place was messed up, and it killed me knowing he already had spent so much time down here.

I focused my eyes and spotted him from across the way, and my heart sank. A flash of white caught my multiple eyeballs as he shifted inside his crate.

Frick. Frick. Frick.

They still hadn't healed him, and he looked so much worse than when I first came down here. There was more blood, more cuts and more bruises—

The Luxian guard with fuchsia eyes stalked toward Sie's cage. I perked up on my prickly legs—the freaking things kept sticking to the large amounts of web I made. I hated transforming into spiders—most times they were more annoying than useful.

But this was the guard we were waiting on. I just had to wait until he had to go to the bathroom so Dove and I could corner him, and then I'd transform—

Frick.

He whipped out his manhood and started pissing on my best friend. Sie hissed through his teeth, pushing away from the stream of urine as he crawled toward the back of the cage. The clothes he was wearing were worn and battered, the metal edges of the grate digging into his skin.

Just when I thought I couldn't hate this place any more, I watched in disgust as the guard's pee went onto all the prisoners in the pit below. I swore to myself if I got caught and was thrown down there, I'd shift into a worm and live out my days without eyes or ears or any body part of importance.

This also completely ruined our plans because now he wouldn't have to go to the bathroom. I really wished I had Sie's telepathy right now because I had no idea what to do next.

"Unchain him and bring him to the torture room," the fuchsia-pee-on-people guard ordered another one.

Sie didn't even flinch as they manhandled him and half dragged him across the concrete floors. I ran as fast as my eight legs would allow—which was actually surprisingly fast for being so small. I had no idea how I was going to stomach watching whatever torture they were about to do to Sie, but Dovelyn and I were going to have to improvise.

I just hoped my best friend would be able to stay alive for the next twenty-four hours until we did.

SIX
SIE

RATTLING sounds brought me back to consciousness.

Fuchsia was standing outside my cage again, only this time, instead of his usual menacing look, he was fumbling over keys before he had my cell door creaking open. I knew it had been a couple of hours since he last visited me—the piss on my clothes had finally dried, although the stench lingered.

I fucking hated him. He always managed to find new ways to get under my skin, and peeing on me earlier—that was the fucking cherry on top.

He was dragging me through the halls before I registered what was happening. My feet kept slipping out from under me as I tried to keep up with his long strides.

And then I realized I wasn't writhing in agony as we walked. He was holding me by my good arm, mercifully leaving my mangled, broken one untouched.

It wasn't until we were turning down another hallway that I realized he was abnormally quiet. Usually he'd be throwing retort after retort about Scotlind, and whenever he'd grow bored of that, he'd tell me exactly what he had planned in the torture room. It added to my dread, knowing what was to come as I was forced to walk down the long hallways.

I was nothing more than a walking corpse, and I tried my damned best to keep it that way. I didn't want to feel, didn't want to think, didn't want to exist.

I ran into his back as he abruptly stopped. We were in a closed hallway, one without all the prisoner cages. I looked up and saw another guard standing in front of us.

"Where are you taking him?" the guard asked. I didn't recognize him. Besides Fuchsia and the illusion user, they were all starting to blend together.

Fuchsia cleared his throat before answering. "The torture rooms."

The other guard smirked. "Going for round two, Nial?"

Nial—Fuchsia had a name, not that I wanted to remember it.

"Uh—yes," he stuttered.

"Well, don't let me stop you." He shifted out of the way for us to pass, but Fushia didn't move.

We stayed in the hallway for *long* seconds before he leaned me against a wall. If I had the strength, I would have used the freedom to fucking pummel him. I wanted nothing more than to beat him to a pulp, but even leaning against the wall was taxing. Chills were working their way through my body, and my vision was going in and out.

"Oh, my shoe. I need to tie it."

I blinked again, trying to focus on what he was doing as he bent down and started *un*-tying his boots before slowly redoing them.

The other guard went to grab me. "I'll bring him to the room for ya, Nial. You don't want to leave someone like him out for too long."

"No," Fuchsia-Nial half screamed, then cleared his throat again. "Um, I'll do it."

The guard cocked a brow, watching as Fuchsia grabbed me again— still by my good arm—and started guiding me past the hallway.

"Shit," he murmured under his breath as we walked through another section of cages. The torture room was just at the other end.

My vision blurred as someone opened the door for us, and Fuchsia brought me inside for the second time today.

"Nial, what are you doing back?" Brown asked. He was my second least favorite person here, after Fuchsia. I only recognized him by his deep-set brown eyes. He possessed illusion, and the two of them worked together to make it their mission to fucking shatter me.

"Ah, you know me, I just couldn't wait to hack into him again." Fuchsia started bringing me further into the room.

Multiple tables were lined throughout the space. They wanted the loners—the prisoners in the cages—to be tortured together. If ours wasn't as bad, we had the misery of hearing and seeing what was being done to others.

It sparked competition within the guards to see who could get their prisoner to scream the loudest. Some even took bets.

I didn't need my vision clear to know the floor had grates every ten feet for excessive blood to drain and every weapon imaginable was hung up along the walls. This room was ingrained in my fucking memory.

Only one other *loner* was in the room with us now. He was strapped to one of the tables having his fingernails slowly removed.

Brown-eyes put down his instrument, saving the *loner* from losing another nail. I glimpsed three bloodied fingers before I looked away. "Want me to do the honors?" he asked, then gestured toward the poor guy strapped to the table. "He can wait."

"No, don't let me stop you," Fuchsia said as he clumsily pushed me down onto a table across from them. I cursed as my bad arm hit the metal. "I have something… um special planned for him."

Brown-eyes shrugged, and I didn't need to look to know he went back to torturing the loner. I focused on my breathing, trying to block out his screams, as I prepared for the pain that would soon follow me.

In through my nose, out through my mouth.

Fuchsia strapped me onto the table.

Slow, deep breaths. Think of nothing. I am nothing.

"Uh, let's see. Yeah, this will do." Fuchsia plucked a knife off the wall and stalked toward me. And then with his free hand he…

scratched his ear. I closed my eyes. I was seriously on the verge of becoming delusional because I swore the man I hated so much just reminded me of Peter. The motion was so eerily similar to how he used to tug on his ear when he wanted me to enter his mind. Fuck. I missed him. I never got to see him after he went back to Lux. I prayed he made it out alive, but he wasn't at my coronation...

Cold metal grazed my uninjured forearm.

In through my nose, out through my mouth.

"Right," Fuchsia's voice sounded again, and the slow drag of it all was killing me. I usually would have been half bloodied by now. My only saving grace with him was his impatience. He always escalated things too quickly, but if he planned on taking his time now...

In through my nose, out through my mouth.

I could do this. The physical torture was always better than the mental ones. The illusions were what I couldn't stomach.

I waited for the slice of cold metal to burn, to feel the sting as it sank into me, but it never came. Instead, I felt sweaty hands against my neck. The gentle touch to the area was so surprising that I jerked. Before I could open my eyes, Fuchsia's fingers pressed down, applying pressure to that perfect spot before I passed out into beautiful oblivion.

———

I CAME BACK to myself with my back pressed against a wall in a bathroom. Fuchsia was standing over me with... the fucking Luxian Princess.

It took me minutes of blinking and adjusting my eyes before I realized neither of them were looking at me. I turned my head to the side and saw... Fuchsia again, only he was unconscious.

The Fuchsia that was standing over me kept tugging on his ear. "Sie, it's me. We're getting you out of here."

I was fucking losing it, or delusional, or brown-eyes had me in another illusion in the torture room. Either way, I knew this wasn't real. I had too many visions of Peter and Scotlind rescuing me, only to wake up in the same cage.

"We don't have time for you to coddle him," the princess spat, her voice was a lethal whisper. "Get the guard and let's go."

"Right," Fuchsia said. Then he squared his shoulders before bending down, hovering over the two of us and punched the already unconscious Fuchsia in the face. I couldn't process what was happening as punch after punch was thrown until his features were a bloodied mess, and he was no longer recognizable.

I looked down at my body. I wasn't in my piss-prison uniform anymore. Instead, bloodied Fuchsia was in it and new, *clean* clothes were on me.

I didn't have any new cuts on me either. Nothing to show for my time in the torture room. I tried to remember what happened and couldn't. All I could recall was pressure placed over my neck before I blacked out. My arm was still mangled. The bone sticking out made me want to pass out all over again, and if I wasn't in so much pain, the agony from it would be all I could focus on. But the chills were worsening. I could feel a sweat starting to break out...

Maybe this was what dying felt like. Maybe the closer you came to that bridge, the crazier your mind worked.

The princess disappeared, completely vanishing before my eyes as Fuchsia picked up the other one, positioning his mangled face toward his chest, and started walking away with him.

"Don't move," Fuchsia called over his shoulder. His voice sounded eerily familiar, but I knew it was just my brain playing tricks on me. "We'll be right back, Sie."

Then I was alone again. I couldn't move even if I wanted to.

I leaned my head back against the wall, closing my eyes, too exhausted to try and break out of the illusion.

SEVEN
SCOTLIND

"I'm sorry I didn't tell you," Tezya broke the silence the next morning. We'd barely spoken since Kallon first portaled us back, and other than him telling me to take the bed later that night, this was the first time he was talking to me. He must have sensed with his ability that I needed space, needed time to sort out my feelings, and even though we were alone, I wasn't ready.

I had thought about talking to him numerous times throughout the awkward silence-filled night. I even played out various conversations inside my head, but I never got the courage to speak.

And when I wasn't thinking about being alone with Tezya and what to say to him, I was worried sick for Peter and Dovelyn. Kallon should be relatively safe since she was waiting outside the trench—not that swimming in frigid water was easy, even with Dovelyn's protective shield. But if Peter and Dovelyn got trapped inside the prison, if they didn't make it out... I couldn't think about it. It's the reason Kallon wanted to stay close to them and not just portal back after twenty-four hours. If something went wrong, she needed to know right away.

I'd been sitting on the edge of the bed with my back turned to Tezya since I'd woken up. Even with the sheer curtains pulled shut, I could still make out human figures moving about and starting their day.

I barely slept throughout the night, even though Tezya left the bed empty. He stayed awake, staring at the motel door, just as anxious about what was happening as I was. His sister went in with Peter, and as much as I didn't particularly care for Dovelyn, I knew she meant a lot to Tezya, and she was risking her life because of it.

I turned my head to look at him. He was still leaning against the far wall with his arms crossed over his chest. His shirt was off and his black pants were rolled past his calves. I had used my abilities to pull the water off of us last night, before changing into warmer clothes, and Tezya had created a small floating fire above us until the embers wore off. But we recovered from the hypothermia of the trench way too quickly. The mortal territory we were stuck in was humid and smothering, feeling more like we were trapped in a ball full of steam than a room. And the worst part of this place was that Kallon told me it was close to the end of winter, meaning it only got worse as the months dragged on. Lux was hot, but without an air user's shield, the humidity of this place felt like a whole new world.

"Is that really necessary?" I asked him, gesturing to the shirt he had tossed over the bed. Even though it was boiling in here, and my own clothes were soaked through, he didn't *have* to take his shirt off.

"It's hot in here," was all he said.

"Aren't you worried about a mortal seeing you through the window?" His black Luxian markings were on full display, appearing over his skin through the sweat.

"Dove put a shield over the window and door. If anyone looks in, the room will appear empty. No one can see us."

I swallowed. Hard.

"It's another reason we're heading north today. We won't have to worry about the heat or the constant rain that happens here. The humans will start raising questions if our markings appear out of thin air."

I didn't respond. I didn't know where to begin. I could barely focus without his shirt on—I hated that I couldn't stop staring, that he looked way too hot half naked and covered in sweat—so I turned back around.

A long moment passed, and I thought we'd go back to ignoring each other, but then he said, "I'm sorry, Scotlind. I didn't mean to hurt you." He must have sensed my emotions, had known that my own thoughts were still lingering on him. There were more important things to think about right now than our relationship, or lack thereof. But I couldn't help it. Being stuck with Tezya all night had my thoughts drifting to him just as much as it did my friends.

"You promised me," I started, turning back around on the bed to face him. "You promised me no more lies." My mind whirled on everything he kept from me. I didn't know if he was ever honest with me—from being the prince, to the prophecy, to what I'd overheard from his conversation with Dovelyn. Had he known the entire time why I was sent to Tennebris? He told me about my real parents after Yule. Had he known it was his sister's fault that they died?

Tezya's crystal blue eyes met mine. I could just make out the specks of silver in them from where I sat on the bed. Some days, I swore the specks grew and took over the coloring. "I know, and I regret it." He rubbed his finger over his palm, over his scab from where we created our bond.

"Do you regret not telling me, or do you regret that I found out?" I didn't pause long enough for him to answer before I continued, "Would you have ever told me? If you hadn't needed to use your compulsion to get us past the guards that day, would you have told me the truth?"

"It's complicated, Rumor."

"No, it's really not." When he didn't respond after the first millisecond, I added, "Forget I said anything."

"I don't want to forget, please. Let me try to explain."

"No." I turned back around to stare out the window. "I don't want to talk to you."

A moment passed, and I didn't know if he would press further, but then he sighed, "You can bathe if you want. They have a shower here, not a tub, in case you were wondering."

"I wasn't."

"Okay, well I'm showering."

I didn't answer. I didn't want to think about him bathing. My mind kept replaying being in the bath with him after he finished his punishment for keeping my ability a secret. It was the first time I'd been able to go into one since Kole.

I was thankful I now had a positive memory, that Kole wasn't consuming my thoughts, but I couldn't get rid of the hurt I felt from him not telling me the truth. I trusted him fully, so stupidly, foolishly fully. That night when he said *no more lies*, I believed him, and I never looked back. I gave him blind faith when I barely knew him, only to find out he kept the biggest secrets of all from me.

I felt stupid.

He made me believe the prophecy was about *me* when it was about *him* all along. He warned me to stay away from Sie, that a child with him would become the chosen one. It gave me conflicting thoughts. I didn't understand why I was so attracted to Tezya if I was destined to be with Sie, because that's how I interpreted what he said to me. Why didn't he just tell me? What was the purpose of me thinking it was about Sie?

The sound of water came from behind me, and a second later, I felt it in my veins. Now that I was learning to master my powers, I noticed it everywhere. It called to me, begging me to wield it—drops of sweat dripping down someone's back, to the lingering dew over the morning grass. Everywhere water was, it sang to me, begging me to manipulate it. And whenever someone else was using their abilities, my enhancement called to that, begging to merge with whatever power they were using.

I instantly regretted my decision to not bathe. I missed the way water used to soothe me. Before everything happened, back when I was at school in LakeWood, soaking in the tub was my go-to way of calming down. Now, I was an anxious mess, and my emotions were all over the place.

The room we were stuck in was sticky. My clothes were clinging to me, adding to another layer of my anxiety. I focused on my own sweat, moving the liquid as I guided it off me until my clothes were dry and a small puddle formed at my feet, but I knew the smell lingered. It was another reason why I regretted declining the shower, but I wasn't about to admit that now.

I needed to do something other than just sit here. I was terrified for my friends and doing nothing was only letting my thoughts fester. I didn't think they'd kill Dovelyn or Kallon. They were too important to the King—Dove because she was the princess and Kallon for her portals—but they were still committing treason. They all were in order to help us.

But Peter… he wasn't important to the crown. If he got caught, he wouldn't be held to the same standards as them. He was the one I was worried about the most. He was also the most likely person to do something unplanned in order to save Sie.

I kept picturing Peter's body hanging limply from the ceiling, with his dress in shreds and his back in ribbons. I shook my head, feeling my heart rate accelerate. He went through all of that just to be my maid, and I knew his friendship with Sie was even stronger. There was nothing he wouldn't do to save him.

The sun was rising higher in the sky, filling the tiny room with a translucent warm light. Once they were back, we'd leave this place to head north—whatever that meant.

I'd been so focused on the task at hand, on busying myself with trying to rescue Sie, that I never actually thought about what would happen if we did.

I tried not to think about what it would mean if—*when*—Sie returned. Would he look the same as I last saw him, or would he be even more sickly than I remembered? He hadn't been locked in the underwater prison for long, but a lot could happen in a short period of time. I knew firsthand what even a few days of being locked in a cell could do to your body, and Peter said he'd die without seeing a healer…

Did they torture him? Was he being fed? Allowed water? I had to remind myself he knowingly sent me to the same fate. He handed me over to the Lux King with no explanation. I was sentenced to twenty-seven days in a cage. Twenty-seven days of having a whip ruin my back, of being tortured for information about him. And before that, I was starved and left in solitude in the Tennebrisian dungeons, and he never once tried to speak with me. Never once tried to help me.

Our last conversation flashed in my memory. How *he* was mad at *me* for being with Tezya. How *he* said that he would forgive *me*. How he wanted to be with me. I honestly had no idea what my feelings were anymore. I knew I wasn't rescuing him just because of the guilt. I cared for him to some degree, but things were different with Tezya. It was real with him. I knew it wasn't my powers pretending and manifesting into thinking we were one. I *felt* the bond work. Deep in my bones and to my core, I could feel Tezya's connection to me and mine to him. Whereas Sie just thought he felt a connection. He mistook my enhancement for the bond. It wasn't real. The attraction we had for each other was, but not the connection.

I huffed. It *was* real with Tezya. But now I couldn't decipher reality from his lies, and I wasn't sure where it left us.

More steam wafted into the room as Tezya opened the door and walked in. A towel was wrapped around his hips. I hated that I looked, that I kept staring.

My body leaned toward him on instinct. I was drawn to him. To the water, to his soul, to everything.

Droplets sprayed onto me as he shook out his bone-white hair. The pieces in the front were getting longer and starting to block his eyes. I watched as he raised his arm, dragging his fingers through the strands, and pushing them away from his face. My eyes trailed down his arm, scanning his markings as they wrapped around his bicep.

The flames on him were beautiful. I had memorized each one from when he was forced to stab himself, and I had to watch. I wasn't scared of his fire, not after that day. Looking at the markings on his skin was the first time I thought flames were beautiful instead of terrifying.

I thought I had memorized every part of him. I thought I knew him so well after that day. But he had more markings—Tennebrisian markings. There was another part of him I knew nothing about.

I was so focused on gawking at his Luxian markings scattered across his broad chest, arms, and up his neck that I didn't realize I'd been staring at him. But when I looked up, I found him staring right back. My eyes flicked to his scab over his palm before I met his gaze again.

He took a step closer, then another. I stood from the bed, unsure what I was planning on doing or why I moved in the first place, but I wanted to be near him. I *needed* to be near him. I wanted to kiss him, I wanted to trace my hands across his stomach, and feel everything and nothing all at once. Whenever I was with him, it was so easy to get lost, so easy to forget about everything around us.

"Scotlind, I—" His words were interrupted as purple and black smoke filled the room. The next breath, Kallon, Dovelyn, and Peter portaled in. The princess fell to her knees, collapsing onto the ground before I caught a glimpse of black hair.

Sie was sagged between Peter and Kallon.

They did it.

EIGHT

TEZYA

I COULDN'T TELL if I was more relieved or pissed off. I desperately needed to talk with Scottie. I needed to fix things before Sie showed up. Some selfish part of me didn't want to rescue him. I was scared as hell for what would happen after she saw him.

But I was worried about my friends more, and I was so fucking grateful to see they were all alive. I knew they were more than capable. We'd pulled off enough undercover missions together in the past for me to know they could handle this, but it was the first time I had to sit back and wait.

Dovelyn could have managed to make me invisible—she was the strongest air user, even stronger than Arcane—but she didn't trust Scottie. I couldn't argue with her lack of training, even if I thought she was capable. It was a rule *I* made for the Luxian soldiers—they had to have five years of intensive training before they even saw a battle, and that was after thirteen years of training during school. But when Scottie used her enhancement to attach to Kal's portal, I was going to disagree with Dovelyn and let both of us stay.

But then Dove had a vision, and I felt it. I couldn't argue it, couldn't risk it, risk *her*. Me staying behind was more about making sure Rumor didn't try to follow us or do something stupid while she waited.

"You did it," Scottie breathed, her voice was soft, barely a whisper. Sie's eyes flicked open at the sound, his focus narrowing in on her. He murmured something inaudible as Peter shifted to support his weight. Then his dark eyes rolled in the back of his head right before he lost consciousness again. I reached out to him with my senses. He was burning up. Pain radiated from him in crippling waves. I focused on it as I inspected his body. A flash of bone was jutting out of his arm just like Peter had said, and without seeing a healer, he was a ticking bomb.

I let my senses roam over the rest of my friends. My power instantly went to Dovelyn. Her pain was coming to me the strongest. I scanned my sister—she was still cradling herself on the ground, but she was mostly unharmed, exhausted and drained, but otherwise okay. It took me another second to register her pain as emotional and not physical.

I scanned Kallon next. Her body was weak from treading water too long and every inch of her was frozen over. I was about to ask Rumor to use her water ability, but I didn't have to. Without missing a beat, Scottie pulled the water off them, and in one loud splash, sent it falling down the drain in the shower. I sent small fire balls throughout the room to help warm them, adding extra around Kallon.

I scanned Peter next. He had minor cuts over his body, but his main injury was to his left side. It was completely bruised over with small bits of coral lodged into his skin.

My sister and him were both completely tapped out. They used everything they had to rescue Sie, but they were all alive. Peter and Dovelyn just needed time to restore their reserves, and Kallon had to warm up and rest.

Peter gently set Sie down on the mattress and started tending to him, careful to avoid his broken arm.

"Is he going to be okay?" Scottie asked as she slowly, hesitantly, walked over to them.

"He needs a healer soon to fix his arm and break his fever, but he'll live," I said. Scotlind was in worse shape from the time she spent in the dungeons and some twisted part of me was glad to see him suffering. He deserved to know what he put her through when he sentenced her to Lux, when he abandoned her to the hands of the Lux King. I was glad he could no longer call her his wife. He didn't deserve her concern or worry.

A deeper part of me thought I didn't deserve her either.

"We need to move out, *now*," Kallon said, her eyes flaring. I rarely saw her worried. She mastered the art of a blank expression long ago. We all had to, from years of being under Athler's watch.

"What happened?" I asked.

"We tripped the alarms on our way out. We realized too late that they placed trackers on all the prisoners, and when we tried to exit through the opening, the whole prison shut down." I looked Sie over again as Peter was talking and noticed a chunk of his skin and muscle was missing from his upper arm. They must have found the tracker and cut it out of him, but it was still too late. Even if Peter managed to destroy the grate, they'd know Sie was alive now. This place was going to be crawling with Luxians soon.

"We were being chased out of the prison and had to move fast," he continued, still focusing on his friend. "When we broke the surface, we didn't account for Kallon being visible and right over the trench opening."

"They saw you." I turned to Kallon, but my sister cut me off.

"It was stupid, so stupid. I swore I left a shield over you, Kal. I really thought I did, but my mind… I was…"

Dove didn't need to finish. I knew her well enough, and it was written all over her face before she left. She tried to act like nothing bothered her, but she had been worried about Brock. She was almost in tears before they portaled to the trench.

"It's okay, Dove. It's not your fault. You did," Kallon said gently. "You had a shield over me, but about halfway through, the shield went out. I was so worried. I thought something happened to you…" Kallon had tears pooling, but she didn't let them fall. I looked up at her, her yellow eyes briefly drifted to mine.

It made sense now why Kallon wasn't doing well. She stayed behind, swimming in the ocean, without protection for hours, waiting to find out if something happened to them.

"When it got close to the twenty-four hour mark and you guys weren't back, I let my fear get the best of me, so I started to swim toward the trench. I'm so sorry, I—"

"I need to go back to Lux now," Dove broke, interrupting Kallon. "I have to get him."

"You can't. If they saw Kal at the prison, the King will be the first person to know," I said and hated that it was the truth. "If you go back to Lux now to get Rainer and Brock, you'll be captured, Dove."

"I don't care. I'm going. Kallon, portal me now." She pulled herself off the floor.

"Dove, we need to think strategically about this," Kallon said slowly. I could sense guilt and unease radiating off her. "Tezya is right. We shouldn't go back. We need to head north. The King probably already knows, but Rainer is smart. Once he hears what happened, he'll get Brock out and meet us at the camp."

"No, he won't," Dovelyn screamed. "Rainer can't even find him! The only person who saw Brock was Tezya and that was the day *she* blinded him. No one has seen him since. No one knows where he is. He's going to hurt him if we leave him there, Tez." The tears she'd been holding back broke free and poured down her pale cheeks as she turned to me. "You know what he does. You know what he will put him through simply because he knows..." her voice broke off in a loud sob. "Because he knows I care for him, and now my father will realize we're all gone. He'll connect the dots that we were the ones who broke Sie out of the prison... He's going to take all of his anger out on him. He's going to kill him."

"He won't kill him," I said, but Dovelyn was right. The King was a sadistic asshole, and once he realized we disobeyed him, that we committed an act of treason—because leaving the Luxian city, not only with Scottie and Peter, but now rescuing Sie from the prison would be seen as an act of war—I didn't know what the King would do...

"Let me go," she said, looking straight at me, and it broke me to see her in so much pain. Dovelyn never cried, and she never begged, so to see her breaking now... "I'll warn Rainer and find Brock."

"They're going to have a trap for you. He knows you'll come for him—"

"I'll have my shield up the entire time," she cut me off. "No one will see me."

"The King will have Athler watching Brock. If you go, his second will sense your emotions unless you're shielded, and you're too drained to maintain both with your invisibility. They'll capture you, Dove."

"Then I'll be captured. I don't care. I just need Kallon to portal me to our spot. Give me a day. Just one day. That's all I'm asking. If I can't find him, I'll come back. But I have to try, Tez. I have to. You would if you were me."

And I would. I would break mountains to get to Scottie. I would rather be caught and captured with her than have her in the hands of the Lux King alone. "Alright," I conceded. "But your reserves won't last an entire day."

Kallon cut in. "I'll give you three hours, Dove. Then I'm coming back for you and Rainer."

"Fine," she said as she swiped at her cheeks.

Kallon started opening the portal, twisting and bending the already built one from the prison so it could take them back to Lux. "I'll be right back. Get yourselves ready," she said as she eyed my appearance. "I'm portaling you all as soon as I'm back. This territory is about to be crawling with Luxians."

Dovelyn lifted her hands and casted invisibility over the two of them right before they jumped into the purple and black hole.

I stared after them, praying she would be able to find Brock and Rainer without getting caught. I couldn't stomach the thought of her father having her too. He would never kill Dovelyn, but there were worse things he'd do to destroy her.

"I know it's hot as balls in this place," Peter remarked, breaking the silence, "but you might want to put some clothes on. I doubt mortals walk around looking like that."

I completely forgot I only had my towel on. I looked over at Peter. He was hovering over Sie who was now starting to stir. Scottie lingered behind them both.

I turned around without responding and walked into the bathroom, letting the door slam behind me.

———

IT DIDN'T TAKE LONG for Kallon to return. She portaled us two at a time to the outside entrance of the camp. I knew she was exhausted, but her reserves were nowhere near depleted by the time we finally made it.

Commander Dravenburg was already waiting for us with his arms crossed over his chest. I knew my vague message would have pissed him off, but it wasn't worth the risk to give him a heads up on exactly who we'd be bringing to the camp. I didn't want to tip anyone off that we were attempting to rescue Sie until after it was done.

His hazel eyes scanned our group ruthlessly. Kallon with beads of sweat clinging to her despite the frigid temperatures, making her saffron and black bangs stick to her forehead; Peter holding up the semi-conscious prince; and Scotlind, who was turning her head from side to side taking everything in.

We were standing in snow half a foot deep, our previous clothes nowhere near functional for the weather. I always forgot how cold it was in this territory. It was nearing the end of winter, maybe only a month left, but this year was worse than previous ones.

It didn't look like a camp, but we hadn't fully entered yet. The shields the air users created here were the strongest I'd ever seen, thanks to Wells' creations. No Advenian could portal or teleport in. The only way into the camp was by foot.

"Tezya, I would say I'm happy to see you, but I'm afraid under these circumstances, I'm not," Dravenburg spoke, his eyes flicking over to Sie before meeting mine again.

"We always knew this day would come," was all I said, because it was all I could say. I hated that I was shattering his well-constructed bubble.

"Yes, well I just hoped my children could have gotten a bit older first."

"You know I will do everything I can to keep Wells and Savannah out of this."

He chuckled darkly. "Good luck with my daughter. That girl was born into this world ready for a fight."

"Speaking of Sav, where is she?" I missed her, I always did when I was stuck in Lux for too long.

"Anxiously awaiting your arrival. Come, we will be starting dinner shortly." He hesitated for a moment, eyeing Sie again. "I'll bring your *friends* to the healers."

"Thank you," I replied.

Dravenburg gave a curt nod, then turned around and stalked off what appeared to be a cliff with a large drop into the ocean. To everyone else, it would have seemed like he plummeted into the rocks. The fake waves roared below as they slammed against them. Scottie yelped, thinking the mortal commander had just jumped to his death as he immediately vanished from view.

"What are you doing?" Scottie yelled as I took a step to follow Dravenburg. "Are you crazy?"

I turned to look at her. She was shivering, her chattering was so loud, her words were almost inaudible. It would be warmer as soon as we crossed. The temperatures inside the shield were tepid, similar to the ones surrounding Lux and Tennebris.

Her sapphire eyes were wild as she looked from me to the cliff. The color was such a deep blue, it matched the illusion of the ocean below. I couldn't help but smile. "It's the way into the camp," I replied, then followed Dravenburg through the shield.

It beeped as I passed through, revealing a grassy field that stretched for miles. Tents were haphazardly erected throughout the plane, with electricity and fire users heating the space.

Behind me, I could see Kallon and Scottie talking, one of the perks to the shield—it only created the illusion on one side. If any mortal approached the area, our scouts would know. But mortals didn't often travel this far north in Maine. It was one of the reasons we picked the location. And if they did come here, not many dared to step too close to the cliffs. Air users on watch generated strong gusts of winds whenever a human was spotted nearby, and most stayed far away from fear of falling to their death.

Kallon was practically dragging Scottie through the shield, and Peter hesitantly followed, carrying Sie with him. As soon as Scottie passed through, she visibly relaxed. The shield sounded with four beeps, annotating the number of Advenians that passed through. Wells found a way to incorporate and meld mortal technology with our abilities back when Arcane used to visit. The two of them used to spend hours messing around, combining Advenian powers with mortal sciences. That was before they had a falling out. Before things changed for Arcane, and his relationship with the King grew more complicated.

I never envied him, being the heir to the throne was something I'd run far and fast from. And despite my brother actually wanting it, the Lux King wouldn't let him near the crown until he was well and dead.

Kallon stepped up beside me. "I'm going to my tent. I need a lot of ale and sleep," she said, then leaned forward to whisper in my ear. "If I were you, I would explain this to her before she finds out from someone else." Kallon nodded toward Scottie who was staring at the massiveness of the camp with equal bits of awe and confusion. Dravenburg had already ushered Peter and Sie away to the healer's tent, leaving just the two of us.

"Come on, Rumor. I'll take you to your tent."

She nodded, but didn't say anything. We walked past the training rings first. Advenians of all ages were going about their day.

A varying amount of clothes and mortal shirts—all thanks to Savannah, who claimed every Advenian needed to be introduced to mortal fashion—lined the grass as most of the men opted to train barebacked.

Scottie halted as she noticed them. Golden markings sprang to life on Tennebrisians who were using their abilities, and Luxians' black markings were on display as their skin became coated with sweat. Some women and children were scattered throughout the grounds, fighting right alongside the former soldiers.

I waited for Scottie to say something, to ask me what she was seeing, but she didn't. She collected herself and began following me again. Loud cheers and shouts followed long after we passed, but the silence from Scottie felt deafening. I wanted to know what she was thinking.

I guided her centrally. Everything of importance was located inward and spanned out from the dining tent, with the exception of the training rings—but that was only because there were too many noise complaints. The rings never closed, and most Advenians kept training well into the night.

"You can sleep here," I said, stopping in front of Arcane's tent. I couldn't stand the idea of her sleeping in the communal ones, and my brother's was next to mine and had been left vacant for years.

She walked past me as I pulled open the tent flaps. The ground was lined in furs with only a makeshift bed and a basin inside. The closest communal bath house was located half a mile from here.

"I don't understand," she said, whirling on me. "What is this place?" I went to answer, but she cut me off, "And be honest with me, Tezya. No more lies."

"This place is called Brighta. It's a camp for Advenians that have nowhere to go."

"Advenians?" Her brows furrowed. "I saw both kingdoms' markings back there."

I nodded, taking a step closer to her. "It's a refuge for both Tennebris and Lux. Although far more Luxians live here, both are welcome."

"Refuge? They were *training* outside."

"Yes, there is training too. A lot of things happen here."

"Like what? What is this place? I still don't understand—"

"Rumor, welcome to the rebellion."

NINE
SCOTLIND

My mouth dropped.

The rebellion. Tezya brought me to the rebellion. The same rebellion he had destroyed over and over again by the King's orders. "I don't understand. The stories—they said you left the battlefield in ashes."

"I did leave it in ashes. It was just never Advenian ashes."

"So, you never killed them? Any of them?"

"I have killed, Rumor. But I try not to."

"How? How did you do it?" Because the size of this camp... There were thousands of men here. Even more women and children.

"Anytime the rebellion started up again, my orders were to kill everyone. The Lux King didn't want anyone left alive, even for questioning, so I made sure that's what everyone thought happened. If thousands of soldiers believed all the rebels died, no one gave what I was doing a second thought."

"How does everyone think you killed them, though?"

"It would start off like a normal battle," Tezya said. "Men would die. Rebels would die. My soldiers died. Brock and Rainer would help me locate whoever was leading the attack as quickly as possible. Once we did, I would fight their commander, not to kill, but I'd make it long enough to give me the opportunity to talk with them. If they refused to hear me out, I'd compel them without anyone seeing."

"You compelled them?" I was still trying to wrap my head around him having compulsion—but to know he regularly used it…

"Yes." He was staring at me, giving me time to process everything, not saying anything else until I was ready.

"Isn't that risky?" I finally asked. "Having people know you have a dark ability?"

"Yes," he admitted. "But if they refused to speak with me I would've had to kill them, so I thought it was worth the risk."

I tried to not let it bother me—that Tezya told rebels he was fighting against the truth about him, but not me. It was stupid, jealous even. What he was saying only proved he was a good person, that he put others before himself, and here I was finding a way to turn it around to be about me. I hated it, hated that I kept doing it…

I also hated that I couldn't get past the fact that he had compulsion. It was wrong. I knew I didn't only feel that way because of my past. I hated the ability to my core. I hated knowing Tezya possessed it, and I still couldn't wrap my head around how he was able to hide it from everyone so easily, especially if rebels now knew inside the camp.

"I'd compel them without anyone seeing, Rumor," he said, like he knew where my thoughts went. "Not even Brock or Rainer saw me use it, and it was only to get them to hear me out. Then I'd compel them to forget I was half Tennebrisian, but that was all I'd ever done. I never once forced anyone to come here. I couldn't risk bringing anyone here until I knew they wouldn't cause harm to the camp or to the people who already lived here. So I'd make their leaders hear me out, then I'd explain what the camp was. I would try to convince them to come with me. Most took a long time to persuade, sometimes forcing us to battle for days. They usually thought I was leading them into a trap, and with all the rumors about me, it was easy to believe."

He shook his head as if remembering moments of battle. "So we did fight—for days, sometimes weeks—but once they agreed, I would orchestrate a fake defeat. I called my men back. They thought it just meant the end of the battle, my finishing move. Once we were two halves, split down the middle, I'd call my flames to form a wall so high and thick, the soldiers couldn't see through it. They couldn't see Kallon creating a portal. It would take hours to do it, sometimes an entire day, draining Kallon of all her magic in order to get the remaining men out and safely into Brighta. I tried my best to keep the flames contained, but in order to block out what she was doing, the fire had to be large. By the time she finished, I usually burned through many trees and bushes. The soldiers thought I was just taking my time killing them slowly. They call it the *bonfire*."

"The women and children? Were they a part of the rebellion? Were they fighting too?"

He shook his head. "No. Some train now, but it's by choice. They never fought in the original battles. Once I returned from the fight, the King would order me to kill the families of the deceased rebels. He didn't want anyone alive who had thoughts of demolishing the current ranking system. It didn't matter to him if it was a helpless infant, he wanted everyone dead. So Kallon and I would portal the families through, faking their deaths, while pretending we killed them."

My gut twisted at thinking back to all the kids I saw in the camp. All the children the King ordered Tezya to murder. Relief washed through me. Tezya never killed them. It was the one part of him that never fit. I couldn't make sense of someone hating the system, hating the King, hating how our society operated, but then following through on orders to make sure it continued to thrive.

"So what is everyone doing here?"

"Waiting, training, living their lives in the meantime. It's always been our plan to fight back, but we aren't ready yet. Our numbers are good, a match against Lux and Tennebris if needed, but we don't have the level of experience the soldiers in Lux have. The demands the King puts on me to train them so thoroughly... I tried to mimic it here, but they just don't have the stamina and many of the civilians just want to live in peace. Most of the Advenians at this camp are made up of zeroes, ones, and twos. There are higher ranks among them, but not as many as I would have liked, and despite knowing Advenians are capable of fighting with little to no powers, I can't deny that it helps to use abilities. The Luxian army is bred of only fours and fives. They're the strongest men in Lux and training is all they've ever known."

"You said you aren't ready yet, what do you mean?" I asked.

"We just started a war, Rumor."

"Because of Sie? Because we rescued him?"

"Yes. You, Peter, Sie… the King isn't stupid. It started the day I broke you and Peter out. He knows what we declared by leaving."

"I didn't mean for it—"

"You didn't," he interrupted. "The war isn't because of you or Sie, even if you were the catalyst. It was bound to happen sooner or later. With Sie off the Tennebrisian throne, the Lux King plans to manipulate and control the Dark Kingdom. Synder doesn't have a real claim to power, so he'd allow it if it meant he got to wear the crown. He's too daft to realize he would never be the one in control. The Lux King is already one step closer to getting what he wants."

"Which is what?"

"Everything. He wants everything. Do you remember me telling you he plans to take over the humans when we visited Florida for the first time together?"

I nodded.

"He wants to keep the ranking system the way it is. He doesn't want people to challenge it, but it's more than that. With the way it's set up now, the strong rule. In Lux, no one questions his authority. His bloodline has been ruling since our kind lived on Allium. The Council members are selected by *him*, and they're all rank fives who agree with his ideologies. He has the strongest army out of the two kingdoms. But it's not enough for him. He wants this *world*. He wants to take over the humans. He wants land, to expand, to be the singular ruler of the entire planet."

"But the humans overpopulate us," I said, recalling our history. It was why our kind resigned to hiding in the first place. I hadn't comprehended how small we were in comparison until I went to the mortal territory with Tezya. I was blown away by how many humans I saw and that was just one area, one tiny blip on the planet. I remembered the maps we were shown during Human Relation lectures back in LakeWood... There was no way he could pull it off.

"I know, but he's been working with Arcane, developing serums that, if they succeed, could be utilized for mass compulsion. It's another reason he wanted Sie off the throne. He needs to control the Dark Kingdom, and Sie was too strong for the court. He never would have been able to do it during his rule, but now..."

"Synder is ruling," I finished for him.

"Which means *the King* is really the one ruling." Tezya took another step toward me, and I realized how close we were standing. I was so engulfed in our conversation, in the casualness of it—despite the horrible topic—that I forgot things were different. I looked down at my palm. My scab from Tezya was still raised and prominent. The one from Sie was hidden beneath—a thin, white scar, barely visible, but it still left its mark. A mark that would never leave. It would always be a part of me. They both would.

I closed my fist. "Do you think Arcane will figure out a way to develop a compulsion serum?"

"It's likely," Tezya said. "He was successful with making Alluse serums. His next task was making a serum out of you. You're the only living enhancement user, and the Lux King has an obsession for seeking power. It's his only weakness. It makes him predictable. He sees you as a tool to become stronger now. He planned on keeping you chained at his side, forcing you to constantly use enhancement on his abilities. But if there was a way to harness your blood, that all he had to do was use a serum and become stronger—"

I thought back to the week I was chained to the King's side and a chill ran through me. Arcane sampled my blood every day, but at the time, I had no idea what it was for. The exhaustion of constantly using my enhancement on the King was getting to me, how I was forced to follow him everywhere, his sick nickname for me... *pet.*

Tezya stopped speaking for a moment, assessing me. "If Arcane pulled that off," he started again slowly. "If he found a way to do that with your blood, he'd easily be able to make compulsion serums. Yours would be the most complicated because he would have to alter your powers. You can only enhance others, not yourself, and the King seeks to reserve that. He wants to drink the serum and have it make *his* abilities stronger, not others."

It dawned on me then. "The King was using me as a trial before having Arcane work on a compulsion user? And if he got a serum that made himself stronger in the process, it would have been a win-win."

"Yes. Why do you think he's kept Kole around?"

Kole. A compulsion user. He was going to use him to create a mass serum, and Tennebris willingly handed the Lux King everything he needed. I always thought it was weird he was treated with respect in the opposing kingdom, but now everything was coming together. And Kole had no idea he was just livestock the King was waiting to slaughter.

"So like I said, it's not because of you that this war started. It started years ago. It's just now coming to head. But we have the advantage of surprise if we attack first. The King will believe we're a small group. He doesn't realize the vastness of the camp. He has no idea I saved everyone he ordered me to kill."

Only then did I realize I was standing in the middle of a camp with thousands of rank zero sympathizers—and not just that, they didn't like the way everyone was treated, they wanted a better world—they were ready to attack the King, ready to protect the mortals, ready to change the system. Ready to do everything I ever wanted.

I was standing in the middle of the rebellion, and the Lux King had no idea what was coming for him.

Bells clanged throughout the camp.

"Dinner," Tezya said, noting my confusion. "We can check on Sie first if you'd like. Then, it's time for you to meet the rebels."

TEN
SIE

I woke up in a tent. Peter was dozing off on a shit ton of fluffy pillows a short distance away, and I felt... comfortable. Those same fluffy pillows were behind my head, not a jagged grate digging into my skin. And for once, the air was clean—I couldn't smell urine and death and decay.

"Where am I?" I asked, my voice cracked as I spoke. My throat burned and felt like acid was being poured down it. I needed water.

Peter shot up. "What? What?" His eyes widened as he took me in. "You're awake. Thank the Goddess. I was sick of carrying you everywhere, and I really didn't want to have to drag you to dinner. You gained some weight despite being starved and all."

"Peter, I'm serious. Where the fuck am I?" I turned my head as I sat up, surprised to not see shackles chained to my wrists. I lifted my arms, inspecting them. No bone was jutting out of my left forearm. The guards broke it right before they shoved me back into my cell— my *cell*.

My shoulders slumped as realization dawned on me. "It's another hallucination." Fuck illusion users. I hated their powers the most.

I hadn't realized I'd spoken the words out loud until the illusion of

Peter's thick brows furrowed. "No, you're free, Sie. You're safe now. We got you out."

I closed my eyes and tried to block out his words. I didn't want to hear it. I didn't want to give in to this hope, only to wake up, drench in sweat as the fever took over my body. I didn't want to feel the throbbing agony of my forearm as I cradled it close to my chest.

At least this illusion was better than the other ones they used on me. I missed Peter, but I knew by now they only sent me good illusions when I was at my breaking point. It'd give me such hope only to come back to reality on the jagged crate that dug into my skin, only to hear the sounds coming from the *Puteus* below, only to be starving and in pain and brought right back into the torture room.

The "good" ones were mostly about Scotlind because whenever she was in my illusions, they destroyed me the most. Sometimes they just sent me images of her—of her rescuing me, her telling me she still loved me. They'd watch me leap for joy, only for me to realize it was an illusion the moment I was elated, and the mockery the fuchsia-eyed guard would hurl my way afterward was worse than any physical torture. He promised me numerous times a day he was going to bring Scotlind to the prison, that he'd fuck and maim her right in front of me, before he'd force me to watch her die in the pit below.

He had shown me exactly what he'd do to her in my illusions too, forcing me to watch it all on repeat until I was screaming.

"Scottie's here in case you wanted to know," my *imaginary* friend said. Fuck, I'd give so much right now to be able to see either of them. I missed Peter and Scotlind. It hurt worse than my arm or the fever or whatever hell the guards threw at me.

I exhaled sharply and took three steadying breaths. She's not real. This isn't real. My wife didn't come for me.

My insides curled as I thought of the two months she spent in different dungeons. Peter told me some of what had happened to her when she was in Lux, and I loathed myself for it. I was disgusted that I sent her there willingly. I barely put up a fight when the Luxian royals came to collect her. I didn't even look at her as she was pulled away, covered head to toe in shackles. I was too scared that if I'd looked, I would have attempted to teleport her away right then and there, only getting us both caught in the process. I had convinced myself that the only way to save her was by buying time, that I had to become the king first before I could act. I was so stupid, and now I would never get to tell her how sorry I was for it all. I'd never be able to look into her beautiful blue eyes again. And I deserved it, deserved *this*.

I couldn't stomach another night of their mind games. Hearing her name brought back the last illusion they forced me to endure.

The illusion user that visited my cell invaded my mind, found and warped my worst nightmare, and brought it to fruition. I was forced to spend hours watching Scottie and the Fire Prince have sex. He would fuck her, and the worst part of the whole thing was that she liked it. She didn't care that I was there. That I could see everything. That she was breaking whatever remained of my shattered heart. I was nothing to her anymore.

And even though I knew it was an illusion—I knew it wasn't real—some part of me couldn't look past it, couldn't let myself believe she wasn't with him in real life too.

Yeah, I wasn't putting up with another illusion right now. Even if it was only Peter.

I went to punch the crated wall with my good arm. All I saw was an endless, open tent in front of me, but I knew my fist would meet with the clang of metal, and then the pain from it would relieve me from this agony. I would once again wake up in my prison of hell.

I waited for the pain to shoot up my shoulder, to see my cellmate, Nidiniri, scurrying to the far corner of his own crate, to look down at the depths of the *Puteus* through the holes in my cage.

Except this time, I fell forward. I met no resistance. Punching my surroundings was how I always broke through the trance of the illusion.

They must have moved me from my cell while I was sleeping and threw me into a larger one. I was getting faster at recognizing the illusions and breaking out of them.

"Shit, Sie," Peter said as he rushed over to my hunched form. I must've fallen off the illusion-bed of pillows when I attempted to throw the punch. I was laying face down on soft furs.

But something was off. The texture felt so real and unlike the cold, dry cell. For a prison that claimed to be hidden underwater, there was none of the substance around. I licked my cracked lips, wishing to be bathed in the fluid. Wishing for my time with Scottie by the sapphire lake again. I wanted these furs to be her silken skin…

There was so much I wanted that I would never get now.

I would give up the five brand from my wrist if it meant I could be with her again. I couldn't stop replaying the last time I saw her. How they dragged me away and left her with *him*. I didn't want the Fire Prince breathing. I didn't want him alive. My fingers curled into the furs, thinking about how his fingers roamed over her bare back the night before my coronation.

And she was still in Lux, with *him*, and I would die in this prison, forced to watch endless illusions of them together until it killed me.

Peter grabbed my hand and the touch felt so damn real. "Sie, you aren't in the prison. We rescued you."

I looked down at the palm my friend was holding. The scar from my blood bond with Scottie was now a thin, white line. I thought of her new cut and the implications of it. Did the Fire Prince force her to make it? What else did he make her do? The worst part about my sentence in the prison was that I would never get to murder him for what he had done to her.

My prayers were being answered because the prick walked into the tent the next moment. He paused by the entrance, looking down at me on the ground. I wanted to give him a matching scar on the other side of his face. I didn't care that this was only an illusion. It would feel damn good to beat the living shit out of him.

I sprang to my feet, surprised that my body felt nimble. A smile spread over my lips as this was finally an illusion I would enjoy. I was waiting to meet the resistance of the chains, breaking the spell on my mind, but it never came. I was thankful for this kind of torture. If I couldn't kill the Fire Prince in real life, I'd happily settle for this.

The prince's silver eyes flashed. I grinned further, my lip splitting as blood trickled down my chin from how chapped and dry they were. I went to bring my fist down onto his face, but he moved out of the way the second before it collided. Peter was up before I could attempt to throw another, and the two of them had me pinned to the ground.

I swore as I struggled beneath both of their weights. "I'm going to fucking murder you," I promised him. The fever wreaked havoc on my body and left me weaker than I should have been, and I never properly recovered from all the poison I'd been consuming in Tennebris. But if I was at my full strength—

"Whoa. He's part of the reason you're alive and breathing outside of a cell right now," my friend said.

The Fire Prince pressed down on my shoulder. "And I'll throw you back into one if you don't calm down."

My eyes really were playing tricks on me because sapphire ones filled the tent as the flaps swayed again. "What are you doing to him?"

"He tried to kill your lover boy," Peter declared as both him and Tezya shoved off of me. Scottie's eyes narrowed on Peter, but she said nothing. Didn't even deny she loved the prick.

I stood, still shocked I wasn't hitting any resistance.

"If you're done acting like an animal and promise not to attack any of the people here, you can come to dinner," the Prince of Lux said through gritted teeth.

I started pacing, half enjoying the freedom of walking and half wanting the illusion to end. It was always harder to come out of the longer ones. *This isn't real. This isn't real. This isn't real.* I started mumbling, praying to snap out of it.

My eyes scanned the tent, confused as to why this illusion was lasting, why I wasn't brought back to reality yet. I waited for whatever they were going to throw at me next. I couldn't stomach seeing Scottie and Tezya at it again. I had to break free before that happened…

"You're not back in the prison, Sie," Peter said again as he patted my forearm. I looked down at where his hand met mine. My skin was closed. My arm was healed. I rolled my shoulders, finding stiffness there, but I felt everything. My body wasn't consumed by fever anymore.

"This isn't an illusion," he added as he assessed me, somehow knowing what I was struggling with. My friend tugged on his earlobe, and I entered his mind out of habit. *You're free, Sie. We got you out. You're safe now.*

I looked into my friend's mossy green eyes as he telepathically said over and over again that I was free. The illusions never did this. No one but Peter knew about our telltale sign.

I met Scottie's gaze next as I stopped pacing and started to allow Peter's words to sink in. She'd never looked so real before. My eyes scanned every inch of her body until they landed on her scarred hand. Her new scab was glaring back at me. I fisted my own palm in response. They never depicted her with another scar. The illusion users in the prison only projected her with a matching one to mine. The news of her with the Fire Prince hadn't spread, probably kept under wraps by the King.

This was real.

Fuck.

She got me out. I looked between Peter, her, and the Prince of Lux, not understanding what happened, but I desperately needed to talk to her.

"Where am I?" I finally asked.

"Well ain't that the question of the week," Peter grinned, looking toward the man I hated with all my being.

"I'll tell you, but only if you prove I can trust you. For now, all you need to know is you aren't on Luxian or Tennebrisian soil. Now, do you want to eat or not?"

I gritted my teeth and forced myself to say, "Fine," because my stomach was growling, and I felt like I was going to pass out if I didn't get food. But— "Scotlind, can we talk?"

"Um," she hesitated, and I didn't miss the subtle glance she gave Tezya. "I think it's better if we eat first." With that, she walked out of the tent with the Fire Prince trailing behind her.

Peter grumbled under his breath, "A 'thank you' would have been nice," before following both of them out into wherever the hell I was now.

ELEVEN
SCOTLIND

My chest was rising and falling out of rhythm, and I couldn't steady my heart long enough to hear properly. I was terrified of what would happen when Tezya and Sie saw each other, but I wasn't expecting to see Tezya holding him down or Sie trying to attack him. I was in more trouble than I thought.

I did my best to ignore the two of them following me. Peter came up next to me, grinning stupidly from ear to ear.

"What?" I snapped at him.

"Nothing. I'm just really, *really* going to enjoy what you do next. Which is what, by the way?"

I gritted my teeth because I had absolutely no idea what to do.

"Rumor," Tezya's voice caught me off guard from behind me. "This way." He pointed toward a large tent off to my left.

"Right," I said as I turned to follow him. I had no idea why I decided I could lead the way to dinner. I'd never been here before and had no idea where anything was located.

I followed Tezya toward the dining hall with my head down. I could feel Peter still grinning beside me and knew Sie was somewhere behind us. Loud chatter and the clanging of drinks echoed throughout the tent—tent wasn't the right word for it. It expanded so far in either direction that it seemed more like a building than fabric thrown together. There was a singular step to get inside with plank flooring covering the ground, giving the illusion it was a room.

A slight hush went over the hundreds of Advenians crammed inside the massive space, but it never fully quieted. An unsettling feeling washed over me as everyone's eyes momentarily glanced our way. Numerous heads bobbed in time with one another before I realized they were just recognizing Tezya. It was eerie to see so many faces, knowing the King of Lux ordered them all dead. That they would have all been dead if it wasn't for him.

A girl with lavender hair chopped to her shoulders ran over as soon as she saw us. "Tez!" she screamed and jumped into his arms. He picked her up, her feet lifting off the ground as he twirled her in a circle.

"Sav, I've missed you." He smiled once he set her back down. She was tall, about a whole head over me, but Tezya still towered over her.

A flash of saffron and black whipped through the crowd as Kallon walked over to us, a pitcher of ale in her hand. It was the longest time I'd seen her sporting the same hair colors. "Let me introduce you," Kallon grinned as she came up next to her.

The lavender-haired girl smiled and it was warm and sweet. She was breathtaking in a unique way. I'd never seen a female like her before. Her energy matched her bouncy form. A thick silver hoop jutted from the side of one nostril and large feathered earrings dangled from her ears.

My eyes drifted down her outfit. She wore a similar shirt to the one Tezya gave me when we visited the mortal world for the first time. It had the same ugly green man on it holding a beverage. This time reading, *the froth is strong with this one.* A jacket was tied around her waist, leaving a small sliver of her abdomen on display from where the shirt cropped. I couldn't help but notice she didn't have any scars—at least none that were showing—and I wondered what that was like.

"Sav, this is Scottie, Peter, and Sie. Everyone, this is Savannah Dravenburg," Kallon said, in between taking a sip from her ale.

"Nice to meet you all." Savannah grinned, and I hated how musically sweet her voice sounded. My gut twisted with unexpected jealousy as I kept wondering who she was to Tezya, and the image of him picking her up as she jumped into his arms kept replaying in my head.

"Sav is the daughter of the commander who runs the camp," Kallon added.

"And how do you all know each other?" the girl asked, tucking a strand of her purple hair behind her ear. More earrings went up the entire length of her earlobe.

Kallon answered her. "Well, Scottie here was married to Sie, who used to be the Dark Prince of Tennebris, but he isn't anymore. He's technically a convict now. They annulled their marriage prior to him becoming a criminal-on-the-run-fugitive, and now she has a thing for my fiancé. Really, I can't blame the girl, she has a hot prince complex."

My jaw dropped. "Thanks for that, Kallon," I muttered, heat rising to my cheeks.

"I'm just stating facts, babes." Kallon winked.

Peter grinned so wide I thought his dimples would reach the inside of his skull. "I like you. A lot."

Kallon returned his smile and offered him a sip of her ale. "And this is Peter, from Tennebris. No one knows anything about him, except he's friends with these two, and he was kidnapped wearing a dress." She gestured toward Peter who was taking a long sip from Kallon's drink, but I could still see him grinning through the rim of the glass.

"It's better that way," I mumbled, knowing full well Peter was going to hound me for the introduction later.

The lavender-haired girl smirked at me. "You have great taste in men." Her gaze shifted from Tezya to Sie, and I had to roll my shoulders to keep myself from doing anything stupid.

"How come your markings don't fade from your skin," Sie asked her. He'd been quietly taking everything in and hearing his voice shocked me. It was the first time he'd spoken since we left the tent, and I still hadn't comprehended that he was back yet. "There isn't a drop of sweat on you, so I'm assuming you're not wet right now?"

The girl choked on a laugh, and Kallon spit out her drink she had just gotten back from Peter. "That is *not* something you ask a girl in front of others." Kallon chuckled.

"She's human," Tezya answered over the girls' laughter. He was the only person taking his question seriously.

"Human?" Sie repeated softly like he couldn't believe it. I couldn't either. I hadn't anticipated running into a mortal here and with her height and slender frame, she looked Advenian. "Why does she have the Luxian markings then?" Sie asked as he pointed to Savannah. Her tan arms were inked with black designs, but they didn't fade from her skin like ours did. Hers remained present. The phases of the Earth's moon went up her right forearm while her left had a variation of numbers and letters I couldn't make sense of. The sliver of her stomach that was showing had glimpses of black markings, but I couldn't make out what they were.

I assessed her in a new light, taking a good look at her now. Sie was right—she didn't appear to be sweating or have any form of liquid on her skin, so why weren't the designs fading?

"Because they aren't markings, prince," the girl answered Sie. "It's a tattoo."

"What's a tattoo?" Peter asked.

"Think of it like artwork for your skin."

"Is this rare among your kind to be born with art?"

She laughed again. "I wasn't born with it. I went to get it done. It's tiny needles filled with a special ink—"

"You stabbed yourself to look like that?" Peter asked in amusement.

"I wouldn't call it *stabbing*. They're small pinpricks. It barely hurts."

"You're mortal," Sie said, still taking her in. "And you know about us?" He paused to look around the large gathering tent before his eyes rested back on the girl. "How many mortals are in this place?"

"Three," she responded flatly, crossing her arms over her chest. "And seeing as this is my home, it would be odd if I didn't know about your kind."

"Where's your brother?" Tezya asked, ignoring Sie's shocked

expression. Actually, all three of us probably looked dumbfounded as we processed the fact that a human was standing in front of us.

"Wells is here somewhere." She shrugged. "It's burger night, so you know he wouldn't miss it for any chemical compound he could compose in his lab."

Kallon huffed a laugh. "I don't blame him. Allen can make one mean burger, which I desperately need right now to go with my ale."

"Good, I'm starving." Savannah turned around, eyeing the tent. "Let's get a table." She gave one last glance at Sie before locking arms with Kallon and walking off. Seeing them arm in arm, one head full of lavender, the other half black, half yellow, I could see where Kallon got her sense of fashion from. I'd always wondered how her hair kept changing and now figured it had something to do with her.

I was left standing with Peter, Sie, and Tezya. No one spoke as we silently followed them. We blended into the line and waited our turn for food.

I watched Tezya ahead of me, taking in everything he did, mimicking his motions, and out of the corner of my eye, I saw Sie and Peter do the same. I grabbed a circular slab of meat, then a piece of bread shaped the same and a few vegetables.

A little girl, who couldn't have been much older than five, came charging at Tezya. "Tezzia! Tezzia!" she yelled, stumbling on his name. She leapt into his arms, nearly knocking the food out of his hands.

"Lamitte." Tezya smiled. "You grew. How old are you now? Three?"

The girl laughed in his arms as she reverently shook her head. "No, I'm four!"

"Sorry, Tezya," an older version of the girl he was holding said. "I told her not to jump on you like this."

"It's not a problem, Clarice," Tezya said as he gently set the girl back down, and she ran to her mother.

The two of them left, but it didn't stop the numerous Advenians from staring after him. I silently followed him toward the table where Savannah and Kallon were already eating when something dawned on me. So far, Tezya knew everyone by name. Several other people acknowledged him or patted his back as we passed, and almost everyone bowed their heads. Tezya regarded each of them, and despite the recognition, he wasn't getting any special treatment here.

I tried not to dwell on the fact that I'd been openly staring at him, watching as he interacted with everyone. And now, I was full on glaring as he took the open seat next to the mortal.

I purposely sat away from him, forcing myself to look around the tent instead of at him and the girl.

There were variations of eyes within the tent. Most of them were the unique coloring of Lux—silver, purple, aqua, sage, yellow, opal, lavender, coral. But within the unique coloring, I saw mixes of black eyes, some brown, some hazel—the Tennebrisian coloring.

Sie must have noticed too. "Are these people only from Lux?"

"No," Tezya answered. "Advenians from both kingdoms live here."

Peter, only having a plate filled with bread, dropped the roll he was holding. "They live together?"

Tezya nodded. "This is a refuge for *every* rebel. It doesn't matter what kingdom they're from. Most of the time, the rebellions happen in Lux, so there are more Luxians, but Advenians from Tennebris live here too."

"Rebel," Sie repeated, his gaze whipping around the room at the same time Peter asked, "And do they like... sleep with each other?" His voice was obnoxiously loud, to the point of practically screaming it. Every table surrounding ours turned to glare at us.

The lavender-hair girl choked on her food and couldn't stop smiling.

"They usually keep to their own families," Tezya answered. "But what people do in private is their own business. There're no rules like that here."

"Other than the training rings and the dining hall, the two king-doms don't really mix," Kallon said in between bites of food. I looked around, guessing the people in the camp had no idea that Tezya was living proof a child from both kingdoms could exist. They *could* mix. I wondered if that was why there wasn't a rule against it. Did he wish more people were like him?

"Where is everyone else?" Savannah asked, steering the conversation away. "Father said you were staying for good, so I thought Dove, Brock, and Rainer would be here."

Tezya's jaw clicked at the sound of his sister's and friends' names. I only noticed because I realized I had been staring at him *again*. I quickly pulled my gaze away and focused on my food.

"They're still in Lux. I'm due to fetch them in an hour," Kallon answered for him, leaving out the information that they might not come back.

"Once Dovelyn returns you should train with her," Tezya's voice sounded. I looked up when no one answered him and realized he was staring at me.

"Me?" I choked on my first bite of burger, which was a shame because it was so good it melted in my mouth. "She hates me. She'll probably kill me before she actually agrees to train me."

"I'll make sure she doesn't."

"Well, I don't particularly care for her either," I spat. "I don't understand why I would need to train with her. Why can't I train with Kallon?" I didn't add *'or you'* even though I missed him teaching me. Besides hating the Luxian castle and being a prisoner there, I missed training together in the private gym.

"Because I want you to be ready. We will *all* start training," Tezya announced to the table. "There's going to be a war sooner or later."

Savannah was the only person who looked thrilled by the idea, and I wondered if he meant to include her.

"War?" Sie repeated, and I forgot he knew nothing about what was happening.

"You didn't think rescuing you from the prison would come without any consequences, did you?" Kallon arched a thin brow under her bangs.

"Who are all these people?" he asked, ignoring Kallon. "You called them rebels, but the rebellion is dead. You killed them." He was looking right at Tezya now and the fire in his glare was menacing.

"Clearly I didn't," Tezya ground out, not really giving him an answer, before turning back to look at me. "If you can master your enhancement, Rumor, it'll be a huge asset to us," Tezya added. "You need to make sure you aren't subconsciously using it on anyone around you anymore." He didn't need to explain why that was a priority.

"Practicing with an air user will be the best way to see your progress," he continued. "You can enhance Dovelyn's shields and expand her invisibility. See how much you can add to her powers and for how long."

Sie's hands fell against the table with an echoing thud. "You figured out your powers?" His voice was breathless and it brought me back to the lake when he tried to train me.

"Yes," I admitted softly. I didn't say anything else at first. It took me swallowing six times before I got the courage to add, "I have enhancement."

No one spoke after that, and I wondered if he made the same connection Tezya had. That my enhancement was what he felt all those times I wasn't wearing my Alluse necklace. That we never had a blood bond.

Sie didn't say anything, but I noticed his jaw tightening, and his fists remained clenched on top of the table.

He didn't eat for the rest of dinner.

TWELVE
SCOTLIND

Kallon portaled Dovelyn and Rainer back yesterday, and apparently Tezya thought it was still a good idea for her to train me.

I was dreading it. Dovelyn didn't like me on a good day, but now—when Brock was still somewhere in Lux—it wasn't going to be pretty. And to make matters worse, I was already late.

I followed the handwritten directions Kallon had sketched for me earlier today. But her drawing skills were almost as bad as Peter's, and her map was illegible. I'd been walking in circles all morning. It didn't help that all the tents looked identical. Tezya offered to walk me, and now I was regretting being stubborn and saying I could do it on my own.

I looked back down at the map in question. I was supposed to meet Dovelyn toward the back of the camp at the opposite end of the training rings.

When I finally made it past the clearing of trees, I halted. Dovelyn was sitting against the corner of a tent—there was only one in the area. Her legs were pulled tightly into her chest as she sobbed into her knees.

Behind the lone tent were open fields. I could just glimpse one of the border control towers—from Kallon's map there were supposedly twelve—but that was it. There was nothing else here.

I stood there awkwardly, unsure if I should leave. I waited a good minute before deciding to do just that. I turned to walk back the same way I came.

"You don't have to go." Her voice came out in jumbled sobs before I even managed to take a step. Of course she already knew I was here.

"I'm sorry about Brock," I offered. I was upset when they arrived without him. He was quiet and the most closed off out of Tezya's friends, but he was also the kindest. If Brock was still with the Lux King, it was because of me—because of the assembly…

The moment Kallon portaled in without him, Dovelyn used her ability and made herself invisible. Rainer sobbed as he choked on his words while Kallon kept whispering it wasn't his fault, and everything was going to be okay.

But it wasn't.

I thought back to Tezya's punishment, about how cruel and sadistic it was, and that was only because Tezya kept information from him. The King did that to his own son, or at least someone he still believed was his son. I didn't want to think about how enraged he'd be now that we were all gone. We openly committed a crime against the kingdom by freeing not only me and Peter—who were considered his property—but now Sie too. And on top of that, his own children were the ones who did it. I doubted he'd hold back with Brock, and it broke a piece of me. I couldn't imagine how Dovelyn was feeling. I kept envisioning how I would feel if it was Tezya left behind…

Besides him offering to walk me and telling me my training with Dovelyn was still on, I hadn't seen Tezya all morning, and I found myself wondering how he was holding up. I knew it was killing him.

Dovelyn wiped her eyes once, then stood. "Me too."

To my surprise, she didn't say anything else and started training me.

I could sense her abilities as I reached my enhancement out to her. We worked with invisibility first, and by nightfall, I managed to turn a quarter of the camp invisible for an entire minute. Dovelyn explained she normally made shields within a thirty foot radius. Unless she was working with other air users, it was easier to make multiple smaller shields than one larger one.

"That's enough for today," she panted. I wanted to fight her on it and beg her to keep going. I wanted to make the entire camp disappear and for more than just a minute. I needed to master my abilities so I could be an asset. I didn't want my inexperience to be a reason I was left out again.

But I didn't push it. I knew what was behind her sullen face and little words. She was distraught and emotionally drained. A pang of guilt sprang through me as I realized she worked with me in silence, only speaking when absolutely necessary, which was unlike her.

"Thank you for training me," I said as I turned to leave. "I know I'm not your favorite person, but I appreciate it."

"I don't hate you," she replied, surprising me.

I seriously doubted that statement. I raised an eyebrow as I turned around to face her again. "You don't?"

She shook her head softly. "No."

"Right," I huffed a laugh.

"You terrify me."

I narrowed my eyes. "Why?"

"Because I see what you can do to my brother. I love him with all my heart, and I will always pick him over anyone else. If I had to sacrifice everyone in the camp to save him, I would. But I see the way he looks at you... I see the way he loves you. You should talk with him. Hear what he has to say."

"Why are you telling me this?"

"Because you have the opportunity to be with the person you love, and you're wasting it. It infuriates me. Back in Lux, Brock and I could never be together. We both knew it. He's a rank four, and I'm a five. But even if we were the same rank, my father never would have allowed it out of spite. It was the same for Tezya. He never would have been able to be with you if you stayed there." I nodded, knowing the King arranged his engagement to Kallon, even though I hated it. "But my brother always planned on getting you out. Tezya's a dreamer to a fault. He was working on a way to fake your death, to safely get you away from my father without raising questions and risking the camp. He planned on bringing you here. He was going to tell you about all of this when the time was right. But seeing you at dinner that night, chained to my father, it did something to him. He acted rashly. We lost our element of surprise because of it."

I didn't move, scared if I did it would bring her out of her uncharacteristic candor.

"I know what that feels like," she continued, "to love someone so desperately, to be forced to see that person every day, but never have them. It's not something I wanted for my brother. So I tried to stop it before he developed feelings for you. I didn't think his plan would work. I didn't think he'd be able to get you out. Not with my father's new obsession with you now that he knows you have the capability to make him stronger." She wiped at her nose. The tip of it was bright red. "But now, that doesn't matter. The people in this camp may look at Tezya like he is their prince, but he won't act on it. He will lead them, but he has no interest in politics."

"And what does he have an interest in?" I asked.

"You." She paused to look at me. Her silver eyes were biting and restless. "You are free to be together. Once this war starts, that's one of the things these people will fight for. Freedom. Freedom to do what they please. Freedom to love who they want. If we win, you two can be together for good. So don't punish him because he didn't fully open up to you. I would have thought that you of all people would understand him, could relate to the sheer terror it takes to reveal something so ingrained in you to keep locked away. He wanted to tell you he was from both kingdoms, but I convinced him to wait. I forced him not to open up until after he brought you here. I'm the reason he didn't let you in."

"Everyone makes their own choices in the end," was all I could think to say, but my mind was whirling. I could understand the need to keep secrets hidden, how revealing something that big wasn't done lightly. I never had the opportunity to open up to Tezya because he witnessed my entire life on the monitor screens when I was brought into Lux. Would I have been able to tell him all my secrets if he hadn't already seen them, or would I have struggled to open up after so many years of forcing it down?

"What did I overhear that day when you were in his room?" I asked her, hoping her willingness to confess everything would last.

She sighed loudly, pausing long enough I thought she wouldn't answer. "I have visions," she admitted and even the wind stilled. I assumed that was her second power—she brought it up during the conversation I overheard in Lux and then again outside the trench— but I was so mad at the time, I never questioned it.

"My powers manifested at a young age," she continued. "I was foolish and didn't know how to interpret them yet. My father has always been cruel, and as you can imagine, our childhood wasn't a pleasant one. Once he realized I possessed more than just an air ability, he started treating me differently. I no longer got punished alongside my brothers. Instead, I got to sit in on his meetings. I was flaunted about, put on a pedestal. I yearned for his approval when I was younger so I told him everything I saw. I couldn't control the visions that came to me. I still can't to this day. I randomly see flashes of images. Sometimes I can make sense of them, sometimes I can't.

"I saw you decades before you were born. The girl with the unique back markings. At first that's all I saw, just bits of your early life in Lux. I had no idea why you kept showing up, but I knew you were important. Something in my gut told me to never tell my father about the visions I had of you, so I kept you a secret. My visions are usually lone occurrences, small glimpses into the future before it happens, but you were the only thing I kept seeing over and over again. I spent years searching the library, trying to find the meaning of your back markings, looking through our records to see if you were born yet, but you weren't.

"Then I started getting visions of my younger brother. I saw golden markings covering his skin. Tezya was only twenty-five when they started. I didn't want to believe it. I loved my brother, but the images of him terrified me. What the prophecy showed me in my visions... I knew it was bad. So I went to our mother, who was kind and nothing like our father. She loved us, and I knew I could trust her with it.

"That's when I learned the truth about him, that he was both Luxian and Tennebrisian. Only my mother wasn't surprised. Tezya and her already knew what he was and what it meant. But we never told him about the bad visions, at least not at first. My brother never really believed in the prophecy, but I couldn't shake this feeling that my visions of you were entwined with him somehow."

Tears pooled down her face. "My mother, knowing what I saw, knowing the full truth, began to go insane. She loved us all dearly, but Tezya was special to her. She hated our father just as much as we did, if not more. Arcane and I are *his* heirs, but Tezya was brought into this life with a male she once loved from Tennebris. She wanted to protect him." She paused, stifling a sob. "Then one day, she had some of my mind wiped by a compulsion user. She took away the visions I had of him and the prophecy.

"To this day, I still don't know what I saw. The only thing I know now is whatever fate awaits him isn't a good one. Our mother took her life a year later because of it, leaving only a letter behind, telling me to always protect him. She thought with her death, the prophecy would die with it. Only I had another vision. I saw her die. I watched it." She inhaled. "In the vision, she came to Brighta first. Tezya and I didn't even know the camp existed until after everything happened. Then, I watched her take her own life right before she sealed her grave in her blood. I made the mistake of telling Tezya that I believed the Goddesses were showing it to me for a reason. That I thought it meant the key to the prophecy was buried with her."

Her glossy eyes found mine. "Then I had a vision of you again. I hadn't had one in decades, and with everything going on with my family, I forgot about the girl I used to see. It was clear as day, exactly as I'm seeing you now. I saw you marry the Dark Prince, and I got an idea. I knew my father was restless. I knew he wanted to kill whoever the prophecy was about. He doesn't like anything lingering that could threaten his rule. We all grew up knowing the bare details of it—that a boy born from both kingdoms would destroy the current systems.

"I knew if my father ever discovered who Tezya really was, he would chop him to bits and spread the remains of him until there was nothing left. I was so scared for his life. I couldn't lose him. I just couldn't... not after the death of our mother, so I lied. I finally told my father about the visions I had of you. Only I didn't tell him the full truth. I made him believe you and Sie would conceive the chosen one, that he just wasn't born yet. I told him about my visions of you two marrying, of a rank five coming to power on the Dark soil. I convinced him to send you there. I helped orchestrate everything.

"I knew what I saw would come to fruition. I knew you two would marry. That all I had to do was get you to the Dark Kingdom. I saw a vision of you two together in a bathroom. I thought you slept with him. The only thing was, I didn't see everything that happened, only little glimpses of your life.

"I told my father the only way to gain control of Tennebris—which I knew he desperately wanted—was to wait and bide his time. I knew you would be captured eventually, but I thought you'd be pregnant with Sie's child. I thought the King would kill you and the baby, and he'd never think about the prophecy again. But I read the visions wrong. I didn't think you and Tezya would ever meet. I never thought you would survive."

I didn't know what to say or how to process what she was revealing to me. I just stood there, staring at her, listening to the words coming out of her mouth, but it wasn't registering yet.

"I feel this guilt when I look at you," she admitted. "I knew what you were going to face by going to Tennebris, but I sent you anyway. I'm sorry for your pain. I truly am. But by the time you were born, I'd spun so many lies I couldn't take them back even if I wanted to. My father had your fate sealed the moment you took your first breath." She paused for a moment, considering. "I am sorry, Scotlind, but I would do it again if it meant that my brother gets to live."

"You... you planned everything?" I was still stunned, still trying to wrap my head around it.

"Yes." She no longer had tears running down her face. "My father orchestrated your kidnap. The men that took you were hired assassins my father later had killed after you were in Tennebris. We informed only those who had to know and most that were involved would turn up dead after their task was completed. He would bribe them with gold, have them complete what he wanted, and then send more assassins to murder them after it was done."

She took a breath as I held mine. "Your counselor was hired too when you first arrived at LakeWood. She was specifically picked for her abilities. She had you compelled to never be able to speak about who you were until you left school. She worked under Synder. Since he was promised the Tennebrisian throne once everything was said and done, he orchestrated everything on their side. It's why you were chosen for Sie. I told my father every painstaking detail of my visions, and I made them all come true. He listened to everything I told him because I promised him he'd be able to kill the boy the prophecy was about while also getting control of the Dark Throne if he waited long enough."

"I was taken by Kole. They almost killed us in the warehouse..." I didn't need to finish before she nodded.

"A vision," she said as she swiped the snot from her nose again. "That was one I saw clearly. The Lux King had Synder set it up. I knew you two wouldn't die, but it served as the catalyst to get you discovered. To move things forward. I thought I had the timeline right. I thought you had already slept together. I needed you to be pregnant so he would believe the prophecy was over."

She knew. She knew I was going to be tortured and almost killed. She knew what haunted me. She *caused* it.

She caused it all.

"I'm sorry, Scotlind, for everything. But I would do it all again for Tez."

"Does *he* know?" I whispered. I was terrified of her answer, terrified to know if the man I was falling for knew everything his sister had done. I couldn't breathe, couldn't think until she spoke next.

She shook her head. "No. Tezya doesn't know all of that. I told him decades ago about a girl with your back markings. I used to tell my brother everything back then. I wanted to see if he could make sense as to why I was seeing you. I figured he forgot about it. It was nearly a century ago now, but after the day you were brought up from the dungeons, he suspected I had my hands in your fate. We all saw your markings on the monitors. Tezya was livid. He sought me out afterward.

"He only knows I told the King to send for you, but he suspects some of the rest. After your interrogation, my father was half furious you weren't pregnant, but half elated it meant we could use you to get Sie off the throne. He punished me for not properly reading my visions, which was proof enough for Tezya that I was involved, because my father hadn't brought me to the punishment cell for over three decades. Arcane probably goes once a year. It's only Tezya that he regularly uses it on."

"You had my parents killed," I said, my voice was cold and toneless. Everything else she said washed away, and all I could focus on was that one single thing. My parents died the night I was taken.

"I didn't," she said as she looked at me with pity. "I didn't tell them to do that. That was all my father's doing. I had no idea he was going to kill everyone."

Everything stilled. I wanted to hit her, to fight her, to scream, to cry, to do something, anything, but I just kept staring at her in disbelief, unsure which emotion was winning. She was the reason for *everything*. If it wasn't for her, my parents would still be alive. I would have grown up in Lux as Haevely Sirena. I never would have been Scotlind Rumor. None of this would have happened.

"I don't expect your forgiveness. I never anticipated having to see you, as you can imagine. My visions never showed me that my brother would fall in love with you, but I see it now." Her gaze settled on the scab on my palm. "I think the Goddesses gave me the visions of you because it had to happen, all of it. I saw you and Sie together before I even came up with the idea to use you—"

I called to my abilities. I wasn't sure what I planned to do, but as soon as I felt the familiar sensation of water inside of her, I let myself be consumed by it.

I felt nothing but rage. Her mouth flew open—and I knew she was screaming—but I couldn't hear it. All that existed was a high ringing in my ears and the need to avenge my parents, avenge what my life could have been, what it *should* have been…

Every horrible thing I ever went through came crashing through me. I was reliving it all. All the death, all the torture, all the fear…

I felt the draw of water in her bloodstream as I pulled it out. Her shield came up a second later, blocking me from ripping everything out of her until she was nothing more than skin and bones. I wanted to leave her a husk. I wanted her to feel the same hollowed out sensation that was tearing through me.

I watched as sweat poured from her—slow at first and then faster and faster—before her scream finally registered in my ears. I was killing her. I was killing Tezya's sister—someone he cared about…

It brought me back to reality, and I stopped pushing, letting my powers slowly fade back into me. I blinked as her silver eyes came into focus before she collapsed on the ground.

I stayed there for three seconds, long enough to make sure she was still breathing, before I started running.

I hated everything about Dovelyn, and I probably always would, but I didn't want her to die. There was a small nagging part in the back of my mind that was grateful. Tezya was alive because of it.

And as angry as I was, I knew I would do it all again.

For him I would.

THIRTEEN
TEZYA

I FOUND Dovelyn face down on the fields toward the outskirts of the camp. Her eyes fluttered open as I scooped her into my arms, but other than that she barely stirred. My senses rippled toward her. Her breathing was shallow and her skin was ice cold despite being drenched in sweat.

Shit.

I sprinted toward the healer's tent, unsure what had happened to push her to the brink of passing out. I called to my fire, surrounding us in flames as I ran, trying to force some warmth back into her.

It took an hour of the healers pumping her with hydration before Dovelyn stirred again. Her body was still shaking, but her face was finally starting to regain some color.

A healer informed me she was severely dehydrated, and I hated myself for forcing her to train Scotlind. I assumed it'd serve as a distraction. She was hurting because of Brock. I just didn't realize she hadn't been eating or drinking because of it.

It was a stupid idea. I knew they didn't get along. Maybe some part of me was hoping it could change, that if they spent time together, they'd realize they were more alike than they thought.

I was delusional.

"Tezya." Dovelyn stirred.

I leaned over her cot, picking up the glass of water on the stand, before forcing her to drink it. She took a long sip, her fingers shaking slightly around mine as she gripped the cup and nearly finished it.

"Are you okay?"

She nodded, scanning the healer's tent, but didn't elaborate.

"I'm sorry," I said as I set the glass back down.

"For what?"

"For having you train Scotlind. I didn't realize you weren't taking care of yourself, Dove. I should have known. I'm sorry if it was too much with Brock…"

She shook her head a little too forcefully, then rubbed her temples. "I'm fine, Tez. We've all been through worse, and I *am* taking care of myself."

I scrunched my eyebrows. "The healers said you were severely dehydrated. I know you're upset, but you still have to eat."

She scoffed, but it came out more of a huffed laugh. She threw her head back against the wooden backboard. "I am."

"Then what happened?"

"Scottie tried to kill me." I stilled, unsure what to make of that statement. Dovelyn slowly picked her head back up, her silver eyes meeting mine. "And she would have, *could* have. She almost did."

"Where is she?"

"She's fine," she scoffed again, but a sly smile formed over her cracked lips. "I'm glad that's all you care about though. Where your girlfriend is, instead of how your sister is doing."

I didn't comment on the girlfriend part. Scotlind wasn't mine, even if I wanted her to be. "What happened?" I asked again. Regardless that neither one of them liked each other, I couldn't figure out what would drive Rumor to murder. She had plenty of reasons throughout her life —numerous people who wronged her—but she never did. She didn't have a vengeful bone in her body. So what did Dovelyn do that threw her over the edge?

"She tried to pull all the water out of my body."

"Okay," I said slowly, unsure where this was going. I couldn't decide what I wanted to know more: *why* she almost killed Dovelyn or *how* she did it. I told her water was everywhere and in everything. Advenian blood was made up of sixty percent of it, so I knew it was possible. But to have that kind of control to separate it and with no experience…

"Tezya, she was seconds away from doing it when I erected a shield," she admitted. "She was going to shift every drop of water out of my cells and drain me. You know how they always say if you can create instead of manipulate, you're a higher rank?"

I nodded.

"Well it's not only because creating takes more skill. Usually, anyone who can create an elemental ability naturally has more reserves."

I nodded again, already knowing all of this.

"And you know that I have the largest air reserves?" she asked, and I knew she wasn't saying it to brag. She was just stating a fact. Her Trials had all of Lux talking about her for years. Her reserves were off the charts.

"Yes, Dovelyn, I'm aware. What are you getting at?"

"Scottie's water ability is stronger than my air ability, despite the fact that she can only manipulate. I think she's a lot stronger than we think."

"What makes you say that?" It wouldn't surprise me. I remembered how she drained the entire pool back in Lux and that was fairly early into her training. It took most Advenians years to master their element effortlessly, and she was learning really fast, unnaturally fast. The way she was manipulating and moving water matched someone who had been training for decades, and she'd only just started weeks ago. But I was surprised Dovelyn had noticed. She wasn't someone who was easily impressed.

"Because she would have killed me if she wasn't accidentally saving me at the same time. My air shield was weakening. I was on the verge of dropping it. I think Scottie could sense it with her other ability. I would have died if she hadn't used her enhancement to strengthen my shield. Her water ability would have overpowered my air."

"Shit," I cursed. If the King knew how powerful she was, he would be after her even more than he already was. And she used both of her abilities at once. It was incredibly hard to do and taxing beyond belief. If you wanted a way to completely drain everything you had, that was how you did it.

It was all the more reason to train her. I knew she was improving. She could decide what ability to focus on in controlled settings with her enhancement and was starting to pick up on different powers, but if she were to fight in this war, I didn't want to risk her accidentally making the abilities of whoever she was up against stronger. She had a habit of losing control when her emotions were heightened, and I didn't want to give anyone an advantage over her.

"Why?" I asked.

"Why, what?"

"Why did she try to kill you, Dove?"

She was silent for a long moment that I didn't think she was going to tell me. Her eyes were searching mine, debating. I knew she was keeping secrets from me. She and our mother had been my entire life, but I was done looking the other way. I waited for her to collect herself.

Then she told me everything.

FOURTEEN
SCOTLIND

I'D REFUSED to train with Dovelyn again, and mercifully, Tezya didn't question me on it.

Instead, all I'd been doing was letting my thoughts fester, and I found myself thinking about Vallie a lot.

I missed her. I was happy she wasn't here, that she was safe and far away from the mess I'd gotten myself into, but I desperately wanted to talk to her about everything.

She'd be happy here too. Vallie always had a fascination with the mortal territory and would probably hound the lavender-haired girl for every nitty-gritty detail about her life.

I knew deep down she'd agree with what the rebellion was fighting for, even though we never talked about it.

We both tried to enjoy the little time we had together in school, and I never once brought up my past. But now, knowing my counselor had compelled me to keep the truth from her, I was even more pissed off. It was worse knowing I'd probably never get the chance to tell her. My mind replayed my entire childhood up until I left LakeWood. I went through all the times I wanted to tell Vallie I was Luxian, but whenever I opened my mouth to say the words—I couldn't.

Everything about my life was a lie. A lie that Dovelyn concocted.

I hated her. Half of me wished I had killed her that day, but then another part of me understood it, even if I wasn't ready to admit it yet.

And when I wasn't contemplating everything I went through, I found myself staring at Tezya from afar, watching him when I didn't think he'd notice. But Sie had. I knew he was watching me just like I was watching Tezya. He had asked to speak with me in private numerous times throughout the week, but I'd been avoiding him, finding excuse after excuse to push it off. I didn't know what to say to him, and I wasn't ready for what he wanted to say to me.

I'd been alone in my tent for the past hour, thinking everything over, when Peter found me. "Dravenburg called a war meeting."

———

We were the last two Advenians to enter the tent.

I was looking at Dravenburg in a different light, knowing he was mortal and the owner of the camp—or co-owner. I didn't understand Tezya's relationship with him or how a human family got involved in the first place.

If I hadn't known Savannah was human, I would have sworn she was an Advenian. It wasn't just that she had the same slender and tall frame or that her tattoos looked like permanent Luxian markings. It was more in how she presented herself. She was in a camp full of lethal beings, but she wasn't scared that everyone around her had powers she was susceptible to. We were always taught that our kind was superior to humans, but if she was intimidated, she didn't show it.

My gaze snagged on Tezya next. He ignored his seat. His fingers mindlessly rubbing at the scab on his palm. He stopped the moment his eyes locked with mine. The commotion around me stilled, and all I could focus on were the blue and silver in his irises, trying to figure out which color was winning at the moment.

Kallon clapped a hand on my back, breaking our gazes. "Have a seat, babes."

I took the chair she was gesturing to and found two black eyes focused on me. Peter was sitting next to Sie and was rambling his ear off while Sie was looking directly at me.

I was surprised Tezya let him join the meeting, not that Sie didn't deserve to be here, but it meant Tezya trusted him enough with whatever was about to be said. There were forty or so Advenians in the tent altogether, plus the two mortals standing next to Tezya.

Rainer smiled at me from across the room. I hadn't seen him since he arrived. His dark skin seemed to glow against his unnaturally white smile. He swept his black curls off his forehead, exposing his sage colored eyes. He reminded me of Peter—not because of their striking green eyes—but because they were both warm and positive. It was refreshing to be around. I gave a small wave back.

Dravenburg cleared his throat, calling everyone to attention, as Tezya stepped forward to speak.

"I want to be proactive," Tezya started, and I had to make an effort to focus on his words and not at how close he was standing to the human girl. "We still have the benefit of surprise since the King isn't aware of our numbers. But the news of Sie escaping the prison is starting to spread. He will double his defenses if he hasn't already. The longer we wait, the harder it will be to make a move. What we have been doing here isn't enough anymore. We don't have the luxury of waiting."

"What are you suggesting?" Dravenburg asked.

"We need to uncover the prophecy."

"No." Dovelyn sprang from her seat so fast that her chair fell to the ground. "That is out of the question." It was my first time seeing her since she confessed everything to me, and I wasn't sure how I felt about it.

One of the Advenians from the camp asked, "What prophecy? How come I've never heard of it?"

Kallon answered next to me, "The prophecy started during the Ability War back on Allium. The servants of the Goddesses spoke about it before the planet was destroyed. They claimed it was the words of Pylemo herself. Once our kind came here, the kings from both sides kept the prophecy a secret. They didn't want it to come true because it meant they would have to give up their crowns."

Peter leaned back in his seat, resting his ankle over his knee. "So does anyone care to enlighten us on what the prophecy is exactly?"

Kallon's yellow eyes flicked over him before she continued, "Legend claims a boy born from both kingdoms—a boy who possesses both golden and black markings—will bring an end to the current courts until there's no longer a Light and Dark Kingdom."

"It's a waste of time," Dovelyn interrupted. "We have no way of opening the tomb to even know if it would be helpful."

"It's worth a try," Tezya said. "If it can help bring an end to separate kingdoms, maybe it's the answer we need. Maybe it means this camp. We've been living together in harmony for a while, why can't—"

"You are forcing connections, trying to convince yourself of it, Tezya, when in reality, it could damn us all along with the current rulers."

"If that's the case, then I won't go through with it. But on the off chance it's what we need to gain advantage, how can we not try?"

I knew what Dovelyn and Tezya weren't admitting. The one thing they weren't telling the group. They both knew if Tezya fulfilled the prophecy, it could very well be damning to *him*.

"What are you talking about?" Dravenburg asked, shooing away Dovelyn's concern. "What good is the prophecy without the Advenian born from both kingdoms?"

In answer, Tezya's body lit up in golden spirals. I saw the slight tremor of hesitation he had before he compelled Savannah, "Fetch me that map." His voice had the same familiar tones I heard many times before as his compulsion swept over the human. The lavender-haired girl moved without wanting to and brought the map to Tezya, setting it down on the table in front of him.

I stared at his markings as they came to life—his *golden* markings. I memorized every curve of the Luxian flames on his skin when he was sweating during his punishment. But this was something else. An entirely different side to him that I hadn't known existed. And he was revealing it to everyone.

"I'm from both kingdoms," he announced, and my mouth gaped open as I stared at him.

As soon as Savannah took a step back, Tezya let his golden markings fade into him.

The mortal girl only stared at him in shock, not understanding why she'd just listened to him. Honestly the entire tent was openly staring. No one said anything as an eerie silence stretched through the tent.

My heart stopped at the vulnerability in what he was doing. What he was laying out before everyone, at the risk he was putting himself in.

Sie stood, his eyes focused solely on Tezya. "You have compulsion," he finally said what was on everyone's mind. Like he needed to hear Tezya confirm it to believe it, even though we literally just *saw* him use his abilities.

Even I was still having a hard time wrapping my head around it, and I already knew. But knowing it and seeing it were two entirely different things. The first time Tezya used his compulsion in front of me, I was in a daze, but now I couldn't deny it.

Kallon swore next to me, and across the room, Peter's eyes looked like they were about to pop out of his head.

"Yes." Tezya nodded. "I'm half Luxian and half Tennebrisian."

Minutes seemed to tick by, until someone broke the silence again. "I thought…" they started, then audibly swallowed. "I thought a baby wouldn't survive from both kingdoms, how are you alive?"

"It's a lie they started back on Allium during the Ability War. I think the kingdoms used it as a method to control us. They wanted separate rules, and there's no better way of guaranteeing that than by fear. So like I said, I think we need to figure out what the prophecy is."

"Okay, so how do we uncover it?" Dravenburg asked.

Tezya stepped up to the map. "I was hoping you'd tell me. It's sealed inside my mother's tomb. From the visions Dovelyn had of her death, she saw her seal her grave in blood, and she only did that when she was hiding something." He swallowed, and I watched his Adam's apple bob as he said, "I think the prophecy is buried with her."

It was an effort to keep my mouth from dropping. I felt for Dovelyn. I couldn't imagine being forced to watch her mother's death through her visions, knowing it was because of what she told her. But I was more shocked Tezya was willing to unbury her for it.

"I know you know where she's buried, Dravenburg. You have to see the benefit in recovering it."

"It's too far away," Dravenburg said after a minute but still didn't point to where it was on the map. "And I'm the only one who knows where it is. I can't leave my children or the camp when this is the most vulnerable Brighta has ever been."

"You don't have to," Savannah said. Dravenburg's hazel eyes glared at his daughter as she continued. "I may have stolen the files you have on their mother, *and,*" she said as she enunciated the word, "I may have snuck out and found the grave's exact location."

"Why on earth would you do that?" her father growled.

She shrugged. "I was bored and curious."

"How far away is it?" Kallon asked, speaking for the first time since Tezya announced he was from both kingdoms. She honestly seemed the most shocked out of everyone in the tent, and that was saying something.

"About a day on foot," the human replied.

"You're asking to lose two days of travel to and from, and however long it takes to try to uncover it once there. It's better we stay here and train," Dovelyn said, but she was grasping at straws.

"Only one day of travel," Tezya amended. "Once there, Kallon can work on setting up a portal for us to return to the outskirts of the camp. We wouldn't need a lot of people. Everyone else can keep training—"

Dravenburg cut him off, finally turning away from glaring at his daughter. "No."

"It's worth the risk," Tezya shot back.

"The risk of my daughter?"

"I can take care of myself, Dad," Savannah snapped. "I know the way there with my eyes closed. I'll be fine."

"Things are different now, Savannah. You can't just go hiking and wander alone anymore. This isn't just a drop in visit. They're fugitives now and both kingdoms are probably hunting them all down as we speak." Dravenburg's voice was starting to rise, and I could see the tension radiating from him by his stiff posture.

"I know that better than anyone," Tezya said softly. "I know what the Lux King is capable of. I am asking to do this because I believe it'll help. Even the shields of the camp won't be enough to stop him. We can't hide forever. He will find us, and when he does, if we do nothing, we won't be ready."

When Dravenburg still didn't say anything, Tezya added, "I want to give our people the best advantage we can. I don't want to wait until war shows up at our camp. If we do, there will be little we can do to keep it away from the humans. I want to bring it to Lux. I want the advantage. We need to be proactive. If this prophecy can give us even a glimmer of a chance at that, I want to take it. So yes, I believe it's worth the risk."

Dravenburg pinched the bridge of his nose. "You know how we do things in Brighta. A vote then. All in favor of seeking out the prophecy with a separate vote for what we find."

I noted Dravenburg's words. He didn't want Tezya to go behind anyone's back with what was revealed. It was strategic. Find out what the prophecy meant, then weigh the risk as a group together later. Yet, I couldn't raise my hand. I found myself unable to fathom putting Tezya at risk. I knew it was foolish. That it made me weak and selfish. I was willing to give up something that could change things for the good of our people, only to save one Advenian. I was putting Tezya above everyone in both kingdoms, above humans too. I started to understand some of what Dovelyn was feeling, because even though my mind told me that raising my hand was the right thing to do, my heart couldn't do it. I didn't want him to do this.

I looked around the room. Everyone raised their hands except Dravenburg, Dovelyn, and me.

Dravenburg's voice echoed, "It's settled then. Tezya, form a small group. Savannah will take you to your mother's grave at dawn."

The girl squealed as she clapped her hands together, and I had to bite down on my jealousy.

She was going to lead him, somewhere in the mortal territory, and the idea of them being alone together hit me like a brick.

FIFTEEN
TEZYA

"I WANT TO GO WITH YOU."

I was surprised to find Scottie in my tent later that night. She'd barely spoken to me since we first arrived, and it was killing me. I was forcing myself to give her space. I knew she needed time to process everything, but seeing her in front of me now, I had no idea why I was waiting.

Dawn was a few hours away, and I hadn't figured out who was coming with me. The only people I knew were going were Savannah and Kallon, and I was fine with keeping it just the three of us. The more people who traveled, the bigger the risk. We would be vulnerable out in the open, not protected by the camp's shield, and I knew the Lux King probably had the entire mortal territory crawling with spies to locate us. It was only a matter of time until they made it north.

He wouldn't kill me. He'd want me alive, but everyone else...

"You're better off staying behind to train," I replied honestly. "I don't care who you train with, but you need to work on your enhancement."

"I'll train with Dovelyn again if you let me go with you."

"Why?" I asked. I didn't blame her for not wanting my sister to train her anymore. Hell, I was furious at Dovelyn after she told me everything, and I wanted to kill her myself. But I also knew Dove was Scottie's best bet at learning her enhancement.

She shrugged. "As much as I don't particularly like her, I want to get better. I want to help, Tezya. I don't want to be left behind anymore because I'm not trained."

"It's not a good idea for you to go, Rumor, but it has nothing to do with you not being trained."

She crossed her arms. "Then why?"

"The more people that go, the bigger chance we're taking at drawing attention."

"Please, Tezya. I promise I won't get in the way."

I met her eyes and saw the pleading look in them. I could sense her, feel how badly she wanted it.

"Okay." I rubbed at my scab, giving in to her too quickly. "But you have to listen to me. If we get caught, you have to leave with Kallon, no exceptions." I could tell she was about to fight me on it. She was stubborn to a fault, but if she wanted to come, she had to realize how dangerous it could be. "I don't want you in his hands again," I said, lowering my voice. The thought of the Lux King having Scotlind sent a newfound fear down my spine.

She narrowed her eyes. "And what about you?"

"I'll manage."

Her eyes flared at my words, but she tried to mask it. The brief moment of worry that crossed her expression was gone in a second. "Fine," she covered, then walked out of my tent without another word.

———

"WE HAVE to stop at Ichi's restaurant first," Savannah said as I met her at the border of the shield.

"Are we borrowing his car?"

"No." She didn't bother to look at me as she started laying winter coats out on the grass. "The hike isn't accessible to any roads. We're walking."

"Then why are we wasting time stopping at Ichi's?"

"I need coffee," Savannah replied like it was the most obvious answer, which knowing her, it was. "A large one. The largest cup I can get my hands on."

"We don't have time for that, Sav."

She whipped her lavender hair in my direction. "Of course we have time. We always have time for coffee, Tez."

I rolled my eyes. "You were supposed to eat before we leave."

"Well, I didn't. I'm not used to eating at the ass-crack-of-dawn, so we're stopping." I went to protest, but she cut me off, "I'm human, remember? You don't want me passing out from starvation, and then you'd no longer have a guide to lead you through Maine. Besides," she drawled slowly as a wide grin stretched over her face, and she grabbed onto my arm, "Ichihana would have your balls if he knew you were in town and didn't stop in to say hi."

Kallon was walking toward us and instantly perked up. "Yay! We're going to see Ichi? I've been dying for his ramen."

Sav rubbed her belly with her free hand. "Ramen and coffee, the perfect mix."

"The weirdest mix," Dove replied as she approached. I went to her tent last night and told her not to come with us, but she shrugged it off. I knew this would be hard for her, but I was happy to see her here regardless. I hadn't put much thought into what we were actually doing, what it would mean to see our mother's grave for the first time. Selfishly, I was happy my sister would be with me. A small part of me thought it was wrong that Arcane wasn't with us too. We all loved our mother. She was the only reason the three of us were so close, and Arcane took her death the hardest. He became a shell of who he used to be, worse than Dovelyn and I ever were.

Rumor and Sie were trailing behind my sister. Scottie was walking a few steps ahead of him, looking ready to bite his head off before her gaze drifted to Savannah's hand still on my arm.

"She's not going," the Dark Prince announced.

"Yes, I am," Scotlind seethed.

"It'll be too dangerous. She's lived as a nix her entire life. She isn't trained like the rest of you."

Scottie bristled, but I didn't miss the quick glance she casted down at both of her zeroes. I was livid. No way would this prick make her feel incompetent or less of herself. I wanted her to train so she could reach her full potential, not because I thought she was lacking.

I took a step toward him, stepping away from Savannah. "You do not get to decide who goes and who doesn't. This is a free group, everyone gets to make the choice for themselves. And," I added, my voice lowering to a growl, "I trained her myself. She *is* fucking capable, so if you ever say otherwise again, you'll find yourself on your ass."

"You can't beat me up."

"If you ever insinuate she isn't capable of *anything* ever again, I would take my time knocking you on your ass. But I didn't mean me." I settled my gaze on Rumor. "I'm sure she'd be happy to prove you wrong."

I gave a half smile as the prince glowered at me. Scottie's eyes trailed to my cheek. I always found her staring at my scar. She wasn't the only one, everyone gawked at it, but most did in disgust. Scottie's assessment was different, it *felt* different. She seemed more intrigued and curious about it than anything else, like she almost preferred it.

"One rule at this camp, Noren, don't ever use the word nix. Better yet, don't ever insinuate anyone of a lesser rank isn't as strong as someone with a higher rank. Sav has no powers, and she can hold her own against the Advenians here."

Sie's dark eyes flicked to where Savannah was standing with her arms crossed. He stared at her with an assessing gaze, one she wasn't backing down from.

"It's an open party then?" he asked. "Everyone can decide for themselves if they want to come?"

"Yes. It's Rumor's decision if she wants to go. Not yours. Not mine. Not anyone else but *hers*."

"Then I'm coming too."

I realized my mistake as soon as Sie said it.

Savannah clapped her hands together. "Great. Now that that's settled, let's go. I want to be at Ichi's restaurant before the sun is up. If I don't get coffee in my system soon, you're all going to regret it."

With that, Sav strutted through the shield with no fear that she was leading our kind's most wanted Advenians.

I gestured to the pile of winter clothes Savannah just laid out. Everyone piled on as many layers as we could before following her out into the thick snow.

Through the shield, I could still make out the low sounding beeps with my heightened hearing. Six noises sounded, letting the border control know we left the camp, and I prayed we weren't making a stupid decision by going.

As soon as Scottie stepped through, she turned to stare back at it. I probably took for granted how well the shield worked, how real it all looked. On this side, it appeared again as a massive cliff right into the ocean.

It was a quiet walk to Ichi's ramen shop and one we made frequently, or we used to. Only this time the tension was palpable. Everyone was on edge except Savannah. It wasn't because she didn't know the danger she put herself in, more like she didn't care. It never bothered her. She was the first to volunteer for anything, driving Dravenburg mad. Whereas her brother, Wells, was the opposite. He rarely left the camp and was usually isolated by himself in his lab.

"Thank all things almighty," Sav groaned when Ichi's sign came into view. His shop was located a mile from town, but it didn't make it any less crowded. Everyone gambled the walk, even when the ground was frozen over.

Most of the human population would drive from their homes to get his ramen. But the entrance to Brighta was through a dense forest, and Dravenburg claimed he didn't need or want a vehicle. Not when he had grown up his whole life inside the camp. On the off chance he had to use one, he'd borrow Ichi's.

We'd been coming to Brighta since before Savannah and Wells were even born. Hell, before Dravenburg was born too. The camp was passed down to him from his father and then his father before that.

We knew our mother's grave was on mortal soil, but it was a guess Dravenburg was privy to the location.

We discovered Brighta after her death. It came to Dovelyn in a vision, and we found the camp together. It was only then we learned our mother started the rebellion with Dravenburg's grandfather. Before, Brighta was only a place of refuge, but my mother changed that. When Dove and I first met Dravenburg's grandfather, we'd begged him for the location of her grave, but he refused to give it to us, claiming he was respecting her wishes.

She never wanted us to find it, which was the whole reason she entrusted it to the past mortal commander in the first place. But I still couldn't wrap my head around her being only a day's travel from the camp. I wanted nothing more than for her to still be alive, that she could've seen what the camp became...

A large closed sign was hanging off the glass door as Savannah stepped up to Ichi's restaurant. She reached into her hair, releasing a bobby pin, causing her lavender locks to cover half her face.

She picked the lock and had the door swinging open before Ichi could make it around the pulled curtain in the kitchen. Warm air pushed on our faces as we all stepped inside, desperate to get away from the cold. I held the door open, letting Scottie pass before me.

"Ichi," Savannah grinned, "look who I brought."

The elderly man smiled from ear to ear, his sunken eyes squinting. "It's about time." He beamed, his gaze shifting through us all. "And I see you brought some new friends too."

Sav sat down on one of the open bench tables. "I need the largest coffee you have, Ichi. Then my favorite spicy bowl of ramen, then another cup of coffee to go."

"It's only seven in the morning, and you want *ramen* now?"

"Please," Savannah pleaded, her lip pouting over.

"You know you should just work here for how much you deplete my stock." Ichihana frowned as he watched her position her bobby pin back into her hair. "And I've told you numerous times to use the bell and stop breaking in. You give me a heart attack every time I wake up and find the coffee machine turned on in the middle of the night."

"But my father's coffee is nowhere near as good as yours." She smiled.

Ichi was a lifelong friend of Dravenburg, making him an uncle figure to Savannah and Wells. He didn't know the full extent of what we all were, but I assumed he had his suspicions.

"It's good to see you, Ichi," I said as I gave him a pat on the back. "This is Rumor and Sie. Friends of ours." Sie gave me a death glare at the mention of Scottie's last name. It only made me want to call her it more. She wasn't a Noren, and she was definitely not his wife, no matter what claim he thought he possessed over her, and I had no issues reminding him of it.

"Nice to meet you both. Any friend of theirs is a friend of mine," he said as he pulled Dovelyn and Kallon into a hug at the same time. "I'll go warm up some ramen."

"And coffee," Savannah hollered as he disappeared behind the curtain again. We all awkwardly sat down around the table. No one spoke, and I was thankful when Ichi re-emerged with a tray of steaming hot ramen bowls and one large, black coffee for Savannah.

Kallon inhaled loudly. "I've missed your ramen back at home, Ichi."

Scottie looked at the dish with curiosity, then watched Kallon dig in. She took her first bite, moaning loudly as she chewed. "What is this stuff?"

Ichi looked at her in confusion. "You've never had ramen before?"

She shook her head as she kept eating, and to my own personal torture, kept moaning. I tried to focus on my own bowl and not think about what it was like to have her moan into my mouth. How it felt to have my hands glide over her body as she carefully sat on top of me in the bath. How I wanted to do so much more than that...

Sie seemed mortified at Scottie's declaration of love for the food and was scowling into his own bowl. Kallon noticed him sulking and smirked. "Don't mind her, she does this often."

Scottie looked up and saw everyone staring at her. Her freckled cheeks turned bright red as she set her fork down—Ichi had the foresight to not give her or Sie any chopsticks, something he did for all new customers.

"Don't pay attention to them," Savannah whispered to Scottie, grinning as she took a sip of her coffee. "Ichi's ramen is the best there is, better than any man. I'll moan over it too once I wake a little more."

Scottie shifted in her seat. "Who's the ugly green man on your shirt? I've seen him before," she asked as Sav started shrugging off her jacket.

"It's only the greatest Jedi of all time, and I know you have. Whose shirt do you think you wore when you and Tezya went to his condo in Florida?"

I could feel the tension radiating off of Sie. He curled his fists under the table as he drew a deep breath in through his nose, but my abilities were also picking up on unease from Scottie.

"The mortal clothes I wore were *yours?*"

"Yup," Savannah said as she took another long sip of coffee, then twirled large amounts of noodles over her chopsticks. Scottie's shoulders tensed as she glanced between me and Savannah.

"Tezya reckoned we were about the same size and asked to borrow some clothes when he took you." Savannah shrugged. "Although I'm surprised you didn't drown in them, you're so short," she added, and Scottie flinched at the word *drown*, but Sav didn't notice. She was too focused on the steam radiating from her noodles as she obnoxiously blew on them.

"You let *him* take you to the mortal territory before?" Sie asked, his voice gone cold.

"Oh, she let him do a lot more than that." Kallon grinned.

I was about to lay into Sie, because he was pissing me off, and I was losing my patience, but Scottie beat me to it. "I did. His condo was much more welcoming and spacious than the dungeon you put me in."

I smirked as he rightfully shut up. I was fucking loving this newfound brazen side to her.

Everyone finished their ramen bowls except for Sie, and Savannah stole a cup of coffee to go before we said our goodbyes to Ichi.

As we stepped out of his shop, Dovelyn took my hand. She'd been abnormally quiet ever since we left Brighta. I looked down at my sister, and the realization of what was about to happen finally sunk in. We were going to see our mother—or the bones that were left of her—for the first time in ninety years.

Finally, we'd uncover why she sacrificed her life in order to keep the prophecy hidden.

I squeezed Dovelyn's hand, praying we were ready.

SIXTEEN
SCOTLIND

THIS TRIP WAS HELL. Snow started falling in thick clumps over us, and the cold felt like it was a part of me. It was something I hadn't felt since that frozen beach when I was seven. It was also something I never wanted to experience again. My right calf seemed to ache, and I hated the white fluff and the memories it conjured. At least we had thick coats on, not that it made much of a difference.

But the frigid temperatures and the trek through rough terrain weren't even the worst part—it was the awkward moments of silence.

I looked up, seeing the back of Tezya's head. His bone-white hair was slicked back in sweat despite the cold. We were all exhausted. Cold. Tired. Irritable. And despite it all, Savannah led us up a steep mountain without faltering once. I was seriously second guessing the fact that our kind called mortals weak.

Kallon and Savannah went into bits of banter periodically, but it was too infrequent. We had to be quiet so we didn't draw attention to ourselves and neither girl knew how to whisper.

Dovelyn and Tezya were wary. I knew it was more than just the thought of being seen by a Luxian soldier. They were both nervous to go to their mother's grave.

Then there was Sie.

I couldn't sort out my feelings for him. I was angry and pissed most of the time, and the resentment kept rising to the surface whenever he talked to me.

He left me. He sentenced me to the dungeons. He shipped me off to Lux.

All those nights of praying to see his dark eyes, praying he'd rescue me, were catching up. I knew he didn't plan for it to happen. He wasn't a horrible person. He just got stuck in a bad situation and acted the way he *thought* was best. I just couldn't help but take it personally.

Would I have done the same thing as Sie if our situations were reversed? Would I have willingly handed over the person I claimed to love to my enemy, knowing full well what would happen to them? Tezya turned his head, and when I caught a glimpse of his scar, I knew my answer immediately. I wouldn't have done that to him. His punishment kept replaying in my head, and I knew I would have done anything *but* hand him over.

I kept seeing Tezya drive the dagger into his thigh, kept seeing all the blood. I saw him holding the ropes as he was forced to stand there while Brock whipped his already flayed back. I saw the tip of the dagger vanish as he was forced to stab himself over and over…

"We'll camp here for the night," Savannah called out against the bitter wind, saving me from my thoughts.

"I thought it's only a day's walk? We should push through the night," Tezya said as he scanned our surroundings. "We don't want to risk being out longer than we have to."

"We're camping because I lied to my father about how far away it was," she said as she threw her pack down onto the ground. The tip of her nose was bright red, and small bits of snow were sticking to the hoop coming out of her right nostril. "If he knew how long it'd take, he would've said no."

"Doesn't he know the location of the tomb?" Kallon asked.

"Aware of it, yes. Knows the exact amount of time it takes to travel there by foot? No. The only thing he knows is it's in Maine."

"You said you already visited the grave?" Kallon arched a thin brow.

"Yup," she nodded, her lavender hair falling out of her hood and covering the tops of her shoulders. "I was honest about that."

"But these conditions are—" Sie stopped mid sentence, but we all knew where his train of thought was going.

"Hard to trek for a human? Yeah, I get it." Kallon and Tezya both grinned as Savannah continued, "The sooner you stop underestimating people you perceive as weak, the wiser you'll become. Strength doesn't equal intelligence and being stupid will get you killed."

I caught a glimpse of Sie's stunned expression as he eyed the girl. She definitely had guts. Sie was the strongest Tennebrisian alive, and besides Dovelyn who possessed an air shield, we were all at his mercy... Not even Tezya was safe being half Tennebrisian, because with Sie's total mind control, he could compel any of us.

"I'm absolutely miserable," Kallon muttered as she plopped down next to Savannah, throwing her arm over her shoulder. "Why did you do this by yourself before?"

She shrugged. "I like being outside and away from the camp. It's nice to see new things."

"I think every Advenian can agree with you there," Dovelyn admitted, speaking for the first time. When everyone turned to look at her, she added, "Why else do you think my father wishes to expand? Why he seeks to rule over the humans? He wants your world. He's grown bored of being the king of only an island."

We were all quiet after that.

Eventually, everyone drifted off into sleep, taking shifts on lookout.

It was my turn to keep watch, and I wished I was back in Florida. I swore to myself I'd never complain about humidity or heat ever again. My teeth were chattering so loud I couldn't even hear if anyone was approaching our makeshift camp. We were high up on the mountain range and the night didn't do us any favors as the temperatures continued to drop. There was nothing to block out the wind. Dovelyn had a shield over us, but at some point, she let it drop as she fell asleep. Selfishly, I wanted to wake her up and have her create one from partition, but I couldn't ask her to permanently give up a piece of her reserve just so I could be warm.

The only thing we had on us were the bedrolls we carried in our packs, and despite them being extremely thick, it felt like paper. The wind was still cutting through it.

I whipped my head to the right as a twig snapped. Tezya crouched down and kneeled beside me. I could see his breath leave his mouth, mixing with mine. He didn't say anything as he held his hand up. The next second, a tight ball of flames floated above his fingers, and my face flooded with warmth.

"I thought you said it was too risky to have a fire," I attempted to whisper, but my teeth were still chattering. "That it would draw too much attention."

"I know, but I think the cold is more likely to kill you than a Luxian soldier at this point."

"Plus, no one can get any sleep," Kallon groaned from a few spaces away. "Your teeth sound like thunder."

"It sounds like a whole freaking drumline in a marching band," Savannah added. I didn't know what a drumline or marching band was, but I assumed by Kallon's laughter, it wasn't good.

"Just until you warm up," Tezya said softly, ignoring their comments, but we stayed like that my entire watch.

———

"How did you and your family come into all of this?" I asked Savannah the next morning.

Once she saw me plait my hair into the twin braids I used to wear all the time, she asked me to do the same to hers. She threw a short purple plait over her shoulder. "It's entirely too early in the morning for that question, especially when there isn't any coffee."

"Oh."

I guess I didn't hide my disappointment because she turned to look at me and answered, "We were born into it. Somewhere down the line, centuries ago, when Advenians first tried to live among humans, one of my ancestors befriended someone from your kind. We were always a refuge for Advenians who didn't believe in the ranking system. Our camp was established around the time rank zeroes started. It wasn't pretty in the beginning, or so I'd been told. My father said they didn't always exist, that only ranks one through five were on Allium. So naturally when zeroes came about, they started killing them, claiming they were mixed with human blood." She scoffed at her own words, before continuing, "At some point it turned from refuge to rebellion, but it was small. It wasn't until Tezya came that Brighta started to grow. He expanded it, made it more. He brought thousands of Advenians into the camp, whereas before it took centuries to get a quarter of the numbers. It's mostly what it is today because of him."

I nodded but realized she probably couldn't see it over the thick hood I had pulled over my head.

"Since we're asking personal questions, what's the deal with you and Tezya? And for that matter, you and Mr. Grumpy Gills?" She gestured to Sie ahead of us.

"It's a long story."

"Good thing we have a *long* time."

I did not want to explain my past with Sie and Tezya when they were both within earshot of hearing it. She seemed to grasp my hesitancy. "Another time then. We'll have a girls' night when we get back and you can tell me all about it."

"A girls' night?" Kallon squealed as she came up behind us. "We should dye Scottie's hair. What color should we do? Pink? Or blue to match her eyes?"

"I'm okay, thanks."

"Suit yourself." Kallon shrugged. "Once we get back, I'm going to go red."

The two of them discussed hair colors and whatever the difference was between balayage and ombre for a while. I found myself falling out of step with them without meaning to.

"Why are you avoiding me?" Sie's voice came up behind me. I hadn't realized he'd fallen back too.

"I'm not avoiding you," I said too quickly. I was definitely avoiding him. Both him and Tezya, for that matter.

"Yes, you are, Scotlind. I want to talk about things."

"The last time we 'talked' about things, your father had me in shackles and chained me in the dungeons the next day." I turned to look at him. "You could have talked to me during any of the weeks I was there."

He flinched. "I was trying to protect you. They wanted me to kill you."

"Did you ever stop and think that maybe that would have been a mercy? You of all people should have known what it was like for me. You were there."

"What are you talking about?"

"Being locked up, chained in the dungeons with nothing but darkness. It felt like Kole was drowning me over and over again. I couldn't escape it. I couldn't breathe. And every time the doors opened, I prayed I'd see you. I prayed you'd get me out of there. But then you shipped me off to the person you warned me to stay away from at our wedding." I paused to calm my racing heart. I really did not want to have this conversation right now, but now that I started, I couldn't stop. I was word vomiting without wanting to, and the months of pent-up anger were pouring out of me. "I'm just not over it yet, Sie."

"So that's it? You're done being my wife?"

"I was never really your wife."

He flinched again before he cooled his expression. "You were to me," he whispered.

I didn't answer. I didn't know how to.

"We're bonded, Scotlind. How do you explain that?"

I shook my head. "We aren't. I have enhancement. That's what you were feeling whenever I wasn't wearing the Alluse necklace."

"You're wrong. I felt it. I felt the bond—"

"No, you didn't."

He let out a frustrated sigh, running a gloved hand through his hair. "That's just what *he* wants you to think."

I shook my head, agitated that he thought I was so easily brainwashed by Tezya. "No—*I'm* telling you what you felt wasn't the bond. Not anyone else."

"Who told you about enhancement, Scotlind? He just wants you to think it was nothing—"

"I know because I know what the bond really feels like," I snapped.

He stopped in his tracks, glancing up at Tezya, before looking back at me. "You fucked him, didn't you?"

Tezya stopped ahead of us. I could just barely make out his fingers curling at his sides. I was immediately aware of how no one else was talking. How he shouted the last statement, and it seemed to echo off the mountain. Not that it mattered, Tezya had heightened senses, and he most likely heard every single word that was said.

"Will you two shut up?" Dovelyn snapped. "I'll kill you myself if we get caught because of this stupid fight."

Sie didn't wait for my reply as he stormed off ahead of me.

SEVENTEEN
TEZYA

THE REST of the trek to the grave was just as abhorrent as the first half. Everyone was eerily quiet after Rumor's and Sie's outburst. I had to fight the urge to punch him myself. The tension between the two of them was palpable and only growing, but it wasn't fair for me to intervene. She deserved space to work out her feelings, and I had to suck it up, no matter how badly I hated it.

When we first rescued Sie, I was terrified she would go running back to him, and selfishly, I was elated when she didn't. Remembering how I found her in the dungeons, I could see why she held onto some resentment. Her back was a thick mangle of scars that distorted her markings. Brock tried to heal them back at the castle, but he said the injuries weren't all fresh. I thought of her tallies on her forearm and hated myself for not realizing what was happening sooner. She was tortured for twenty-seven days within my reach, and I had no idea. She was on the brink of death when I found her, and I knew firsthand those feelings never dissipated, that they hurt worse than any physical scar left on the skin.

I could understand Sie's frustrations, although it didn't warrant him acting like a total dick. He did what he thought was right, and as a result, he lost the girl he loved. I would be just as bitter and pissed off if I lost her too.

I scoffed. I *had* lost her. I barely had her to begin with, and I already lost what little I had of her. I was delusional if I thought any differently. She'd barely spoken to me since she found out I'd been lying to her.

But I kept catching her staring at me when she thought I wasn't looking. I could hear the slight hitch of her breath whenever I came close. I prayed to Pylemo every damn second of every day that I could find a way to regain her trust.

I wanted to tell Scottie everything back in Lux, but after the King tortured me, I knew I couldn't. He was keeping her close on purpose, and all I kept thinking about was how I wouldn't have been able to handle it if our situations were reversed. If he ever brought her into that room instead of me...

I couldn't risk it with the compulsion user still there. I didn't doubt the King would use Kole again to go into her mind, and I'd be damned if I gave him any reason to hurt her.

I swallowed, trying to push it from my mind.

The limp in my leg was almost gone, thanks to the Luxian healers at the camp, but it would leave another scar. The King picked his punishment well, targeting my leg would have left me weak for months if I was still back in Lux. I was never allowed to see a healer.

And that was his punishment for keeping Scotlind's second ability a secret... If he knew she was harboring information about the prophecy, if I had told her everything and he found out... I shuddered. I didn't care what he'd do to me, but if he hurt her... There wouldn't be anything left of her after he was done, and I knew he would only keep me alive long enough to watch it.

"We're here," Sav shouted over the roar of the ocean, forcing me back into the moment. We were long off the mountain pass, but the area wasn't any less forgiving. It took half a day trekking through semi flat terrain before we could smell the salty spray of the ocean. Miles of icy, large boulders separated us from the water, forcing us to climb them.

By the time we made it to the water, a storm was coming in. The clouds darkened, and the tide rose to our right. The more we climbed, the worse it got. The waves started spanning high above our heads, reaching the height of the boulders, threatening to join us with the sea.

The only thing that saved us was Dovelyn's constant shield, blocking the brunt of the water, and Scottie using her powers to slow it down. After an hour, water started seeping past her shield, gently spraying us, making us decide we'd risk having a fire if it meant warmth. We were all too exhausted and too cold to care. I had tightly bound balls of flames following everyone, but it did nothing to squelch the chill. Hours later, I was starting to feel my own powers drain from reforming the flames every time the water wiped them out.

Snow was whipping into us from the wind, mixing with our already drenched clothes. It left the ground slippery, making it impossible not to fall on the rocks. I had no idea how Savannah made this trek alone or why.

I looked up at where she stopped ahead of me. Her hood was down with her short lavender hair falling out of her braids and blowing all over the place. She turned to face me. "It's over there." Multiple strands of her wet lavender locks were stuck to her chin as she tried—and failed—to wipe them away with one hand while pointing with her other. The boulders cleared ahead of us and turned into a large clearing about fifty feet past the ocean. There was one singular stone positioned directly in the center of the snow—no. Not a stone, a makeshift tomb.

My gut fell through me. I couldn't breathe. *MaryLynn N.* was splattered over the stone in a red smear that resembled blood. Which would have been impossible for it to remain after all these decades, except I could smell the magic holding the prophecy within.

My mother's abilities were unique, like Dovelyn's, they were one of a kind. Her powers allowed her to create blood seals. I remembered the King dragging her to parts of the castle and forcing her to use her gifts for him when she was still alive.

She could create barriers and seals, blocking entrances to anything or anyone. When we were little, she did the same to our private rooms back when we all shared quarters. It was our only sanctuary in the castle, the only time we ever got to feel like a family without the King's looming presence.

No one fully understood what she was capable of, but I knew with certainty I was looking at the last remnants of her power.

Everyone started walking toward her grave, but I stood there, still as the stone before me. I was frozen. The waves were beginning to crash over me as Dovelyn got further away, but I still couldn't move. Guilt was riddling and festering inside me. My mother died for this. She believed in it enough to end her life so I never saw what she took to the grave.

Scottie came up beside me and only then did I realize I was still standing on the rock. She was pushing back the waves as best as she could. A pallor had filled her sun-kissed skin, and I knew that she had sweat mixed with the water that was splashed all over her. She was struggling against the ocean, yet she didn't tell me to move.

"Are you okay?" she asked softly.

I shook my head. I couldn't speak. My emotions were stirring at the surface, emotions I'd been pushing down for nearly a century. But one thought kept outweighing the others. If we open the tomb, my mother's death would have been for nothing. If we went through with this, I was cursing her.

At the same time, I couldn't fathom *not* opening it. One life wasn't worth the chance of saving countless others. Dovelyn confessed shortly after our mother killed herself that she believed she was trying to protect me from my fate—she thought I was going to die. But if this prophecy meant I had to give up my life, I would do it. I couldn't *not* save innocent Advenians just because my mother didn't want me to. I couldn't *not* go through with this even if I was going against her. Because if the King wins, the life keeping me grounded on this slippery rock would be lost with it. I wasn't willing to lose this war over my feelings, but more than anything, I wasn't willing to lose *her*.

"You aren't cursing her," Scotlind said softly. "Your mother loved you and that won't change. Regardless of your actions today, it doesn't take away the love she had for you."

I looked at her in shock. Her eyes were just as wide as mine, a deep sapphire blue matching the ocean at our backs.

I hadn't realized I said the words out loud. I swallowed hard and a lump stirred in my throat. My lips were cracked and dry, and my tongue felt like sandpaper. That's when I noticed her hand. She had grabbed mine. Our hands were clasped over our scabs, and I realized, somehow, she had gotten into my mind, or I got into hers.

She withdrew her hand quickly, maybe realizing the same thing. "We should go."

I took one shuddering breath before I started making my way toward the grave. I was staring at my feet, too much of a coward to look at Dovelyn right now—if she was crying, I might give in to her.

I had to remind myself this was what I wanted, even if I was hurting my family in the process.

I wanted the chance at freedom. I wanted to destroy the King. I wanted Scotlind to live in a world without anyone hunting her down. I wanted to spare my siblings from their father's rage. I wanted to save my own people from his brutality and control. I wanted to save the humans before he tried to take over them too.

I knew in my bones this was the right decision. I just wish I could've gone back a century and saved my mother too. If I could have prevented her from killing herself, if I could have done more... After all these years, the ache I felt with her absence still destroyed me. It killed Arcane and Dovelyn too. Our mother was all the good things in this world. She was the one person who showed us love, who took on the brunt of the King's rage to spare us. Every day I wished she was still with us—

I staggered back into Scottie, not registering what had happened until I felt the sting on my cheek the next second. Sie's dark eyes were honed in on me. He was about to throw a second punch when Scottie stepped out from behind me and jumped. They toppled to the ground, their bodies entwining into a tangle of limbs. A loud crack sounded as Sie's head slammed into the tomb, his blood spilling onto the rock.

"What the hell are you doing?" Scottie seethed, her breathing ragged, and hearing her voice broke me out of my trance. I pulled her off of Sie and shoved her behind me, not wanting to wait to see how he would react.

"It's one thing to pick him over me," he spat, his eyes narrowed on us. He still hadn't moved from the ground. "And it's another to flaunt it in front of everyone."

Scottie huffed, her chest rising and falling in anger as I kept her pulled back. "I'm not flaunting anything. Can't you see—"

"Not trying to break up this lover's quarrel," Savannah interjected, "but this storm is only getting worse, and I'm freezing my bum off. And seeing as we're stuck here until we figure out how to open the rock, we need to get started."

Scottie stared at Sie for another long second before she nodded and stepped out of my grip.

Savannah stepped up to the Dark Prince, extending a hand. He stared at her for a moment before accepting it. "You alright?"

"I will be as soon as I get away from here," he grumbled.

"I didn't mean your pride. I meant your head. You're bleeding."

"I'm fine," he snapped, not bothering to wipe the blood that was starting to run down his temple.

"Great. So, how do we open it?" Sav asked, rocking back on her heels, and gesturing toward the stone that was now covered in his blood.

Kallon was a few feet away, working on creating a portal to take us home.

I stepped up to my mother's tomb and placed a hand over the stone. As soon as I did, I felt the surge of her magic infused in it. She used a variation of a blood seal on it, and the second I touched it, more words materialized under her name.

"Whoa," Savannah noted as she came up next to me. "Ew, why does everything have to be written in blood?"

A lover. A sister. A brother.

"I don't understand," Dovelyn whispered. "I'm assuming it's a clue. That you need all three to unlock the tomb, but what does the *N* mean? Our last name begins with an X."

MaryLynn N.

"I have no idea," I admitted. I hadn't noticed it before.

"What about her middle name?" Scottie asked.

I shook my head. "Her middle name was Lira."

"Her maiden name?"

"Wayrin," Dovelyn answered. "Her maiden name was Wayrin."

"Um guys, forget the *N*, the word brother is turning from red to black," Savannah gasped.

I looked at the stone and watched as the word changed colors, then engraved into the stone itself.

"Is it because Arcane isn't here?" Kallon suggested taking a break from creating the portal to stare at the grave. "You have Dove here as your sister, Scottie here as your lover. Maybe it won't open unless Arcane is nearby."

Everyone ignored Sie's rage over Kallon's choice of words. I stole a glance at Scottie to see what she made of it, but she didn't seem phased. She was entranced by the tomb as she leaned forward, brushing her hand over the now engraved brother.

"Goddess above," Kallon breathed as she stared at the stone. I followed her gaze and watched as the word lover darkened before engraving itself along with the word brother. The only word left in blood was sister.

Scottie jolted back as she realized what she'd done. She gripped her wrist, covering her zero, and stared at her palm. I looked between Scottie's hand and the slab of stone. A drop of blood had embedded into the crevice where she brushed her hand over it.

Everyone's gaze landed on her. She was frozen, still staring at her palm like it burned her. The chapped air must have caused the scab to dry and crack open again. I felt it against my own palm when she grabbed my hand on the rocks. I swore it was what caused our connection.

"Sie, your last name is Noren," Dovelyn said, her silver eyes never leaving the stone.

It wasn't meant to be a question, but Sie answered anyway, "Yeah. Why does that matter?"

"MaryLynn Noren. That's what the N stands for."

"What are you talking about?" Sie snapped.

"Tezya is my half brother. My mother... she had an affair with someone from Tennebris. That's how Tezya possesses abilities from both kingdoms. Her lover had compulsion. Is that not the power that runs in your family line?" Dovelyn asked.

Sie paled. "That's not possible."

But Dovelyn cut him off. "My mother's affair was over a century before you were even born. She loved him. The man used to be on the Dark's High Council. I still remember him to this day. He visited us often, staying in Lux on a work visa. I was young when it happened, but I swore I would never forget his eyes. The way they always found my mother's. It was the first time I saw her truly happy. But then he had to return home and shortly after, Tezya was born." I swallowed as she continued, "The man my mother loved was named Maverich. I never learned his last name, but his first name was Maverich."

Scottie faltered as she looked between Sie and me.

"No. That's not possible—" Before Sie could finish, Dovelyn removed a small dagger that was strapped to her thigh. I could do nothing but watch as she dragged the blade over her skin, then let her blood drip onto the stone.

The word sister changed from blood-red to black until it was engraved along with *lover* and *brother* forever etched into the stone.

A faint click sounded, and the tomb lifted off the ground.

<h1 style="text-align:center">EIGHTEEN</h1>

<h2 style="text-align:center">SIE</h2>

I STARED in disbelief as the tomb opened. No one said anything. But I couldn't unsee it now. The resemblance between Tezya and me. We were about the same height, almost the same build. We shared the same straight nose. The same jawline. We both had my father's—*our father's*—thick brows. I wanted to vomit. The only difference between us was his Luxian coloring. His hair was bone-white while mine was jet black. And his eyes were a mix of crystal blue and silver, the disgusting color the same as his half siblings of Lux. While mine were so dark most days I couldn't find my pupils in the mix of my irises.

We were brothers.

He was my fucking brother. The ocean was roaring angrily at my back, warning us we were running out of time, but I couldn't get myself to move. Moments before, I would have done anything to speed up time, to uncover this stupid prophecy so I could get off this damn boulder-filled beach.

I still couldn't believe Scotlind tackled me. My head throbbed, but not from hitting the stone and cracking it open. It was screaming at me that she chose him. She picked him. And now that *him* was my damn brother.

Kallon was the first to break the silence. "Let's talk about this back at the camp," she said, gently gripping her hand over Tezya's elbow. He was staring at me in disbelief, and I at him, but neither of us moved. The wind was plastering my long hair over my eyes, but I couldn't get myself to run my fingers through it. "The portal's ready, we need to get whatever this prophecy is and go."

Neither of us moved. We were frozen in time, caught in a staring contest where no one would win, but I saw Dovelyn nodding in the distance. She took a step toward her mother's grave until she was standing in front of it. The tomb had lifted off the ground for a split second when all three words were etched into it, before it slammed right back into its original spot. I didn't see anything useful other than the theatrics of it all. There was nothing that would give us a clue to the prophecy.

Dovelyn placed both her hands on the stone, a part of her touching all three words, before she screamed.

It released Tezya from his stupor as he rushed toward his sister. He tried to pry her hands off the stone, but she didn't budge.

"Help me," he shouted over her ear-piercing shrieks. Savannah, Kallon, and Scotlind all ran toward them, grabbing the princess and pulling at her desperately. I still didn't move, I couldn't. I barely knew what to think, so I just stood there watching the girl as she wailed in agony. Dovelyn's eyes were wholly blue. There was no pupil, no iris, no whites to any of it. The milky color consumed her sight as her head tipped back and convulsing overtook her body.

Then, as quickly as it started, it stopped. Dovelyn blinked the silver back into her eyes and stepped away from the grave. Tezya steadied her as she collapsed into him. Tears were pouring down her face.

"I saw everything," she said weakly to her brother. "My visions... the ones she took away, they all came back."

Then she fainted.

———

PETER WAS SITTING with me in our shared tent. A week had passed since we returned and the Luxian Princess still hadn't opened up about what she saw. She'd been unconscious for two days and then refused to talk after that. 'Refused' was generous, she'd been *unable* to talk, at least, in a civilized manner. She turned full psycho, reciting lines here and there that made no sense, and couldn't manage to stay conscious for more than a few hours at a time. Her eyes would shift from silver to milky blue during her manic rants and it looked downright terrifying.

"Want to fight?" Peter asked from the cot opposite me. It used to be my outlet for everything. Whenever I was angry or stressed, I would spar, kicking and punching the built up tension out of me, but ever since we got back from the trip, I didn't want to do anything.

My father was bitter my entire life. I knew he never loved my mother, that all he cared about was power, about making the Noren name infamous, about making sure Tennebris was as strong as Lux. Did he only want power so he could change things? Was there more to him I didn't know? He wasn't a good man by any means. He was a complete asshole to everyone I knew. But ever since I lost Scotlind, I'd been just as bitter as he was.

No. I wasn't going to go there. *I was not my father.* I refused to become him.

Maybe a good sparring match would help clear my head. Before I could answer Peter, the flaps to our tent opened. Tezya was standing at the entrance. "Mind if I come in? I'd like to talk."

"You're his family," Peter beamed as he rose from his cot, then slapped me across the back, "of course you can come in." I was going to fucking murder him. His dimpled-grin didn't falter as I gave him a death stare.

When we first came back, I told Peter everything. He listened intently, making sure I was okay first. Then, once he realized I was fine—or as good as I could be with finding out I had a brother about a century older than me and it happened to be the one person I fucking hated—he'd been making fun of me relentlessly. He claimed it was karma for leaving him behind with Rainer while we went on the trip.

Peter walked out of the tent, still grinning, leaving me alone with

Tezya. He remained at the entrance for a moment before coming inside.

"I'm sorry," he said as he sat down on Peter's cot across from me.

Sorry for what? Sorry we're related? Sorry he stole my wife?

Before I could figure out how I wanted to respond, he continued, "I know this isn't easy and it's not what either of us wanted or expected, but I'm not going to stop loving her just because you're my brother. I know you care about her—"

I cut him off. "If you only came in here to discuss Scotlind, then get out. I don't want to talk to you about her."

"Well somebody should. Look, neither of us want to have this conversation, but we need to. I came in here to tell you she went through hell because of you. If she ever finds it in herself to forgive you, I'll accept it. If she chooses you, I'll let her do it. We both hurt her in different ways, and she's been hurt her entire life, so if she finds any means of happiness, we both need to suck it up and let her take it."

"That's easy for you to say when we both know she's going to choose you," I seethed.

Tezya let out a long breath, and for a moment, he looked just as devastated as I felt. "Maybe. She wasn't lying when she said we're bonded."

"Well I thought I was with her too, so you might not want to get your hopes up," I snapped before I thought better of it.

"There's a difference," he said, leveling a glare at me. "I don't *think* we are, I *know* we are. And if she decides to not be with me, I'll accept it. It'll fucking kill me, but at least she'd be happy. After everything she's been through, she deserves that without your added guilt. You can't blame her for the actions she took when you threw her into the fire. It was *your* decision to annul your marriage, *your* decision to send her away. You need to accept your own mistakes and stop projecting them onto her. You don't understand what she went through because of *your* choices."

Images of her being sent to Lux flashed in my mind. She was skinny, too skinny for her frame, and she looked so damned weak. It was all I could think about back in the prison—how I subjected her to the same thing.

"How she left your dungeons in Tennebris was nothing compared to how she was treated in Lux," he continued.

"I know what happened to her," I ground out. Peter told me bits and pieces of what happened, and I didn't want to hear any more of it. And I especially didn't want to hear it from *him*.

"No, you don't know. I wish I found her sooner. I had no idea they were torturing her for information about you. Every damn day for twenty-seven days they starved her, kept her chained in a fucking cage so small she had to lay curled on her side, only to be dragged out, chained to a wall and whipped. She was barely alive when I found her. Her entire fucking life has been haunting her. It took a while for her to be able to act like a normal Advenian again. So it really fucking pisses me off when you wallow in your own self-pity because you lost her, because she found a sliver of happiness without you. I don't care what happens to me, but if you hurt her again, I won't hold back. It doesn't make a difference if we're related or not. She comes first, so you *will* suck it up and stop causing her more grief."

"Get out," I gritted through my teeth. My fists were curling at my sides, and it took every ounce of self control I had not to fucking fight him.

He eyed me for a long moment before finally listening. As soon as he left, I felt a tear fall down my face. I wiped it away, hating it. I never cried. But his words... hearing how Scottie suffered because of me. He was right.

I hated that he was fucking right.

NINETEEN
SCOTLIND

I had to see Tezya. I didn't care what time it was, what he was doing, or who he was with. The sudden urge to be near him came so abruptly my chest ached, and I panicked when I couldn't find him right away.

I ran to his tent, pulling the flaps open, only to find it empty. I searched the dining tent, the training rings, the common center... I was desperate by the time I ran into Kallon, knocking into her and spilling her ale.

"He's in the war tent," she said as she wiped her hands against her pants. How she knew what I wanted before I even asked was beyond me. I think I muttered a thank you before I started taking off in the direction of the tent, thankful that after a couple of weeks here, I was slowly learning my way around. "But don't bother him now, they're in a meeting!"

Her words were lost on me as I broke out into a full blown sprint toward one of the larger tents they used for meetings. I knew I shouldn't interrupt. I knew he had more important things to attend to than me, but ever since our hands reconnected on the rocks, I couldn't stop thinking about him. It felt like my soul was on a string that kept tugging me closer and closer to him.

I tried to push my feelings aside, to give Tezya time. He was distraught after everything that happened with Dovelyn. I overheard Savannah talking him off the ledge once Kallon portaled everyone back. Only it had been a week now and the princess still hadn't talked.

I was the only Advenian here happy for her silence. If whatever she saw meant more pain for him, I never wanted her to speak again.

I was panting by the time I burst into the tent. Everyone turned to glare at me, but all I saw were crystal blue eyes with traces of silver and a thick, jagged scar. My eyes never left Tezya's as I willed myself to steady my breathing and tried to calm down. I didn't even know why I was so worked up to begin with.

"Everyone out." His voice was cold. Menacing. Demanding.

"But we need to—" Dravenburg started.

"I. Said. Get. Out."

Neither of us moved as everyone rushed out of the tent.

Once we were alone, I panted, "I had to see you."

"I can see that."

I truly hadn't thought about what I wanted to say or what I wanted to do once I found him.

"How are you?" I asked, then immediately cursed myself for asking such a stupid question. He just found out his sister wasn't in her right mind after venturing to their mother's grave for the first time. I knew he felt responsible, even if it wasn't his fault.

On top of that, he found out Sie was his half brother, which I wasn't ready to wrap my head around either. And he was, moments ago, in the middle of a meeting about a war, and we were no closer to finding out what the prophecy meant or what he had to do. *Yet, I'm standing here asking him how he's doing?* "Never mind. Don't answer that."

He smiled, and I watched his scar rise on his cheek. "I'm fine, Rumor." When I didn't say anything else, he added, "I'm assuming you didn't interrupt the meeting to ask me how I'm doing?"

I nodded.

He arched a brow. "And?"

"I want to talk," I admitted softly. His lips parted as I added, "About us."

Tezya gestured to the table in front of him. Now filled with empty chairs from everyone he had just kicked out. There was a map laid out across it. Tennebris and Lux were marked in red with other drawings I wasn't familiar with. "I didn't mean to interrupt," I started.

"You didn't."

I definitely did, but I wasn't about to press because I was happy he stopped the meeting. My pulse was bounding, and I couldn't wait a second longer to talk to him. I wanted to know everything. I needed to know.

I was finally ready.

He watched me intently as I walked around the table and sat in the chair next to the one he took.

The tent wasn't anything special. Besides the maps and a few cabinets that held files, all it had were chairs and one long wooden table toward the back. Even the ground was devoid of anything but fresh grass. It was a deep green, despite all the countless boots that stomped over the soil. I imagined a Luxian ground user had something to do with the lack of mud. Only the sleeping tents had furs laid out and the dining tent had step-up wooden planking. Everything else throughout the entire camp was just grass; plain, simple, and to the point.

"Why didn't you tell me the truth?"

He didn't answer right away, and I realized he was waiting for me to elaborate. There was so much he kept from me, so I started with, "Why did you make me believe the prophecy was about me and Sie? You made me think it'd be my child with him. It messed with me. This whole time I thought I was supposed to be bonded with him, until we... until you cut my hand that night, and I knew. I knew it was you because I felt it. So why did you lie to me if you knew you were the chosen one?" He cringed at my words, but I didn't stop. "Why did you tell me to stay away from Sie when it didn't matter?"

Dovelyn's words came back to me. That I, above all people, should understand how Tezya felt. I was terrified to open up about growing up in a different kingdom. Yet Tezya was born from both. To be the prophecy child, the one both rulers feared. The one they wanted to kill and had made an elaborate, ill-led plan to do just that. I could understand his hesitancy, but I was still hurt by it.

"I was jealous," he said, surprising me. "I mostly acted out of jealousy. I saw everything on the monitors the day I brought you up from the dungeons. I was forced to watch him kiss you in his bathroom. I knew you two had a history beyond just being obligated to wed, and I couldn't explain why, but it made me jealous as hell. Even before I truly met you, when you were chained in that chair covered in your own piss and blood, I was jealous. It was selfish, and I didn't have any good reasons. I didn't even know you, but I didn't want you with him.

"As for everything else," he drew in a breath as he placed his forearms on the table before us. "I found out about the prophecy at a young age. I knew I was different when I started getting what I wanted. I didn't realize it—my skin turning golden under my clothes as I compelled the servants for assortments of foods or to let me wander the halls late at night. I had no idea what I was doing, but my mother did. For years, she sheltered me. Raising me solely, never risking using a servant after my Tennebrisian powers manifested. She warned me, scared me so thoroughly to never use that side of me, to never breathe a word of it to anyone. It was drilled into me every second of every day. She told me if anyone found out, the King would kill me, but he wouldn't stop there. He'd kill my sister and brother too. I loved my family, and the King's *lessons* never stopped. Even when I was kept in isolation, I knew and understood his ruthlessness. I knew my mother's threats were warranted. I'd seen the King try again and again to hunt down the prophecy, had seen him use Dovelyn's visions to do it.

"Growing up, I didn't want to believe it. I didn't want to give the King a reason to kill my siblings. He tortured us our whole lives over nothing, finding stupid excuses to bring us into that room. I knew if I let slip who I really was, the things he'd do to us would be worse than anything I could imagine. I always felt like he held a power over me because of it, even though he had no idea.

"When I was younger, all I wanted was to live with my siblings in peace. I was terrified of being the reason he hurt Dove or Arcane, so I pushed that part of me down, never using my Tennebrisian powers. But after my mother died, everything changed. I started practicing in secret. I knew I had to become strong. I planned to get revenge on the King for everything he's ever done. I wanted him dead, and our people needed him off the throne. So I started harnessing my Dark abilities whenever I was alone, knowing someday I'd need them. I made myself into a weapon so he couldn't deny me a spot in the army. I fought my way to the top until I led it.

"I already knew about Brighta. Dovelyn and I discovered it a month after our mother's death. She had a vision about the place existing and swore it was our mother urging us to come here. At the time, it was a small refuge only just starting to become a rebellion. Dravenburg wasn't even born yet. We started visiting as our own means to escape Lux. But once the rebellion started to pick up, things changed. The first time the King ordered me to kill all the wives and children after a battle—he wanted me to go into their homes and slaughter them in the middle of the night—I knew I wasn't going to go through with it. So I brought them here and have been doing the same ever since.

"The camp will always be a place of refuge, but it has also turned into its own rebellion and has grown over the past couple of decades. Many Advenians aren't satisfied with staying here their whole lives. They want to fight back. They hate the Lux King and the ranking system from both kingdoms. Most of the battles didn't end immediately. There are families who lost loved ones before we could bring them here. They have a reason to be mad, and now they have a reason to want change.

"Tennebrisians and Luxians have been living here for as long as I can remember. We live without rank. If a child is born within the camp, they won't get branded. Everyone is equal here, everyone is just as important as the next." He took a deep breath. "Secretly, selfishly, I hoped there'd be more people like me. But over the past century most of the Advenians in the camp have kept to their own families, only coexisting but never mixing.

"But then I learned about you—a Luxian who had been living in Tennebris. I was intrigued by you. Some part of me wanted you to be pregnant when we went to collect you. If you were, maybe my mother was wrong about the prophecy. But then I saw you, and I instantly regretted that wish. I didn't want anyone else with this burden, especially you.

"Then, I was forced to train you, and I started to care for you despite trying not to. I was terrified the King would hurt you. I knew you were vulnerable as long as you stayed there. Even after the results with the healer came back and the King found out the prophecy wasn't about you, the threat was still real. He would have killed you both if he saw you together, so I gave you the warning to stay clear of Sie because of it. If he even had the slightest inkling you were pregnant, he wouldn't have hesitated to murder you both. I didn't want to give the King a reason to kill you, but more than that, I didn't want Sie's hands on you. Some part of me knew I told you to stay away from him partly out of jealousy. I know that's fucked up, and I'm sorry."

I stayed quiet. The only sound in the tent was my breathing, leaving me in uneven waves as I listened to Tezya talk and open up about everything.

"I wanted to tell you. I thought about it, weighing the risks and going over my options. I'm sorry I didn't, Rumor. It was never my intention to lie to you."

"Then why did you? You could have just told me all of that..." I thought back to our promise the night I found out he was the Fire Prince, the night we said no more lies.

"Because I would rather risk you being pissed off at me like you are now, than you being in the hands of the Lux King again. It had nothing to do with not trusting you because I trust you with my life. But I didn't want to put that burden on you. I didn't want to make you more of a target than you already were. The King's fascination with you meant you were being watched too closely. I didn't put it past him to use Kole on you again."

I shuddered thinking back to the monitor room and how everyone saw everything inside my mind, how I'd never felt so violated before, so exposed.

"I know it isn't an excuse, but I was terrified of what he would do to you if he found out that you knew about me," he continued. "What he did to me that night, that was nothing, *nothing* compared to what he would have done to someone if he learned they had information on the prophecy."

I swallowed. "You don't get to decide what's a burden to me."

"I can see that now." He turned his wrist over. I caught a glimpse of his five brand before he drew his arm off the table. It made me wonder what his rank truly was because he had to surpass a rank five. He was declared that strong from his Luxian abilities alone.

I turned to face him, finally meeting his gaze. "I can't take any more lies. I don't want to keep things from each other. I want to know everything, no matter the burden, no matter the risk."

He met my stare and there was a seriousness there I'd never seen before, making his features hard. "Okay."

"Promise me," I whispered, my voice barely audible. "Promise me and actually mean it this time."

"I promise, Scotlind."

There was a moment of silence, neither of us knowing what to do. We stared at each other, unmoving before my body became aware of how close he was. My breathing grew heavier. Somehow while he was talking I had leaned toward him. His gaze shifted from my eyes to my mouth as my lips parted.

He hesitated for a moment, staring at my lips. I thought he was going to finally close the small gap between us. But then he leaned back in his chair, his legs spread in a relaxed posture, even though he looked anything but. He ran his fingers through his hair, pushing the white strands out of his eyes.

His chair dragged across the grass as he abruptly stood. I didn't want him to go. I wanted him to kiss me. I was sick of the distance I was forcing between us, but I realized it was my turn to open up.

He was trying to be respectful by giving me space. He didn't think I knew what I wanted. He thought I still needed to figure out my feelings between him and Sie. But the truth was, I already knew it was him before I even came in here. I reached out and caught his wrist with my hand, stopping him before he could walk away.

He went deathly still, completely unmoving. My pulse was pounding and all of a sudden everything was spinning around him.

"I want…" I swallowed and tried again, my hand was still clamped over his wrist as I tugged him back down into his chair. "I want this. Whatever this is between us."

His eyes flared, and I swore he stopped breathing. "Say it, Rumor. I need you to say it." His voice was demanding and low, sending shivers down my spine.

"I want… I want *you*." I met his silver gaze.

"I want you too, Scotlind Mae Rumor," he breathed, a sly smile peppering his lips. "I've wanted you since the moment I laid eyes on you." He shifted my grip on his wrist, moving to interlock our fingers. The contact wasn't nearly enough. I wanted more. I tried to scoot my chair closer to his, but it was stuck in the grass and wouldn't budge.

Tezya groaned, ripping his fingers from mine to wrap both hands around the wooden legs and pulled my chair until it collided with his. I fell into his chest. The smell of him, his touch against my skin… all of it was overwhelming and intoxicating. I'd wanted this for so long, wanted *him* for so long.

His hands immediately moved from the chair legs to my neck. The scab on his palm ran over my bare skin as he brushed my hair to the side. My own breathing hitched, his lips were so close to mine that I could smell the mint on his mouth.

His thumb brushed down my cheek before he slid it across my lips. I parted for him involuntarily, a moan escaping from me on instinct. He leaned forward, pulling my face toward his and silencing my moan with his lips.

My eyes fluttered closed, narrowing all my sensations on the way his mouth felt pressed against mine. His touch was soft at first, just a featherlight press of his lips before it was gone.

He pulled back too soon, his hands still holding the back of my neck, locking me in place. He met my gaze as I blinked my eyes back open. He was waiting, assessing, making sure it was what I really wanted. I exhaled into his mouth, my breath having nowhere to go but into him.

"Please," I panted. "I don't want you to stop."

He didn't hesitate after that, tilting my head up to meet his before claiming my mouth once again.

TWENTY
SCOTLIND

Our teeth collided as his lips crashed against mine. Only this time he wasn't gentle or slow.

I didn't want him to be. I wanted more. Needed more. I needed to breathe him in and get lost in his essence. I moved from my chair, slowly straddling him, never breaking our kiss as I crawled onto his lap.

He groaned the moment my hips rolled over him, his lips moving against mine, completely consuming me. I gasped as his fingers wound between my hair, pulling and tightening to the point of pain. I leaned back, giving him more access while my own hands roamed over his face.

Before I could think, he slid his tongue into my mouth. And the sensation, feeling it meet with my own, I melted—

He took full control like he was ravenous, like he had held back for so long and was finally cut free, and I was fine with it—fine with being destroyed by him.

He slid his hands down my throat before he grabbed onto my hips, dragging me further into his lap. I exhaled loudly as I felt him harden against me. My stomach dropped, and I wanted more. I wanted to explore every inch of him, to memorize his body like it was my own.

My hands found their way under his shirt, feeling the muscles over his stomach move beneath my fingers before I pulled the material over his head in between frantic kisses. My fingers ran over his bare abdomen, tracing over some of the scars he had there until they stopped above the trail of hair leading down.

I went to kiss him again, needing the contact, but he pulled back. I stared at his lips, mad they weren't still on me.

"Why did you stop?" I half panted, half pouted as I rolled my hips over him, wanting more.

"I love you," he whispered, his breath was just as ragged as mine, and I stilled. "I fucking love you with everything I am."

My heart fluttered as a cheesy, full-tooth grin escaped me. I leaned forward, my hands wrapping around his neck before I started trailing feather-light kisses over every inch of his scar, my smile lingering as I kissed my way down his jaw. "Say it again."

His head tilted back. "I love you, Scotlind Rumor."

Once I reached the end of the jagged line, my mouth meeting with smooth skin, I continued kissing down his neck, mumbling in between each one. *"I."* My lips pressed into the crevice of his collar-bone. *"Love."* My tongue slid out, meeting with the sensitive skin there as I trailed down even lower. *"You."* I reached up, weaving my hands through his hair. The texture of his short buzz met my fingers before I reached higher to grab onto the longer locks at the top. I took hold of his head, turning it so I had better access to his neck. *"Too."* I savored the way I sent shivers down his body, how I could feel him shake beneath me, how I knew my touch affected him.

As soon as the words left my mouth, Tezya stood, taking me with him. Our chair clattered to the ground as he lifted me out of it, my legs instinctively wrapping tighter around him. One of his hands pressed against my bare back under my shirt. The other embedded into my hair again as he slammed me down against the war table. He spread my hips wider before stepping between them. Distinctly, I heard one of the maps tear as I ground my hips against his, but I didn't care. I couldn't think about anything but him.

He kept kissing me as he guided me down until I was sprawled out on the table before him. Then he was standing over me, removing his mouth from mine. I pouted for a split second before I realized what he was doing.

He reached for his pants, his eyes never leaving mine. I thought he was going to remove them, but then he pulled a dagger out. My brows furrowed when he didn't toss it aside and kept the blade in his palm.

"I've wanted to see you. To see *all* of you." My breath hitched as he bent over me. He placed the blade between his teeth as he gripped me by my hips, scooting me to the edge of the table. Once I was directly before him, he grabbed the knife from his mouth and pulled my pants away from my skin, dragging the blade down the length of them. "I've been dreaming about this ever since that night in the bath... I've thought about all the things I'd do to you once I healed."

I stared up at him as my pants split in two before falling off my body. He was looking at me with an overwhelming hunger I wanted to get lost in. He moved to my shirt next and cut the material until it no longer clung to my chest. I gasped, feeling the cold blade against my bare skin as he cut off my underwear and bra next.

I held my breath, feeling vulnerable and confident all at once. I was laying naked before him, biting my lip between my teeth as he took his time looking at me.

His breath hitched before he blew it out. "Fuck. You're perfect, Rumor." A thud sounded as he threw the dagger and it sank into the wood a good distance away from me.

He stepped between my legs, his fingers running over my right calf, and I shuddered as he met the rough skin there. He lifted my leg up in the air and rested my ankle over his shoulder, exposing me fully below. Turning his head, he kissed the ruined flesh left from the fire. "Every inch of you is gorgeous," he said, his tone serious. "I love every part of you, but I won't ever let fire hurt you again. I won't let one more scar mark your body."

He pressed his lips to my calf again before sending slow, agonizing kisses up my leg. I moaned loudly, becoming utterly aware of the cool draft and how exposed I was in this position. I bent forward with the intention of kissing him, but his other hand shot up and pushed me back down, pinning me against the table.

"I'm not done enjoying you," he growled as he kissed over my knee and started up the length of my thigh. I didn't have time to think about it before the hand holding me down simultaneously moved up my stomach and started grazing my breasts.

My back arched, shifting my hips in an attempt to position his head where I wanted it, where I *needed* it. Everything he was doing kept building and building, the sensation overwhelming even though he was barely touching me. Every time his lips reached higher up my leg, a shiver ran down my spine and sent my entire body tingling. I gasped, a tremble working its way through me. I wanted him to keep going, to reach the point that burned for him.

Right as his lips were between my thighs, when I could feel his warm breath directly on top of me, he stopped. He gently set my right leg back down. Once it was free, I wound it around his knee, locking him into me. He grinned down, raising my left leg and repeated the agonizingly slow process, watching me the entire time.

I couldn't stop panting, couldn't stop my chest from moving up and down in ragged movements, even as his other hand cupped my breasts before finding and pinching my nipples between his fingers. I was squirming and bucking under him, and he was enjoying it.

"Tezya," I moaned as my hands threaded into the longer strands of his hair. I tried bending his knee with my right leg, forcing him down where I wanted him. "Please." I couldn't take it anymore. His touch felt like everything, but not nearly enough.

He was halfway up my left thigh, his body hunched over mine, as his silver gaze locked onto mine. A smile curved his lips in between kisses, and he laughed at my poor attempt to move him before he finally gave in and kneeled on the grass before me. His face now directly in line with the table—directly in line with me laying naked on top of it.

He was grinning as he kissed me, continuing up my leg, still teasing, until his lips finally—*finally*—met with what I wanted. I arched around him until nothing of my upper back was left on the table. My abdomen cradling his head, locking him in place as he kissed and licked and devoured every inch of me.

Every sensation flowed at once, all ending in one point. His mouth... his lips... his tongue... the way his scar felt as it brushed against my inner thigh...

I couldn't take it. Time was lost on me. I didn't know or care if it had been minutes or seconds that passed, I was already about to shatter. The pressure kept building and building, threatening to consume me. His thumb replaced his tongue over my clit as he gently made tantalizing circles. Then he moved his head lower, and I half screamed as his tongue went inside me, mixing and blending with the movement of his finger. The combination of them together was too much.

"Tezya, I—" I didn't know what I was going to say as the sensation overwhelmed me. My vision blurred as my hips started rocking on their own accord against his face. My fingers tightened in his hair, trapping him there. Then I lost it. I wasn't sure how much time had passed before I was coming undone. The feeling was spiraling out of me in waves as I slowly, so slowly, started regaining my senses.

First, I heard myself panting, my breathing no longer belonged to me. Then, I felt my hand cramp as I realized I was still holding his head captive, my grip over his hair nearly ripping the strands off his head. I could feel sweat starting to form behind my knees, one still bent over his shoulder, the other had moved around his back when he kneeled down.

My vision came into focus a second later as Tezya looked up at me and smiled. I watched as his tongue slowly slipped out of his mouth, licking his lips as he savored me on them.

"Fuck, you taste good."

I loosened my grip on his hair, but I didn't let go. Instead, I used my hold to pull his head back up to mine.

I needed more.

Reaching for his pants, I started unbuttoning them in a haste, not stopping until they were a pile of fabric on the floor. My throat ran dry as he sprung out of them, taking in every beautiful, scarred inch of his body. He waited, letting me soak him in like he had me, and it wasn't until our eyes locked that he repositioned himself against me.

I gasped as soon as I felt his length press into me. With one hand, he guided the tip of his cock so it just barely rested inside me before gripping the edge of the wooden table around either side of my thighs. He stilled, staring down at me, his face turning serious.

"What's wrong?" I asked. I wanted him to press further in, to completely fill me. I needed to be close to him—needed our bodies to become one.

"Your first time should not be on a fucking table."

I reached up, bending forward to wrap my hands around his neck, kissing his thought away. "Tezya, I want you. Like this. Right now. On this table." I jutted my hips toward him for emphasis, and he moaned as the tip of him thrusted inside me. My eyelids fluttered back as a loud gasp escaped me. I had no idea what having sex would feel like, but I didn't imagine this. My adrenaline was working in overdrive as I adjusted to the feeling, half in pain, half in pleasure, and I couldn't tell which sensation was winning. But I didn't want him to stop.

Tezya leaned forward, gently guiding me back down against the cold table, but I barely felt it. His hands rested around my cheeks as he kissed me, this time soft and slow. "You're not playing fair when you do something like that," he teased, but he was smiling as he kissed me.

"I mean it. I don't want this any differently." I cupped his face, capturing anything else he wanted to say with a kiss. We stayed like that, he didn't move further into me or pull out as he kissed my lips gently, as I kissed him back just as slowly, savoring him.

"Are you sure?" Tezya asked between breathy kisses. "I can do this right with—"

"Yes," I cut him off with another kiss. "Tezya. Please."

He was quiet for a minute, studying my face, before he conceded, "This might hurt. Tell me if you need me to stop."

I nodded slowly. His hands found mine, our fingers interlocking above my head as he slid the rest of the way in, completely filling me. I cried out at the first thrust. A sharp jolt of pain shot through me, all ending to where he was inside of me. He paused for a moment, resting his forehead against mine. "Is this okay?"

I didn't respond at first, needing to sort through how I was feeling. "Just. Go. Slow." I panted the words out in small breaths, breathing heavily into his mouth.

"Tell me if it's too much," he said again. When I nodded, he found my lips, kissing me through it, soft and gentle as he moved in and out.

Again and again. He pulled out slowly, unhurried, before gently easing back in, stretching me bit by bit as I got used to the feel of him. Each one was met with a kiss, his breathing quicker than usual. Mine was just as rushed and winded.

I could tell he was holding back, waiting until I adjusted. I focused on kissing him, on the feeling of his lips against mine and tried to block out the searing pain that was mixed with pleasure.

Eventually my thighs relaxed, and my posture became less rigid. The next time he pushed forward, he slid further in, almost completely inside. I could feel myself growing wet, taking the pain away with it as I adjusted to the feeling of him. My eyes closed as my head tilted back. Tezya noticed my change but was still holding back, hesitating. "Does it still hurt?" he whispered.

I shook my head, unable to muster many words. "Good. It feels... good... now. I want... more."

He smiled, quickening the pace in an instant, finally letting himself move the way he needed. I inhaled sharply as he grabbed my chin by my jaw, turning my head to the side. His teeth dragged over the flesh he just made raw.

"You're mine," he said as he sucked my neck. The feeling of his lips on my skin, of him moving inside me, was becoming my undoing. He wasn't holding back now, he wasn't slowing. My only answer was a moan. I couldn't form words, couldn't think.

"Fuck. You feel so good." His one hand gripped my hip, his strength punishing. His other kneading my breast, his thumb grazing across my nipple. I couldn't control the noises that left me. I couldn't control the shake that started in my legs as they wrapped around his hips, trapping him against me.

This feeling was everything. I had no idea where he started and I stopped, and I didn't want to find out. I wanted to be together, to always be a tangle of limbs and ragged panting forever.

My back arched off the table, putting him deeper inside me, but in the process, my head whipped back and thudded against the wood.

"Oww," I groaned, rubbing the back of it. We both laughed, Tezya smiling as he leaned down and started kissing my neck, then cradled my head in his hands so it wasn't pressed into the hard surface anymore. My eyes kept fluttering, my nails scraping down his back, indenting into the scars across his body.

It still wasn't enough. I needed *everything*. I still wanted more, needed to be closer to him.

I reached my arm across his chest and yanked the dagger out of the wood. His eyes flashed, his movements slowed but didn't stop. His hands left my head and slid down me until they rested at my hips.

"I want to," I stuttered, barely getting the words out. His eyebrows furrowed in confusion until I turned my hand over.

"Are you sure?" His eyes widened as he stilled, completely stopping now, but he didn't pull out of me. "If we do this, it can't be undone."

"I'm sure." And I was. I wanted to complete the bond. I'd never been so certain about anything in my entire life. Because when something horrible happened, he was the only person I wanted comforting me. When I had exciting news, he was the first one I wanted to share it with. And when the nights grew as cold and dark as that tub had felt, I wanted his flames to melt the frozen water off my body. I wanted his fire to consume and devour me until I was only ash in his hands and there was nothing left of my existence.

I was nothing more than a moth attracted to the fiery blaze that was him, and I was no longer scared of being burned.

TWENTY-ONE
TEZYA

I STILLED, watching as Scotlind gently dragged the blade across her scab, reopening it. Her sapphire eyes were a deep blue as she pressed the hilt of the dagger into my own hand, waiting for me to do the same. I repositioned it, turning the blade over. As I did, I felt the back of her with my cock. I still hadn't pulled out—didn't ever want to. But fuck. She felt so damn good that it was hard to focus on the task. But I wanted this more than the feeling of being inside of her. I wanted all of her, every single damning inch.

She watched as I reopened the scab on my own hand, not nearly as careful as she had been with hers. I wanted it to leave a mark whenever it healed. It would be the only scar I'd cherish. Every time I saw it or ran my fingers over the rough edges, it would bring me back to this moment with her. I had too many scars, and so did she, but this one was different. It was hope amongst suffering. It was a good memory instead of the horrors I tried to drown out and forget.

I took in every inch of her. The image of her laying bare before me. Her smile and how her left side rose slightly higher than her right. The freckles splattered across her nose. The way she'd slowly dragged her lips between her teeth, and the slow blinks she didn't even realize she was doing whenever she wanted to soak in a moment. Pylemo, I loved her. I had never loved anything as much as I loved her, and I never would again.

As soon as the blood flowed from my palm, I collected a small drop of it with my finger. Scottie bent forward on the table, the motion driving me deeper into her as she brought my finger into her mouth. I almost melted from the sensation, imagining her lips around another part of me—later. We'd do that later. Right now, this was all I wanted.

She flicked her tongue over the pad of my finger before removing her mouth and doing the same with her own. A jolt rushed through me as soon as I tasted her blood on my tongue, our bond coming alive again with an electric shock. Our hands met immediately, neither of us uttering a word. We didn't need to anymore. I felt the surge of energy intensify as soon as our blood connected, our souls bleeding into one another, becoming one from the inside out.

I knew she felt the same rush of emotions because her aura became alive, developing into a living, breathing thing for me to witness. I felt her pleasure as my own, and by her moan, I knew she felt mine as I started slowly moving my hips again. Our thoughts, our emotions, our *everything* was bleeding together.

The dagger clattered onto the table as I dropped it, but I barely heard it. All of my focus was directed on her. I gently tilted her head up to look at me, needing to see the emotion on her face instead of just feeling it.

With my heightened senses, I was used to feeling everything more intensely. Every pain, every pleasure, every touch was amplified, but Rumor was only just experiencing it now. It was overwhelming her, and I wanted more of her to unravel before me. I wanted to consume every part of her. She felt so damn good and right and perfect.

Tezya, she whimpered, but I think it was only in her mind.

"You're mine," I growled as I thrusted into her again and again, feeling the adrenaline fill our veins in unison.

Her answer was a moan as I lifted her off the table with me still inside her. I moved her everywhere, soaking in the different sensations with each new position. Standing with her in my arms. The chair. Against the post. On her stomach on the ground. Every single place in this tent I made her mine.

And with each damning, blissful moment, I felt the blood bond lock into place.

TWENTY-TWO
SCOTLIND

"I don't want to go," I murmured, pressing soft kisses along Tezya's jaw. "Let's do that again."

His groaning response had me nipping his ear before I started kissing down his neck. I could feel that he wanted to take me again, his erection was throbbing against my stomach as I laid on top of him. My legs had fallen around his hips, and despite the shake to them, I wanted more. His thoughts started seeping and mixing with mine, and I swore he was going to give in.

"We can't. I've already postponed the meeting long enough. Dravenburg is going to have my head for it. He's probably already plotting my death for stopping it when I did."

I turned my head to the side, peering over his jaw to look out the tent flaps, with each gust of wind I caught sight of the darkening sky. It was morning when I found him, and I hadn't realized how much time had passed since I first interrupted the meeting until now. We were still naked, using his clothes as bedding as I twisted off his stomach to curl into his side instead, but when I looked up at his face, his expression changed.

"What's wrong?"

"I'm terrified," he admitted. "I won't survive it if he takes you."

"If *who* takes me, Tezya?" I couldn't follow his train of thought.

"The King—if he gets his hands on you again…" He looked like he was about to cry. "Scotlind, you have no idea." He shuddered, letting out a breath. "You have no idea what it did to me seeing you chained at the dinner table." I'd never seen him so vulnerable, so serious. I knew that dinner affected him. He acted rashly, breaking Peter and I out of the castle that night because of it.

"Tezya, I'll be fine—"

"He's going to come after you," he said, cutting me off. "Besides wanting your abilities, now that Sie is out of the prison, his focus will be to separate the two of you. Promise me no matter what happens, no matter what he tries to do to lure you in, you won't…"

I kissed him, stopping his words. "I promise, Tezya."

Then I kept kissing him. He had a small ball of fire glowing above us, but it didn't fully keep out the draft.

"You're shivering," he murmured into my mouth. I wasn't sure how long we stayed like that, how long our mouths moved against each other.

"I can think of a few ways for you to warm me," I hummed as I thought of all the things we did today. I replayed the visions in my mind, knowing Tezya could see them. The blood bond was new and fragile, but I felt it grow the longer he held me. The strands were snapping into place, stitching together tighter and tighter as the day dragged on. With it, our senses were merging, our minds becoming an open pathway without either of us having telepathy.

After our second time having sex, when we finally bothered with words, I asked him if it was common, but he didn't know. We had no idea how or why we were able to communicate without speaking or if it'd even last.

Either way, I liked it. I liked knowing his thoughts. In hindsight, it probably should have scared the crap out of me, knowing none of my own were sacred anymore. I'd never be able to hide anything from him ever again. But it did the opposite. It gave me comfort, made me feel like we were truly one; two souls made for each other.

"Oh, shit," he cursed.

"What?" I asked as I pushed up on my elbows to look at him, my hair dropped over his face like a canopy.

"I forgot I ruined your clothes."

"Oh."

"Here, wear this." He reached his arm out from under me, passing me his shirt. I stood reluctantly, not entirely wanting to be separated from him.

It smelled like him at least, and I couldn't stop grinning as I shrugged it on. But my smile faltered as soon as I saw his frown. "What?"

"It barely covers your ass. I don't want you walking around a camp full of Advenians wearing only that."

I had no idea why that made my stomach do summersaults, but it did. I bit my lip as I looked down at him. His markings were barely visible, almost translucent, as the sweat on him was starting to dry. His white hair was slicked back and his freaking body...

He rose from the ground, pulling his pants up as he went. I couldn't help but stare when he didn't fasten the button, letting them loosely hang off his hips. He was so ungoddessly attractive, and he was all mine.

"It covers me," I said as I looked down at his shirt. It rested slightly above my knees, and I was pretty sure the King forced me to wear more revealing dresses when he made me sit on Tezya's lap during the annual meetings.

He closed the gap between us in two strides. "I'm going to get you more clothes." His hands immediately found my waist as I stood on my tip-toes to kiss him back.

"Uh-huh. And where's the guy who couldn't wait to take me to the Luxian nude beaches?"

"That guy decided he doesn't want to share you."

A giggle escaped me as his grip tightened around me, pulling me further into his chest. I wrapped my arms around his neck, wanting his lips on me again.

Tezya stiffened a second before I heard the flaps of the tent open. I whirled to see who had entered, and my heart stopped as Sie froze in his tracks. I scanned what was left of the war tent. We'd completely ruined it. The chairs were thrown. Everything that was once on the table was now in shreds, the maps were completely destroyed. My ripped clothes were still scattered on the ground, the dagger thrown somewhere across the table. And I was in Tezya's bare arms, his shirt now hiked halfway up my stomach, revealing *everything* as he held me.

Sie's dark eyes flashed in shock for a split second, but then it was gone. Tezya released me but didn't let go of my hand. I used my free one to nervously pull down on his shirt, suddenly wishing I had more fabric on.

Sie cleared his throat, his expression was cold. "Your sister started speaking." He turned around and stormed out of the tent without another word, leaving the flaps fluttering behind him.

Tezya was still for one second before he bolted out of the tent with me in tow, not caring that he didn't have a shirt on or that I still didn't have pants. I wanted to say something, to ask him to wait, but I was just as nervous as he was for what Dovelyn would say. Any embarrassment I might have had vanished and only one thought consumed me —*Why now?*

I didn't have time to process Sie walking in on us or the crowd gathering around the princess outside the dining hall.

Tezya stilled, his hand squeezing mine as Dovelyn's voice rang out to us, except it didn't quite sound like her. There was something off about it. Something darker, something lower…

"*The world must start anew. Forged in peace, one shall be born with the powers of two.*
Light and Dark will come together. The chosen one will be the tether.
Beneath the Goddesses' feet, is the information you seek.
To manipulate Pylemo's gifted fire, the son must use it against his claimed sire.
But without a sacrifice from Light and blood spilled from Dark, the chosen one will lose his spark."

· · ·

DOVELYN'S EYES were the same milky blue from when we were at their mother's grave. She spoke in a rushed tone, like she couldn't hold the words in even if she wanted to. She chanted the same rhyme over and over until the crowd parted and her milky eyes rested on Tezya. Something about him made her stop her frantic chanting, but her eyes didn't return to normal. She just kept staring at him, frozen in time. If she had pupils, they would have been blown wide.

Then as quickly as she stopped, a scream rippled from her lungs before her voice broke with pleading sobs, and she fell to her knees. "He will die. He will die. Gone. Gone. Gone. Please. I can't lose him."

Tears were running down her pale face. "Okay," she shrieked in resignation, her body sagging on the ground as everyone collectively took a step back. "His fire must be used. Chosen. Chosen. He was chosen by Pylemo. He is the only one who can kill him. Must do it. Too strong. He is too strong. Not balanced. Scale tipped. Use all the fire. Use everything. Everything until there is none. Everything until *he* is gone."

Her head was tilted up toward the sky as her voice continued to ring out, carrying her broken sentences throughout the entire camp.

She's talking to someone, I said to Tezya as I squeezed his hand because there was no doubt Dovelyn was having a conversation with someone who wasn't there.

I know, he answered in my mind.

Tezya dropped my grip and pushed his way through the crowd toward his sister. It wasn't until he pressed a hand on Dovelyn's slim shoulder that she leaned into his touch and the rambling stopped entirely. I couldn't hear what he said to her, but I watched as Tezya disappeared, cradling Dove in his arms as he led her back toward his tent.

My bare feet were glued to the spot in the grass where I was standing. Everyone around me was clearing out, slowly getting back to their day as the commotion died down. But I couldn't move. I didn't have it in me to be bothered by the glares I was receiving from my lack of clothing. My mind kept stewing over what Dovelyn had said, and the three words that now haunted me...

He will die.

TWENTY-THREE
SIE

"ARE THERE ANY OTHER TAKERS?"

A crowd had gathered around me, but no one stepped forward. My chest wheezed from exertion, and it was an effort to steady my breathing enough to talk. I'd been in the training rings for the past three hours, fighting whoever would challenge me.

The only thing I was thankful for right now was that the rings never closed. They were positioned far enough away from the communal sleeping tents that anyone could train anytime they wanted. Electric users scattered lanterns around the area, casting the rings in a dim glow. Not that it was needed tonight, the moon was so bright it felt more like dawn than dusk.

The only issue was, I was nowhere near done letting out my aggressions, but I had already made a dent on the Advenians who called this camp their home. I was running out of willing fighters.

It felt strange to spar people from both Lux and Tennebris. I still couldn't wrap my head around how they'd been living in peace in their own made-up society without anyone ever knowing.

"I can go again," Peter said. He'd spent the entire time by my side, even though I knew he was beyond exhausted.

"Are you sure—" I started to ask, but Peter already stepped into the ring. There was a circle drawn into the earth, partially from a ground user, partially from an air user. The two powers worked together to protect anyone who watched from the outside—which was a shit ton of people. I was surprised so many Advenians trained and used the rings.

I smiled as soon as his fist collided with my arm. This was what I was built for. This was what I was good at. What my father had trained me to do. Kicking. Punching. Fighting. Zoning the whole fucking world out. My father's old phrase came back to me, *"Once you're the king, people will only seek you out because of your status, so get comfortable with being alone. Build a shield for yourself and never let anyone breach it. Love will leave you broken, and fragility makes you weak."*

I never fully understood the meaning of his words until now. My father had lived through what he preached to me all those years ago. I always thought he was just bitter. But now I could see it was his own way of protecting me. He'd experienced heartbreak. I always knew he didn't love my mother, that what they shared was only a mutual agreement to breed. I just never knew he'd fallen in love with a Luxian before her, and it just had to be the fucking Fire Prince's dead mother.

I was more pissed off at myself for not heeding his advice. That despite knowing what my father told me was true—love would only hurt me—I still wanted it. I thought I had it with her.

She completed the blood bond with Tezya.

I just barely dodged Peter's kick, and only missed his counter punch because I teleported out of the way. My body ignited in golden spirals as I called to my abilities. I felt my reserve dwindle, knowing only rest would replenish them, but I didn't care. I needed to clear my head, and I was nowhere near done.

He's my brother. My fucking brother.

I grunted as Peter slammed his foot into my ribs with more power than he normally possessed. He usually stood slightly smaller than me, but he used his ability to shift and transform into me again. The first time he did it I freaked on him. "I don't want to look at my reflection right now," I spat. But then I realized he was challenging me to an even match, giving me what I really wanted.

I had just walked in on the two of them fucking. My worst nightmare from the prison was coming true...

Peter transformed out of the spitting image of myself and turned into a bear for a split second. His claws slashed my shoulder before he quickly shifted back into me, saving me from the brunt of the damage.

Tezya had the fucking nerve to lecture me, telling me I hurt Scotlind. It felt like a sick joke.

I screamed as I lunged toward Peter, my anger having no outlet but this. I didn't hold back my throw as I went right for his jugular. He staggered before falling over on his ass. His hands were wrapped around his throat as he was forced back into his own body. He went into a coughing spell before spitting up blood. Everyone watching around the circle simultaneously backed up.

Shit. Shit. Shit. I thought he saw me coming. I thought he was going to dodge. "Are you okay?" I asked as I rushed to help him.

"Just peachy," he rasped, but he looked anything but. It was his fifth time fighting me, and it showed. He stepped in whenever others hesitated, and each time he shifted into a version of me, so I could have a fair fight. But all the transformations were dwindling his reserves. Not to mention I found some sick pleasure in beating the shit out of myself and kept forgetting it was actually my friend.

He gestured to begin again.

"No." I shook my head. "You can barely stand up straight. Fuck, Peter, I'm sorry."

"I'm fine," he lied. "I'll let you know when I need to stop." But he wasn't shifting back into me again. He was too drained. His blonde hair was stained darker from the coating of sweat that lingered, and his hands were shaking beneath his scabbed knuckles.

"No, I'm not fighting you anymore."

Peter opened his mouth to protest when a female voice called out, "Mind if I have a go?"

I tried to mask my shock as Savannah stepped into the ring. She'd clearly been watching the fight and saw what just happened. I was surprised she wanted to spar me after witnessing it. The more fights I had, the less Advenians that wanted to challenge me.

Out of the corner of my eye, I saw Peter still rubbing his throat. Someone passed him a jug of water as he stepped aside, leaving only me and the human in the ring.

"This isn't a place for a mortal. It's ability sparring." I gestured toward the circle drawn in the dirt, enclosing us in. The rings itself consisted of packed dirt, soft enough that when you fell, it cushioned the blow. The areas in between each of the rings had lush grass that never seemed to get muddy, even though thousands of Advenians stomped through it day after day. Most rested in between fights, but some just came to spectate. Either way, the place was packed.

"Humor me then, prince." She smiled, and I had no idea why she wasn't backing down. She should be scared. She started tying her lavender hair up as she took another step closer to me.

I went to protest, but she stopped me. "First off, the rings are for *everyone*. Advenians, humans, guys, girls, adults, children. We're *all* allowed to train here. So don't tell me I can't. And second off, I know you aren't fighting right now so you can show off your teleporting skills. You want a real fight. You want to let your anger out, and you see, I want to do just that too." She finished tying her hair up. "So fight me without using your abilities."

"What do you have to be angry about?" I asked in disbelief.

Her eyes narrowed, and I swore I saw a glimmer of lavender reflect off her gray irises. "I'm not asking you why you're fighting."

Humiliation filled me. Everyone in the fucking camp knew that Scottie and Tezya were now bonded. When I found Peter after Dovelyn's outburst and told him what I saw, he wasn't surprised. He'd told me half the camp *heard* them bonding. "Courtesy ah-la fabric for walls," he tried to joke, but it only pissed me off more. And now, this damn mortal had the nerve to think she could fight me. My life was a fucking pathetic joke...

"Fine," I growled. "But I'm not holding back just because you're human. Don't come crying to me when you regret it."

She just grinned, flashing a straight, white smile that looked so sweet and innocent, I was in a stupor when she attacked first. I'd always thought humans would be slow, but she moved with agility.

She landed a kick to my cheek before I even got into my fighting stance.

I rubbed my jaw. It didn't hurt. She wasn't particularly strong compared to our kind, but I was amazed she was able to hit me at all. I went to attack, but she was faster, doing some sort of flip in the air to avoid my oncoming move.

Laughter echoed in the ring. "In order to make me cry with regret, as you claimed, you'll have to actually hit me, prince."

Kallon—Tezya's so-called fiancée—made her way to the front. I only noticed because one half of her head was a flaming red-orange, and I bristled. How in the hell could she wear the color of fire when the person she was supposed to marry just slept with someone else. But she didn't look like her entire world just shattered. Maybe she didn't know yet. I scoffed—I doubted that. According to Peter, the entire camp now knew, and anytime Scottie and Tezya were together, she never seemed bothered.

"She's fast, prince," Kallon taunted with a light smile. "It's the only way she wins fights. No one can land a hit on her."

My eyes flicked from Kallon to Savannah. Both of the girls were tall. Kallon still stood inches above the mortal, but I was surprised that she didn't tower over her. I always imagined humans would be small, but she looked more Advenian than Scotlind. Whatever muscle she had on her body was zeroed out by her narrowed frame.

She held her hands up, and I caught sight of bare wrists. It was weird to not see a burn on them. She had to be around our age, and if she was an Advenian she would have been branded. Yet, humans walked this planet without anyone knowing what they were capable of until it was too late.

Scottie's wrists flashed in my mind from when she was first branded. Her right wrist was still more raised to this day. She would forever have a reminder on her skin that she's considered weak. Our kind would judge her before she would get the chance to say hello. Hell, sometimes I judged what she was capable of. Had years of growing up with my father unconsciously brainwashed me? Because I did look at the ranking system and believed in it. I never agreed with how my father treated zeroes, but I still always thought of them as lesser.

I ran my hands through my hair. Savannah halted in the ring, giving me a minute. I never shared the same beliefs as Scottie. She so passionately wanted to get rid of the ranking system, but did I? What did I want? I had no fucking clue what I believed in anymore. I thought about what Scottie asked me back on the lake… that if I could change things, would I? Was the ranking system truly fair? I tried to remember if I knew any ranked servants, but every damn one of them was a zero.

I didn't want to think about it, about any of it. I could barely sort through my thoughts on my wife, let alone on how the Advenians governed—"She's not even my damned *wife* anymore."

"What?" Savannah asked, startled. She'd been moving around the ring with me, not attacking, seeming to notice that my mind was lost in my own fight.

Fuck. I just said that out loud. Instead of answering, I attacked, but this time when she leapt out of the way, flipping gracefully in the air, I used my abilities. I met her halfway, teleporting to where she was jumping and crashed into her. We both tumbled to the ground, our legs entwining with one another. Mine with golden swirls, and hers sun-speckled and bare.

Her lavender hair flared out around her, coming out of the twist she had it in.

She puffed out a breath. "Can't breathe."

Shit. I was crushing her. I quickly jumped off the girl, and at the last second, decided to extend my hand to her. She regarded it but didn't take it, hopping to her feet swiftly on her own. She started dusting off her clothes, even though the dirt left no traces on her from the magic. "That wasn't fair. We agreed on no abilities."

"You said that, not me," I told her as she rubbed the back of her neck. "I never once said I fought fair." I started walking away, finally calling it for the night.

I left the girl standing in the middle of the ring and didn't look back.

TWENTY-FOUR
TEZYA

I HEADED BACK to the war tent after Dovelyn finally drifted off to sleep. Hours had passed, making it closer to dawn the next day, and I hadn't seen Rumor since.

Dovelyn's eyes were bloodshot from all the crying. If she remembered what she'd been chanting, she didn't say. The only thing she kept repeating was, "Please don't die." She'd pleaded with me for hours, sobbing and repeating the same three words over and over again, before finally accepting my answer that I wouldn't.

I didn't know what the damn prophecy showed her, but I felt responsible. Dovelyn didn't want to find the grave. She didn't want to uncover the prophecy, and I practically forced her to by making Dravenburg take a vote. I knew she'd be outnumbered. That everyone would want a chance at an advantage against the King.

I hadn't realized it would affect her this much. Maybe this was why our mother took away Dovelyn's memories in the first place. Maybe she didn't take her own life to spare me from the prophecy, but to prevent this from happening to Dove, and I ruined everything.

My sister's suffering was because of me.

It's not your fault, Scottie's voice filled my head a moment later. I glanced up and saw her standing at the entrance of the war tent. She was looking right at me but hadn't opened her mouth, our connection doing the work for her. I couldn't muster a reply because we both knew it was. Instead, I gave her a weak smile and took her hand in mine before walking into the tent together.

Scottie had changed into new clothes, but there was nothing we could do to hide what we had done earlier. We never got the chance to clean up the tent after hours of using it, and it showed.

Dravenburg glared at me the moment we entered, and I swore his ears were producing steam. "You completely ruined it. You ripped my map."

Scottie winced. I squeezed her hand but didn't let go. "Actually, it was my map," was all I said as I led us toward the front. Every Advenian important to the camp was either sitting or standing inside. Scottie's cheeks were flaming red by the time we made it to Dravenburg.

Relax, it's fine. We did nothing wrong, I told her, gesturing for her to take a seat.

Tell that to Dravenburg. I'm pretty sure he wants to kill me right now.

I laughed out loud and everyone turned to look at me. Dravenburg did look ready to murder us, and Savannah kept staring at the map and frowning. I took the seat next to Scottie, forcing myself not to think about what we'd done earlier. I was half tempted to kick everyone out again, but I knew Dravenburg was right for calling a meeting—we needed to talk.

I pushed my thoughts of her away. Getting a hard-on in the middle of the meeting wasn't high on my list.

Instead, I focused on how we could win this war, preferably before it even began. I didn't particularly want to fight the men I trained from the Luxian army, and the fewer battles fought, the more lives saved. Some of the soldiers from Lux would probably switch sides once they realized what was happening, but most were loyal to the King.

Dravenburg cleared his throat, starting the meeting. "For anyone who didn't witness it, can someone recite Princess Dovelyn's *words?*"

Savannah uncrossed her legs and leaned back in her chair, reaching for a piece of paper she had folded in the pocket of her jeans. "I wrote it down after about the tenth time Dove chanted it." Her father nodded for her to read it. "The world must start anew. Forged in peace, one shall be born with the powers of two. Light and Dark will come together. The chosen one will be the tether. Beneath the Goddesses' feet, is the information you seek. To manipulate Pylemo's gifted fire, the son must use it against his claimed sire. But without a sacrifice from Light and blood spilled from Dark, the chosen one will lose his spark."

Everyone was quiet, letting her words sink in. I hadn't been able to process it until now. All my focus went into making sure my sister was okay. But now I couldn't stop thinking about what winning this war—what killing the King—would take.

"Well, the beginning is pretty obvious," Kal spoke. "Tezya was born with two powers, and he helped shape Brighta, bringing Tennebrisians and Luxians together. He also possesses the Goddess' favored ability of fire, and his claimed sire is the Lux King, so Tezya needs to be the one to kill him. What I don't get is, what's the sacrifice from Light and blood from Dark?"

No one answered as her question settled around the room.

"We need to go back to Lux," I finally said.

"Are you crazy?" Scottie seethed. Her hair whipped across my shoulder as she snapped her head in my direction.

"We don't have a choice, Rumor," I answered gently. "I've used my fire on the King countless times. He also possesses the ability, as well as air to make shields, so it does nothing to him. We need to figure out what Dovelyn was alluding to. She called it Goddesses' fire, so it has to be something more than me just using my ability, and I think the answer is in Lux."

"I agree with Tezya," Wells said. I hadn't noticed him standing there until he spoke.

"Wells." I smiled as I stood and walked toward Savannah's younger brother, clapping him over the back. He pulled me into a hug, tucking his head into my shoulder. Dravenburg, Wells, and Sav were the only mortals in the camp. Most of the time, I forgot Savannah wasn't one of us with her reckless behavior. But looking at Wells, it was undeniable. He was as human as you could get.

"I've missed you, Tez." He smiled as he pushed his glasses up the bridge of his nose with one finger. He looked nothing like his sister. His brown glasses matched his spiral curls atop his head. His eyes were the same shape as Savannah's, but where her coloring was a hazel-gray, his was a pale brown. They stood about the same height and both had lean frames, but Savannah was corded in muscles from years of training with Advenians in the rings, while Wells was all skin and bones. The only things he lifted were vials and serums in his lab. The only real resemblance they had to each other was their skin tone. But Savannah's skin was tanned from hours under the sun, while Wells was naturally dark.

"Save the greetings and pointless chit-chat for later," Dravenburg grumbled, rubbing his thick, graying beard. "Why do you think he should go, Wells?"

"Because the Lux King needs to die, and the answer on how to do that will be at the Goddesses' feet."

"There are many statues of Pylemo. How do we know they're referring to one in Lux? I'm sure Tennebris is loaded with them too," Rainer said, pulling his hair up into a high bun—his telltale sign he was concentrating.

"*Ex Cinere Renasci.*"

"What—?"

"It means rebirth from ashes," Wells answered Rainer. "It's the name of the statue by the bay. Pylemo is the Goddess of fertility and Tezya's ability is fire, so that statue is the most logical choice."

Dravenburg stiffened. He was furious when he first discovered Arcane used to sneak him into the Luxian city any time the King was in Tennebris for meetings. Everyone knew Wells and Arcane had a past. They still loved each other, even though neither of them would admit it.

"I agree," Kallon said. "The statue was built in honor of Lakimi, and it's the only statue that depicts her bare feet."

I hated that particular statue. My old room overlooked it, and with my heightened senses, I could depict the exact details of the golden memorial.

Our history claimed Pylemo birthed the lesser Goddesses during the first ever Lakimi, and in honor of them, she decided to give us the gift of fertility too. It was the reason the statue was created, but I'd always felt it looked out of place amongst the simplicity of the bay. She was portrayed completely naked standing with her hands raised toward the sky while the twelve lesser Goddesses all bowed at her feet.

To me it looked like the lesser Goddesses had their noses forever stuck in the dirt and was a constant reminder they weren't seen as Pylemo's equal. They were supposed to be her children, that only together, with all twelve of their strengths combined, could they equate to her.

"You don't actually believe what Dovelyn was saying, though, do you?" Rainer asked. "She was talking nonsense."

"Not nonsense, but riddles, and yes, I do believe it," Wells shot back. He normally remained quiet during these meetings, never uttering a word, if he even managed to leave his lab to attend them in the first place. He hated the attention they brought and hated crowds even more. But I was thankful he was on my side. I had to find out how to use my fire to defeat the King, which meant I had to go back to Lux. And I knew Wells wanted the same thing, just for more personal reasons.

"If the only way to kill the King is through whatever is at her feet, then it's worth the risk," Wells continued. "If Tezya can bring it back to me, I can properly examine it..."

"*Worth the risk?*" Savannah interjected sarcastically. "You're talking about sending Tezya into a lion's den where everyone will be after him. The King probably has a reward on his head so high that any friends he had in Lux would turn on him. And to make matters worse, none of you even know what you're looking for. What if it's nothing? What if it's not even an object?"

"So Tez goes in strategically. He can be in and out before they even see him coming."

"All this is going to do is get him caught," Savannah spat at her brother.

"Dovelyn said it was the only way to defeat—"

"Killing the Lux King isn't going to magically make Arcane come back to you."

Silence filled the room. I knew this was the one subject Savannah and Wells never agreed on. She hated that her brother fell in love with the eldest Luxian Prince. She supported him during their short-lived relationship, but ever since things ended badly, she's never forgiven Arcane for hurting him.

Even though there's only a year difference between them, she took on the protective older sister role a little too seriously. Not that it wasn't warranted. My brother could be a selfish dick at times, and I knew when they ended things, neither of them were the same afterward.

"Arcane is easier to manage than my father," Dovelyn said. Everyone turned to look at her as she entered the tent. Dark circles were painted under her eyes, and she was thinner and paler than normal. "And what I said earlier was true. We need to kill the King. He's too powerful." She turned to look at me, and my heart sagged in relief. It was the first time all week she was speaking in coherent sentences. "I know you, Tez, and I know you're going to go after this prophecy with or without my help." She turned away to scan the rest of the room. "So if there's a sliver of hope my brother can come out of this alive, then it's worth the risk. We need to find whatever is at the Goddesses' feet to see if it can save him."

"What answers do you think it will hold?" Kallon asked, and everyone collectively held their breath, wondering if Dovelyn knew more about it.

She shook her head. "I don't know, but I'm praying it will tell us what it means by a sacrifice of Light and blood spilled from Dark."

"There's no way of knowing until we go," Wells said.

Kallon nodded. "If we're lucky, it'll be both—how to save Tezya and how to kill the King."

"What are the King's powers?" Sie asked, speaking for the first time. I looked over at him. Peter and him both had cuts and bruises scattered across every inch of them. Sie's knuckles were scabbed over, and the blonde was sporting a busted lip, a swollen eye, and a darkening bruise over his throat. The pair honestly looked worse than when they came back from the prison.

Dovelyn glanced at him. "Everything. He possesses *everything*. Any ability in Lux that exists, he has. And now he'll want *her*." Everyone's eyes turned to Scottie. "We're all targets, but getting her back will be my father's number one priority. He wants Arcane to continue his experiments on her, to see if he can create a reverse serum to make himself stronger. He wants her enhancement. It's the only ability in Lux he doesn't have yet. But he'll also want her back to set an example. She was his prisoner, and he lost her. He can't stand to look weak, so he won't stop until she's in chains by his side again."

My sister didn't admit Rumor was also his top priority because he doesn't know the truth. The King still believes her lie that the prophecy is about Scottie and Sie, and with Sie out of prison, he will make it his mission to kill him and capture her before it can happen. I closed my fist over our bond. For the first time in my life I regretted that I kept who I was a secret because now it was putting *her* at risk. If he knew I was the one the prophecy was about, he wouldn't be going after her.

"What are you suggesting?" Kallon asked Dovelyn cautiously.

"We use her as bait."

"No," I cut Dovelyn off at the same time Sie did.

She huffed. "Calm down. She won't get caught. We need Arcane distracted long enough for Tezya to go to the statue. He'll be anxious to get back in our father's favor after he *lost* her on his watch. By now, the King knows she's missing, and Arcane is suffering because of it."

Wells' brows furrowed before he directed his gaze toward the ground, staring at his high-top sneakers.

"You just want a chance to search for Brock again," Rainer said, tucking a loose spiral curl behind his ear that fell out of his bun.

Dovelyn shrugged, not bothering to deny it. "And you don't? He's your friend too, and he's being tortured. We need to get him out of there."

I grimaced, my heart aching for my best friend or whatever was left of him. "I agree. We need to look for Brock when we go. But we go in with a solid plan. If it gets too risky, we leave."

"I'm in," Kallon said, but I could tell Rainer still wasn't convinced. He wanted Brock back just as much as the rest of us, but he was always the most hesitant—the most cautious out of the group—especially if there was a potential of getting caught. It was good. Sometimes the rest of us were too rash. We'd act without thinking of the consequences, and Rainer taught me to center myself, to think everything through before I went head first into something.

"What's your plan?" I asked Dove. "And we aren't using Rumor as bait, so think of something else."

"I'll do it," Scottie said next to me, and I tensed. "If being a distraction means we can find the *answers* to…" She paused. "I'll do it."

The answer to keep me alive was what she didn't say. I hated how Dovelyn was convincing everyone my death was inevitable. But if I had to sacrifice someone from the Light Kingdom in order to save myself, I wouldn't do it. Even if that meant I had to die alongside the King. All I wanted to know was how to use my fire because what I had now wasn't enough.

"I don't like the idea of using you," I said out loud. Then only to her, I added, *We don't even know if I'll die, just because Dovelyn thinks so, doesn't mean it's true—*

"I want to help," Scottie said, cutting me off. "I'm going with. You can use me in your plan, Dovelyn."

"Great. Here's how it's going to work. Kallon portals us in, and I'll use my ability to cast invisibility over us. As soon as we get to Lux, we separate. I'll go to the castle and search for Brock. Scottie goes to the ocean side to draw Arcane out. Kallon and Tezya will go to the statue by the bayside. Once you two find what you need, Kallon portals you guys to Scottie, then to me and Brock."

"How are we going to stay invisible if you're separating from us to find Brock?" Kallon asked. "I know you can separate your magic, but we're not going to be staying in one place. It'll be too much for you to divide your ability between three different spots."

"And how do you expect Rumor to lure Arcane out without getting caught?" I added, not liking her plan one bit.

Dovelyn crossed her arms, then shrugged. "I can manage the three locations, but I'll train Scottie with her enhancement until we leave. She can link to my ability within the radius I'll be traveling. She was already able to do it the first day I trained her with objects I shielded."

"An object and moving people are entirely different things—"

"I can do it," Scottie interrupted me. I searched her mind, testing the limits of our new connection. She was confident, yes, but it derived from determination, not experience.

"It's out of the question—"

"She stays invisible until the last second," Dovelyn cut me off. "We all go to our spots." She pointed to three spots on a larger—newer—map of Lux that Scottie and I hadn't ruined. "Kallon already has portals created in these areas." She traced her fingers over the locations. Lux was crawling with portals Kallon had made over the years. "I'll get a head start. Just give me enough time to search for Brock while you two make your way to the town's center by the bay. Go into the side streets, and spread rumors that someone who looks like Scottie is in Lux. The news will travel to Arcane. After that, Scottie will unlink her invisibility."

"No," I said. "There are too many variables."

"Then pray Pylemo is on our side. If things go wrong, Kallon can portal to us immediately, and we'll all leave."

"There's no way of keeping Scotlind safe during this—"

Kallon cut me off, asking her own question, "And how will we communicate if we're all in different areas?"

Dovelyn shrugged. "I'd heard rumors you two were busy while I wasn't feeling like myself." Scottie stiffened next to me, my senses and our connection radiating to her. I could tell she was uncomfortable with the direction this was going. "I was hoping now that you're bonded, you could help with that. How strong is it? Do you have telepathy?"

"Yes," I admitted, ignoring the death glare Sie was giving me. "But it's not reliable. We don't know how it works yet." Scottie and I hadn't even been able to discuss the changes that were happening to us. Hell, it hadn't even been an entire twenty-four hours since we created the bond. Sometimes our minds just found each other, but I didn't know how it worked yet. I didn't even know if it was something we could control. "I don't know if there're limits yet. It might only work in close proximity."

"Then test it here before we leave. See how far you can go while still being able to communicate, and we'll make sure not to go a step further than that."

"You can't portal back here," Dravenburg said. "I won't allow it. If you're followed, you'll be bringing the enemy to our camp. You can risk yourselves for this if you want, but you won't risk the standing of this camp, my people, or my children."

"If we don't come back within twelve hours, then assume things went south," Dove said. I was surprised by how much she was acting like her old self again, considering she'd been unconscious just hours before. "Dravenburg, you can move the camp to the backup location if we don't return. Only Tezya knows where it is in our group, and he can't be compelled, so everyone in the camp will be safe."

The backup camp was a good call. Dravenburg and I made it decades ago, and we were the only ones who knew the exact location. It was significantly smaller than this one, and only had the bare necessities, but it would keep everyone safe if Brighta was ever discovered.

"Okay," Kallon agreed. "I'll go over all my portals with Tezya and Dovelyn before we leave. We'll confirm we weren't followed before coming back to the camp."

Everyone nodded.

"Great," Dovelyn clapped her hands together. "It's settled then. We'll go once we hear word that the King is leaving the city. He's going to have to travel to Tennebris soon to meet with Synder. So then we'll only be risking Arcane."

"And his second," I said as everyone turned to me. "There's no way he'll leave the city unprotected. He'll leave Athler in charge like he always does. Rumor isn't going up against them alone." I knew I couldn't stop Scotlind from going, but I wasn't about to agree to a plan where she'd go up against them by herself.

"I'll go," Sie spoke. "I can compel anyone that sees us to forget we were there. It will still give us the element of surprise."

"Your compulsion won't matter. Every Luxian guard is wearing Alluse now," Rainer said. "At least the ones in close proximity to the King. After you guys left, Athler and the King ordered every Alluse citizen to come to the castle the night he found out you guys escaped, and most never returned home. I don't know what happened to them."

"Shit," I cursed. "Why didn't you tell us this before?"

"Honestly, I forgot about it. A lot happened after you left. The King kinda went crazy."

"You should stay behind, prince," Dovelyn said to Sie. "If you can't use your compulsion, you won't be of use to us."

"I can teleport," he said. "If you plan to use her as bait, I'll watch her. If Athler or Arcane get too close, I'll teleport her away." He met my gaze before he added, "We both don't like the idea of using her as a distraction, and with the plan you have now, you're leaving her vulnerable. You need me."

Scottie's eyes widened at the realization he would still choose to protect her even after she picked me. Hell, I was surprised by it. He met her shocked stare for a moment before looking back at me.

"You need me," he said again, and I did.

"Fine," I said, ignoring the shock from Scotlind next to me. If he was going to offer her any kind of protection while I was going to be on the other side of the city, I'd take it.

TWENTY-FIVE
SCOTLIND

"This plan has a lot of flaws," Tezya said to me. "If anything goes wrong, I want to know immediately." He kissed me thoroughly before leaving the tent. We didn't know when the King would be leaving Lux, so we had to be ready. We were trying to figure out how far our communication could go. Every day, we tested our bond, but we weren't any closer to figuring it out.

Neither of us fully understood it, and we had no comparison. Blood bonds had been a forbidden practice for centuries now, ever since King Arcane the Third brought our kind to Earth. They didn't want it known that Advenians of different ranks could be together. That the Goddesses would bless a union from someone who was strong and weak—not when they were implementing same rank marriages. And they especially didn't want us to know a bonded couple could be from both kingdoms.

Tennebris also abandoned the tradition since coming here. From what we could tell, we were the first bonded pair on Earth.

Everything was trial and error. I couldn't read Tezya's thoughts consciously anymore. It was only in the initial moments of opening the bond that everything was fully open. Now, I could sense a tangible divide. It was thin, but I knew it was there.

When our emotions were high, the small line that separated our minds severed, and only then would our thoughts flow from one another without our control. It left us sporadically and randomly knowing the other's feelings.

The only thing that seemed to stay consistent was we could intentionally speak to one another like a telepathic user, but it took a lot of concentration.

Do you think our connection will fade? I asked him. I was sitting by the entrance of the camp as he walked further and further away from me.

I don't know, he admitted. I could hear his voice growing fainter the further he walked. *Telepathy is a rumored blood bond trait, so I think we'll always be able to talk like this.*

What about emotion sharing? I asked. *Do you think there's a chance that will stay too?*

Maybe. It's only happened when our scars touch, he answered. *I don't know if our hands are now a point of contact or if it's just from our blood mixing from when we first created the bond.* He was quiet for a moment. *It could also just be something we have to train.*

I nodded, even though he couldn't see me, before looking down at my palm. It was still scabbed over from reopening it. As soon as it healed, we'd get our answer—

I'm at the far side of the camp by the fields, Tezya said, breaking my train of thought. *This should be enough distance. The locations Dovelyn picked aren't further than this.*

So what now? I asked back.

Now, we just wait until Kallon hears word the King left. She has a few spies in Lux—select people she trusts. It shouldn't be long. Supposedly he set up a meeting with Synder. His voice was growing clearer in my head, and I knew he was making his way back to me. *The rebellion is picking up again, and since they can't send me to lead the Luxian army to eliminate them, they're going to want to talk about it. Both kingdoms will want it dealt with and quickly. A lot of citizens in Tennebris aren't happy with Sie's imprisonment. Ever since you came to Lux, Synder's been changing the laws over there. It hasn't been pretty for rank zeroes. The people in Lux aren't happy either. There's talk going on about our disappearances. A lot of Advenians think the two events are related. And without me leading the Luxian army, the King is struggling to demolish the rumors.*

Isn't this the rebellion?

Yes, the Advenians here were once part of the rebellion. They still technically are, but more are forming every day. All it takes is a few people to band together to spread word. Most people, from both kingdoms, aren't happy with the way things are. They want change. The only issue is, we don't know where they're located now. If the King sends the army to fight them, they'll be slaughtered. The Luxian soldiers are ruthless. They've been trained and bred to be. Unless we can find the rebellion first and tell them about this place, it won't be pretty.

Can we do that? Can we find them?

"Hopefully." It took me a second to realize he said it out loud as he closed the distance between us and pulled me into a hug. "Once we return, it'll be another thing for us to do. I think more Advenians will join us once they see what we've started. Many people aren't rising up because they don't believe they stand a chance. It's a known fact that if you're caught in the rebellion, your entire family line will be killed. I'm hoping once they see everyone's still alive, it'll change things. I honestly think we can do this, Rumor. We can change everything."

I nodded but couldn't find my voice. All I kept thinking about was the cost.

He will die. Those three words haunted me. I couldn't stop replaying Dovelyn's voice as she chanted it over and over again. Her milky eyes transformed in my mind, and I saw flashes of Tezya's lifeless body instead.

Tezya noticed my mood shift. His callused hands cupped my cheeks, forcing me to look at him. "I'm going to be fine."

"But what if—"

He cut me off, his lips lightly pressing into mine. "I'll be fine, Rumor," he whispered into my mouth.

I went to try to speak again, but he didn't let me, his lips kept moving against mine, silencing anything I wanted to say. "The only thing," he groaned, his hands gripping my hair, "I want you to say right now is my name."

———

HEAT instantly clung to my clothes as Kallon portaled us into Lux. We left the chill back at the camp, but I felt it lingering in us all. Tezya was scared. I could tell he was second-guessing coming here. He wasn't worried about himself, but the risk of putting the rest of us in danger was weighing on him. He didn't want me to be the distraction, and he was terrified Athler would fall for the bait instead of Arcane. He'd made me promise a million times over that if I saw him, I'd get out immediately.

I couldn't see anyone. Dovelyn's invisibility was already over the five of us. The only reason I knew Tezya was still next to me was because we were holding hands. He ran a finger down my scar, giving my palm a tight squeeze, before letting go.

Be careful, he said into my mind as he left with Kallon. No one dared to speak out loud. I knew Dovelyn fled the moment we arrived, wanting as much time to try and find Brock as possible. We all knew this was probably her last attempt at finding him before this war truly began.

I felt a tug on my shoulder. **Come on, let's go**, Sie said telepathically. We walked in silence. I had to focus to keep Dovelyn's invisibility going through my enhancement while maintaining my connection with Tezya. We only just started, and I was already feeling the toll. I wasn't used to stretching myself thin. I was barely used to using my abilities at all. But I was happy to do it. Even if it was draining, I wanted to help.

I wanted to prove to everyone I was more than capable. It was why I had been training with Dovelyn any free chance I had back at the camp before we came here.

I was thankful for her invisibility now. I didn't want Sie to see my body trembling or the sweat dripping down my back and soaking through my shirt. I knew I could do this, could push through the immediate drain I felt. I just had to get used to it first.

Everything okay? Tezya's voice sounded, and it was weird to hear both him and Sie inside my mind.

Yes, I answered. *Everything good with you and Kallon?*

Yeah, we just got to the statue. Kal and I are scoping it out right now. We're giving Dovelyn a few more minutes to find Brock before we start.

How long? Sie.

I think we're almost to the ocean, I said to Sie, trying to recall the way from the map Tezya made us all memorize. I'd never been to the public Luxian beaches before, so I was forced to spend every second I wasn't training with my abilities or practicing my bond with Tezya to study Lux.

I was told Sie had done the same, but I hadn't seen him until this morning. We were walking away from the castle toward the southern tip of the island, trying to put as much distance between us and Tezya as possible. We just had to reach the portal spot before they started, and then we'd only have a few minutes to lure Arcane out for Dovelyn to get Brock.

That's not what I meant. How long have you been in love with him?

Oh—OH. I was silent for a minute, unsure how and if I should answer him, but he deserved to know and somehow not being able to see his face gave me the strength to say, *I'm not sure, but I think for a while now. He's not a bad person like half the Advenians believe he is, and he's helped me when I needed him the most.*

Helped you when you needed him... Sie repeated my words softly, like he had to make sense of them. His sigh resounded through my head. **It was never my intention to leave you, Scotlind. I never meant to hurt you.**

I know.

Would things have been different? If we weren't caught at the lake, if you stayed in Tennebris, would you have loved me?

Yes, I answered honestly, but it was because I didn't know what love was then. What I felt for Sie was different than Tezya, but I still trusted him. I still cared for him, still had an attraction to him that wouldn't fade. At the very least, I liked him, and I think it would have grown into something more. I was starting to fall for him when every-thing happened... A pang of guilt weaved its way through me because I knew I was hurting him, and it didn't matter if he hurt me in the past too. I didn't want to cause him pain. So I added, *I care about you, Sie, I think some part of me always will.*

But it's not enough. You picked him. Another sigh. **My fucking brother.**

I'm sorry, but I think it was always meant to—

My words were cut off by an ear-splintering explosion. I whipped my head in the direction of the sound, knowing Sie was most likely doing the same. The castle was just a speck in the distance, standing lower but wider than all the high towering buildings of the city. I scanned our area but didn't see any smoke.

Shit, Sie said into my mind at the same time Tezya asked, *What happened? Are you okay?*

I tried to focus on Tezya. We were at a far point, and his voice was growing quiet. *I'm fine,* I lied because my reserves were depleting faster than I'd thought. I tucked my hands under my arms to stop the shaking, even though I knew no one could see them. *What happened?*

I think something happened to Dove. We need to get out of here now. Kallon and I are going to destroy the bottom half of the statue. Don't expose yourself, Rumor. We don't need a distraction anymore. You and Sie get to the portal and wait for us. We'll get you as soon as we find Dove.

No, don't—I tried to say more, but it didn't go through. My legs were shaking, and I could barely stand. I didn't want Tezya to destroy the statue with Arcane still in the castle. It was too dangerous. I didn't care if our cover was already blown. I didn't want any attention turning to him. Worry flooded me. If he was captured... I staggered forward and crashed into something hard.

"Are you okay?" Sie whispered in my ear as he held me up. "You're trembling." He wasn't speaking telepathically.

"I don't feel—"

That's when I saw him. I was looking up into familiar dark eyes. Sie materialized out of thin air as Dovelyn's invisibility went away. A soft clapping noise sounded from behind us as Arcane and Athler came into view. They had black masks covering their noses and mouths.

"I'm quite impressed," Athler crooned, his voice altered through the mask. The only thing I could see were his dull opal eyes. "You managed to hold off longer than I thought." He was pushing Dovelyn in front of him, a knife held to her throat, as Arcane was holding Brock.

He was alive.

Thick-chained shackles were clamped over his wrists and ankles. He was still a massive, looming figure—still the strongest Advenian I knew—but it was due to his broad frame and height. His muscles were melting off his body from weeks of being the King's captive, and any part of his skin that was exposed through his ragged clothes had varying colors of bruises hidden underneath layers and layers of dried blood.

His left eye was sunken in while his right was swollen shut. I caught a glimpse of red covering each of his fingers, but I refused to look at the cause. And by the way he was limping, his ankles had to be mangled…

Guilt wrecked me because while we'd been safe at the camp, Brock was here, being tortured by Athler and the King.

Sie slowly trailed his hand down my shoulders to wrap around my waist. Once he tightened his hold on me, he teleported—or he tried to teleport. We both fell to the ground a few feet back from where we were originally standing.

Athler's laugh was piercing, echoing through the open rotunda. We never made it to the beach. We were nowhere close to the portal. The streets were eerily quiet. All I heard was the distant lap of waves, teasing us that the ocean was just out of reach.

Opal eyes stared right into mine as Athler pressed the knife further into Dovelyn. Tears streaked down her face, and I knew it wasn't for the blade at her throat, but the man she loved next to her.

"You'll find you won't be able to use your abilities for a long, long time," Athler said, and I knew he was smiling without seeing his mouth.

"What did you do to us?" Sie seethed.

"It's called vapor Alluse. All you have to do is inhale the substance, and you'll be rendered powerless. It's relatively new. Prince Arcane just finished creating it, so beyond knowing it will linger in your systems, side effects haven't fully been worked out, and you both just breathed in a rather large dose."

Terror ripped through me as I realized the vapor was why I felt so drained. Even without the Alluse now coursing through me, I'd used all my enhancement trying to fight it off. The same thing must have happened to Dovelyn. Air users could erect a shield to protect themselves against Alluse, but if the vapor was in the air, if it was too overpowering, it would have completely depleted her reserves. None of us had our abilities, and I had no idea how we were supposed to get out of this.

"What do you want," Sie gritted from behind me, his arm never left my waist as we both slowly stood up.

Athler tilted his head. "I want all of you."

"I'll make a trade," I blurted before I even registered what I said, but I couldn't let us all get caught. If I did, this would all be for nothing. And Tezya... I couldn't imagine what they'd do to him again. I kept picturing that room, that knife in his thigh...

He laughed. "What can you offer us that we can't already take?"

"Let them go free," I gestured toward Brock, Dovelyn, and Sie, "and I'll willingly go with you."

Dovelyn's eyes widened. Brock stirred from where he was barely standing up but didn't say anything. I didn't know if he was even capable of words right now. Sie's grip around me tightened, but I forced myself to shrug him off.

"No," Sie said, but I ignored him, looking only at Athler.

I gestured to Sie. "He escaped the most dangerous prison both kingdoms share, and he was wearing Alluse chains at the time. What makes you think he won't escape your dungeons? Escape and free us all too. You'll be left with nothing when the King comes back."

Athler and Arcane both shuffled from foot to foot. They assessed Sie in a new light, looking at him like he was a threat too dangerous to handle, and by the way Sie was seething over my words, it was working.

I was bluffing. Sie was strong, but without being able to use our abilities, we didn't stand a chance against them. But they seemed to be considering it, so I prayed to Pylemo that I could make this trade before Tezya showed up. Dovelyn said the King's priority would be me, so I just had to convince them to take the bait.

"The last time you were supposed to watch two prisoners, we both escaped. Do you really want to disappoint your father by letting that happen again?"

"I accept," Arcane said, and I knew I struck a nerve with him.

Athler whipped his head to the prince. "Don't be stupid. One prisoner, no matter how badly the King wants her, is not worth more than others."

"I'll switch her for Brock then," Arcane said. Sie was still free. He could escape easily if he wanted, but I knew he wouldn't leave without me. I looked over at the princess and found her already staring at me, a pleading look in her eyes. The knife at her throat had slackened by Athler's shock from Arcane. He wasn't paying attention.

"Let Brock go, and I'll take his place," I said, willing my voice to be steady, to sound sure of myself, but my heart was hammering in my chest, and I couldn't fully comprehend what I was doing. I started slowly making my way toward Brock. Sie went to move as Athler turned his attention back to him.

Arcane straightened. "Deal. You for Brockwich." I could tell they weren't planning on letting Dovelyn go. They'd still try to take us all despite the trade.

I searched my strength for any last remnant of my power. Then, struggling through the emptiness in my veins, I sent one last message to Sie. *Trust me.* The words came out weak, but I knew he heard it. His fists clenched into balls at his side, but he let me go. I needed him to believe I had some sort of plan in order for this to work. Because the reality of this was a fool's errand. I knew that, but I couldn't think about it right now. I just needed to make sure he didn't come after me.

I stopped a few feet in front of Arcane and Brock. "Let him go first."

Arcane thought it over for a moment, weighing his options before he threw Brock on the ground in front of Dovelyn. The moment Brock was out of Arcane's hands, the princess twisted. She moved so fast, her small frame more agile than Athler's. She was out of his grasp and dragging Brock over to Sie before he could blink.

I sprinted in the other direction, praying Athler and Arcane would chase me. A small smile spread over my face once I heard pounding footsteps. I risked a glance behind me and saw opal eyes gunning after me. In the distance, Arcane was chasing Sie, Dovelyn, and Brock, gaining speed as Brock slowed them down.

I focused on the path ahead of me and sprinted as fast as I could toward the castle. Once I made it to the jungle behind it, I could lose Athler under the canopy. Tezya told me Kallon made a portal by the hut decades ago, and if I couldn't escape Lux, or if something happened to the one by the ocean, to meet there. Kallon would come for me.

I knew Dovelyn could manage everything else. She would get everyone to the portal. She just had to escape her older brother.

My entire body felt weak as I sprinted up the long rising incline. I pumped my arms hard, my legs feeling immensely heavy as they pounded against the pavement. I had drained myself too much. But I just had to last long enough to distract Athler so my friends could escape.

I just had to make it to the jungle...

But then I forgot why I was running. I didn't want to leave Lux. In fact, I wanted the opposite. I wanted to be near him, near Athler.

I stopped immediately, my legs coming to a halt as I turned around and found opal eyes. A flash of dull red hair on pale skin came up beside me.

Yes. I wanted this—wanted *him*. My mind went blank as all I thought about were those eyes. Then his veiny hands, about how they would feel touching me. I wanted them on me. No. I *needed* them on me. Desire pulsed through me, making me dizzy. My breath was already coming out in ragged pants from running, and it wasn't subsiding.

I exhaled harder. I couldn't focus on anything but him.

"Do you want me to fuck you?"

I nodded and relief fluttered through me at his returning grin and the attention he was giving me. He'd taken off the hideous mask so I could see his face—his beautifully crafted face—with high narrowed cheekbones and a slanted nose. How have I never found him attractive before?

"Hold out your wrists."

I did immediately.

"Good girl," he crooned.

My heart skipped a beat, and I wanted nothing else but to exist for him. I couldn't hold back my smile as he clamped golden shackles around my two zeroes, and my stomach turned into a pit of butterflies, imagining him taking me in them.

I was making him happy. I *wanted* to make him happy.

"Enough. Release her," Arcane drawled as he came up beside us. "You have her chained, you don't need to keep using your powers on her."

Athler laughed as his ability lifted off me, and my mind was my own again. Realizing what happened, what he'd done to my body... I collapsed, my knees scraping into the pavement as I vomited on the ground next to me.

Disgust ran through me as my adrenaline settled, and my fate was sealed. I couldn't stop gagging. He changed my actions in an instant. He made me want him, made me forget about everything else in the world except for him.

Arcane shared a look with me that I couldn't quite read. His gaze roamed over my flushed cheeks to the vomit on the ground. I prayed everyone else got away, that I didn't just let myself get caught for nothing.

I staggered backward, trying to put space between Athler and myself, but the chains pulled taut. It was already too late. There was no way I'd be able to escape now.

I wasn't making it to the hut.

TWENTY-SIX
TEZYA

"Check all the portals," I shouted to Kallon, not caring who heard us now. "I'll cover the area by foot. Something's wrong."

I turned away from the bay and started sprinting to where Scottie was supposed to be. I felt our connection teeter in and out right after the explosion, fading weaker and weaker until it was nothing. First her panic came through, then desire, before pure terror overtook her. I couldn't make sense of the shift of emotions, but my gut told me it was Athler.

"Tezya, wait!" Kallon screamed, but I didn't stop. I just prayed she could cover more ground without me and I wasn't making a mistake by separating. Something told me Scottie was somewhere else, that she wasn't by the portal.

Distinctly, I heard the gasps from a few Luxian citizens who saw me tear through the streets. Some shouted the youngest prince was back in the city, others screamed for soldiers to take me down. Dovelyn's invisibility was gone, but I didn't pause long enough to see or care about the damning consequences.

I tried over and over again to reach out to Scottie, to see if she was okay, but every time I tried, our bond came back empty. I ran through the last rotunda before reaching the first strip of beach when a wave of nauseating voidness stripped me bare. I didn't have time to think about why my powers dissipated. Panic was lacing its way up my spine. I still hadn't seen Scottie.

When I finally made it to the meeting spot by the ocean, I saw Dovelyn and Sie waiting, holding up a half unconscious Brock. A second of relief passed through me at seeing my friend alive, but it vanished as soon as I didn't see beautiful, sapphire eyes along with them.

"Where is she?" My voice was a growl as I circled them.

Dovelyn shifted all of Brock's weight toward Sie. "Be quiet or you're going to attract Athler's attention again. We need to get out of here *now*."

Again.

The word broke me.

Scottie was gone.

"I don't care who the fuck hears. Let the entire fucking city know I'm here. *Where is Rumor?*"

Kallon finally portaled in. Her yellow eyes flashed with relief as she took in Brock. "I checked all my portals—" She whipped her head, scanning the rest of us, coming to the same realization I had. "Where's Scottie? What happened?"

"Athler," Dovelyn answered, confirming my fucking nightmare. "He found us before we could do anything. Arcane made some sort of vapor out of Alluse. He set it off in the rotunda." She turned to me. "All our powers are gone, Tez. We can't fight back, not like this."

"None of you have your abilities?" Kallon paled, fear taking over her face.

"I don't care about our damn powers right now. What the fuck happened to Scottie? WHERE IS SHE?"

Sie was the one who answered. "She made a trade with Arcane and Athler. Us for her."

"And you *let* her?" I spat. "You were supposed to protect her. The whole reason you came along was to make sure nothing like this happened!"

"I tried to teleport us away, but I couldn't," he snapped back. "She told me to trust her, so I thought…" He ran his hand through his black hair. "I fucking thought she had a plan. I didn't think she'd just hand herself over."

"So Athler has her now?"

"I don't know," he admitted. "She started running toward the castle. Arcane was coming after us, but then he just stopped and turned around."

The hut. She was running toward the hut. "Kallon, portal me to the hut now."

"Tez, I can't. We need to get out of here. We're sitting ducks. If I run into this vapor Alluse too, I won't be able to get any of us back to the camp. We'll all be stuck in Lux."

"I'll fucking run there," I screamed. "I don't care, but I'm not leaving without her!"

Kallon hesitated for a moment. "Okay, Tezya, I will, I will… Don't go on your own. Just let me portal everyone else back first. If we leave them here, they'll get caught too."

I nodded. I hated the idea of having to wait. It was precious seconds they had Scottie, but I didn't want to risk anyone else. Kallon portaled the three of them back. In all, it only took a minute, but it felt like a lifetime before she grabbed my hand and portaled me to the place I first trained Scotlind.

But it was fucking empty.

I tore the entire hut down. Breaking the sliding glass doors, ripping the bed from the posts on the floor. I scanned the ocean, even swam a mile out to see if she was waiting underwater. I ran through the jungle, then looked through the hut again out of desperation. There was nothing.

"Tezya, she's not here," Kallon said softly.

"Portal me to the castle. I'll get her and meet you at the docks in an hour."

A tear ran down Kallon's face. "Tez, you can't. If you go after her, you'll only get yourself caught too. You have no abilities right now."

I stormed over to her. "Kallon, I don't give a damn if I can't use my powers. The woman I love is in the hands of the most sadistic Advenians I know. You know what they'll do to her. I'm not leaving her here. I can't."

"Tezya." She was crying now. "It's not safe."

I reached her then. Pulling her arms into mine, begging her to understand. I could run through the jungle, but it'd take me half a day. I needed to be portaled in. I needed to get to her before it was too late, because once they took her inside, they'd have her on so many damn locks and chains it'd be near impossible to get her out. "Kal, please, I need to—"

My sentence was cut off. I hadn't realized where Kallon was standing. I hadn't realized the purple and black smoke until it was too late. Until she fucking portaled us back to the camp.

My knees sank to the ground outside the shield once Kallon released me. The snow started seeping into my wet clothes, but it felt like nothing compared to the numbness inside me.

Distantly, I heard Kallon crying… heard her sob, "Your fire is too important to risk, Tez. I'm sorry. I'm so sorry."

I called to my Dark ability, cursing myself that my veins were void of it. If I could, I would've compelled Kallon to portal me back, to drop me off in Lux and leave me there. I'd rescue Scottie by myself if I had to. But no matter how many times I willed my Dark powers to manifest, nothing happened, the vapor Alluse was already consuming too much of my veins.

I screamed, but I couldn't hear it.

I was dragged back through the shield, but I couldn't feel it.

Scottie was left in Lux completely alone.

Without any abilities.

And in the hands of Athler.

TWENTY-SEVEN
SCOTLIND

DARKNESS ENGULFED ME. A bag was thrown over my head, but I knew I was being dragged through the castle. I just didn't know which part of it they were taking me to.

"Send word to the King," Athler ordered. "Tell him we have an urgent matter, and he'll want to return immediately." The only response was fading footsteps. I couldn't tell what scared me more—seeing the Lux King in person or Athler using his ability again.

My elbows slammed against the floor as I was thrown into a room. A click sounded, then brightness flooded my vision. Brown eyes burned into me as the bag over my head was removed.

"Scotlind..." The words came out more like a question, and for a brief moment, a look of shock ran across Kole's face before it was gone.

"Chain her to the floor," Arcane said. His voice was so much lighter than Athler's, less grating.

Kole nodded as he pulled the chains around my wrists. Using his free hand, he lifted a rug to reveal a circular hook embedded into the floor. He dragged my shackles down, connecting them to the hook, and I realized I was in the King's personal chambers. It was the same room he ordered Tezya and I to come to before the meeting with

Tennebris. I remembered the rug—noticing the bump under it even then—and the large mantle across from it where he stood as he assessed us.

Disgust filled me, making me want to vomit all over again. The King had a permanent place for a prisoner in the middle of his room...

I pulled at the lock, but it wouldn't budge. I kept trying and trying as realization of what I did finally caught up to me—

"If you keep fighting, I'll chain your ankles and neck down too." Athler let out an amused chuckle, before turning to Kole. "Compel her. The Alluse we used in the vapor was Vir so abilities will work on her."

Kole straightened, his voice taut. "What do you want the compulsion to be?"

"I want information. I want to know where she's been and what they've been up to. Once the King comes back we'll hook her up in the monitor room." Athler turned his glare toward Arcane. "And she better reveal *everything* about your siblings' whereabouts since you couldn't manage to capture any of them, not even the stupid brute who was half dead."

Arcane didn't reply.

Relief flooded me for a brief moment. Everyone escaped and was safe. But the feeling was washed away as quick as it came before the terror set in. The camp. They couldn't find out about the camp. Once I was in the monitor room, I'd be forced to reveal everything that had happened since we escaped. The King would know the truth about Tezya. He would find out the rebellion was still very much alive and ready to fight against him. I prayed Tezya and Dravenburg would be able to evacuate everyone to the new location before that happened, but I would still ruin our only advantage in this war. I would be forced to reveal our hand, forced to tell the King everything about the prophecy and about Tezya. And if that happened, he'd make it his mission to kill *him* first.

I backed away from Kole as his fingers gripped my chin, and horror sank its teeth into me. I watched the golden spirals appear on his hand.

No, no, no.

"Where have you been hiding?"

His voice was musical, the same familiar octave I remembered, but it felt different. I could tell he was using his ability, but I wasn't compelled to answer him. I said nothing, the shock was all consuming for a heartbeat. Then another.

He compelled me again, but the urge to obey didn't come. I had no idea how or why his compulsion wasn't working, but I wasn't going to waste it.

I'd forced myself to obey, to pretend. If I could lead them astray... If I could manage to keep everything about Tezya and the camp a secret, we could still win. "We were staying close to Tezya's condo in the mortal territory."

"Who's with you?" Athler stated the question to Kole, who repeated it with compulsion.

"Sie, Kallon, Dovelyn, and Tezya," I replied automatically. I only told them what they already saw. They'd seen Sie and the princess, and I knew it wouldn't be believable if I said Tezya wasn't with us. They also had to assume we had Kallon since she'd been missing, and her portals were the only feasible way we were coming and going.

Kole froze for a moment, and I was worried I gave something away. "You left here with Peter. If Sie's with you, there's no way he would have abandoned him."

Crap. Crap. Crap.

I willed myself to stay calm, to think rationally, but my heart was jackhammering in my chest. "Peter didn't make it," I lied, half choking on the words. The sorrow that filled my voice wasn't hard to fake. Thinking back to the state Tezya and I found him in, it wouldn't be hard to believe he was dead.

"What were you doing in Lux?" Kole repeated Athler's question as he stared at me. I held my breath, praying my face wasn't giving anything away.

"We came back for Brock," I answered. Simple truths, nothing to condemn Brighta's goals.

"What are Dovelyn and Tezya planning?"

"Nothing."

Athler's eyes narrowed. "She's lying. Tezya and Dovelyn possess too much ambition and pride to sit back and do nothing."

"They just wanted to get away from you and the King," I spat back. "Seeing how cruel you are to them, I'm sure you won't find it that hard to imagine why."

Athler smiled at me, his thin lips cracking as he stepped forward, bending down at the waist until his eyes were level with mine. I stiffened as his fingers traced over my upper thigh, the same spot Tezya was forced to stab.

Kole kept my chains pulled taut so I couldn't pull away. I could barely lift my hands off the floor. "What you saw that day," Athler breathed as his long fingernails dug into my flesh, "was nothing. The punishment we gave to Tezya was child's play. So trust me when I say the boy has lived through a century of my lessons and one little dagger in the thigh isn't enough to make him crawl to the mortals and hide. He knows how to live in pain. In fact, I recall a marvelous memory when Tezya almost had his face cut in half from one of my lessons. Do you remember that, Arcane?"

Arcane's fists tightened at his sides, but he replied with a simple, "Yes." Knowing Athler was the reason Tezya had his scar made me want to rip through my chains and claw his throat out.

Athler chuckled. "So I'll ask you one more time, what are they planning?"

"I'm telling you the truth. They aren't planning anything. They just wanted to get away from *you*." My breathing hitched as Athler inhaled, and I flinched.

"If they aren't planning anything, why would they bother rescuing Sie? I don't believe the princes were ever friendly toward one another. In fact, I might even go as far to say they hate each other."

I didn't answer. I didn't know how.

"And while you're stewing over your answer, let me tell you Dovelyn was spotted in the prison the day he escaped, so if you try to claim she had nothing to do with it, I'll know."

An unsettling silence filled the room. Athler withdrew his fingernails from my thigh and proceeded to smear the lingering blood over my skin. Without looking down, I could feel the four letters he was tracing onto me.

L

I

A

R

"She's not lying," Arcane said. "She was compelled to answer. If she says my siblings aren't planning anything, then they aren't."

"Make her prove it." Athler turned to Kole. He rose and took a few steps back, allowing Kole the freedom and creativity to test me. I waited to see what he'd do.

Kole looked from Athler to me, before compelling, "Stop breathing."

I held my breath, willing my pulse to steady and my chest to still.

My lungs started to become heavy. A slow, growing agony flowing through them, making me feel like I was catching on fire from the inside out.

A minute passed, and the burning wasn't stopping. It was morphing, becoming unbearable. I told myself over and over I was fine. I could do this. For Tezya, for Brighta, I could do this, even if it felt exactly like being drowned in that bath again. Even as I saw Kole's two brown eyes, the only difference now was he wasn't laughing. He was staring right at me, like he could see through it all, like he knew something I didn't.

But my body begged for me to inhale—to take a breath. My mind screamed that I was going to die to prove a point. Darkness started to seep into my vision, and I had to fight to not pass out... or give in.

The suffering grew—intensified to a point I couldn't handle. It was worse than anything I'd ever felt before. My skin was peeling off my body. Every bone felt like it was being crushed slowly. My mind felt like it was being stabbed over and over again...

I started writhing on the floor. I knew my face was turning purple, my lungs felt charred. It was a black void, expanding and all consuming, ready to swallow me whole until there was nothing left. Was this what it felt like to die? I always knew whenever the time came, it'd be painful, but I wasn't prepared for *this* kind of torment. I couldn't take it anymore.

I screamed.

"She's not compelled," Athler said, his voice grating, and I realized the pure agony was coming from him. "I changed her pheromones. Regardless of how much pain I caused her, she should have been forced to suffer in silence."

Arcane and Kole turned to look at me, but Athler was staring directly at the eldest prince. "What kind of Alluse did you use? Are you sure it was Vir and not complete?"

"Yes, I'm sure. The vapor worked. Maybe something is wrong with the compulsion user," Arcane drawled. "You were able to manipulate her pheromones just now, were you not? That is proof the Alluse worked perfectly."

Athler slapped Kole across the face. He staggered backward, tripping over me. "I ordered you to compel her."

Kole glared up at him. "I *did* compel her." He stood, straightening his jacket. "And you're not allowed to touch me. I'm here on a work visa by my king."

"If you're on a work visa and you can't properly work, then you'll be disposed of however I deem fit. The visa is only valid if you can perform."

Kole's jaw ticked. "If you didn't inject yourselves with Sui Alluse, I'd compel *you* for proof. I have no idea why it's not working, but it's not my powers."

"Go fetch a servant," Athler ordered. Kole was silent for a moment. His chest puffed before he finally stormed out of the room.

"You better be right about the King wanting her." Athler turned to Arcane. "I don't want a word about Sie or Dovelyn being here. If he finds out they got away, he'll have our heads."

"You mean *your* head," Arcane clarified, his voice calm. "I'm the heir, which is nothing but a fancy title while the King still breathes. I hold no power yet. But you're his second, and that means when the King is gone, you're the one in charge."

I stared up at the eldest prince. I hadn't had many interactions with him beyond the week he was ordered to sample my blood, and even then he was straightforward, quiet, and to the point. He never hurt me, never took more than he needed, and I couldn't help but wonder what game he was playing now.

Was he happy to make the trade? Did he let his sister go on purpose? I had no idea the kind of relationship the three siblings had —only that Tezya had said none of them were spared from the King's *punishments* growing up. Was Arcane secretly trying to protect Dovelyn from that?

Arcane was supposed to make a mass compulsion serum. Did he do the opposite? Did he create a vapor serum that blocked compulsion instead? Was he the reason I wasn't being compelled right now?

Athler took a possessive step toward the eldest prince. "Then I'll have your head before he has mine, and I promise you it won't be pretty. If you say a word, you'll regret it."

Kole pushed the door back open, cutting the tension as he dragged a servant into the room.

He was shaking with sweat pooling under his arms and a large zero on his wrist that matched mine. His eyes widened, his expression pleading and begging me to help him.

"Compel him," Athler ordered.

Kole's body flared again in golden spirals. "Stand up." The servant stood on shaking legs. "Sit back down." The servant sat. "Stand." He rose again. "Hop on one foot."

"See," Kole said, turning to face the other two males in the room. "It isn't me. I can use my compulsion just fine."

"Anyone can follow simple commands," Athler replied, seeming bored. "That isn't very convincing."

"What do you want him to do then?"

Athler smiled, handing Kole a dagger. "I want you to compel him to do something I know he'd never willingly do. Have him slit his throat."

The boy staggered backward, tripping over my chains. His aqua eyes found mine again. "Please, no. I swear I didn't do anything. I was just cleaning the dishes as I was told. Please, don't kill me."

"Stop this," I begged as Kole took a step toward him. His brown gaze slid to mine. He looked like he was going to protest. He turned the handle over in his hand, stalling, waiting for Athler to take the order back. "Please," I said to Kole. The boy staggered behind me, his fingers pressing into my shoulders, nearly breaking my clavicles as his nails dug into my skin. I felt warm liquid seep into my clothes from behind me the second before the smell of urine filled the air. He started sobbing.

"Unless you want to speak willingly," Athler deadpanned. "Tell us what we want to know."

I didn't say anything. I couldn't. There were thousands of lives at the camp. How many women, children, and men would they kill if I gave them the information they wanted? I looked up and found Arcane staring down at me. He was still, so unmoving, and I remembered he knew about the camp too. He was in love with Wells. Arcane knew everything Athler wanted to know, and yet he didn't say anything either. He didn't want me to tell him.

"Then we need proof that Kole's compulsion is working. Do it," Athler ordered.

Kole grabbed the boy by his arms, yanking him off of me. "Stop fighting." His body stilled. The only indication he was scared was the wet spot on his pants and the tears running down his cheeks. "Take the blade." His hand reached for the knife.

"Please, don't—" I cried.

"Slit your throat." Kole didn't look away as the boy obeyed. Gurgling noises filled the room for one second, two, three—then it was over. He collapsed on the ground next to me with a thud.

"Leave the boy there." Athler grinned down at me. "I have a feeling there will be more to follow until she learns to behave." He turned to Kole. "Watch over her until the King arrives."

Kole stared at the dead servant as Athler and Arcane left the room, leaving us alone.

TWENTY-EIGHT
SIE

Every Advenian that was able to was helping hold Tezya back. He was kicking and punching at anything he could, screaming at Kallon to take him back. I didn't pity her, because at the moment, Tezya looked like he was ready to strangle her. She stayed a good distance back, tears streaming down her cheeks.

"I'm sorry, Tez," she kept repeating, but the words were lost on him.

Dovelyn left her brother screaming and thrashing on the ground to follow the healers who took Brock into the medical tent. It felt ironic. The bitch got what she wanted and didn't care what it cost her brother... or me.

"What's wrong?" Savannah asked as she approached. She looked between Kallon, Tezya, and me, then at all the Advenians it took to hold him back from killing the two-haired girl.

"Scottie was left behind," Kallon said softly, and even though Tezya's screams were echoing throughout the camp, Kallon's voice could be heard by everyone.

Savannah's eyes flared, but she didn't respond. She whipped a tiny object out of her pocket and approached Tezya, injecting something under his skin. Within seconds he started relaxing under everyone's grip, his movements slowing. His eyes grew heavy-lidded before he collapsed with a thud onto the grass.

"What did you give him?" I asked her.

"A sedative," Savannah responded, not looking at me as she recapped the needle. "A heavy one. I didn't feel like having him murder my best friend today. Help me get him to his tent."

I stepped toward Savannah, picking Tezya up by the shoulders. Kallon stayed back, sobbing, the guilt weighing heavily on her. But I couldn't shake the guilt I felt too.

Trust me.

I thought she had a plan. But now she was imprisoned again, and I did nothing to save her.

Again.

Peter ran up to me. "What happened?" I knew he was searching for her, his eyes roaming the crowd. She was his friend too.

"They have Scotlind," I answered. I didn't look at his face as I walked past—I couldn't. Tezya's body was heavy, and for some reason soaking wet, making carrying him harder.

Peter turned around immediately, sprinting to catch up to me. "Is she okay? How did they capture her? What happened to Tezya? When can we go get her? Do you have a plan? We need to find a way to get Scottie—"

"I know, Peter," I said, shutting him up. "We'll get her back." And I prayed to Pylemo we could.

TWENTY-NINE
SCOTLIND

I TRIED NOT TO CRY. I tried to look anywhere but at the dead servant that was left lifeless next to me. His blood had poured down his neck and made its way to where I was chained to the floor. I could still smell his urine that dripped down my back. I still heard his screams, still felt the sting of his nails digging into my shoulder...

"Where did you go?" Kole asked. I looked up and found him already staring at me.

"You can't honestly think I'm stupid enough to answer you. I'm not telling you anything."

"You'd be smart to," he said after a long pause. "They're only going to make this a lot worse for you. You're going to tell them everything anyway, so take my advice and do it sooner."

"There's nothing they can do to get me to talk."

"You're wrong. They have—" He was cut off by the sound of footsteps. The Lux King pushed his bedroom door open and halted once he saw me chained to the floor. Kole rose from his chair and bowed his head. I didn't move, not that I could even if I wanted to.

He smiled. "Bring her to the monitor room."

"She can't be compelled," Athler's voice rang out, and I flinched. I didn't see him standing behind the King until he spoke. "She won't give up any information that way."

The King flexed his neck in irritation. "Why?" He asked it calmly, but his expression was anything but.

"We don't know," the eldest prince cut in. "The Vir Alluse works. Athler was able to use his abilities on her." The King turned his attention toward Kole, who surprisingly held his ground. "And it's not him. He's still able to compel other Advenians."

"Fine. There are other ways to get her to talk."

"I don't think torture will work on her," Arcane added. "It didn't before when she was questioned regarding Sie Noren."

The King looked from me to the dead servant. "Then, we won't torture *her*." Kole's jaw ticked as the King turned to him. "Unchain her."

I was familiar with where they were taking me. The long, winding stairway, the deserted halls. I was going to the dungeons. My body revolted thinking about the days I had spent crammed into a small cage. Then again as I thought of the room Tezya was forced to stab himself in.

My fists were clenched, hiding the thicker, newer scar from my blood bond with him. I looked down at my forearm. The twenty-seven tallies were now tiny, barely visible, thin white lines. Both scars from this place. One good. One bad.

"Scottie?" That voice. I'd recognize it anywhere, even though it had been months since I heard it. My heart broke in pieces, and my vision blurred as tears instantly welled in my eyes. "Scottie, is that you?"

A slap resonated off the stone wall and sobbing followed that echoed mine. I blinked away my tears to see my best friend holding a palm against her now pink cheek. Vallie. I couldn't speak. I couldn't hear what anyone was saying around me. Her bright red hair was caked in dirt, the curls limp around her face. Her normally red lips were cracked and dry. Her skin was bare, only a few moles were scattered across her pale cheeks. She was still gorgeous, even with layers of mud and dirt covering her, but to see her treated like this…

I stiffened as the King noticed her too. "This is her friend?" he asked Kole.

"They both are." Kole's jaw was clenched. It was the only indication he didn't like this as he nodded toward the next cell, and my heart split in half all over again. Miles. He was chained against the wall, a gag in his mouth preventing him from speaking. His hair was straggly and long against his shoulders, and he looked even thinner than his abnormally lean frame. They were both starved... Tears pooled down my face faster as I imagined how long they'd been down here. "If you want her to cooperate, you can use him too."

I lunged, wrapping the loose ends of my chains around Kole's neck. His face turned red as horrific choking sounds came from him. Kole grabbed at my arms, attempting to yank me off him, but I didn't budge.

It was one thing to hurt me but to hurt Vallie... Vallie who was too sweet and pure for this world. Vallie who wouldn't hurt a fly. She didn't deserve to be tangled in this mess purely because she knew me. I didn't want her to be exposed to this kind of treatment. I'd prayed every day she was living peacefully with Miles, far away from all of this. That she was happy and safe and free. It was the only thing that made our time apart from each other tolerable.

But she was here, in the Luxian dungeons, and chained.

The King's laugh blended in with the sound of Kole's choking. I was only ripped off of him when his face started to turn purple.

"B...it...ch..." Kole gasped as he bent over, clutching his throat.

The King motioned the soldiers behind me. "She needs different chains."

They obeyed immediately. The moment my current shackles were unlocked, my arms were yanked behind my back. New chains clamped over my wrists from behind, but they didn't stop there. They placed chains over my ankles as I desperately kicked and shoved and screamed to get to Vallie. Then they connected the links from my wrists to ankles so I could barely move without toppling over.

"This'll be fun." The King smiled as he took a possessive step toward Vallie. She backed away from him, but it only caused her to slam against the soldier holding her down. "Wash her up and take her to see Semander. He'll know what I want done to her."

"No," I screamed as Vallie was dragged away from me, her own wails mirroring mine. I tried to lunge toward her but the movement caused me to lose my balance and fall. With my hands tied behind me, I couldn't brace myself as my head slammed onto the stone with a crack. Someone pulled me up by the middle links in the chain, causing my knees to bend. My vision blurred, and my right eye burned as blood dripped into it, but I couldn't wipe it away.

Miles' chains were rattling as he pulled against them. Mumbled protests were slipping through his gag. His eyes were wide and pleading with me as we were both forced to watch them drag Vallie away.

"Bring her to the underbelly," the King ordered. The soldiers looked nervously at one another before shoving me forward.

I could do nothing as I was pulled away from Miles and forced to walk further into the dungeons. It grew colder and darker. Larger cells changed to smaller ones until we reached a section that was nothing but cages. But they were different from the cages I was kept in, and I realized there had to be different entrances and sections down here.

These were dark, no lights illuminating the damp area, not even small taunting windows paved the pathway for us. The only reason we could see anything at all was because a fire user had a floating ball of flames hovering over us as we walked. I tried not to stare at the poor Advenians who were forced into a fetal position in order to fit inside the rusty bars. I could still feel the cramp in my neck and the stiffness in my legs from being stuck like that for days. My only liberation was when they *questioned* me about Sie.

The King removed a pin from his shirt as we reached a dead end and pricked his finger. He smeared a small drop of blood onto the empty stone wall ahead of us and a door materialized, swinging open on a gust of air magic.

I was half dragged, half carried down a steep flight of steps. Only seeing out of my one eye now, I was forced to squint. The lights were brighter here, illuminating the marbled floors and alabaster walls.

Everything looked too pristine, too shiny, to be considered part of the dungeons. Instead of a rustic metallic gray coating the cells, it was a sparkling silver.

I was standing in between two rows of cages. And inside were Advenians chained to the walls by their necks. There were hundreds and hundreds of them from what I could glimpse. Most shuddered at the sight of the King, others gave him death glares. Some were so far gone they could barely muster the strength to lift their heads.

Only their chains kept them from being able to touch one another. Holes were dug in the floor under them, and I assumed it was so they could relieve themselves.

The King didn't pay them any attention.

"King Arcane." A healer bowed. "You've already visited today for your dose. Do you require another?"

That's when I noticed the Advenians' skin. They looked more like husks than actual people. The long rectangular cell to the left housed Advenians with varying cuts scattered all over their naked bodies. The ones on the right had a tube sticking out of their veins that poured their blood into buckets.

"Just here for a tour. Get back to work," he remarked.

The King pointed toward the right. "These are Alluse users. We drain and replace their blood continuously. Arcane is able to make serums and now vapors out of the blood we collect." Healers were scattered throughout the cages, working on some of the ones who were too pale to be considered normal. "And this side," he gestured toward the left cage, the one with all the cuts marring their bodies, "is for my personal use."

I was pushed forward as we walked down the narrowed hall of chained Advenians. "You see, I can take whatever I want. All these people had an ability I once desired." He stopped walking and turned to face me. "And now their abilities are *mine*." He smiled as my eyes widened. "My power is unique. All I have to do is drink the blood of a Luxian, and I'm free to use their abilities. One small drop and it becomes mine."

A ball of flames burst from his palm so close to me I could feel the heat radiating from it. I leaned back, my head slamming into one of the soldiers holding me upright. "Oh, that's right. I forgot. You don't like fire. It's what killed your parents." Then the ball of fire turned to water, dousing the flame. The King reached forward, pressing his hand against my chest. I screamed as my body revolted, an agonizing shock shooting through me. It only lasted a second, but it was enough that if I wasn't being held up, I would have fallen over. "Electricity."

The King vanished, but I felt his fingers slide up my arm as he whispered, "Air and invisibility." A burning agony flooded my stomach, and I screamed.

I glanced down and blinked as I saw blood seeping through my shirt. The King materialized with a dagger. He stabbed my stomach before he replaced the blade with his hand and a blue glow radiated from it. "Healing." He smiled after releasing me. "I possess any ability from Lux I want. All I need is a small drop of blood every day, and it's all mine."

"Why are you showing me this?" I whispered, my voice was barely audible. A mix of horror and repulsion were crashing into me. How long had all these people been trapped down here?

"I'm showing you this because once I'm through with you, this is where you're going to end up. Arcane is working on a way to alter your blood so that when I drink from you, *I* become stronger. When he does, you'll live out your remaining days down here. But for now," his hand possessively trailed down my cheek, "I have other needs for you."

The King turned toward Kole who'd been following behind the soldiers. He was as pale as the Advenians drained of blood. "Chain her back up in my chambers."

THIRTY
SIE

Dravenburg called another meeting in the war tent. It was the fifth one in the past two days, and no one had made any decisions yet. The camp had two clear leaders, Tezya and Dravenburg, but neither of them had the final say in anything. Everything had to be settled by a vote, which made the process agonizingly slow.

I was sitting next to the princess. To my surprise, she'd been present for each meeting. It was the only time she left the healer's tent. She looked like absolute shit. I hadn't seen the Fire Prince since we first came back without Scottie, but I was pretty sure he was worse.

Rainer and Kallon approached the princess. "How's Brock?" the male asked.

"He's doing better. They think he'll be fine in a couple of weeks."

"Can he see?" Kallon asked, pulling her lips into her mouth with her teeth. The girl's eyes were swollen and it was the longest I'd seen her hair stay the same color. Even her bangs were plastered to her forehead from a layer of grease.

"I don't know yet. They did an examination on him when he first arrived, but he's been unconscious since. They won't know for sure until he wakes up."

I was surprised the guy was alive. Seeing his injuries made my stomach turn. He didn't have any fingernails left and a piece of his right pinky was missing. To top it off, I overheard one of the healers mentioning almost all of his ribs were fractured, and his left foot was so shattered, they weren't sure if it was salvageable yet. He was broken, from the outside of his skin being bruised and cut in almost every way imaginable, to them nearly destroying every organ and bone on the inside.

And I had left Scottie in the hands of the same people who did that to the massive brute…

Trust me. Her words haunted me. I was happy I hadn't seen the Fire Prince because I didn't think I'd be able to look him in the eye. *You were supposed to protect her.* The other six words that were seared into my memory.

To make things worse, they convinced me to use my total mind control on him, and I compelled Tezya to not go after Scotlind alone. I was the only Advenian alive who could force him to stay… because he was my half brother. I couldn't wrap my head around it yet. I still had no fucking idea how the prince kept a massive secret like that hidden for so long.

I thought back to when Scotlind and I were betrothed. As if I wasn't fucked up in the head enough, my brain kept running through constant cycles of horrible memories—from everything I'd ever done wrong to her, right up until now—to when I left her in Lux for the second time.

I couldn't shake the night Alec brought Scotlind to the party before our tour. I kept seeing the hatred on her face when she was forced to pretend to be compelled. It made me wonder if the prince ever had to act compelled before. If it was difficult not showing that side of him and having to pretend compulsion worked on him.

I highly doubted it. He was the commander of the Luxian army. I doubted the King ever let any of his children go without some sort of Alluse protection. They probably were fucking coddled like babies. Everyone in Lux had to have known that, so no one would risk using compulsion on him. Not that tons of Tennebrisians were even stationed in Lux to begin with. Work visas were becoming more rare and harder to obtain. Now you had to get approval by both Advenian Councils.

But compelling him reminded me exactly why I hated using my ability. I hated how much I fucking craved the power. I could compel *anyone*. Well, anyone except a Luxian air user who casted shields or an Alluse user. Sometimes I hated how much I loved using it, but I loved even more that no one could do the same to me.

The moment I called my powers back, guilt always lingered. It reminded me of my father, of when he had forced me to do things against my will as a child. The comparison made me sick to my stomach. I didn't want to be anything like him.

But I had to compel Tezya. The guy was stupid enough to go marching into Lux alone for her. I could see everyone's reasoning in having me do it, but now, I was on the top of his shit list along with the dual-colored hair girl.

Peter patted my shoulder as he took the empty seat to my left. "Any news?" he asked.

I shook my head. If anyone heard anything about Scottie, I'd been kept in the dark. I looked up at Dravenburg who was talking to a few soldiers in the camp. It was still odd to see Luxians and Tennebrisians living together and knowing they had been for decades, even weirder that a mortal was overseeing them. They all coexisted peacefully, even with the three humans.

My eyes wandered to Savannah. She had an ugly green creature on her shirt again, the material stopping just shy of her pants, revealing a thin band of bare skin. She tucked a wavy strand of her hair behind her ear, the lavender color reflecting in her gray eyes. That's when I noticed she was glaring at me, and I'd been stupidly staring at her like an idiot.

"I guess she hasn't forgiven you for cheating in your fight," Peter leaned in to whisper in my ear.

"I didn't cheat," I said and forced myself to tear my gaze away from her.

"Try telling that to her. She's looking at you like she's planning your death."

"I don't care what she thinks."

"Uh-huh. Sure," he replied as he pulled a croissant out of his pocket and started eating it.

I was about to retort back on—one: why the fuck he was carrying around a piece of bread, and two: I really didn't give a shit about the human—when Tezya entered the tent. A hush fell over everyone as they stared at him. It was the first meeting he was attending since he came back without Scotlind.

He didn't say anything. He didn't even look at Kallon, Dovelyn, or me as he slumped into a seat next to the mortals.

Dravenburg tapped his fist onto the wooden table. "First things first. We need to relocate. The girl is held captive by the Lux King, and she's seen enough to damage us. Even though she doesn't know the exact location of the camp, she can give away enough insight that it's only a matter of time until they find us here. We need to move out before they do."

"Scottie wouldn't give up any information," Kallon spoke softly.

"She can be compelled," Peter said and everyone turned to look at him. "The Lux King has a compulsion user by his side. He has a way to hook her up to monitors and go through her memories."

Dovelyn nodded in agreement, but I was studying the Fire Prince. His head remained down as he stared blankly at the ground. He was so still, so unmoving.

Dravenburg interjected. "Exactly. We have to expect the girl will give away every advantage we have. The King most likely knows the prophecy is about Tezya, and that we possess what we need to see it through."

I straightened. I forgot all about our original mission, how we went to Lux for information on how to kill the King. Dravenburg gestured toward Kallon who pulled a ring out of her pocket.

"That's it?" someone asked. "This is going to help us defeat the Lux King?"

"It's a damn ring. The woman I love is being held captive all for a fucking piece of jewelry." It was the first time Tezya spoke. His words were slow as he enunciated each one. No one spoke as the quiet swept through the tent and lingered.

"We'll get her back," Savannah said after a moment.

"How? You won't even let me fucking try." His eyes were bloodshot as they found mine, as he remembered me compelling him. Well fuck. He turned toward his sister, rising from his chair. "Your vision is going to come true. Are you happy now? She's at your father's side just like you said. Goddess fucking knows what he's going to do to her until she breaks."

I had no idea what the two siblings were talking about or what they thought Scottie would do, but as I looked around the room, everyone seemed just as confused as I was.

"Tezya, I didn't wish for this to happen."

He sighed heavily. "I know, Dove, but you didn't stop it either. You didn't question it for one second. You didn't care what would happen to her. You have Brock and that's all you wanted. Scottie was yet again at the mercy of your scheming."

"And what should I have done? Brock was dying! Scottie saw that and decided to help. Do you wish he wasn't back with us? Do you wish the King still had him?"

"No," he said softly, defeated, as he crumbled back into his seat. "No. I just don't want her in his hands." He was quiet for a moment as he stared at his palm. "I can feel her. Just brief moments of panic and pain. I don't know how or what they're doing to her, but we've lived through it enough, Dove, to know it's fucking hell. I can't speak to her. I can't reach out through the bond, but I *feel* her. Do you know what that's like? To feel the pain and agony from the person you love, but you're so fucking helpless to do anything about it?"

"I know what you want to do, Tezya, and it's not smart," Kallon whispered.

"You don't need to risk anyone. Just me. Just fucking release his compulsion and portal me into Lux. That's all I'm asking."

"That's out of the question," Dravenburg said.

"Why?" Tezya challenged. His chest was puffed, and he looked ready to set the entire camp on fire.

"You're too important to risk."

He fumed. "It's my fucking life, Drave. I get to decide when to risk it—"

"No, you don't. Because if you die trying to rescue her—which is nearly impossible with a group of people, nonetheless, you alone—it'll ruin everything we've been doing here. This war is bigger than one girl. You are bigger than one girl. We need you. You have a camp full of people that you brought here in the hopes of one day leading into battle, and now the time has come to do just that, and you want to throw it all away for *one* person? If we believe this prophecy, *you* are the only one who can stop the King, so like it or not, you're needed alive more than her."

Tezya closed and opened his fist, staring at his scar. I could tell he was weighing everything over, trying to decide between duty and what he actually wanted to do. *Welcome to my world*, I wanted to say to him. That same duty was what caused me to lose Scotlind in the first place.

"We'll figure out a way to get her back. We need to plan an attack on Lux soon. We'll work her rescue into it," Dovelyn said.

"That's bullshit," Tezya spat. "We both know we can't attack Lux until I figure out how to harness Pylemo's fire, and who fucking knows how long that'll take. I'm not waiting—"

Dravenburg cut him off. "We can agree to evacuate and move everyone first," he said. "We can't stay here, and Brighta is our top priority at the moment."

Tezya met my gaze for a moment with a pleading look, but I knew what he wanted was futile. The King wouldn't let Scottie leave his side now that he had her again. Rescuing her would be damn near impossible.

———

TEZYA FOUND me after the meeting.

"Sie," he yelled my name as spit flew out of his mouth. "I want a word, *alone*."

Peter halted by my side, ready for anything. We were halfway back to our tent, and surprisingly, no one else was around us. "It's okay," I told Peter. "I'll meet up with you later."

He looked between Tezya and me before finally shrugging and walking off. I turned to face the prince, knowing this interaction was inevitable the moment I compelled him.

But what surprised the hell out of me was that his enraged, feral expression turned to anguish. "Please," he begged. "Please, remove the compulsion."

I shook my head. "You heard Dravenburg in there. I can't—"

"Fuck that," he spat as he ran his fingers through his white locks. The motion of it reminded me so much of... *me*. "Do you know what it's like to want to save her, but you physically can't?" He took a step closer to me, closing the distance between us until we were nose to nose. "With every fucking fiber of my being, I want to walk out of this camp and go to her. I don't give two fucking shits if no one will help me or if that means I'd have to walk on foot across the whole damn continent and swim across the ocean to get to her, I'd fucking do it. But I can't." He ran his fingers through his hair again, then exhaled. "He has her because of me." He started pacing. "It was my decision to go to Lux. I agreed to her being a distraction. I agreed to split up. I should have done more. I should have—"

"You aren't solely to blame, Tezya. You aren't the reason she's captured right now." I don't know why I decided to remind him of that because I didn't have a death wish, but the guilt was eating away at me, and it was strange to see him falling apart. *Trust me.* I was supposed to protect her. Tezya even went as far to meet with me before we left and threatened my life if I failed to put her first. He warned me Dovelyn wouldn't and with him being across the city, he couldn't be the one to do it. I was supposed to, and I failed again. I let her walk right into Athler's arms. I let her go.

Trust me.

"Then help me, please," he begged as he turned toward me. I'd never seen him look so distraught before. The Fire Prince never begged. I shook my head, hating myself for it, but Dravenburg was right. We needed him. Tezya had to understand that too.

"Please… you don't know the King. He's a ruthless and cruel ruler, but that is nothing—*nothing*—compared to how he is behind closed doors. He's a sadist, and he's going to break her, Sie. He's going to fucking savor in it too. Please, just help me, if not for me, then for her. Just let me save her before it's too late."

"Tezya, I can't…"

"You don't have to take any part in it," he half screamed, frustration written all over him. "I'll go alone. JUST. BREAK. THE. COMPULSION."

"I will help you, Tezya, but not like this. Not when your rage is going to get you killed first."

"Then when? When will you help me? Because the more time that passes, the longer he's fucking torturing her. She's going to die."

"Your sister made it pretty clear before we went to Lux that the King wanted her alive. He wants her powers."

"There are worse things he can do to her than kill her." He started pacing again. His face was stone cold like he lived through it and seeing the jagged cut across his face, I started to wonder if I was wrong about him. I assumed his scars were a result of being in the army, but the way he spoke about the King with such emotion, such hatred… It made me wonder if I got the better end of the stick being raised by my—*our*—father.

"The compulsion I put on you doesn't stop you from saving her."

Tezya stopped in his tracks and halted his pacing to face me. "What do you mean? I've tried numerous times to leave the camp, but every time I get close to the shield, it fucking stops me. It's like a barrier forms out of nothing that prevents me from passing. I physically can't leave."

"The compulsion I put on you doesn't prevent you from saving her. It just prevents you from saving her alone without a solid plan, like you want to do right now, which is only going to get you killed."

I stumbled backward, landing flat on my ass. My mouth throbbed, and my teeth ached from where he just threw a punch. Tezya was panting over me, not bothering to hold back his rage. I pulled myself up until I was resting on my elbows.

"I promise I'll help you save her." I spit out blood before running my tongue along my teeth to make sure they were all there. "We'll find a way. We just have to be smart about it."

A tear slid down his cheek and rolled onto his scar. He held up his fists, ready to fight as he gestured for me to stand. I accepted his offer. He needed this. He needed to let off some steam, and I was happy to oblige.

Finally, I'd be able to spar someone who could give me an even match.

THIRTY-ONE
SCOTLIND

Kole had tied my arms and legs to the ground behind me, forcing me to sit on my knees and stare at the bedroom door. He looked at me afterward, long enough that I thought he was going to say something, but then he stormed out of the room, leaving me with only the dead servant's rotting body for company.

I had no idea how long I was left alone, trying not to hyperventilate, before the King walked in.

He nudged the dead servant's head with his boot, turning his neck so his vacant eyes were staring at me. "I think this will serve as a reminder," he crooned. "We wouldn't want your friend to share the same fate as him, now would we?"

He crouched low, his boots stepping over the dried blood, so his face was directly in front of me. "Where's my daughter?"

I didn't answer.

"Where's my son?"

I bit the inside of my cheek. I could feel the vapor Alluse fading from my system, and with it, I started to feel Tezya's emotions again. Only little bits here and there. Anger. Guilt. Worry. Rage. Hopelessness.

I tried to reach out—to talk to him—but he was too far away or maybe the bond was fading. I had no idea how it worked, but all I got were random feelings at random times. Feelings that made everything worse. Was he still in Lux? Was he back at the camp? Would they evacuate and move everyone? The only comfort I got was knowing he wasn't with the King. He wouldn't be asking where they were if he had them. Tezya was safe.

But it also confirmed no one was coming for me. I could have accepted my fate if I was the only one who'd suffer from it. But now that the King had Vallie and Miles... I didn't know what to do.

"You'll regret not telling me." He straightened, then motioned toward the door. Soldiers were waiting on the other side. They dragged Vallie into the room, then left without a word.

She was crying softly, her amber eyes were swollen and red, but otherwise she looked okay, or as good as she could be. I didn't see any visible signs of torture. She was washed and dressed in a thin white slip. Even after being starved, she still held onto her feminine figure, and the fabric of her gown did little to cover her.

"Come here," he ordered.

Her bare feet started padding across the marbled floor, but she froze once she looked down and saw the decaying body next to me.

"I said come here."

Her full lips trembled as she started walking again, slowly, softly, hesitantly. She stopped once she stood in front of the King. Her feet were just out of reach from the pool of dried blood. I could tell her breathing was ragged, she was struggling to take a full breath.

The King's eyes drank her in. "It's a shame I'll have to ruin you." The King turned to me. "This is your last chance. Who will you pick? My son or her?"

I couldn't. I couldn't choose. Giving up information on Tezya would be equivalent to murdering thousands of Advenians and destroying any chance of ever defeating him. And there would be no way of knowing if he'd even honor his word. He could still kill Vallie after I told him everything. But to not say anything—I couldn't let him hurt her.

Vallie noted my hesitancy. "It's okay," she sobbed. She knew nothing about Tezya, of what he was trying to accomplish, but yet she was giving me permission to not speak. Even though she was scared, even after knowing the King would harm her if I didn't talk…

Tears swelled in my eyes, matching hers. Vallie was too good. Too good for me, too good for this world. "Please," I begged the King as hopelessness settled inside me. "Please, don't hurt her."

"That's really up to you." He walked across the room toward the oversized mantle. I twisted on the ground so I could still see him. Vallie was left standing in front of me, her body hadn't stopped trembling.

He dragged a chair across the room with one hand, a dagger glinting in his other.

"Does this look familiar?" he asked as he twirled the blade. "It's the same one my son stabbed himself with in order to protect you."

Vallie gasped, finally noticing what was in the King's hand, the terror of the situation fully sinking in. Her eyes flicked from the blade to the slit across the dead servant's neck. She went to take a step back, but the King stopped her. "I didn't say you could move." He waved his hands, using stolen ground magic, creating roots out of nothing before winding them up Vallie's legs and holding her in place.

"What do you want to know?" I whispered, my voice defeated through sobs.

"Everything." He smiled triumphantly. "I'll start with easy questions. For every question you don't answer, your friend will pay the price."

The King snapped his fingers, and the doors opened again. Athler stepped inside, taking the blade from his hand.

"It's been a while since I've participated in one of these." He grinned as he looked Vallie up and down, his tongue darting out, licking his cracked lips.

The King took a seat in the chair he just dragged over as he asked his first question. "Is my son alive?"

"Yes."

"Where is he?"

I didn't answer.

Athler grabbed Vallie's wrist and made a small cut on her forearm. The size of it wasn't much more than the length of my fingernail, but it was deep enough to draw blood. She winced as she tried to pull her arm away.

"How did you get free?"

"Tezya got us out," I said, debating what I could admit to in order to protect Vallie without leaving Brighta vulnerable.

"How?"

"He told the soldiers it was on your orders. No one questioned him."

The King straightened. "One of my soldiers claimed he was compelled. Explain."

I racked my brain for what to say. My gaze briefly flitted to Vallie who was still rooted in her spot next to Athler, forced still by the vines the King created. Athler started to raise the dagger.

"Peter, the Tennebrisian who pretended to be my maid, he had compulsion," I blurted, praying I could get through this without hurting Vallie.

"You're lying. Synder sent me the boy's file from his Trials. He can shapeshift, which would explain how he infiltrated my castle for so long, but it said nothing about compulsion."

I gave my best shrug. "I don't know why he never showed that power during his Trials. A lot of Advenians keep parts of their abilities a secret. Maybe he knew his shapeshifting was enough to rank him a four and decided not to use it."

"No one in their right mind would keep an entire ability a secret. Parts of their abilities I could believe, but an entire ability would never happen. You're talking about the differences between ranks."

"I guess not everyone puts their worth into a pointless number."

The King narrowed his eyes, and in response, Athler cut into Vallie.

"I answered your question," I seethed, my chains rattled, almost causing me to fall on my face again. "It's not my fault I don't understand the mind of someone who isn't here."

"I don't want excuses, I want answers. And we cut your friend based on your attitude, not your answer, so it would be wise to behave and learn some manners. Now," the King said as he leaned back in the chair, looking like the epitome of comfort. "What's my son planning?"

I paused for a moment, trying to figure out how to answer. "He just wanted to get away from you."

Athler added two more cuts into Vallie's arms. This time she screamed.

"Stop! Please... I answered your question," I started to cry.

"I don't want lies," the King drawled. "Athler can smell your pheromones. He can decipher when you tell the truth and that was now two lies you told us."

———

THE NIGHT FELT LIKE A LIFETIME. Vallie's arm was as red as her hair by the time the King and Athler finished. I answered every question they asked me, but they still cut into her, claiming I was lying. I tried to steady my breathing, to calm my racing heart, but every time I didn't tell the truth, they knew. Even when I only told half truths, they started picking up on it. I had never felt so helpless before.

"Don't cry," the King whispered into Vallie's ear as he brushed her hair over her shoulder. She was still trapped by his vines and every time she struggled against them, they tightened. "I'm done hurting you, *for now*."

That only made her sob more.

The King looked at Athler like he was expecting something.

Athler smirked, and I could do nothing but watch as he crossed the room, finding a clean blade and a goblet. He cut his arm and filled the glass with his own blood before passing it off to the King.

Vallie shrieked against the vines as the King drank from the cup. Droplets of blood lingered on his lips as Athler's powers became his for the next twenty-four hours. I thought back to all the Advenians chained in the lower levels of the dungeons, of how many powers the King possessed if he drank from that many people every day. He had every ability known to Lux because he stole it.

I cowered in my chains, realizing how powerful that made him, now understanding why my enhancement always felt off around him. There was always too much to enhance.

He snapped his fingers, and the vines immediately disappeared, releasing Vallie from its menacing grip. She staggered forward, red marks denting across her calves and thighs from where they had wrapped around her.

"It's a shame you weren't born Luxian. If you were, you wouldn't have needed to see my healer." Vallie winced as his fingers grazed across her hips. More tears spilled down her cheeks as she tried to pull away. He grabbed Vallie's bloodied arm. "Stop resisting," he purred, and I wanted to vomit as Vallie's movements stilled. Her posture started to relax into him instead of away, and I knew he was using Athler's ability. It was worse than compulsion because while it was happening, I knew Vallie would *think* she wanted it, but the moment it'd wear off, the moment he would let her feelings be hers again, everything would come crashing back.

"I have a thing for redheads," he said as his gaze took in every inch of her. He twirled her hair, twisting it around his finger. Then his voice lowered to a whisper, but I heard every syllable. "You want to please me."

"Yes." Her voice was breathless.

"Good girl," the King murmured. "Come with me." Before he dragged Vallie away, he met my stare. "Pheromones are perhaps my favorite ability. So many marvelous things can be done with it."

I watched in horror as he led my best friend into the next room. I caught a glimpse of a bed looming in the distance before he shut the double doors, blocking me from view and trapping her inside. And I could do nothing, absolutely nothing but sit on the cold, dried blood of the dead servant and wait.

I didn't think things could get worse, but I was wrong. I pulled at my chains as I heard my friend's cries change from agony to pleasure.

I hated him. I hated him so much. It was a different level of fucked up to change the way someone was feeling, to force them to like you, to force them to do things they didn't actually want to do.

Athler only stared. The bloodied dagger he used on Vallie was still in his hand as he twirled it over and over again, taunting me.

It felt like an eternity before the doors to the King's bedroom finally opened, and he threw Vallie onto the floor. She screamed as her legs tripped over the dead servant, causing her to land hard on her side.

"Bring the compulsion user in to watch them and have him tie her up on the other side of the room."

Athler nodded and followed the King out of the room. Kole entered a second later. He paused, staring at Vallie crying on the floor. The white slip she had on earlier was gone, leaving her completely naked.

Kole walked toward her, his movements slowed as he guided her toward the opposite end of the room. She blindly followed him and didn't protest as he gently clamped shackles around her wrists, covering her rank two brand. I tried to crawl toward her, but my chains pulled taut, and I fell on my face.

"Vallie, I—" I didn't know what to say. *I'm sorry* wasn't enough.

She turned away from me and curled up into a ball on the floor. But before she did, I caught sight of her eyes, and they looked more dead than the boy's next to me.

THIRTY-TWO
SIE

"I KNOW how to get her back." Wells—the mortal boy—came up to Tezya at breakfast two weeks later. Peter and I were sitting a few tables down from Tezya and his friends, but everyone quieted to listen.

The dining tent and training rings at the evacuation camp were the only areas that were the same size as the previous one. Everything else suffered. There were more communal tents than anyone cared for, almost no one had their own. And instead of multiple bath houses, there was only one now. It was all small—too damn small for the amount of Advenians that claimed it as their home.

It had taken us a total of five days to move out and another two to properly set up new shields. Every air user of Lux and illusion user of Tennebris were called to help with the task. And now everyone was settling in and adjusting, getting used to the new camp. Everyone except for Wells. He seemed almost as miserable as Tezya, which was hard to imagine.

The previous camp's location was positioned over an old home, which I only found out while we were evacuating. It had been converted into the human's lab. It took a day alone to move all of the things he had jammed inside the place. And he somehow still managed to claim two entire tents for himself when most Advenians were stuck sleeping on the ground. One tent was for his personal use while the other was for his new makeshift lab. But since he was the main reason the shields were working so well, no one complained about it. That and the fact that he was their leader's only son.

Despite the cramped living situations, if I hadn't known any better, I would have thought this was always the main camp. They even still called it Brighta. The only person who acted differently was the Fire Prince. He hadn't been the same since we returned without Scotlind. He barely spoke to anyone.

The strangest thing was that after our fight two weeks ago, he started following me to the training rings every morning. It was our new unspoken agreement. The two of us sparred daily. Never saying a word to the other, we just fought, easily flowing into a rhythm of beating the shit out of each other.

We weren't on good terms by any means—we just decided to use each other to help cope with how miserable we felt. We were evenly matched, and despite hating to admit it, he was good. Where I lacked in strength, I made up for in agility. The Fire Prince's punches were more focused and powerful, although he was still nimble. He had maybe an inch on me and was a bit more broad, but the extra muscles didn't slow him down much. Neither of us held back and neither of us saw a healer afterward.

Savannah came rushing into the dining tent after her brother. "No," she snapped at Wells. "It's too risky."

"It'll work," her brother responded.

Tezya straightened in his seat. The bruises I'd given him earlier this morning did nothing to hinder his movements. I stood from my table, making my way toward theirs. I knew Peter was following me without having to look.

"What's your plan?" I asked Wells, not caring if I wasn't invited into the conversation.

"Offer to trade me for Scotlind."

"The King will never agree," Rainer deadpanned in between a bite of eggs. He was sitting next to the Fire Prince and was the only one who hadn't stopped eating throughout the entire encounter. Peter glanced at his plate, eyeing his bread, but I elbowed him hard in the ribs before he made a dive for it. He was pissed at me that I made him spar longer than usual this morning, and by the time we got here, all the croissants were gone.

Wells turned toward Tezya, who'd been staring at him in a stilled silence he seemed to have adopted. "Don't trade with the King. Make it with Arcane." His voice faltered slightly as he said the eldest prince's name, but he kept going, "He'll agree. You know he'll agree."

"And then what?" Savannah snapped. "What do you think will happen to you when Arcane's father realizes he's been hiding a human in his bedroom?"

"We won't actually go through with the trade. Set the terms and meet him on *our* ground. It's the only way we can get Scotlind out of the castle long enough for us to rescue her."

"Are you sure you want to do this, Wells?" Dovelyn asked. "He won't come alone."

"And neither will we." Wells nodded, a little breathless. "Set up an ambush. If it's on our terms, we'll have the advantage."

"That might work," Kallon said softly. The girl's hair was half black, half aqua today. She'd been sitting at the table with Tezya, but Rainer was in between them as a buffer and neither of them had spoken to one another as far as I knew. Savannah looked at her friend in earnest, probably pissed she didn't side with her and wasn't automatically shutting down the idea.

"Why would you risk your life for her?" I asked Wells because as far as I knew he never even met Scotlind.

"Arcane is an asset to the King. You said yourself that he created a vapor out of Alluse. If we do this, if we can get Scotlind back and capture Arcane in the process, it might give you the edge you need in this war. If they both stay in Lux, we'll never have the chance," the boy said as he fidgeted with his thick-framed glasses. He then proceeded to take them off and wipe them across his shirt even though there wasn't a smudge on them. "I'd been thinking about it more and more since you came back. The idea for a trade came to me this morning."

"And what makes you so confident the prince will agree to it?"

"He will," Dovelyn answered me. "Arcane has been desperate to talk to Wells ever since their... fight." I turned to stare at the mortal. He seemed shocked by what the princess was saying, but he did a good job masking it. "My brother cares very little about a lot of things, but the few things he does decide to give his attention to, he becomes obsessive. If Wells offers a trade, my brother will agree."

"So we kidnap Arcane, and then he can't make anymore Alluse vapors or serums," Kallon said more to herself as she set her amber-filled drink back onto the table.

"Exactly," Wells grinned, pushing his glasses back up his nose. "They'll eventually run out of the stock they have. I've been in Arcane's lab before, there's not a single Luxian who works for him that's capable of what he can do. He's unmatched, irreplaceable... If we can convince him to be on our side..."

"My brother isn't going to automatically join our side," Dovelyn interrupted. "He'll agree to the trade, but he won't change his beliefs."

"We'd have to keep him locked up, Wells," Sav said, crossing her arms over her chest. "Are you prepared for that?"

He swallowed hard, his Adam's apple bobbing in his throat. "It's worth a shot. I can't think of any other way to get Scotlind back."

"Dravenburg won't approve it," Rainer said as he started biting into his croissant, and Peter visibly tensed next to me. "The vote will probably fail."

"Then don't vote," Dove cut him off, surprising everyone, me included.

I looked around the crowded tent, raising an eyebrow. "I'm pretty sure someone here will tell Dravenburg before we even walk out of the tent."

Everyone was staring in our direction.

The princess smirked. "I'm an air user, Dark Prince. I put a shield over us the moment you and Wells approached."

"So my dad doesn't need to know a thing until it's too late." Wells grinned.

Everyone turned toward Tezya as if he had the final say. I was surprised he'd been quiet this long. He stood. "I'd agree to any plan that gets me out of this camp." He threw his fork down on the table, leaving his food untouched. We watched as he stormed out of the tent without another word.

"So does that mean he's in?" Peter asked, swiping the roll from his plate.

Dovelyn nodded. "Yeah. He's going to contact Arcane."

THIRTY-THREE
SCOTLIND

I WANTED to vomit as I forced myself to take another bite. They stopped having soldiers hand feed me after I sank my teeth into them one too many times. Now my hands were chained in front of me—for the duration of my meals only—with only enough slack to allow me to bring my fingers to my lips.

Vallie was chained to the floor from across me, starving, while I was ordered to lick my plate clean after every meal. They'd give her just enough scraps to stay alive, only feeding her every couple of days.

The meat stirred in my stomach and it took everything in me to keep it down. Across the room, Vallie's stomach growled. Her hips and curves were melting away. I could see her rib cage protruding, her shoulders caving. The King starved her—starved her, tortured her, and abused her in every way possible. Anytime I didn't cooperate, he took it out on her.

I only kept track of the days by how many meals I was forced to eat and how many Vallie was neglected. Every day was the same endless cycle.

Arcane would find me in the morning to collect samples of my blood for his tests, and occasionally, he'd bring me into his lab if he needed more. I should have liked it when I got to leave. It was my only reprieve, the only little bit of freedom I got, but I hated it.

I felt like I was suffocating within the white walls and pristine floors of his lab. Everything was too clean. Vials of blood lined counter after counter. Every so often, another Advenian would be chained to a chair, moaning in agony. I tried not to focus on the tests being done. I tried even harder not to focus on the state of the Advenians that were strapped down. They were all on the brink of death, and I knew I was destined for the same fate once Arcane succeeded with my own blood serum—once he found a way to reverse my ability.

Did he know that? Did he know his father kept hundreds of people chained below the castle? I couldn't get a read on the eldest prince. I couldn't figure out if he was helping or hurting us. But if he knew about the hidden dungeon and was making Alluse serums for the King, there was no way he could be on our side.

I shuddered, thinking about the right side of that room, how all the Advenians were drained, their blood pouring into buckets beneath them. Then I thought of the left side, the side the King drank and stole from every single day. I tried not to, but all I saw were hundreds of cuts marking their bodies and how I'd end up there soon.

After Arcane was finished with me every morning, he'd deposit me back into the King's antechamber. The dead boy was starting to decay, and the smell was sickening. The blood had seeped and permanently stained the floor, but no servants were allowed to mop it—*him*—up. It was meant to serve as a reminder that if I didn't obey, Vallie would join him. It was a delicate balance I was failing at.

They questioned me every day, always asking the same things. Where was Tezya? What was he planning? How did we escape?

When the vapor finally wore off, my chains were replaced with Vir Alluse ones, but I still couldn't be compelled.

They had Kole try every day on the off chance whatever was preventing me would magically go away. But I was never forced to obey. The compulsion wouldn't work. I wondered if Arcane was putting something in my food, some serum that prevented compulsion.

I straightened in my chains as the King walked into the room. The fireplace was on today, but it didn't emanate any heat like the ones in Tennebris. Unlike the rest of Lux, the King's rooms were cold.

"Every day you resist me, resist *this*, it directly affects her," the King said as he watched me finish the meal I was forced to eat. "I need you alive and healthy, but her," he gestured to Vallie, "she doesn't matter."

I looked over at Vallie. She rose from her fetal position and was sitting with her hands in front of her, trying to block most of her body from view as she glared up at the King. Her chains had more slack than mine, giving enough length to allow her to walk if she wanted. But as I stared at her, I didn't think she could stand even if she wanted to.

A tear slid down my cheek. I was at a loss for what I could do for her. I didn't know how to keep her safe anymore and the more days that passed, the more and more I contemplated just giving in and telling the King everything he wanted. They were killing her slowly and forcing me to watch.

"I'm going to show you mercy today." His gaze flicked over Vallie, drinking her in. "And to prove how generous I can be, I'm going to give *this* redheaded friend a break."

I narrowed my eyes, unsure what he meant by that, but I didn't have to wait long to find out. He grinned down at me as the door burst open. Miles was brought forth in chains by Kole. More guilt riddled me, and I knew it would be the death of me. I forgot about my other friend. I forgot they still had Miles in the dungeons. I was so focused on Vallie that I hadn't worried about what they'd been doing to him.

Miles lunged, his shackles pulling and straining against his wrists. I couldn't tell which one of us he was trying to get to before the King's voice overpowered his screams. "Silence him," he ordered, growing bored, "or I'll do it for you."

"Stand still," Kole sneered, but Miles didn't stop, and seeing that, seeing him fight broke me further. Miles was a ranked Tennebrisian, he couldn't be compelled, but it didn't matter. Kole overpowered him in every way. He was contained even if he didn't stop. Kole's voice lowered to a whisper. It was so quiet that I had no idea how I heard it. "You need to calm down, or he'll make it worse for her."

Miles stopped then, falling slack in his menacing grip. Kole's eyes were on Vallie before he turned to look at me. His gaze narrowed, noticing me staring.

Vallie stirred in her own shackles across the room. I shuddered as Miles' gaze took in the sight of me, then the dead boy, before finally settling on his twin. Starved, naked, bruised, with dried blood crusted over her delicate skin. The empty plate by my chains felt disgusting as I saw Miles note the way his twin's body caved in. How her lips were dry and cracked and bleeding. How the skin around her eyes was sullen and sunken in. And me, who was fed, clothed, and didn't have a speck to show for any maltreatment.

The King assessed me, watching me take in my other friend. "You have caused me a great deal of pain. You, my son, the Dark Prince... It seems there are many civilians who support the three of you. Some have twisted what happened when you and my son *left* and unfortunately the rumors of the Dark Prince's escape haven't been silenced. The rebellion is stirring again, and I plan on using you to stop it."

A feeling of doom washed over me. The King had an obsessive fascination with Vallie. He kept her in a condition just enough to keep her alive, but he got off on her struggle. I prayed to the Goddesses every day that it was enough to keep her breathing. But Miles... him being here didn't sit right. I couldn't gauge the lengths the King would take on him. I scanned Miles from head to toe. He looked thinner than he was before. His red hair grew past his shoulders, and a thick beard peppered his normally clean-shaven jaw. How long had they had my friends imprisoned before I came?

"What do you want?" I forced myself to say, the bite of food I just shoved down felt lodged in my throat.

"We're planning a broadcast, and I want you to do exactly as I say. If you don't," he paused before turning his attention to Miles. The next second Miles was drowning. The King was using water creation, forming a tight bubble around his head. I watched in horror as my friend struggled against Kole's grip. He was screaming, sucking in endless cycles of water over and over again. Bubbles ebbed around the water, but the King held his stolen ability.

I knew that pain. I knew what Miles was feeling…

"Please, please, stop. I'll do anything. Just let him go," I screamed, but I barely heard my words over Vallie's shrieks. I realized she was begging, pleading for Kole to help, to do something, anything. He was the only one unchained besides the King.

Save him. Help him. Please. Kole! Do something. No. Please. Miles! KOLE! Her screams echoed in my ears, sinking into my bones.

"Shall I demonstrate all my abilities?" The King's voice was eerily quiet, but somehow I heard him perfectly over the panic in the room. Miles' body revolted as the King added electricity into the mix. The floor shook as he created vines out of nothing. The mossy branches jutted out and replaced Kole's hold on Miles, winding up his legs and arms, locking him in place. Kole took a step back as he watched. His gaze flicked to Vallie's. She was standing now, pulling against her chains, as she screamed for Kole, begging him to help. His hard expression faltered, and he took a single step toward Miles.

The King smiled, releasing the water for a moment, but before I had time to relax, to think it was over, fire replaced where the water had been. An air shield was pocketed over the flames, keeping all the smoke contained around Miles' face. Terror wrecked me as I watched his body sag into the vines holding him up.

No.

No.

No.

His head was burned off, reduced to nothing but ash. There wasn't even blood seeping from his neck. It was all charred. The King retracted the vines and his body flopped onto the floor. The thud resounded in my ears, repeating over and over again.

I would never hear his laugh. I would never be able to listen to him talk again. He would never smile. Never be able to speak to his twin. Never read a book with me or study the mortal maps with his sister.

Vallie's screams were piercing like a dagger stabbing my heart over and over again. It was endless. I was stuck in this moment of terror, unable to escape. Forced on repeat.

Distantly, I heard the King order someone to gag Vallie. Tears pooled down her face as soldiers I hadn't seen before entered and forced her jaw open. They clamped her mouth down around a gag, but muffled screams still ripped from her. I'd never seen her so feral, so ready to murder each and every being in the room. Kole just stared at her in disbelief. I couldn't read the expression on his face.

The King turned to me. My gut twisted as he smiled. *Smiled.* "If you don't do exactly as you're told, she'll be next. When it's time, you'll be washed and briefed on exactly what I need from you. But mark my words, if you stray even a hair from what is expected, I'll make the girl's death twice as long and twice as painful as the boy's. Consider this your only warning."

Then he left us. Left me alone with Vallie, still kicking and screaming through her gag. Her wrists and ankles were bleeding from where she kept pulling her shackles taut, trying relentlessly to break free. I stared at her, then to my headless friend on the ground between us.

Her twin was dead—Miles was dead.

THIRTY-FOUR

SIE

"LET'S GO," Savannah called over her shoulder. I nodded and followed her to the border of the camp. If everything went to plan we'd be rescuing Scotlind and kidnapping Arcane tomorrow.

Tezya and the eldest prince had been communicating, and I was surprised to see Wells was right. Arcane agreed immediately. I underestimated the love he had for the mortal. The fact that he'd risk the King's wrath just to see him again was absurd. But I guess that's what love did. It made you stupid and had you acting irrationally.

What shocked me the most was that it took them four days to agree on a meeting place. Tezya was pissed. Every day Arcane dismissed a new location was another day Scotlind was the King's prisoner and already too many days had passed.

Neutral territory on human ground, far from mortal civilians was what Arcane finally agreed on. He just had no idea we moved locations, so the meeting spot was close to the new camp. Savannah, having suggested it, was taking me there now to scope it out.

For it not being a far walk, it felt long, and Savannah kept finding ways to annoy me. She was sipping loudly on her coffee, claiming it was too early in the morning. She wasn't exactly chipper. It would have been easier if Kallon portaled us, seeing as she already had one in place, but I was curious. I wanted to see more of the mortal lands, and the camp was starting to feel more and more like a giant cage.

Plus, it wasn't like I didn't have time to spare. I hated doing nothing. And despite sparring with Tezya every morning, my days were bleak. It was strange to think that my time with him would be the highlight of my day. But it wasn't his company I craved. Lately, I only lived for the thrill of the fight, for the pure bliss of complete dissociation. I wanted to taste blood in my lungs and feel the sweat drip down my back until all I could focus on was the task at hand. And that was the only thing Tezya gave me—an even match.

"This is it," Savannah said as she spun around. Her eyes were wide, and I found myself staring at the silver hoop coming out of her nostril. The tip of her nose was red, and the cold air was leaving her lips in thick puffs.

I forced my gaze away from her face to scan the perimeter. It wasn't bad. The ground had a slight incline to it, giving us the advantage of better vantage points.

We were standing in the middle of a small clearing. The grass was long and untamed beneath a thick layer of snow, only exposed through our sunken foot tracks. It gave the allure that it was forgotten. Ice clung to the bare trees circling the open pane, and even though everything was dead and neglected, it still looked beautiful. The sun reflected off the snow, casting everything in a soft sparkle.

The Dark Kingdom's cold season was only just starting. Tennebris would be completely covered in darkness in a few short weeks. It was strange to me. I was still trying to get used to the fact that they had sunlight all year round, that it came and set each day.

"There isn't much cover," I said, forcing myself back to why we were here. "With the leaves off the trees, we won't be able to hide."

"I know," she admitted as she turned away from me to scan the area too. "Kallon will be stationed a mile or so back. Part of Arcane's terms was that Tezya comes alone. He'll sense if she created a portal too close to the meeting spot. You'll be over there." She pointed to a large fallen trunk not too far away. "If things go sour, you're going to teleport us to her. She'll be waiting at the other end, ready to portal in case we need an out."

"Won't he be able to sense the rest of us standing by?"

She shrugged. "Probably not. A portal draws a lot of energy and the air around it shifts and pulls. A person doesn't change it much as long as we hide behind a tree or an object. Arcane picks up on everything. He notices even small details. With Dovelyn's invisibility, we'll probably have a minute or two before he senses us."

It was strange—she knew more about the Luxian heir than I did. But I guess it made sense if her brother used to date him, and she grew up around Advenians her whole life. I pushed it out of my mind and asked, "Alright, and if things go right?"

I didn't think this plan was smart. So many things could go wrong. I knew Savannah hated the idea even more than I did with her brother directly at risk. I wanted Scotlind back. I still wanted to try, but I couldn't shake the feeling that this felt too easy.

"If things go right," she said, "my brother will be safe, and Arcane will be a prisoner at the camp." Rainer and Wells were working on a place to hold the eldest prince if we were successful. "And," Savannah continued, "you'll both have your *girl* back."

My girl. I scoffed. "She isn't mine."

She tilted her head to the side to assess me. "Could have fooled me with the way you look at her all the time."

I narrowed my eyes. "It's none of your business."

She shrugged. "Seeing as we're risking my brother and the safety of the camp to get this girl back, I would say it's a little bit my business. I don't see how one girl is worth all of this."

Was she? Was Scotlind worth risking the camp? Her sapphire eyes seemed to stare at me even though I knew she was in Lux at the King's mercy. I owed her this much. I owed it to her to be the one to rescue her this time. Sending her to Lux in the first place was my biggest regret. I was constantly thinking about how things would have played out differently if I'd just rescued her in the Tennebrisian dungeons, if we ran away together and escaped all of this, leaving our world behind. But somehow I didn't think Scottie would have been happy. She wasn't the type to be content while others suffered. I knew she wanted to change things. Knew her dreams were equal parts risky and terrifying, but she would have always regretted not fighting back. She would have resented me if I had taken her away back then. And now, if we can manage to save her, she'd finally get the chance to do what she always wanted.

"Scotlind would think it was worth it if it was you in her place. She wouldn't hesitate to risk her life to save someone she didn't know," I finally said because it was the truth. She would have stopped at nothing to help someone. She fought fearlessly for those who needed it. "She was only captured because she saved us, giving us time to escape. If it wasn't for her we would all be rotting in the dungeons in Lux right now."

Savannah nodded. Her lavender hair falling over her face before she tucked a strand back. More silver jewelry lined the curve of her ear.

We both mindlessly went to work, scoping out the rest of the area in silence. When we finished and were certain there wouldn't be any surprises, she said, "I have a question about your abilities."

"Okay." I didn't know if I was going to answer her or not. I hadn't spoken a lick of my powers to these people or to anyone really. It was technically considered rude to ask abrupt questions in Tennebris, but my interest was piqued.

"If you teleport today, would it drain all of your reserves or would you still be good for tomorrow?"

"Why?" I asked. I was even more surprised she understood how our abilities worked. That she knew about reserves and how only time refilled them. I guess having best friends as powerful Advenians would do that.

"Because I want you to take me somewhere."

"I can jump and be fine by tonight."

"Great," she smirked, closing the distance between us. I stilled as her hand slid into mine, surprised that they were just as callused. I could feel her knuckles jut out from the rest of her fingers. "I'll tell you which direction to go."

The girl was crazy. The fact that this didn't scare her, the fact that *I* didn't scare her. Half of Tennebris was terrified of me, and they had some sort of power to defend themselves with. But she had nothing, yet she wasn't intimidated at all.

I had to be just as insane to agree, to actually use my ability for a mortal's request, but gazing into her eyes, she didn't look very human.

THIRTY-FIVE
SCOTLIND

I JUMPED at the sound of her voice. I was numb, frozen in time, that I'd forgotten where I was and what had happened. I tried to disassociate, to imagine any other outcome of my life other than what it actually was.

Four days had passed. Four days of not speaking. Four days of not being able to stomach looking at Vallie, of being too much of a coward to muster the courage. Her nickname for me flashed in my mind: *Scottie-cat*. Because growing up Vallie was always the fearless one. I just put on a brave face and pretended—pretended because I had no other choice.

But I couldn't pretend what happened away. I couldn't pretend Miles was still alive.

Arcane came to sample my blood every morning, my only indication another day had ticked by. I was thankful the King was preoccupied with preparing for the broadcast that he didn't force me to eat my daily meal. I preferred the hunger. If there was anything in my stomach, I would have just vomited it up the moment I was forced to shove it down.

He barely slept in his bed, which meant it had been four days since he used Athler's pheromones and forced Vallie into it. We were chained in his antechamber room. Forced to do nothing but try and avoid looking at what was left of Miles.

The stench of all the death was appalling, but the King's pride wouldn't move the dead servant or my friend from the floor. Miles was starting to decay now. I knew the servant was worse, but I couldn't brave a look. All I could do was stare forward and pretend he wasn't there. But we were forced to stare at Miles... He was positioned in between Vallie and me in a way that made it impossible not to see what was left of him whenever I looked at her. My vision tunneled in on him before I quickly jerked my head up to find Vallie already staring at me.

"What?" I asked. My voice was raw. We hadn't spoken. I'd thought about what to say every second of every day that had passed, trying to figure out how to apologize. But every time I tried to speak, words never came out. I didn't know where to start. I couldn't fix this.

"I said I need you to do something for me."

"Anything," I breathed. I would do anything for her.

"I need you to not go through with whatever the King wants from you," she whispered, surprising me.

"What? Vallie, I can't. If I don't..." I hesitated, trying to avoid looking at what was left of Miles, but it was impossible. I focused on the chain link in front of me, on where it connected to the floor. I counted them numerous times. There were fifty of them in total—at least the portion of it I could see. "Vallie, if I don't do it, he'll kill you too."

"I know."

My eyes snapped up, meeting her gaze, and I was surprised to find them clear. Some time during the third day she stopped crying, but her eyes were still red and swollen. She was determined, her mind made up. "Don't let him die in vain. Don't let the King win. Whatever it is he wants you to do, don't do it."

"No." I shook my head, tears falling down my cheeks. "No. I won't let you die. I can't..."

"Dying is better than this." Her voice was barely a whisper and the way her words cracked...

"I can't, Vallie. I need you." Guilt took over me. I should have tried talking to her. I should have tried to say anything these past four days, but whenever we were left alone, Vallie curled up in a ball on the floor, turning away from me—away from Miles—and sobbed.

But I should have noticed the change in her the past day when the crying stopped. I could tell she was tired. She was a ghost of the lively friend that had been my family. I could see it in her eyes that she wanted to give up, could see it so clearly that it broke me. But I wouldn't let her. I couldn't lose her too.

She was about to answer when the door jerked open. A soldier strode in and walked straight toward me, sidestepping over what was left of Miles on his way. He unchained my shackles from the floor but kept them linked over my wrists.

"It's time," was all he said.

I couldn't look at Vallie as I was led out of the room, couldn't stomach to see her disappointment because I knew I would do whatever the King wanted of me. I wouldn't lose her too.

———

MY BODY WAS pink by the time I was scrubbed clean. Other than my visits to Arcane's lab, it was the first time I'd been let out of the King's antechamber. I hated that Vallie was left alone. She was by herself in the room where her twin's body was rotting.

I still couldn't process that Miles was dead, still didn't fully believe it. It all happened so fast. With all the weeks of torture Vallie went through, I assumed when Miles was brought in, the King would torture him too. I thought I'd have time to figure out how to save him, to save both of them. The King was creative in how he punished Vallie. He did it in a way that hurt her but never killed her. But now I realized it was only selfish acts that kept her alive. Acts that kept his bed warm.

I'm going to show you mercy today. And to prove how generous I can be, I'm going to give this *redheaded friend a break.* That's what the King had said moments before he murdered Miles in front of us. I didn't even have time to think about what the King would do to him before he burned his head off. I didn't even get to tell Miles anything. There were so many things I wanted to say: *I miss you. I'm sorry. I wish the three of us were on that planet we talked about as children...* But I said none of that. And now I'd never be able to tell him anything ever again.

Miles' screams would haunt me, muffled through the air shield that the King kept perfectly molded around his head. I kept seeing his face melt off, leaving nothing left of his features, leaving nothing left at all—just an empty body.

Fire.

The King ultimately used fire to kill him. Fire that also killed my parents. Fire that haunted me my entire life. Fire that the man I loved possessed. Tezya's fire. I knew it was just another move he made to play mind tricks with me, but it was working. I was starting to fall apart. Vallie and Miles were the only family I'd ever known. They were all I had and now half of that family was gone.

Dead.

Miles was dead.

And now Vallie was so beyond destroyed she wanted to die too.

I wasn't paying attention to where I was being dragged until I was inside a ballroom. Four familiar thrones were erected on a raised platform. The King lounged on the largest one. Arcane took up his seat on the second. He was stoic as he watched me approach. Dovelyn's seat was vacant, but my gut twisted when I saw the fourth. Tezya's throne was now occupied by Athler. This was the same ballroom Kallon had portaled me into for Yule. The night I found out Tezya was the youngest Prince of Lux.

"Impressive what a wash and a nice gown can do for the appearance," the King murmured as he assessed me.

Everything about my appearance was pristine, so at odds with how I felt on the inside. Even my chains were swapped with new ones. The servant's urine and blood had dried on the ones I was originally wearing. Now they were silver, matching the decor in Lux. I could feel the Alluse sinking into my veins, mirroring how I felt—numb. Empty. Nothing.

The dress I was forced to wear was thin. The white silky material had high slits running up both my thighs, revealing my legs and exposing the brutal scar Kole had given me from my hip to knee. But it was nothing. Nothing compared to the scar over my heart from watching Miles die, of knowing it was all my fault, of knowing Vallie was suffering because of it.

"Bring her forward."

The soldiers didn't hesitate as they led me up the steps of the dais. My bare feet padded the cold marble, filling my body with dread. They didn't stop until I was standing directly in front of him, and I could feel his breath against my throat. The King went to reach for my chains but grabbed my palm instead, his fingers digging into the bare skin right before my wrist met with metal as he turned my hand over. "What is this?"

"Nothing," I blurted.

He smiled. "I hadn't noticed it before, but my servants informed me of your scar when they were cleaning you up. You've been doing a good job of keeping your palm hidden from me, and I want to know why." He dragged his finger over the thin, white scar. "This," he murmured, "I remember. This is your blood bond mark with the Dark Prince. But this one," he dug into my scar with Tezya, the wound almost entirely healed now from the weeks that had passed. "This is new."

"I tripped while holding a dagger. I landed on the blade wrong," I lied. My heart was pounding, and it took every ounce of self-control I had to remain calm.

He laughed. "You tell such terrible lies. I would bet my life that my son now bears the same scar across his palm. But what I'm not sure of is if the bond took."

I tried to pull my hand away but his grip tightened around my wrist. "I've always been curious about the bonds and how they work. It's forbidden in Lux to complete them, so we haven't had a bonded match since our kind first settled here." His smile was vile as he looked up from my palm to stare at me. "You will be punished for breaking the law, but I figured we could have a little fun first. I'm curious how connected you two are. For example, if I cut into you, would he feel it?"

I pulled away again and this time he let me. I staggered back before regaining my balance, almost falling off the dais.

"We'll find out soon enough because my son will come for you after this. We'll have plenty of time to test the limits of your new bond, and I have a lot planned for it." He rose from the throne, towering over me. "In the meantime, we have a broadcast to air."

I stiffened as he passed my chains over to Arcane. "Run tests on her blood and compare it to our databases. See if your brother's blood is mixed in her palm."

Arcane nodded.

"The broadcast is in two hours. Make sure whatever you do to her doesn't show, and don't be late."

"Yes, sir," Arcane said as he started to walk toward his lab, forcing me to follow him by my chains.

"And Scotlind," the King added just before we reached the doors of the ballroom, "I don't think I need to remind you that if you mess up, your friend will be the one who pays the price."

THIRTY-SIX
SIE

When Savannah asked me to take her somewhere, I assumed it was close by, but I was beginning to question her judgment for what she considered a short trip.

Beads of sweat were dripping down my temples by the time she finally announced we were here. But I wasn't about to admit I felt exhilarated instead of exhausted. It was the most amount of jumps I'd made in a long time, and it felt freeing to move that openly.

I was starting to notice the effects on my body from weeks of *not* consuming a daily poison. I was getting stronger, getting back to my old self again, and it felt fucking good.

I found I liked doing new things—things I never would have even considered before my time in the prison. My memories were tampered with. I had to constantly convince myself I was free, that I wasn't stuck in some illusion a Tennebrisian guard projected onto me.

I was still having trouble waking up every morning. Even when I spent time with Peter, I found myself touching my forearm just to check for broken bones.

And despite the fact that this human girl annoyed me to no end, I savored that I knew I was in the present moment with her. I wasn't cast in another illusion thousands of feet underwater in some suspended cage. I was out because there was no way in hell my mind could have conjured up something like Savannah. Whenever I was with her, I didn't have to question my reality.

It made her annoyingly intoxicating.

I'd never let anyone dictate where I'd jump before, and I must be starting to go insane because I agreed almost immediately when she had asked. Maybe I just wanted to be with her for a little while longer. Maybe I didn't want my mind to play tricks on me. Maybe I just didn't want to think about Scotlind and how I failed her again… *Trust me.*

Fuck trust.

I just wanted a small reprieve from the current fuckery that was my life. I didn't want to go back to a camp that was too cramped. I didn't want to worry about whether or not this plan would work. And I definitely didn't want to fucking think about what would happen if it did work. Scottie still wouldn't be mine. I lost her and no plan I conjured would bring her back to me in the way I wanted.

"It's called the dead river," Savannah said as she headed for the bank. "I come here whenever I want to feel alive."

I scanned the area, wiping the sweat off my forehead despite the chill in the air. There wasn't another soul in sight, but the river still performed. A constant current flowed down the base with an occasional fish splashing and breaking the surface. Wildlife was hidden from us, but if I listened closely, I could hear that we were still surrounded by it. Lavender flowers, the same shade as Savannah's hair, were sprouting on the other side of the bank. I couldn't understand how something so delicate survived in a harsh climate. My breath was a constant cloud of smoke in front of me, and if it weren't for the layers of clothes we were provided before we set out to scope the meeting grounds, my balls would have frozen off.

Savannah made her way toward the river's edge, and despite the freezing temperatures, she sank into the snow, curling her feet behind her. "What are you doing?"

"Enjoying the water."

"I mean, what are you doing here? Why did you want to come? Why make me bring you?"

"To enjoy the water," she repeated as if that answer should've been obvious.

I ran my fingers through my hair in frustration. I was long overdue for a cut, it was almost as long as hers, stopping just above my shoulders. "You did not just make me teleport you for the past hour so you could look at *water*. There's water back at the camp."

She turned to glare at me, her palms sinking further into the snow, and fuck, she looked serene amongst the white powder. She was so out of place, just like the purple flowers amongst the winter, but yet somehow she still belonged.

I had no idea how she was managing because humans were even less adapted to temperature changes than Advenians. Tennebris was colder around the border of the shields, but we were never outside long enough to feel the numbness from it.

"I didn't make you do anything. You agreed. And the water isn't the same at the camp. I like it here better."

"Why?" I asked as I started making my way toward her on the bank, mainly because I had nothing else to do.

"Because no one ever comes here. I like being alone and not in a camp full of Advenians—"

She cut herself off, but she didn't have to finish her thought for me to imagine what she was going to say. I felt the same way. Even though I was in awe at what Tezya created, I fucking hated it. The camp was everything Scotlind ever wanted. She had asked me if it was possible one of the nights at the lake when we were still married, and I told her no. It felt like a reminder of everything I lost, and for once in my life, I didn't know what to do next. I was supposed to be the king. I was supposed to be with Scotlind. And all the fucking Advenians at the camp who stared at me everywhere I went... they knew it. They knew, and I was growing sick of their judgment.

I sat down next to her in the snow but didn't say anything. I didn't know what Savannah's life was like, but I saw the way some of the soldiers interacted with her. How she'd get pissed off whenever one of them called her *Lavender*. At first, I hated myself for watching her. The fact that I even knew what she did in her spare time was infuriating.

But it was only because she was my reminder that I was free. That was it.

We were silent for a while. I wasn't sure how long we sat there with the snow seeping into our clothes. But I felt like, for the first time since I was rescued, I could breathe. I could just exist without the constant reminder of everything I'd lost.

"Come on, follow me." She stood, wiping her palms across her thighs. "There's a hidden path to the river about a half mile down."

"What do you mean *hidden*?" I asked, but she was already walking away from me. Sighing loudly, I followed her more out of frustration. I was tempted as hell to just leave her here, but I didn't doubt she'd eventually find her way back to the new camp. She seemed to have a knack for navigating the mortal territory, and to my surprise, had a fair amount of knowledge of both Advenian kingdoms too.

And I had no desire to deal with a pissed off Dravenburg if I came back without his only daughter. Despite her never listening to him and constantly running away, he was overprotective to a fault.

A soft hum sounded as Savannah vanished before my eyes. It looked like the river just stopped, meeting with a harsh tree line too thick to walk through. There was no way in hell I'd fit through the gap, but the girl just disappeared. I hesitated for a moment before following her. As soon as I did, the river stretched out before me. The temperature rose multiple degrees, the warmth a telltale sign this was the work of an air user.

"Why is there a shield in the middle of the mortal territory?" I asked in a daze. A few paces out, the river dropped into a pounding waterfall. The sound was deafening. I turned back to face where we just came from. Snow and ice stood at my back, but past the shield everything was vibrant and green. More of the lavender flowers were scattered throughout the riverbank.

Air shields fascinated the hell out of me. How one thing could do so much: control the temperature, cast invisibility, block sounds, act as a protection barrier. It was the one ability I wished Tennebris had. It was a match against the Dark's psychic powers, and one of two abilities that blocked out Tennebrisian compulsion.

"Because Dove and I love this place so much, we wanted it just for ourselves."

"And did you find this place by stealing a folder and wandering through the middle of nowhere?" I asked.

She leveled a stare with me. "I like to hike and be outside."

"I didn't really take the princess to be a nature buff," I said, and for some reason it didn't surprise me that Savannah was. But Dovelyn coming here sounded laughable. I didn't really take her for anything other than a stuck-up snob who wouldn't sit on anything that wasn't cushioned or cleaned prior, but I didn't add that part.

She huffed a laugh to herself. "She's not, but this place is special to me, so she sucks it up. We needed a place to escape to, and we both fell in love with the solitude of it. And since I love it here and come much more frequently than she does, she overlooks the whole water thing."

"Water thing?"

"Oh, yeah. Dovelyn hates water, and I mean *hates* it."

"Good to know," I started to say, but she was already walking over to the cliff's edge where the waterfall started, removing her clothes as she went. She stepped out of her pants first, walking backwards, and not taking her eyes off me. Her shirt came off next. Feathered wings covered her rib cage and dipped over her stomach. I was mesmerized by it until she spun around and her bra came off next.

The same flowers that spanned the area of this place went up her spine. The clusters stacked on top of each other in a vertical manner, covering each knob of her vertebrae. They didn't hold any color, just the bare bones of the flowers that I wouldn't have known they were meant to be purple if we weren't surrounded by them now.

I couldn't get over my fascination with her markings—or mortal tattoos as she called them—it was weird to see black patterns over someone's body when they weren't exposed to water. I kept staring at them, too busy getting lost in the designs, that I wasn't prepared for her to jump. I hadn't even noticed she fully undressed before she leapt off the soft grass and fell into the roaring water below. Her thick winter clothes were in piles before the bank.

"Fuck." I bolted toward the edge, then teleported the rest of the way. I managed to catch her awkwardly right before she landed in the uproar, but we were tumbling too fast. I couldn't teleport us away before we were sinking into its depths, the pounding water above pushing us further and further into the deep. I felt her wet skin against mine as she pushed me off and swam to the surface. The heavy coat I was still wearing was weighing me down, taking me longer to swim to the top.

When we both sprang free, inhaling mouthfuls of air, she spun to look at me. "Why did you do that?"

"I saved you," I answered. "You fell into the water. I think a thank you would be nice."

She laughed. Hard. The sound was light and carefree. I watched her bob in the water a good distance away from me, her chin dipping under the surface with each giggle. I was surprised to find the temperature tepid, enjoyable almost.

"I jumped, you idiot, *on purpose*, and now your clothes will be soaking wet when we head back."

Irritation rang through me. I hadn't thought of that. I looked up at where we came from, at least fifty feet above us. "You could have died."

"I've made this jump multiple times before."

I stared at her in shock. She was a human. *Mortal.* Their bodies were supposed to be so fucking fragile. And yet she willingly did this. "Why did you jump?"

She splashed water at my face. "For fun. Haven't you ever done anything for fun before?"

No. But I wasn't about to tell her that. "Aren't you scared of dying?" I asked instead of answering. I tried to focus on our conversation and not on the fact that she was naked, or that the water was clear, despite it being dark, and it did little to hide her body. She dipped underwater, and I held my breath as she started swimming toward me. I couldn't look away.

"No, I'm not scared of dying," she answered when she came back up for air, only a few inches in front of me now. Her hair was now a deep purple instead of its usual light lavender coloring. "I'm scared of not living."

THIRTY-SEVEN
SCOTLIND

MY FEET WERE FROZEN against the cold floor of the laboratory, but I could barely feel it. Arcane didn't say a word to me the entire walk, and my nerves were eating me alive at what the King was going to do. He knew about us, knew that Tezya and I were bonded, and he had a plan to bring Tezya here...

Dread filled me as I recalled the conversation I overheard between Tezya and Dovelyn before everything went to shit. *I saw people die right in front of her, and she didn't do anything to stop it. She didn't even blink or seem surprised by it either. She just watched.*

Was this what Dovelyn saw? Did she see this happening? Would this be the moment I ruin everything? Could I really sit by and do nothing as the King continues to murder people?

"Everyone out," Arcane ordered as we walked in. He dropped my chains and left me standing by the door. His lab was busier than normal with tons of Advenians scurrying about. I realized it was the first time I'd been brought here in the afternoon and not in the dead of night or the early hours of the morning. It was also the first time he made everyone else vacate.

He nodded toward an empty test chair, gesturing for me to take a seat. I walked slowly, almost tripping over the chains now that they were loosely hanging around me and not pulled taut. Once I sat, he gently unclamped them before replacing them with the shackles built into the armrests.

I felt fire in my veins as my powers slowly receded back into me. It was the only time I felt Tezya's emotions. When I first was captured, I could feel him periodically even while wearing the Vir Alluse, but now I was fully cut off from him, except for the split second it took for them to replace my chains. It was the only glimpse I got that he was still alive before it felt like a part of me was cut off again. Except this time, the connection didn't fade. I could still feel Tezya as the new chains clamped over my skin.

I looked up at the eldest prince in question as he finished fastening my wrists into the arm rests, then continued with my ankles at the base of the chair. Why wasn't he using Alluse? As soon as the vapor wore off, I'd always been put in Alluse chains.

"Don't get any ideas," he said, seeming to read my thoughts. "I'm stronger than you, and you'll regret it if you try anything."

A dome-like shield fell over us as he turned to me. "There's a silencing bubble in the shield so the monitors won't pick anything up." He gestured to the corners of the room where cameras were positioned throughout the lab. In all the mornings I'd been dragged down here, I never noticed them before. We were being watched.

I scanned the shimmery air the prince created. It was different from any shield I'd ever seen before. A faint flow of silver was mixed into it, matching his eyes. I stared at him. He looked so much like Dovelyn with his long sleek hair tied behind his back. I used to be envious of it when I first saw them. Not the silver coloring but the silkiness to it. My own brown strands were brittle and dry, despite the effort the servants put into my appearance today. Not that any of it mattered anymore. My best friend was suffering somewhere above me, forced to sit in the same room as her decaying twin, and I'd soon be rotting in a plated cell, levels below the dungeons for the King to drink from until the day I died.

I gritted my teeth. I had to get Vallie out before that happened, before I couldn't do anything anymore.

Arcane moved swiftly, hooking up numerous monitors and sensors across my body. Once the screens flared to life with numbers and symbols I couldn't comprehend, he pulled a large-bore needle out of a drawer. I knew what was coming next as he threaded the tip into my vein and connected it to a tube that drained into a small collection bag. I watched as my blood poured out of me. Would he really be able to tell if Tezya was bonded to me? Had my blood somehow changed since we completed the bond?

Arcane worked in silence, but I couldn't stop gawking at him. Something was different. I felt him somehow as he methodically worked, and I got a sudden urge to trust him, which was crazy and absolutely ridiculous. He was part of the reason I was captured in the first place, and he currently had me chained to a chair to run tests on my blood. How could I think he was remotely good? I blew out a breath, concluding I had gone insane.

But I still couldn't shake the feeling that there was more to him than the facade of being the King's obedient heir. Was it because of Tezya? Arcane was his half brother, and now that I was mated to Tezya, did that mean I'd feel differently toward his siblings? Sie was also Tezya's brother, and I still had no idea what to make of that. Not that it mattered. I wasn't going to see either of them ever again.

My fists clenched at my sides.

Arcane noted the movement and eyed me curiously, and something else came to mind. I was positive he was the reason I couldn't be compelled anymore. I knew he was protecting the camp. If he didn't care about it, he would have just told Athler and his father the location.

"Why did you make the trade for me?" I asked. He said we had a silencing bubble around us, so I took a chance.

He didn't answer. Of course he wouldn't. He never spoke to me, so why would this be any different? But it *felt* different. I pushed forward.

"Was it because of Dovelyn?" I asked. "Did you make the trade to protect her?" I was shocked when he agreed to it, and even more shocked that it actually worked. He was the one who chased them when Athler ran after me, and Arcane came back empty handed. Was it on purpose? Did he let them all escape? I watched him closely and noticed his jaw tick. He still didn't answer.

"You love them," I said, realizing it was true. He loved Tezya and Dovelyn. I had no idea how I knew that, I just did. "You don't really like your father at all. You're only doing his bidding to save them from the burden of it."

"Mind your tongue," he growled, and I was surprised to hear such venom in his voice. "Or I'll take it from your mouth. What you're saying is treason, and I won't stand to hear it."

I sank into my seat, not bothered by his threat, because for some reason, I knew it wasn't real. He wouldn't do that. And then an idea came to me.

"You do realize you can do more for the human you're in love with if you go against your father, right?"

"How do you know about Wells?" His eyes went wide in terror as he bent down to cup my chin, forcing me to meet his gaze. His emotions surged into me. Complete and utter fear mixed with disbelief flooded my bones. It was written all over his face.

I smiled. I had him. I hit his weak spot. I couldn't admit I knew Wells because it would confirm Tezya went to the camp, but if I could get Arcane to bring it up first... "I don't know anything about a *Wells*." I smiled sweetly as I enunciated his name. "I was only referring to the conversation you had with Dovelyn and Tezya when I was a prisoner before Tezya broke me out."

Arcane stilled, realizing his mistake as I continued. His grip was still around my jaw. "You told them both that day that you loved a mortal boy and said you were working with your father so you could be together—"

His grip on my jaw hardened to the point where it bruised. He cut me off with a growl. "Don't ever repeat that again."

"Then help me. If you don't want me running to your father and telling him all about the guy you love, do something for me."

"What do you want?" He sneered as he assessed me. "I can't stop this broadcast from happening so if that's what you're about to ask, don't bother. It's too late for that."

"Save my friend." Arcane leaned back slightly at my request. "Please. She's innocent in this. Just get her out of here, and I'll do anything you want."

"I can't help her. My father is obsessed with her. You don't understand what you're asking."

"Please," I added as I looked into his deep silver eyes. They were darker than Tezya's, not having the added pale blue mixed into it.

"No."

Heat rose in me as my anger boiled. "Then I'll tell him about Wells." I wouldn't. I wouldn't risk Savannah's brother. I knew he didn't deserve to be brought into this. But if I could convince Arcane I would, if I could get him to help me…

"My father won't believe you. I never visited the mortal territory like my brother had."

I needed him to believe me, but I was running out of ideas. If I didn't get Vallie out *now*, I was going to do whatever the King asked during the broadcast.

I felt sick. A lightheadedness took over me, and I became feverish. Arcane was still leaning over the chair, staring directly at me, his fingers digging into my chin. I glanced down. The needle that was draining my blood was burning my skin, and the collection bag was full, threatening to explode. The next second, the wires burst into flames, catching on the monitor system.

"Shit," he swore as he leapt off me, out of my line of fire. Without the Alluse chains I could feel the draw to my own powers. I called to the water in the room and doused the fire before the flames burned me.

"Your system is faulty," I commented as I wiggled out of the crisped, charred wires.

Arcane just looked at me, his eyes widened in shock. "Interesting," he murmured so softly I almost missed it.

I was about to ask him what was interesting when the King burst into the lab, confirming he was watching us. He seethed at the eldest prince. "What the fuck happened here?"

The silencing bubble disappeared the instant he arrived. "Faulty machinery," Arcane said.

The King glared at his son as he snapped his fingers. Soldiers rushed into the room and started to surround us. "All you had to do was get a sample of her blood. I told you I needed her unharmed for the broadcast." I looked down and realized my dress was ruined. "We're going to the confinement room," the King added when Arcane didn't respond. "It seems you require a *lesson*."

I swallowed, knowing full well what the King's lessons for his children entailed. Arcane straightened but still didn't say anything.

"Put her chains back on and bring her to the servants. She needs a new dress," the King ordered. "I'm going to teach my son what happens when he disappoints me."

I watched as Arcane followed his father, and as I stared at the back of his silver hair, any hope of saving Vallie before this broadcast went with him.

THIRTY-EIGHT
SCOTLIND

I STILL WASN'T TOLD what I was expected to do during the broadcast. Soldiers dragged me onto an outdoor stage after servants shoved me into a new dress. I was dripping in diamonds and jewels, and my makeup was done perfectly, hiding any dark circles under my eyes.

The new dress I was in was similar to the first—silk, little fabric, and barely covering. It was more cream than white, and I realized one part of the King's plan. Almost every inch of my skin was on full display. It was proof I was left untouched. I'd been fed. My body wasn't too thin for my frame anymore, and there wasn't a single scratch on me—except for the one on my palm. I didn't look like a prisoner at all. To anyone else, I looked healthy. The picture perfect image of a guest.

Dying is better than this. Vallie's last words kept replaying over and over in my head. Would it be a mercy for her if I didn't obey the Lux King? My throat ran dry. I knew the answer to that. She just watched her twin get maimed and murdered before her eyes. Her twin who she loved more than anyone else in the entire world. Her twin who she gave up her dreams of studying the mortal territory for so she didn't have to travel to Lux and be away from him. I was Vallie's best friend, but Miles was half of her, and now that part of her was dead.

And beyond having to relive the horror of his gruesome death over and over again, of having to stare at his headless body, she was tortured, raped, and abused. While I had been kept unharmed, Vallie wasn't. She was living through a nightmare. I knew the answer to my question. I knew what I needed to do. I shouldn't go through with whatever the King demanded. I should set her free, even if that meant destroying myself in the process.

I thought of Sie, of when I was captured by his father, and he had to make the decision to send me to the Lux King instead of killing me himself. Was this how he felt? Because I knew, *I knew*, I couldn't do it. I knew I would obey the King. I would recite every damning word he ordered of me. I would stand in silence. I would look pretty. Hell, I'd smile if he asked me to, if it meant keeping her alive. Because I couldn't live without Vallie.

The Lux King was standing in the center of the stage with Synder as more Tennebrisians started to trickle in. I had no idea what angle they were playing at or what they hoped to accomplish by doing this. It was the first time a broadcast was going out from both kingdoms, the first time they were making one together.

I was left mostly alone, standing off to the side. I assumed it was late in the afternoon, but the sun was still high in the sky, beating down against my back, as everyone worked to set up. Monitors were being stationed throughout the area, and massive cameras were positioned at every corner, exposing every inch of the stage.

The King noticed me. "You look *well*," he said as he approached.

I straightened my shoulders. "You forgot one minor detail," I sneered as I held my wrists up before him, my chains rattling against all the jewelry I was wearing. "It will be hard to pass me off as anything but a prisoner while I'm wearing these."

He smiled and it was all but serpentine. "Do you see that man over there?" he whispered into my ear as he leaned forward. I could feel his breath caress my bare shoulder. My eyes went in the direction he was pointing, and I nodded. "He's a Vir Alluse user. He'll be casting his ability on you the entire time your chains are off so you won't be able to use your abilities. And as far as those go…" He burned the metal off my wrists and ankles. I screamed in surprise as it melted. The King flicked his wrists and blew the remaining ash away on a gust of wind so the stage was left pristine. Then, he used his healing magic to erase the bruises where the shackles had been—the only indication I wasn't here by choice was now gone.

The moment I was free, I felt new chains clamp around my wrists, neck, stomach, and ankles. I gasped as I looked down at my body but saw nothing. "Your new *shackles* are created by my air ability. If I tighten everything just right, they work just as good as metal ones." An immense pressure pressed against all sides of me, everywhere his air touched, agony followed. He walked, and I fell forward, following him on an invisible tether. He stopped in the middle of the stage. "You will stand here for the duration of the broadcast. You will not show any expressions of malcontent or disagreement. You will follow along with everything being spoken today. You don't even have to say a word. All I need is for you to stand there and look pretty. If you do anything I don't agree with, your friend will be dead. Do you understand?"

I nodded.

"That's not enough. Say it. Say you understand because this broadcast is going out to *everyone*. All of Tennebris and Lux will be watching today, and I need to hear that you won't disobey me."

"I understand." I gritted my teeth.

"Good." He smiled. The back of his knuckles grazed my bare arms. "I crave obedience. There is something so satisfying about it, but I don't like leaving things to chance. I still can't comprehend how or why you can't be compelled, but there are other ways to force you to submit."

Arcane emerged with Athler on cue. Both of them had changed, and I couldn't help but notice the stiff way the eldest prince now walked. Arcane didn't speak as he made his way to stand by my side. The King's second crept up behind him. He looked so jarring under the sun. The only color to him were thin blue veins that wrapped around the length of his arms, and his dull, red hair that was so wispy, I could see through it.

"If you don't smile pretty enough or go along with what we want, Athler will adjust your pheromones."

"No—" I started, but my words were cut off. I couldn't speak. I looked down at my thigh, the top of it was exposed through the two running slits up my dress. Arcane was withdrawing a needle from my skin. I tried to form words, but nothing came out. I looked up at the King in horror.

"I believe my son told you about Brockwich's ability." He paused, allowing me time to answer. It was a sick joke. I couldn't speak. I couldn't even make a sound. "He can take away different senses." He paused again to smile briefly. "Arcane has been sampling his blood and studying his powers."

I glanced at Arcane, wondering what he told the King about the day I was captured. Was Arcane hiding things? Did the King still believe they had Brock? I knew Brock got out. Everyone did. They admitted it themselves. Arcane's expression was taut, masking whatever he was thinking as he met my stare.

"And my son found a way to single out and manipulate each of the senses. He altered them and created new abilities through serums. You won't be able to speak for a very long time."

Horror filled me. I wanted to scream, but I couldn't—

The King's grin widened. "Now, let's begin."

———

THE LUX KING SPOKE FIRST. Most of the cameras were positioned toward him, but I felt some focused on Arcane and me as we stood slightly off to the left of the stage.

There were thousands of Advenians in the audience now and even more watching through the screens. I was told the broadcast was mandated and airing for everyone to see. Was Tezya watching somewhere? Were they forcing Vallie to watch back in the King's room?

I could feel so many eyes on me from the audience below the stage.

Their judgment was palpable, wondering what I had to do with this mandate.

"Thank you all for setting time aside from your busy day to listen in today," the King began. I huffed, but no sound came out. It wasn't like anyone here had a choice. A wave of calmness washed through me like a shiver down my spine. It melted my resentment, my anger, and even though I knew it was Athler's abilities affecting me, I could do nothing to stop myself from standing up straighter, from looking longingly and hopeful at the King I hated as he continued. Internally I was shrieking. I was ripping through layers and layers of myself, trying to fight to my core, to gain control, but I had none. I was the perfect puppet.

Alec and Reagan stepped onto the stage next to Synder, waiting and listening patiently while the Lux King continued addressing the audience. Not a flicker of emotion showed on my face at the sight of them. Reagan wore a black, strapless gown that hugged her frame. Her blonde hair was twisted into an intricate bun, drawing attention to her bare shoulders. Her expression was serene until she saw me standing next to the eldest prince. I could feel her enmity radiating toward me before she quickly composed herself and looked back toward the crowd.

Alec winked as he took in my dress and kept staring. He didn't look away. His frame had broadened since the last time I saw him, and he looked more like the kings on the stage than the boy who tormented and compelled me back in Tennebris.

"I want to cut to the chase," the King's loud voice carried toward the audience. "There have been many rumors swirling around about the events that took place not too long ago, and I want to set everything straight. It is my duty as your king to be open and honest with you. Sie Noren has escaped the prison." He paused, letting the statement sink in. Loud gasps and murmuring took over the crowd, and I could only imagine what was happening beyond the screens from everyone watching at home.

The Lux King waited for the crowd to settle before he continued. "Because of this, we're implementing a curfew for your own protection. No one will be out on the streets past eight in the evening. Sie Noren is dangerous, and his escape should not be taken lightly. If you get the opportunity, we give you permission to kill him on the spot. Do not hesitate."

He paused, letting a flicker of grief show on his face. "It pains me to extend a similar statement toward my own children. Dovelyn and Tezya are both under the influence of Sie right now. As many of you are aware, Sie possesses total mind control. That means he can compel anyone from Lux *and* Tennebris, and it is believed he has my children under his coercion as we speak. It makes Sie one of the most dangerous males alive. He can compel anyone from both kingdoms. No one is safe. Even if you are an Alluse or air user of Lux, it is believed he is still using his abilities through Vir Alluse.

"If anyone comes into contact with Princess Dovelyn or Prince Tezya, you are not to engage. Do not believe anything either of them say as they are not in their right minds, and they'll do anything to convince you of Sie's lies and manipulation. We ask that if you see them, you bring them back to us alive. We're aware both the Prince and Princess of Lux are incredibly strong, and if you're a lower rank or do not feel like you are capable of going up against either of them, there will be armed soldiers stationed throughout both kingdoms at all times, monitoring the streets. The soldiers are there for *your* protection." He paused, making a show of acting upset. "I hope and pray my children return to me. I will personally see to their recovery if that happens, but the safety of our kingdoms must remain our top priority. So I urge by law, if anyone has any information on their whereabouts, come forward with it immediately. Anyone found harboring or withholding vital information will be found guilty and charged as an accomplice with the former Dark Prince."

He paused again, slowly surveying everyone in the audience. "Because of the dire situation, we're forced to mandate some new laws. On top of the curfew, you will obey the soldiers. Whatever they ask, you'll oblige. There will be routine home searches and randomized questioning you're not allowed to refuse. But please remember, this is only until we have Sie Noren's head. We're adding these new laws for *your* safety. I cannot stress enough how dangerous he is."

Synder stepped forward, his hair slicked back as he stood next to the Lux King. He looked like a slimy, less lethal version of him. Like a starved snake, who just shed its skin, and has just now realized it can leave its dead scales behind.

"Thank you, King Arcane." Synder nodded as he took over. "I know this has not been easy for either kingdom. For Tennebris, we have been manipulated by Sie Noren in so many ways it's appalling, but rest assured it ends now. And for Luxians, I know how saddening it is to know Sie has your prince and princess under his control. But I need to further shed some light on how dangerous Sie Noren is. You need to know the full extent of what he is capable of.

"There have been some rumors that Sie is good. That he is, in fact, fighting for you, and that is the most horrific and sickening lie he has spun. It pains me to tell you this, but King Arcane and I both found that it is imperative for you all to know the full extent of his plans and what he has already done. Sie Noren is attempting to revert back to the old ways of Allium before rank zeroes existed. He wants to eradicate all zeroes and possibly even ones and twos. He is trying to lure the weaker ranks out by falsifying claims that he will protect and fight for you, but please do not fall prey to his trap. He has and will kill any lesser rank the moment he can. It's what he's been doing this entire time. Many zeroes and low ranking citizens have been going missing as of late and it's because he is murdering them, and he won't stop until only the strong ranks are left."

I looked out at the crowd. There were so many shocked faces who were clinging to every word they were saying. Most were holding onto their loved ones while they listened. Some had tears in their eyes. Others were shaking. Most looked terrified and appalled.

The Lux King began talking again. "Sie has never liked the lower ranks. King Lunder suspected it the moment Sie was crowned prince. We didn't want to believe it, but when Scotlind Rumor was announced as his bride, a Tennebrisian rank zero—" All the cameras turned their attention in my direction, and I could feel the eyes of everyone scrutinizing me. My heart raced, but I couldn't show it. I forgot that no one knew I was really Luxian. The two kings before me never made it public knowledge. The world still believed I was a rank zero Tennebrisian, and I could do nothing to prove them wrong. I tried to call to my powers, to bring my water forth and prove I was from Lux, but the Alluse user was locking them down.

"Sie was disgusted by the notion of having a weaker wife. We have some testimonies and video proof to show you his maltreatment toward her."

Synder nodded toward Reagan who stepped forward, claiming damning words about Sie. I couldn't believe it. I couldn't believe this was happening, that they were making Sie out to be evil and painting this horrid picture of him. When Reagan was finished, Alec and Kole stepped forward next.

"I need to warn you, some of the footage we're about to show you is graphic." My heart fell into my gut at Synder's words. *Footage.* He said footage. Alec smirked at me, but my eyes were set on Kole as he handed a disc over to one of the camera men. The next moment my face flashed on the screen, but it was a still image, the video not yet playing.

Synder kept talking, "You see, Sie set Scotlind up. He framed her and made it look like she had an affair when, in fact, it was all orchestrated by him to get rid of her. And for that, Scotlind, we apologize." A wave of sorrow and sadness washed through my body. I tasted salty tears as my lips parted in shock. For a second, all I felt was hate toward Sie. Everything he'd ever done to me hit me like a tidal wave.

Then it lessened a fraction, and I knew it was Athler manipulating me. I tried again and again to find myself, to gain some control over my emotions, but everything felt amplified. I couldn't shake the sadness away or stop the tears from flowing. I felt the emotions as my own even as some deeper part of me was fighting against the Vir Alluse user.

"Sie has always treated Scotlind terribly. He never wanted her to be his wife. We realized the truth once we had a compulsion user go into

Scotlind's memories and what we found was maltreatment and abuse."

The video started playing. It was edited clips of Sie and me, confirming everything they were saying. The Lux King must have saved this from when I was in the monitor room, but they cut and clipped my memories. They only showed the bad, and I was shocked at how much footage they had.

The video started the moment I was selected as Sie's wife. The disgust on his face was evident as I walked up to the stage. How he refused to look at me, how he stormed away the moment it was done. Then it showed Sie flirting with other girls, and lots of them, and besides Reagan, no two were the same. It played clips from the night of our engagement banquet, to footage I'd never seen before. My chest tightened when the night Alec compelled me to play surrender came up next, of Sie watching me while Reagan and the brunette were kissing his neck and practically sitting on top of him. I was as mortified as the audience—everyone from both kingdoms—watched as I crawled on the floor, as I kissed his boot, as I sat on his lap, and he smirked down at me. His demeanor was relaxed and arrogant, even though I knew the truth. They didn't censor anything. They showed me stripping while Sie did nothing to stop it. Then our wedding night was next. The screen went black, but the sounds were all but damning. It played out the loud, resounding noises of Sie flipping the table over to him pounding against the door, and then the screen flashed to the aftermath the next day. Our room was completely destroyed. Next they aired clips of me limping. I couldn't walk right, but it wasn't from Sie. It was because Kole cut into my leg, but they got the timeline wrong. They made it look like my injuries were from sharing one wedding night with him. I no longer went to my lessons. I looked terrified, scared, and weak. They edited it in a way that looked like he forced himself on me. They showed every horrible thing Sie ever did when we were back in Tennebris. The video ended with our marriage being annulled. The last image was a still of me—proof that I'd been beaten, starved, and on the brink of death.

Everyone in the audience was staring at me. My tears had dried, and Athler didn't need to alter my emotions. Embarrassment and shock coursed through me. My heart was beating out of my chest, and I couldn't suppress my ragged breathing.

Alec stepped forward now. "Sie compelled me to treat his wife like that," he started. "He compelled me many times before that actually, all on rank zeroes. I didn't realize what was happening. I have compulsion myself, but Sie would compel me before the party started. He'd tell me word for word what he wanted me to do to Scotlind, and I..." he stopped speaking like he was fighting what he wanted to say next. "There are even more horrific things he made me do to her that were too graphic to show. I have trouble even thinking about them. He wanted her to suffer, but he didn't want to frame himself for it, so he used his total mind control on me." He shuddered as he turned toward me. "I have nightmares thinking about all the ways I harmed you. I'm so sorry, Scotlind."

I could barely stomach to listen as Alec spun his twisted version of what happened. But one thing was completely certain, after today, Sie would have a massive target on his back. He wouldn't be able to leave the camp without having to worry about every single Advenian from both kingdoms trying to kill him, and I got the sinking feeling he would have been better off left in the prison.

He was as good as dead.

THIRTY-NINE
TEZYA

WELLS CALLED us into his tent just as the broadcast started. He learned how to hack into all official airings years ago. It was deemed a necessary skill by Dravenburg. He wanted to keep up with what was happening in our world, especially during the times it'd take me months to visit. I'd never been more grateful for it than now.

I was out of breath, partly from sprinting to his tent, and partly because of *her*. My heart was racing, and I couldn't stop the ringing in my ears as all my senses solely honed in on Scotlind. She was alive. My eyes kept scanning every inch of her body, searching for any signs of abuse.

I was relieved to find her unharmed, but I didn't for a second believe that meant they weren't torturing her or making her life a living hell. The King was creative when it came to inflicting pain. He knew precisely what to do to hurt the most, while not making it obvious to anyone else. The worst scars he left were invisible.

Alive. Alive. Alive.

I kept repeating the word over and over again, not fully believing it. I couldn't stop staring at her. I had to force myself to actually pay attention and not lose myself at finally seeing her. I ground my teeth together, fighting against my rage over the whole damn situation—

about the King having her in the first place. He was fucking flaunting her. He knew I'd be watching. He knew I'd see her and come running straight into his waiting trap, begging for her back. And fuck, it was working.

I stood paralyzed, half staring at Scotlind, half zoning out what was happening. I was sick, beyond terrified that this was going to mess everything up, that this was what Dovelyn saw in her vision weeks ago.

Every day, I fought against Sie's compulsion. And every day, I got no closer to breaking it. But the trade was supposed to be tomorrow—providing this broadcast didn't fuck everything up.

We were all crammed into Wells' tent, our bodies shoulder to shoulder as we watched the King's lies unfold, leaving us in complete horror. But I barely noticed anyone else. The room was deathly quiet. Everyone was just as shocked about how they were manipulating what happened. They were damning Sie and digging his grave deeper and deeper.

I forced myself to tear my eyes off of Rumor for a split second and was surprised to find him standing directly next to me. His face showed a calm, lethal rage. He didn't do anything but stand there, his eyes fixed on the screen, stuck in pure shock just like I was.

The fucking compulsion user the King kept around came onto the stage, and I was about to lose it when they started playing a video of Sie and Scottie. My fists curled at my sides, and my jaw was clenched so tight I thought my teeth were going to crack. The King had the fucking audacity to put the damning footage on display for the whole fucking world to see. I knew how badly those memories affected her.

The original footage was bad enough, but they tampered with it, making it look worse. If I hadn't seen everything with my own eyes, if I hadn't been there the day the King hooked her up to the monitors, I would've believed what I was watching. But I saw everything she lived through that day, and I hadn't forgotten a single second of it. Everything she experienced was seared into my memory like it was my own.

Sie was a dick to her. He made mistakes. I'd been pissed at him ever since I watched her life unfold. But I knew deep down, even though everything he did was wrong, he acted with her best interest at heart. He was trying to protect her when he ignored her before their marriage, but now it just looked like he was repulsed by her.

They framed it to look like Sie was the reason Scotlind got a zero brand on both of her wrists. They manipulated the video and edited it in such a way to make it seem like he set the whole thing up just to hurt her.

Then, the night she was compelled started playing on the screen, and I was going to fucking lose it. It took everything in me not to break the screen as I watched her undress, as everyone had a full view of her almost naked body. The video kept playing, kept showing more damning footage.

When it finally ended, Alec started talking, further confirming everything we just watched on the screens. I barely heard it. All I could do was focus on her again. I couldn't shake the feeling that something was horribly wrong.

Synder stepped forward after Alec finished. "Sie went as far as murdering King Lunder," he said. "He went to our former king and begged for a new wife, but when Lunder denied the request, he orchestrated his death in retaliation. We have a testimony to prove it."

A healer stepped forward. I knew she was Luxian by her coral eyes. Her legs were shaking slightly beneath her dress as she was forced to walk to the middle of the stage. Sie went deathly still next to me. I heard his breathing hitch and figured he probably knew the girl.

"Moli's a healer who's been stationed in Tennebris. She has been working for the Noren household since Sie was ten and was transferred to tend to him at the castle when he was crowned the prince. Is that correct?" Synder asked her. Moli nodded, a brown spiral curl falling onto her face, covering three triangular moles across her cheek.

"Fuck." Sie's voice was rough, his anger was rivaling mine. It was the only sound that reverberated throughout the tent and it felt deafening.

"Yes," the healer admitted softly.

"And King Lunder's death was not an accident as the Tennebrisian Kingdom was formerly informed, am I correct?"

"Yes, that's correct." Her voice was soft, weak.

"Tell us how he died."

Moli's eyes were brimming with tears, and I could tell she was fighting against something. "Po-poison," she stuttered. "It was poison."

"And you were there when King Lunder's death was announced as an accident? When it was told to everyone that he died from choking?"

The girl's head nodded, the tears that were pooling in her eyes were now falling faster over her dark skin.

"And shortly after Sie was arrested, we found the same exact poison in his room when it was searched," Synder announced. "This healer worked with Sie to kill the king." Gasps coursed through the crowd watching the broadcast live. "Do you deny Sie had the poison in his room? That you were the one who supplied him with it?"

The healer said nothing.

"Fuck." Sie stepped closer to the screen, his fists clenching at his sides. "Fucking deny it, Mols." She still said nothing. It was almost as if she couldn't speak. She was sobbing, but I couldn't hear anything through the crowd's angst.

The Lux King stepped forward. "You are hereby charged with working alongside Sie Axel Noren and assisting him with the murder of the Tennebrisian former ruler, King Hennley Joel Lunder."

Before Moli could react, the Lux King engulfed her entire body in fluid, drowning her a couple feet above the stage for everyone to watch. Scottie took a step forward but halted, almost tripping. The movement was so subtle that most would have missed it, but my eyes were trained on her. She looked furious for the briefest moment before it was washed away, her emotions collected again into a calming mask, and I knew exactly what they were doing to her.

Athler.

Sie was screaming at the screen next to me, begging anyone to save the poor girl, even though no one could hear him. Peter rushed to his side, pulling him back a second before he would have destroyed Wells' monitor.

I saw Savannah out of the corner of my eye, watching him warily. They were killing the healer, drowning her for everyone to see. The girl's hands were clutching her throat, her face scrunched in agony as she struggled to breathe. The Lux King didn't retract his powers until she stilled within the bubble of water he created, until her eyes were unmoving and her mouth slackened. Only then did he wave his hand, and the water dissipated. The girl's body slammed onto the stage with a resounding crack, her leg twisted and snapped as it caught under her and her body collapsed into an odd angle.

Sie cursed, his rage palpable.

"We also have testimonies from multiple rank zero servants who grew up in the Noren household."

They brought Sie's family out in shackles.

"Fuck. Fuck. Fuck. FUCK!" Sie broke through Peter's hold and punched the table next to him.

They all had dark hair, the resemblance between them uncanny, and my gut twisted as I knew immediately who they were. I was staring at my real father—at Sie's father—and that meant... the boy with them was my half brother. He looked almost identical to Sie, just a younger version of him. His hands were clenched beneath chains, and his eyes widened as he took in the healer in a heap on the stage. He stilled, trying to reign in his anger. His wrist wasn't burned, which meant he was too young to be witnessing this...

Peter stilled, giving up on trying to hold Sie back. Even Dovelyn looked shocked as she stared at the screen.

Multiple servants stepped forward, each giving a similar testimony about Sie's childhood, about how he was brainwashed to believe he was better than everyone else. Every story was told in a calculated way, portraying Sie as a modeled version of his father. Each one hinted that there was no coming back from how he was raised. They recalled graphic, detailed memories of Sie being forced to compel them, how if he refused, his younger brother would suffer at their father's hands. The abuse the servants were telling was horrific and sensing Sie's radiating emotions, I didn't think any of it was fabricated.

When they finished, soldiers pushed Sie's father forward.

"Maverich Blanch Noren, you are charged with maltreatment of your servants. You are guilty of murder by default, for brainwashing your son to act upon the ideals you installed in him and for—"

Sie's screams blocked out of the rest of whatever Synder said. The Lux King stepped forward, casting the same water ability over Sie's father—*my* father's—head. They were killing him. Realization dawned on me that I'd never get to meet him. I kept looking at my half brother, praying he wasn't next. He was beaten. Bruises marred his skin, and he wasn't standing up straight. He was fighting against his chains, stepping in front of their mother...

Sie was pounding into the shield Dovelyn placed over the monitor screen, screaming at the broadcast as he was forced to watch his father drown. I knew the method was intentional. Every painstaking detail the King did was intentional. He chose to *drown* them, drown them because that's what happened to Scotlind. Because as much as that night at the warehouse haunted her, it was also a nightmare for Sie. He relived it whenever he couldn't sleep, watching the person he loved almost slip through his fingers. His emotions were the strongest, coming to my abilities like a moth to a flame. I didn't know why I honed in on them because it started to become my own personal hell. I'd lay awake at night wondering what was happening to her, wondering what new horrors would destroy her once I finally got her back. Maybe I figured it was my own form of punishment. I didn't deserve to sleep. I couldn't, not while the King still had her.

The Dark Prince's knuckles started to bleed. He didn't stop punching into Dovelyn's shield. He kept going, kept trying to make his fists connect with the monitor. I knew what he was feeling, what he was picturing—he wanted it to be the King's face instead of a screen.

When Sie's father was thrown on top of the healer's corpse, they started ending the broadcast. "For now, the rest of the Noren family will undergo evaluations to see if they are guilty in aiding Sie." The cameras flashed over Sie's mother and brother. They were holding hands through their chains, his brother still standing protectively in front of her. His eyes were hard, his breathing ragged.

Sie stopped punching Dovelyn's shield and dropped to his knees.

"Greyland." He whispered the name so softly, I wouldn't have heard it without my heightened senses.

The Lux King stepped forward, stepping over the two people he'd just killed. "Please, let this serve as a reminder to you all," he said as the crowd continued to flow out. "Do not trust anything Sie Noren or his accomplices say. They're working against everything we have fought to build. They're trying to eliminate and weed out the lower ranks, while we value all Advenian life, even the life of servants. You're not safe as long as Sie is still alive. But we will protect you. We will get through this hiccup in time together, and I promise you, I will not rest until we have Sie Noren's head on a spike."

I couldn't believe what was happening. No one could. The entire tent was speechless, the silence erie. Sie was on his knees, his head resting in his hands. Blood soaking into his dark hair through his knuckles. I hadn't seen someone break into a protective shield like that before.

"Umm, guys..." Wells said, breaking the silence. I turned to look at him as he stared wide-eyed at the computer he was using. His glasses were almost falling off his nose, but he didn't bother fixing them.

"What is it?" Dovelyn asked, sweat dripping from her brow.

"The broadcast is still airing, but look," he said as he pointed to something in his view. "They shut it off to Tennebris and Lux. This is only playing for us now."

"How's that possible?" Dovelyn asked at the same time Savannah said, "What does that mean?"

"It means the Lux King knows we're watching."

I looked back at the screen. Mass numbers of Luxian soldiers were escorting everyone out of their seats. They were all armed to the teeth and looked more ready to harm them than help them. The King was looking directly at the cameras, a coy smile peppering his lips.

"He's waiting until everyone leaves," I said, realizing what was happening. "He isn't finished yet." My eyes darted back to Scotlind. She was still standing there, but with Athler now preoccupied talking to Synder, her true emotions were slowly coming back. It looked like she was screaming, but she wasn't making a sound.

"I know you're listening, Sie," the Lux King said after everyone cleared out. "If you don't hand yourself over, your mother will be joining your father by the end of the week. And after that, your brother will be next, and I'll make certain his death takes the longest." He paused long enough to smile, before adding, "And although Greyland Noren is rather *enjoyable* to torture, I'm sure you don't want it to get to that."

Sie was fuming.

"And Tezya and Dovelyn. I know you're with the convict." As he was talking, Athler pushed Scottie closer to the King. "Don't think for one second you won't be punished when you return to me, which I know you both will. It's only a matter of time, but what I'll do in the interim as I wait for you…" His fingers wrapped around Scottie's bare thigh through one of the high slits of her gown. She flinched just as the connection went out.

"Bring it back," I yelled, my body instantly taking a step toward the screen. I needed to see her. My rage was boiling at everything the King had done, at how easily he killed them, at how the broadcast ended with more threats I knew he'd act on, and the King's hand around her, the fucking possessiveness he was showing.

If he touched her—

Distantly, I heard Wells typing frantically on his computer. "I can't," he said, stunned. "They wiped my connection." More frantic typing sounded before Wells swore. "Shit. That took me months to set up…"

Did the Lux King know the man he just killed was my mother's former lover? Did he know he was my father? That I was the chosen one the prophecy claimed, the child he always feared, always hunted? Because I could feel it now. I knew it in my bones. The fire inside me heated, boiling my core, calling me toward him, to kill him. I wanted to fucking murder him for everything he's ever done, for everything he still planned to do.

I turned to Sie. He was still on the ground. His chest rising and falling rapidly as he stared at the blank monitor in shock. I was about to say something to him when Dovelyn gasped, "Brock."

Everyone turned toward the opening of the tent. My friend was leaning heavily against the post holding up the structure. He was panting, his entire body drenched in sweat, and I realized he was shaking uncontrollably. It was his first time out of the healer's tent. Hell, I think it was his first time awake. I couldn't tell if he could see us, but I immediately knew what he was doing. I was wondering why I didn't lose my shit. Why neither of us did because they fucked Sie in that broadcast. But Brock was taking away some of our anger, not all of it, but tampering it down so we were calm enough to get through the worst of the airing.

My sister rushed to his side, attempting to wrap her arm around his waist, but he was too large. "Brock, stop. You're too weak." He looked down at Dovelyn, and the moment he did, his concentration broke, stopping him from using his ability. My emotions came flooding back to me in full force, feeling like I was hit with every brick in the world. My quiet rage before was nothing compared to this. An insatiable need for vengeance was blazing into my core, becoming my very essence.

I was about to fucking destroy everything in my path, but before I so much as blinked, Sie fucking lost it.

FORTY

SIE

I COULDN'T BREATHE. I couldn't see, couldn't think. I had to move, had to hit something, had to let my anger out some way, or I was going to combust. It was too much. This was too much. Everything was too fucking much.

Moli was dead.

My father was dead.

And now they had Greyland and my mother.

I couldn't let the King kill them too.

I heard people shouting my name. I felt hands on me, trying to calm me down, urging me to stop, but my rage was all consuming. Now that it was coming to the surface, nothing could tamper it down.

All I kept seeing was my brother chained and beaten.

A flash of lavender whipped before me, and I saw her eyes right before I slammed into the table. Savannah was standing directly in front of me, breathless and gasping for air. Her back was pressed against the edge of wood. My hands were gripping either side of her, caging her in. I was seconds away from either flipping the table, with her in tow, or splitting the wood right down the middle. I couldn't decide what would be more satisfying, probably both.

"What the fuck are you doing?" I panted, trying my damn best to collect myself. Red was still peppering my vision, and she just fucking stepped in front of me like it was nothing. I thought of all the times I'd blacked out before in a manic state, how I lost control of myself and didn't come back from it until it was too late. The damage I could've caused her body—I would've killed her. I didn't move, didn't trust myself to. I just stood there with my arms bracing either side of her, leaning into her space.

"You need to calm down." There was a vial in her hand, and I felt the tip of it pierce my skin. Her gaze was clear as she looked right into my eyes. "I don't want to do this, but I will if I have to." For emphasis, she pushed the needle half an inch further.

I blew out a breath, not realizing how close I was to her. A strand of her purple hair blew across her face, but she didn't move to swipe it away. Instead, she held my gaze, not looking away, not the slightest bit terrified that I could kill her in a split second.

"They're dead," I finally said, not knowing why I felt the need to say it out loud. Everyone saw what happened. Everyone in the tent was watching. "They're all going to die because of me."

My brother—my little brother who had nothing to do with this…

"I know," she said softly. "I'm sorry, Sie."

My knees bucked at her sincerity. She didn't know them. She didn't know Moli or my father, she barely even knew me, yet the way she was looking at me felt like she saw through to my soul. The broadcast was meant to make everyone hate me. It was meant to make everyone so deathly terrified of me that they'd kill me without a second thought.

Guilt washed over me, entwining with my anger and shock. I was hurting more from the loss of my friend—from losing Moli—than I was from my own flesh and blood.

I should have cared more.

There was a small part of me that was devastated I lost my father—a very small, minuscule part. It was a part I didn't want to access. I wasn't ready to face what it meant. He still raised me. He was a horrible fucking Advenian. What the servants said were all true. He used to force me to do terrible things to them and I would—I had to—or he'd take his aggression out on my brother and me.

But now, it didn't matter what I thought of him. He was dead.

The King just murdered him in front of everyone, but my fear for what he might still do to Greyland was outweighing almost any of the grief I had for my father.

Grey was what had me screaming. Grey was what had me needing to destroy everything.

I feared for what he could still take. He fucking destroyed me during the broadcast. I didn't want to be like my father. I hated him. But yet, as I watched the footage back, I couldn't deny that I was him.

I knew the video was edited, that not everything happened the way they portrayed it. But another part of me couldn't deny a lot of what I just watched was raw and real. Some of it actually happened. There were parts of it that didn't have to be manipulated to make me into a monster. *I was one.*

I couldn't stomach watching it. And seeing Scotlind standing on that stage, witnessing everything I'd done to her with a stoic fucking expression, broke me further. She was the one person I had wanted to convince I was good. And seeing her do nothing, watching her just stand idle as they ruined me, felt like she was holding the knife to my throat. I was clinging to the shreds of Scotlind's forgiveness, hoping I could still get her back, but now it was gone. I no longer wanted it.

I didn't know how to process everything I was feeling. The mix of emotions and confusion was too much. On a good day, I could barely get myself to believe I wasn't in another illusion. But this was real. *She* wouldn't be here if it wasn't real. Seeing Savannah confirmed it all happened.

Her eyebrows scrunched under me. Her gaze was assessing. She watched the damning broadcast, everyone had. I didn't know where that put me. Would everyone in the camp believe it? Would *she*? I had no fucking idea why it even mattered to me.

I was still caging her in, my forearms grazing hers. I could feel everyone in the tent watching us, waiting to see if they needed to intervene and protect the mortal from me. They should.

Savannah leaned forward on her tiptoes so we were eye level with one another, my body hunched over, leaning forward without meaning to. I was waiting for her to inject me, waiting for her to push the needle the rest of the way in and take me far away from this torture. I wanted to be gone. I wanted her to put me into oblivion.

But she withdrew the needle. My gaze snagged on her movements as she threw it onto the table out of reach, leaving herself vulnerable. Before I could tell her how stupid that was, that I could kill her if she didn't douse me, she pressed her body against mine and pulled me into a hug.

And I shattered.

———

"MY FATHER DOESN'T KNOW about Tezya," Dovelyn said later that night. "Whatever they're doing to Scotlind, I don't think she's told them anything vital."

Dravenburg still wasn't in the loop about the trade, and we wanted to keep it that way, so Tezya called a private meeting in his tent to go over everything.

I was relaxed enough to sit through it, but it was only due to taking some sort of concoction Savannah gave me to help calm my nerves. She told me her brother created it, a potion of some sort. I downed it in one gulp, not bothering to thank her for it, and then tried my best not to spit it out the next second. It was the most disgusting thing I had ever tasted—worse than the poison. I figured she had offered the same potion to Tezya, but I had no idea if he took it. We were both train wrecks, barely functioning. I tried not to think about how I literally cried into her arms after the broadcast. She mercifully didn't say anything about it, and now, I was purposely avoiding her gaze as we discussed what tomorrow would bring.

"What makes you think that?" Kallon asked.

"Because you don't know my father. All he thinks about is this prophecy. He's consumed by it. He doesn't want it to come true. It's the only thing I've ever known him to be afraid of. If he found out

Tezya is the one it's about, he would've turned everything on him, but instead he requested the both of us alive." The princess paused to look at me. "I don't think you fully realize what the King has done to you, Sie. You have a target on your back. If anyone sees you, they'll kill you without question. He wants to keep Scottie alive so he can use her enhancement and as leverage against Tezya to get him to obey. He still believes you two are the key to the prophecy. It's the main reason he targeted you. He wants you dead. He wants the rebellion squashed and the prophecy threat eliminated. And he wants a way to kill off the lower ranks while placing the blame on someone else. He managed to do all of that and handle you at the same time. That broadcast was—"

The princess didn't need to finish her sentence for me to know where she was going with it. The broadcast was my fucking damnation. It made me out to be the most twisted, vile Advenian alive. There was no way I could come back from how they portrayed me.

I had needed another two doses of Wells' calming potion when Dovelyn first explained the reason Scotlind was sent to Tennebris. The fact that she framed us—that she set everything up and was the reason we had to perform the blood bond at our wedding... I probably would have murdered her if I wasn't more pissed off at the Lux King.

"I'm going to turn myself in," I said into the silence.

"No, you aren't," Peter snapped immediately. "That's completely out of the question." He was probably the only person in this tent who cared.

"It's the most logical thing to do." I shrugged.

"Why do you say that?" Wells asked, his expression was calculated like he'd actually consider it if I gave a good enough reason.

"If he still believes Scottie and I are the key to the prophecy, it will give you guys the upper hand. He'll think he won, and in turn, he'll put his defenses down, giving a clear way for you to attack."

"That still doesn't answer why *you* want to hand yourself in. Last I checked, you didn't care about what we're doing here," the princess challenged.

I gritted my teeth. I wanted my fucking brother back unharmed, but I didn't feel the need to explain that to everyone. I'd hand myself over as long as he went free. I shrugged, trying to act like I didn't give a shit, even though I was dying on the inside. "You said it yourself, princess, I'm a dead man the moment I step out of this camp. Everyone is going to try to kill me, so why delay the inevitable?"

"He *will* kill you, though. He won't put you back into the prison knowing you escaped before. You'll be dead before you even see your family," Savannah said, shifting in her chair. I turned to look at her, surprised she knew what I really wanted. "That's why you want to turn yourself in, right? You want to save your mother and brother."

"Shit." Tezya blew out a breath. "Sie, listen to me. Handing yourself over won't give you what you want. And it won't stop him from killing them. It was a bluff. He wants you to do just that. And if you do, you'd be playing right into—"

"What do you expect me to do then? Nothing?"

"No," Tezya said, running his fingers through his hair. "We'll get your mother and... *brother* back." My eyes narrowed at how he choked over the word.

"If the King has them, they're already dead," Dovelyn said, this time her voice was a tad softer. "We need to be realistic about this."

Tezya ignored her, looking right at me. "After we make the trade in the morning, we'll question my brother for information. Arcane will know where the King is keeping them, and I'll help you get them back myself. He won't kill them right away."

"Whoa. Hold up. You still want to rescue Scotlind?" Savannah balked.

Tezya curled his fist, encompassing his scar with Scottie. I looked down at my own hand, at my own scar. I tried not to think about her, about how she just stood there and did nothing. My father was a dick to her. I didn't expect any sympathy from her when he died, but Moli saved her life. She helped Scottie and me after we came back from the warehouse. She risked her life to heal us, and she just watched her die with no emotion on her face.

Deep down, I knew she couldn't have done anything to stop it. It wouldn't have made a difference, but fuck, if it didn't hurt like hell to watch her just stand there and do nothing. She didn't even flinch as they *drowned* Moli. Drowned her—she knew what that felt like. Kole tried to do the same thing to her. I was forced to relive her drowning in that tub every night in my dreams.

As long as Greyland doesn't die. That's all that matters now. He can't be in my nightmares too. He just can't.

"Why wouldn't we make the trade, Sav?" Tezya fumed, his voice threatening.

"I'm just questioning if this girl is worth risking my brother's life. She did absolutely nothing during the broadcast if you hadn't noticed. And now, Sie's the most wanted person dead or alive."

I met her gaze, surprised by her balls to challenge the Fire Prince and surprised that someone else noticed the same thing I did about Scottie.

"She didn't have a choice. She's their prisoner—"

"Prisoner? Tezya, she wasn't chained. Absolutely nothing was forcing her to stand there. She looked like an untouched goddess. She wasn't injured or harmed or anything. She didn't even blink when—"

"Athler was controlling her," he interjected. "The King's second. He can alter and change someone's pheromones. He uses it to control people." Tezya turned from Savannah to face me. "It's what happened during the annual meeting with Tennebris. It's why Scottie and I were all over each other the day you came. We didn't have a choice. We couldn't help it. He was controlling us, just as he was controlling Scottie during the broadcast. It's why she wasn't reacting."

"Could have fooled me," Savannah contested as she slumped further into her seat, bringing her left leg up onto the chair and cradling it to her chest.

"It's true," Dovelyn said, "about Athler. He most likely was controlling her."

I hadn't thought of that. I knew the King had a second in command and that he was powerful, but he rarely made himself seen.

"I'm getting her back," Tezya said after a moment of silence. "If anyone wants to back out, that's fine, but tell me now. I won't force anyone to be there tomorrow. But I'm going."

Wells spoke first, "Count me in."

Savannah rolled her eyes but didn't protest.

"I'll help," Dovelyn said. "I think it's the most logical thing to do. If we can capture Arcane in the process, it'll stop my father from creating more serums and vapors that'd only be used against us. It's a strategic move besides your feelings for her."

"I want Scottie back too," Peter said. "I'm in."

Kallon and Rainer both nodded in agreement before Tezya turned to me. I was the only one who didn't give my answer.

"I promise I'll help you get the rest of your family back. I just... we just... we have to do this first." Tezya met my gaze. "I promise, Sie."

I wanted to save Scottie, despite my emotions with her being on that stage, despite the fact that she did nothing during that broadcast. It didn't matter if she couldn't control her feelings, it still fucking hurt to see. It still felt like she ripped my heart out of my chest and left me to bleed. But I didn't want her to suffer either. And if Tezya was willing to help me get my family back after this, I would help him. I'd agree to anything.

I shrugged, not having the energy to muster a response.

FORTY-ONE
SCOTLIND

I was screaming but no sounds were escaping my lips. No one could hear me. Arcane dragged me across the stage, and no matter how far away he led me from Moli and Sie's father, I couldn't stop seeing their dead bodies lying there.

Watching them drown brought back the same burning and constriction in my lungs from when Kole held me in the tub. I prayed Sie wasn't watching somewhere, but I knew he was—everyone was—Tezya too.

After everyone filed out of their seats below the stage, the Lux King kept us there, kept the camera's rolling... He addressed them directly, threatening to kill Sie's brother and mother if they didn't hand themselves over to him.

I couldn't breathe, and not being able to speak, not having anyone hear me, made it feel like I was drowning too. I was dying slowly from the pain I was causing everyone around me. I couldn't take any more deaths. I couldn't, and now the King had not only Vallie, but Sie's family too. All three of their lives were in danger, and it was all my fault.

Everything was my fault.

My chest was rising and falling a mile a minute, and my vision was starting to see spots from how frantically I was pulling in the air around me. Arcane was dragging me through an empty hallway, but I couldn't focus, couldn't breathe. I hadn't even realized we had made it back into the castle.

Arcane whirled on me, throwing my back against a wall. "You need to calm down." He eyed me for a moment, thinking something over. "I'd give you the antidote, but I don't trust you not to scream, and I need you to be quiet."

I looked around, not recognizing what part of the castle we were in. It was completely deserted, which meant it was nowhere near Vallie. I tried to speak over and over again. My mouth forming the words: "Where are you taking me? Where is Vallie? Please save Vallie. Vallie. Vallie. Vallie." But nothing left my lips.

Footsteps sounded behind Arcane, and I had no idea what was happening.

"You called for me?"

I knew that voice.

Arcane didn't move as he replied, his silver eyes wholly assessing me. I was still pressed against the wall, his tall frame blocking my view of who approached.

"Yes. I need your help."

FORTY-TWO
TEZYA

THIS WAS IT. I was going to get Rumor back. It was risky using Rainer's lightning, but it would be our best bet at breaking through Arcane's shield—our only chance. Both of my siblings were air users. But while Dovelyn was better at invisibility, Arcane thrived with protection shields. They were nearly impenetrable.

I knew Rainer's lightning would work. It'd get through Arcane's shield and keep him on the ground long enough for us to capture him. He wouldn't risk conjuring his wings if there was a threat of losing them. Both my siblings loved flying—it was something I used to be envious of as a child—and Rainer's lightning would fry my brother's wings down to the bone, making it so he'd never be able to use them again.

But his powers could just as easily harm *her*.

There were too many things that could go wrong. I hated the plan, but I didn't have a choice. With Sie's compulsion, I wasn't allowed to get Rumor myself and this was the only way everyone else had agreed to let me rescue her. This had to work.

Please don't let her get hurt.

I knew Arcane was going to bring someone with him. Even though we both agreed to come alone, he wasn't stupid enough to follow through without backup. He also knew me better to know I wouldn't either. And he wasn't going to waste his reserve on making them invisible—it would all be going into his shield to separate Rumor from me—so whoever he showed up with would be all he brought.

I just couldn't wrap my head around who it would be. It was throwing me off. He didn't have any friends in Lux, and I knew it was intentional. He didn't want to risk having a weakness for his father to exploit. He only ever hung out in our friend group. It was how he met Wells. He was the only person who managed to get under my brother's skin. Arcane's emotional walls were just as strong as the physical shields he created.

And since I had no idea who he was going to show up with today, I had no way of preparing. Arcane knew all my friends. He knew all their powers and what they were capable of. He knew Rainer would be the only one who could get past his shields. It was why he agreed to this. He didn't think I'd use him, not with Scottie involved, not when using his lightning was just as likely to harm her as it would save her. I still couldn't believe we were using him...

Rainer spent the entire week training, trying to strike a target without creating a rippling effect, but it wasn't enough.

This will work. Rumor won't get hurt.

I couldn't stand still.

Maybe love blinded you, caused you to act without thinking properly. Rationality was gone. Maybe that was exactly what I was doing now, except I was putting my friends in the crossfire and setting Scottie up for worse.

"If you keep fidgeting, you're going to blow our cover," Wells whispered. "And that's coming from someone who compulsively can't stop moving."

"He'll be here soon," my sister's voice sounded from my right even though I couldn't see her.

Dovelyn, Sie, and Rainer were all nearby, hidden under her invisibility. But while Sie and Rainer were behind us, waiting in the cover of the clearing for his signal to teleport, Dovelyn was standing out in the open.

Wells and I were the only ones who weren't under my sister's invisibility.

Peter, Savannah, and Kallon were further back in the woods where Kal had a portal set up.

We were all ready, but I couldn't calm down. My pulse was quickening. I kept opening and closing my fist, feeling my scar against my palm. I forced myself to take a breath and glance around. A dense fog was rolling down the hill, obstructing a lot of my view. Savannah was right to suggest the spot. The clearing in front of us was open enough that Arcane couldn't have hidden anyone without coming here prior and knowing he was at the broadcast made me confident he didn't have time for it. The forest behind us was just far enough for Sie's teleportation to reach and thick enough that my brother wouldn't sense Kallon's portal through the wind. If needed, we could lose Arcane in the foliage. And with the dense fog lingering, he wouldn't be able to track us by flying. It was as perfect as we could get it.

But retreating wasn't an option, not for me. I wasn't leaving without her. We never settled on something without a plan B or a means to escape if things went to shit. It was just a plan if things went wrong...

Things wouldn't go wrong. I wasn't leaving without her.

Don't get hurt. Please Pylemo, let us pull this off.

"Do you think he'll come alone?" Sie asked, his voice coming from the tree cover.

I shook my head, knowing he was able to see me just fine even if I couldn't see him.

Dovelyn answered. "He'll have to fly here. Scotlind's tiny, but my brother isn't known for his strength. He won't be able to carry more than two people."

"And he's going to make it on time?" I could hear the doubt in Sie's voice.

"Yes," I answered, the conversation distracting me enough to calm my nerves. At least it was something to focus on. "He uses the wind below and behind him. It helps keep him up and allows him to fly faster at the same time."

We were silent after that. The wait for Arcane to show up with Scottie felt like an eternity.

Then, when I couldn't wait any longer, my heart stopped. Arcane landed before me, his large slate-feathered wings flapped the swirling mist around him. But he was alone. Scotlind wasn't with him.

Arcane eyed me before his gaze traveled longingly to Wells. I sent a silent prayer to Pylemo that he'd be too distracted to pick up on Rainer and Sie. He let his gaze linger there for a moment too long before he spoke, "I don't know why you bother to hide, sister. The wind is telling me you're here."

Dovelyn materialized with a sly grin, but she kept Rainer and Sie hidden in their spots. "I've missed you, Ar."

I didn't give him time to respond. "Where is she?"

Arcane folded his arms across his chest at the same time he dispersed his feathery wings. "You would have to think I'm a fool to bring her right away."

I half growled. "What do you mean?" I could feel her. The only times I couldn't was when she was wearing Alluse, and I was certain she wasn't wearing any now. I didn't say anything to anyone, but I felt our connection growing stronger and stronger the closer Arcane got. It was adding to my paranoia because all I was getting from her was terror and confusion. I thought it'd give her peace of mind to feel me, but instead it was doing the opposite. The further she got from Lux, the worse her feelings became, and I couldn't understand why.

I kept trying to telepathically reach out to her. I swore it was working, but I never got a response back, like something was stopping her from speaking, even in her mind, and that had my gut wrenching.

"I mean, I know you, Tez, and I know Wells. As tempting as your offer was, and," he looked at Wells again, "even though I know you love the Luxian city, I didn't for a second believe you'd willingly come back with me."

"Then why did you come?" Dovelyn asked.

"Call it curiosity." He shrugged. "I wanted to see what you're playing at, besides getting Scotlind back, why did you reach out to me? And," he added a tad softer, "I wanted to see him."

"You know, you could have come back to the camp at any time," Wells said, his tone icy. "I don't understand why you stay with him."

Hearing Wells speak for the first time had Arcane looking up. I knew their last fight was about the same thing. It was the fight that ended their relationship and caused Arcane to avoid the camp for the past three years. They fought over the Lux King, about not agreeing on what next steps to take, and what was right. Wells never spoke about it. He acted like their relationship never happened afterward. I only knew the entirety of their conversation because of my heightened hearing.

"You know why I'm doing this."

Wells took a step forward. "Ar, if there's any good left in you, please just stop working for him and come back to the camp."

The smoke and fog swirled around my brother. "Any good left in me, Wells? Do you even know why I'm doing this? Do you know what I'm sacrificing by staying in Lux?" Arcane shifted, and I noticed his wince, how he stood rigid with his back straight. Athler must have brought him down to the dungeons recently. But for what? Arcane rarely acted out. He was the angel child between the three of us and tried to avoid displeasing the King for the sole purpose of avoiding the punishments that followed.

"Can't you see I'm doing this for *us*? They," Arcane gestured toward Dovelyn and me, "want to someday go back to Allium or to whatever new planet they can claim as their own. They want to leave Earth. Do you know what that means, Wells? It means I would never get to see you again. Our kind needs to stay here, we can't leave. But in order for that to happen, for us to be together, we need to make our presence known. We need to—"

"I know what your father is planning," Wells interrupted. "He plans to overthrow my kind. It doesn't matter how much I love you, nothing is worth *that*. Nothing is worth the lives of millions of humans." Tears slid down Wells' chestnut cheeks at the same time Dovelyn shifted from foot to foot. This conversation felt too personal to be having while everyone listened. I could feel the palpitating emotions coursing through my brother and Wells. They both had pent-up feelings that had been building and building over the last three years.

"You would risk millions of innocent lives just to stay here with me?" Wells' tears turned to anger. "For what, Arcane? A blink in your own very, very long lifespan? You know you'll outlive me. I'll be gone. Dead. And you and your father would have destroyed our Earth in the process. You would have him control and enslave humans, murdering anyone who wouldn't submit? This would carry on for centuries, maybe forever, long after I'd be six feet under."

"Stop—"

"If you still think I'd want to be with you after all of that, after what you plan to do to my kind, you're a fool, and you already lost me."

"I said STOP!" Arcane screamed. The fog rose and shot into the sky as the wind swirled around us. I planted my feet, so I wouldn't fall over. I couldn't risk him sensing Rainer. Dovelyn only stayed put using her own abilities. But Wells staggered. His hands flew up to his face to prevent his glasses from falling off. When the mist cleared, Arcane collected himself. "I wouldn't let it get that far. I'm going to stop him before he tries to enslave the humans. I'm on your side."

"No, you aren't," Wells snapped, and I'd never seen him so riled, so firm about something. "If you're still working for your father, you aren't on our side."

"I'm not working for him. It's just easier, for now, to pretend I am. I have a plan. A plan that will allow both of our kinds to live in peace. We wouldn't have to flee. We wouldn't have to search for another planet. We could live together and be happy."

"Humans would never be okay with this," Well said. "They won't react well to meeting your kind. They fear the unknown. A war would be inevitable. I don't want to spend my life having to fight against you. And it's safer for your kind too... The humans have weapons that could kill an Advenian, regardless of your prolonged lifespan. We possess machinery that could take you all out in seconds, and anyone they don't kill, they'd study and research. You'd be no better than one of the vials in our lab. Either side winning would be detrimental to the other. Can't you see that?"

"It won't be like that. I'm working on something, on a serum. It'll allow for mass compulsion. When we come out to the public, I'd use the serum alongside a compulsion user. I'd get them to listen, to stand down. I'd make them realize we can live together, that we mean no harm. They'd welcome us with open arms. We could have real peace."

I shifted. I knew Arcane was working on a mass compulsion serum by the King's orders. I just had no idea why he had agreed to it. Not that Arcane could refuse orders, but he could have told him it wasn't possible. When the King asked about it at one of our mandatory family dinners, Arcane perked up. I had no idea why at the time, but now it made sense. It was all for Wells, even if it was delusional thinking.

Wells looked just as taken aback. "At what cost?" he breathed. "You think it's better to take away our own ability to think? That's called brainwashing. Tell me, Ar, would you use compulsion on me too?" Arcane flinched at Wells' words. "I don't agree with you, so you'd have to compel me. According to you, there's no harm in that, right?"

When Arcane didn't answer, Wells continued, "Don't lie to me. You know your father won't be happy with ruling alongside the humans. Besides the fact that he regards us as nothing, it's not just about him wanting more land for his people. He wants control. He wants to rule, and he wants power. He wants to overthrow everything."

"I know," Arcane said desperately, his voice rising. "We'd stop him before it gets to that point."

"Why did you let us go, Arcane?" Dovelyn asked, drawing the conversation away before Wells could respond. "Because you did let us go. Athler had Scotlind when you came after us, and then you just stopped."

Arcane sighed, forcing his gaze away from Wells to look at our sister. "Dove, if Father ever gets his hands on you or Tez again, you'll wish you were dead. I don't want that for either of you. You don't understand how livid he was when he realized what you both had done. He already has Athler preparing for your return—" He didn't need to finish for Dove and I to understand what he meant. If we were captured, we'd both be locked up for decades, maybe longer, and he wouldn't go easy on our punishment.

"Where's Scottie?" I asked again, not able to take it any longer. I knew she was nearby, I could feel it, feel her, and I had to see her. "Is she hurt?" The question was burning on my tongue. I couldn't make out her emotions.

"She's fine. More mentally abused than physically."

"If you hurt her—" I started to growl, not believing his words, but he cut me off.

"I didn't. I said she's fine, and I mean it. I only sampled her blood. Beyond some daily needle pokes, she's unharmed." He paused for a moment, seeming to question if he wanted to tell me more.

"Spit it out."

He sighed. "I know you're bonded and so does the King, but it's better if he doesn't understand to what extent."

"What do you mean by that?" I snapped.

"You don't know?" He looked genuinely shocked, then a smirk formed on his lips. "Interesting. I don't think she knows either."

"Where the fuck is she, Arcane?"

My brother met my gaze for a long moment before he arched his back, calling back his wings. "I'm here to make peace, Tez. If you try anything, you'll regret it." Then he lifted off the ground and flew away.

I waited, holding my breath, until he came back.

Please don't let her get hurt.

Three minutes passed and then—

Arcane flew overhead. I saw him carrying two people beneath his wings, but I couldn't make out who the second person was yet. I didn't care. All I could focus on was her as he landed on the grassy patch before us.

She was here, right in front of me. It felt like my soul was being put back together, like I could finally breathe for the first time in weeks. It took everything in me not to rush to her. Until I saw *him*, saw who was holding her. Everything clicked. Her fear, her emotions...

"I thought you agreed to come alone." My voice was a lethal calm, but inside I was fuming. I knew he wouldn't. I knew my brother would have backup, but seeing *who* he brought woke something feral in me. Maybe it was the bond. Maybe it was from being away from her for too long or that I knew she was hurting and I couldn't do anything about it.

"I know my limits, Tez. In battle, you beat me every time. I needed a way to talk to you, and a means of getting out of here too."

"And you think *he'd* stop me?" I glared at the compulsion user who was holding Scottie hostage. She was in the same gown from the broadcast. I remembered every single detail of her from the screen. I kept replaying the image over and over again in my mind. Her blue eyes met mine as I scanned her from head to toe, checking for any injuries even though Arcane told me she was okay.

She was shaking, her chest moving rapidly sucking in air, but I couldn't hear her breathe. I couldn't hear anything.

"No, I don't think he'd stop you. I brought Kole here because if you do anything stupid, he has orders you won't like, things he'll do to Scotlind." On command, his grip tightened around her. Her mouth flew open like she was screaming, but no sounds were coming out.

"What did you do to her?" It took every ounce of self control I had to not go running toward her and rip her from his hands. But if I wanted to get her back, I had to let Rainer and Sie do the work. I just had to keep distracting him, keep him talking. It was the only reason I let Wells and Arcane go so long in the beginning. Rainer had to get ready, and by how much I was fuming, I didn't even register that it started—

Kole and Arcane revolted, lightning twisted under their skin, leaving cauterizing marks. Scottie's agony hit me a second later, the electricity consuming her. I could feel it inside me, running through my own veins, shocking me to my core, and even though I was left unharmed, her pain was destroying me.

The next second, Scottie was gone. I felt Rainer's power fade as she was ripped from Kole, leaving him writhing in agony alone on the snow-covered grass.

It would be harder with Kole here, but the thought of holding him captive at the end of this had me fleeing into action. The lingering effects of Rainer's power felt more electric now, jolting me awake. Sie reappeared without Dove's invisibility, and I sighed in relief as he nodded. The single gesture let me know she was safe. The first half of our plan worked. The half that mattered most to me, and I was really going to enjoy the second half.

Sie tossed me a set of Alluse shackles, the metal felt wrong in my hands, and I thanked the Goddess Kallon thought of bringing an extra pair. Sie lunged toward my brother, while I went for Kole, neither of us saying a word. Rainer kept his ability focused on both of them, leaving them defenseless on the ground.

I knew it was taxing for him. Rainer struggled with maintaining his power, and the fact that this entire clearing wasn't crashing with lightning was enough to tell me he'd been practicing and getting better at his control. Rainer didn't stop until Sie and I had Arcane and Kole locked under the Alluse chains.

We both grinned madly at each other, probably looking half-crazed as Rainer's powers started to subside.

And it might have been the first genuine smile I ever shared with the Dark Prince.

FORTY-THREE
SCOTLIND

Panic filled me. I was back in Brighta, but the camp was different than before. It looked smaller, and I realized they had moved locations because of me. Peter was holding me down as Kallon left to go back through the portal. I didn't know what was happening, why Arcane brought me here, or the reason he involved Kole.

Excruciating pain was still rippling through my body. It was a paralyzing shock that rendered me useless. I couldn't move. I could barely think. All I could focus on was the lightning flickering through me. It was agony and death wrapped in one long torturous, unending moment. Like time stilled, and I was left dying over and over again with no one to save me.

Peter was speaking, but I couldn't hear him. He was holding me on the ground, his arms wrapped around me, and I realized I was shaking. My entire body was covered in pale streaks that looked like white lightning had stained and burned onto my skin. All I could do was stare and watch and feel—

Black and purple mist reappeared, and Kallon portaled Savannah and Wells through. She was gone before I could ask her what happened. Savannah was staring at me, but I couldn't process her emotion, my mind was still whirling in pain.

Kallon was back, dumping Dovelyn and Rainer onto the grass next to us. The latter avoided looking at me. I thought I heard a mumbled *"I'm sorry"* before the portal opened again and Sie and Arcane came through.

Sie had the same white streaks from where he had grabbed me, but his were only on his hands and forearms. Arcane was covered head to toe, and I knew Kole would be too. Did I look that bad? The eldest prince didn't fight back against his chains. He was static, unable to hold himself up. Foam was pouring from his mouth and tears were streaming down his face, matching my own.

Then Kole and Tezya appeared, and everything stopped. Kole was dumped on the grass next to Arcane, but Tezya's eyes found mine, and I lost it. I pushed up from Peter's grip with everything I had, my legs still shaking, as we both met each other halfway. I leapt into his arms, not caring about who was watching as his hand cupped the back of my head and he held me to him.

"I'm so sorry. I'm so fucking sorry, Rumor." He kept repeating over and over again, and it wasn't until I tried to respond that I remembered I still couldn't speak. Tezya stilled as he noticed. My feet hit the soft grass as he gently set me back down, but his arms never left mine, and I was grateful because I would have fallen over without it. I wrapped my hands around my throat, trying to get the words out to explain, but they didn't come.

"What the fuck did you do to her?" Tezya snarled at his brother.

"The antidote... is... in my front pocket," Arcane grunted against the pain, his body still convulsing as he laid on the ground. The metal in his shackles flared and ricocheted with lightning as it gathered around his hands where the scarring was the worst.

Sie stepped forward, grabbing Arcane by his shirt, avoiding the damning chains, and pulled a green vial out of his pocket. He turned it over, inspecting it. "Where's the needle?"

Savannah grabbed the tube from his hands, frowning at it. "It's not an injection. She needs to drink it."

"What did you do to her?" Tezya repeated, his voice menacing as his hand instinctively gripped me tighter.

"I found a way to... manipulate Brock's ability while combining it with another," Arcane ground out as he repositioned himself on the ground. The lightning was slowly receding. I glanced at Kole right as he recovered too. "I found a way to zero in on particular senses he can steal..." There was a long pause as Arcane wiggled his fingers beneath the shackles and found his breath again. "I have vials for each one..." He paused again. "I was able to mix it with a paralytic agent that attacks the vocal cords. The King ordered me to take away her ability to speak before the broadcast." Sie's head snapped up as Arcane kept talking. "If she doesn't drink that," he gestured toward the bottle, "it'll probably be another twelve hours before she can use her voice. If she takes it... give her ten minutes."

Tezya strode forward, his one hand still resting on my waist to hold me up, as he grabbed the tube from Savannah with his other. Then he gently turned toward me. "Here."

I drank from the vial, gagging on the contents that bubbled and clogged my throat. Green liquid spilled from my lips. The feeling of my esophagus starting to expand was the only reason I didn't hurl everything back up.

"I'm taking her to the healer's tent," Tezya announced as I was still choking on the fluid. "I need to make sure she's not injured. Lock them up."

Everything hit me at once. I was free. I was out, away from the Lux King and Athler. But my friend wasn't.

I tried over and over again to form the word I needed to say. I knew Arcane said it would take ten minutes before I could speak, but I willed it sooner, praying my enhancement could somehow work to coincide with the serum, but it was no use.

Tezya saw me struggling. "It's okay, Rumor, don't try to force it. You'll be able to speak soon. You're safe now."

I shook my head, tears streaming down my face, frustrated that he wasn't understanding. It wasn't me I was worried about. I couldn't lose another friend. I couldn't lose Vallie the same way I lost Miles. I tried over and over again to form the words as everyone just stared at me. I willed our telepathy to work, attempting to speak with Tezya mind to mind, but even the voice inside my head was dead.

"She's trying to say... *Vallie*," Kole hissed through the lightning still pulsating around his shackles, but he was sitting up now, his head bowed between his knees. "Your father has Vallie."

FORTY-FOUR
SIE

"ALL I NEED IS your invisibility to keep Vallie hidden once I get to her. I'll do everything else myself," Peter half sneered at Dovelyn later that day. We were in the princess's tent—who somehow managed to snag a private one, while everyone else was still stuck sharing.

"And Kallon," the princess deadpanned, staring at her fingernails. "You would need her to portal you in and out of Lux." Her cool arrogance seemed to have returned now that she had everything she wanted. Brock was awake and recovering, only Scottie paid the price for it.

The princess blew our cover saving the brute and didn't seem to have any remorse or regrets about it. I half wondered if she visited Scottie after she returned this morning… If Tezya would even let her. I didn't know how he could stand looking at his sister. She was selfish as hell and was too caught up in her own world to even care about anyone else. I had no idea why Peter was even bothering with her. She wasn't going to help.

Peter gritted his teeth. "Fine. All I need is you and Kallon, but neither of you have to lift a finger."

The princess scoffed. "The last time we went to Lux we were all almost caught. You have Scotlind back, isn't that enough?"

Peter flexed his fingers and drew out a long breath. It took a lot to piss him off, but I could tell the princess was testing his patience. "If Brock was still there, you'd find it worth it. She's innocent and being tortured by your father, isn't that enough?"

"It's suicide. You can't rescue her alone," was all Dovelyn responded with.

"It was impossible when we rescued *him* from the prison," Peter spat at her and half-heartedly gestured toward me, "but we still did it, and we succeeded. All I'm asking is for us to try."

"That's different. No one was expecting a break-in inside the prison when we got Sie. We succeeded because the guards were relaxed and there were no tip-offs. Vallie is being kept in my father's personal chambers. Do you have any idea how heavily guarded they are?"

Peter bristled, hating her words, hating the reminder of all the different kinds of torments the King was inflicting on her. She was beautiful and kind from the little bit of time I'd spent with her when we toured LakeWood, but she wasn't worth the life of my friend. It was the only thing I agreed with Dovelyn on—that rescuing her alone, right now, was suicide. I knew it wasn't a fair call, but I cared about Peter more than I did her. I was worried if he went into Lux, he wouldn't come back.

But a deeper, more selfish part of me was terrified it'd ruin my chances of getting Greyland back. I needed to wait. I had no leads on my brother or mother.

When we questioned Arcane, he refused to talk. But when we went to Kole next, he told us everything we wanted to know—just not about my family. He answered question after question about Vallie, and the moment he admitted she was chained in the King's room, Peter lost it. I swore he was going to destroy the entire tent when Kole told us that, he was not only torturing her during the day, but forcing her into his bed at night.

I was surprised Kole gave up the information willingly. I had spent hours torturing him for information when he attacked Scotlind back in Tennebris, and he never budged no matter what I did to him. But now, it was too easy. He was telling us everything we wanted to know without hesitation.

Something was off.

"He could be leading you right into a trap," I added because it was the truth. We caught them both easily, and I couldn't shake the feeling that maybe it was on purpose. Did they let themselves get caught to set us up? Kole's rare moment of candor seemed too convenient to be true. And thanks to the Sui Alluse they both ingested right before coming here, I couldn't compel the answers out of them... *yet*.

And I planned to do just that. I needed to ask every question imaginable so I could find Greyland.

"We should wait until the Alluse leaves his system," I said. "I can compel Kole once it does and make sure his story adds up. You just need to wait a little bit longer, Peter."

"No. That's out of the question. I'm getting her *tonight*."

"Then you're being stupid," I hissed. "You should wait until we can all go in together. If I can wait to get my mother and Grey back, so can you. I know it sucks, doing nothing fucking sucks, but if you go now, you risk getting caught, and then no one will be able to save her."

"It's different," Peter snapped. "The Lux King isn't forcing your mother and brother to sleep with him, is he?" I'd never seen Peter so pissed off, so short fused. I blew out a breath, trying not to let it get to me. I knew he was just as terrified as I was.

"I don't know what he's doing to my little brother, and it's fucking killing me. I can't sleep. I can't do anything but worry about him. I want to get him back just as badly as you want to get Vallie, but I realize that means a tiny bit of fucking patience. We need to make sure Kole and Arcane aren't leading us into a fucking trap."

"Kole's not lying," Peter said sternly, "but even if he was, I don't care. I'm going after her, Sie. The longer we wait, the worse it's going to get for *all* of them."

Savannah blew out a breath. She had been listening quietly on the princess's bed, taking everything in. She cocked her head to the side.

"What's up with the male testosterone in this camp going ape-shit over the girls they like?"

Peter whipped his head to glare at her, but he didn't deny it. He couldn't. He never admitted to liking Vallie, and I didn't think he ever would, but I'd never seen him so distraught, so vexed and helpless about something. He was always the calm, optimistic one between the two of us, always finding the positive in every situation, but this was consuming him. It was breaking him.

"I'll do it," Kallon said, surprising the group. "I'll go with you to get her back *now* instead of waiting." I would have thought that she was only agreeing to the plan after what happened with Scottie. Tezya still hadn't forgiven her for portaling him back to the camp without her. Maybe she thought if she returned with her best friend he'd finally let it go. But the Fire Prince wasn't here. He dragged Scottie away the moment the trade was made, forcing her into the healer's tent, even though she was kicking and soundlessly screaming. I didn't envy him right now for trying to tame her.

"Why?" I asked Kallon, scanning her face, never really noticing the fine details in it before. All I ever saw when I looked at her was her multi-colored, ever-changing hair. But today, the colored side was a dark gray, almost matching her normal shade of black. And for some unforeseen reason, I thought of Savannah's eyes. The shading wasn't right. Savannah's were lighter with opal specks infused into them whereas Kallon's hair right now seemed more devoid of color and life. But it was the first time I studied her face without her hair drawing all my attention, and I was surprised that she was beautiful.

Her lips pursed as she met my gaze. "Because Scotlind is my friend, and if this Vallie girl is important to her, then she's important to me too. I know what the King is capable of, and if what the compulsion user said was true, the poor thing has been through enough. She doesn't deserve to be dragged into this mess, and no one deserves what's being done to her."

I exhaled, trying my best to remain calm. If they went for Vallie now, it meant my chances of getting Greyland were slim. They had half-ass information from Kole about Vallie—if they wanted to believe it—but I had nothing. I would be going in blind. I had no idea where he was keeping my family. "This is all pending on Kole telling the truth," I said, trying to talk them out of it.

"He is," Dovelyn said, and I could have punched her. "At least about the part regarding the castle. There is a secret entrance into the King's rooms. If they are occupied with Scotlind and my brother's disappearances, it will give us a chance to break her free without them noticing. *Potentially.*"

"We have to act now while they're looking for Arcane," Peter pleaded. "The King won't be occupied with Vallie, but if we wait too long, he will be. We'll lose our only chance."

"Fine," Dovelyn said, half rolling her eyes, and I was surprised as hell she was agreeing, that she'd do anything to aid anyone else but herself, especially when it didn't benefit her at all. But then again, I was told the princess went into the prison to rescue me. Maybe she only acted like she didn't give a shit about anyone or anything...

Dovelyn looked toward Kallon. "You have a portal set up there, right?"

Fuck. There was no talking them out of it. I zoned out their conversation, leaving them to sort through the logistics of their ill-thought out plan, to focus on the rest of the camp. If they were breaking into Lux, I had to find a way to work my family's rescue into it, even if the idea of not waiting to compel Kole was completely fucking idiotic.

My skin lit up in golden spirals as I focused my telepathy throughout the camp, trying to use it as a locator to find Tezya. It was hard to do with the sheer mass of Advenians that lived here, but I'd been training with my abilities, getting more comfortable using them freely now that my body was poison-free.

I was learning how to use my telepathy at greater distances while simultaneously shifting from mind to mind. Peter helped me. He'd sneak off to different areas of the camp, and I'd try to find him. It was hard as hell and usually gave me a grueling headache afterward.

Before, I'd only ever used telepathy on someone in the same room as me. But I was getting better at it and finding it easier and easier the more I practiced.

Our abilities were a muscle, and I never realized how much I relied on physical fighting over my powers. How much I never worked my abilities and just took them at face value. But being here gave me nothing better to do, so I trained both.

Tezya, luckily, was easier to find in the camp. I assumed it had something to do with us being related, but I didn't want to dwell on what that meant. When I finally found him, still in the healer's tent, I opened my mind to his, using my powers. *I need you here, right now.*

Where are you? His voice sounded a moment later. I was surprised by the lack of questioning.

Dovelyn's tent. They're going after Vallie tonight.

"It's not ideal," Kallon said. Their conversation coming back to me the moment I disconnected from Tezya's mind. "It's about a half mile from the entrance of the tunnel, but if we leave now while it's still dark, we should have enough cover."

"Good." Dovelyn nodded. "You'll only have thirty minutes once we get in."

I was about to stall them when Scotlind cut me off. She pushed open the flap of the tent and halted in front of Peter. She'd changed out of the flimsy gown she was in, and I was thankful, not wanting another reminder of the damn broadcast and what it cost me.

Her words were winded as she fought to catch her breath. "You're going after her," she wheezed.

Peter nodded.

I glared at Tezya who came up behind her. *You fucking told her?* I seethed into his mind.

I didn't tell her anything, he snapped back, *Teleport her away.*

"Don't you dare," Scotlind said out loud, turning to glare at Tezya. "I'm coming with you—"

Tezya's voice cut inside my head, his eyes honed on me, and I knew why he was asking me to do it. Scottie wasn't healed. Her entire body was a well of scars, and he didn't want her to come. *Teleport her now, Sie.*

I called to my powers, grabbing onto Scotlind before she could react, then teleported her to the opposite side of the camp. I vaguely heard her yelling at me as I dropped her onto a grassy field.

I'm sorry, Tezya's voice sounded the second I teleported back, and I realized I was still connected to his mind.

I scanned the empty tent—well almost empty tent. Only Savannah was standing between me and the fading purple and black mist.

"Fuck," I cursed.

"They left," Savannah announced, like I wasn't aware of the obvious. I kept swearing and shouting every curse word imaginable as I started pacing up and down the small-ass tent like if I walked through the evaporating portal mist, it might still work.

Scottie flew into the tent sometime later, panting and drenched in sweat. I didn't have time to worry about the fact that she probably shouldn't have been running. Right now, I didn't care, all I could think about was that my little brother was in Lux, and I was stuck here.

When Tezya promised me he'd help me get my family back, I thought he meant I'd go with him, not stay behind and play fucking babysitter.

I thought I was teleporting Scotlind across the camp to leave *her* behind, not so he could leave me behind too.

Scottie was screaming, at me or in general, I wasn't paying attention long enough to care.

"Scotlind, shut the fuck up," I cursed.

"I'm sorry I'm bothering *you,*" she hissed back. "You're the one who teleported us away."

I started rubbing my temples.

"That's my best friend," she was still screaming. "I can't just sit back and do nothing. And now Tezya went—"

"It's my best friend too," I snapped, and she paused. My anger fumed out as I looked into her sapphire eyes, and I realized I had never yelled at her before, had never even raised my voice. "Peter left to go rescue her. He's out there too. Him, my mother, and my little brother... they're all I have left. Everyone I fucking love is in Lux right now."

She didn't respond, just stared at me. Out of the corner of my eye, I saw lavender hair flash by the tent flaps, and I knew Savannah was leaving.

I let out a heavy sigh. "Just come sit with me," I said once we were alone. I walked over to the spot on the bed Savannah vacated and slumped down onto it. "If they don't come back in a little bit, I'll figure out a way to teleport us there."

I'd teleport us there now, but they'd portal back before I even made it halfway across the mortal territory. It'd take us multiple days to get there, and by that time, we'd be too late.

Scotlind still hadn't moved. "And who's to say you won't leave me behind again?"

"I won't," I ground out, pissed that I even listened to the Fire Prince. "Just sit down," I resigned, softening my voice, as I gestured to a spot on the bed. I wasn't mad at her, and I knew she had just as much reason to be pissed at me as she did Tezya.

Her eyes widened as she took in my arms. White scars ran up both my arms, stopping at my biceps from when I pulled her off of Kole. Rainer's lightning hurt like hell, and I only got the remnants of its effects from touching Scotlind. I wondered how she felt about being covered in them. But judging from the way she was assessing my own arms, I got the sinking feeling she hadn't looked at herself yet. Guilt washed through me because I knew some of her scars were because of me, because I failed to protect her when I should have been there for her. Again.

She hesitated. "Sie, I..."

"Yeah, I know, you love him. I'm not asking you to cuddle with me and magically choose me instead."

"Then what are you asking?"

Hell if I knew, but I was fucking terrified for Peter and Greyland, and I needed a distraction.

And more than that, I was furious I was left behind.

I needed to be the one to save Grey, and if I lost the opportunity because of this... If Tezya didn't come back with my brother, I'd kill him, and then Scotlind would never look me in the eyes again.

I just wanted to forget everything that happened for a damn moment. Pretend that our relationship wasn't completely gone. Pretend that I didn't just watch Moli and my father get murdered like it was nothing more than a fucking spectacle. Pretend that the most sadistic Advenian alive wasn't threatening my little brother's life right now. Pretend that I was okay and not hanging on by fraying threads because I had no fucking idea what to do next.

I knew I couldn't realistically teleport us to Lux. It was across the fucking ocean, and I didn't have the slightest idea which direction to go from the camp. Dravenburg refused to give the new location to us, and no one was allowed to leave to figure out where we were shielded.

Not that any of us listened to his rules when we got Scotlind back this morning, but he didn't know that. We all agreed to keep Kole and Arcane hidden from Dravenburg, and so far, he hadn't noticed Scotlind was back or the extra surveillance we'd been making around Tezya's tent. Wells and Rainer turned it into a makeshift cage prior to the trade, and we all agreed to cycle through shifts watching them. Currently Rainer was stuck on guard duty.

I sighed. There was nothing I could do but wait. So instead I said, "Just sit down. I already have a headache from your screaming, and I don't feel like getting whiplash from your pacing."

Her lips turned up into what I would almost call a smile, but then it was gone. "You promise to teleport us if they don't come back?"

"Yes," I said to her, and I meant it, even though it'd be near impossible. Peter, Greyland, and my mother were all I had left, and all three of them were in Lux.

FORTY-FIVE
SCOTLIND

I SAT on the furthest side of the cot from Sie, curling my legs under me, as I stared at the spot the portal had been. The mist was long gone, but my worry wasn't lessening. I felt like I was breaking all over again.

This morning, Tezya had taken me to see the healer—well dragged me to one—but besides the electricity from Rainer, I was fine. The healers told Tezya they couldn't do anything to heal my body from the lightning, not without potentially causing more damage. They could monitor my vitals and make sure my heart wasn't having an aftershock reaction, but that was it.

"Do it," Tezya spat. "Run every test you have. Make sure she's okay."

I tried not to look down at my hands to see the pale white scars that now ran all over me. It was worse around my stomach and my right forearm where Kole was holding me when Rainer attacked. I only knew because I felt the jagged lines raise and could tell how thick they were.

But I was going to be fine. The scars on my skin were nothing compared to what Vallie was going through.

In all the time I was kept by the King, the only harm done to me were small needle pricks across my arms from where Arcane collected my blood, but the King healed every last one before the broadcast. He even healed the bruises I had over my wrists and ankles where the chains had dug into me. I didn't have a scratch to show from my time in Lux.

They never touched me, only causing harm to Vallie in my place. I prayed to Pylemo over and over again that she was okay. I prayed that the King or Athler hadn't turned their attention toward her yet. And now, I was praying for everyone else too. What if none of them come back?

I kept repeating the King's words—how he had plans for when Tezya came back to Lux. I couldn't stop making up different scenarios of the punishment room, couldn't stop seeing that knife and all of Tezya's blood—

I was pissed at him for leaving me behind, but more than that, I was terrified.

My ability to speak came back shortly after I made it to the healer's tent. But I barely spoke. When Tezya and I connected our hands, everything that happened came flooding into us.

I relived everything he went through while I was gone. I could feel his suffering, his frustration, his rage. Tears broke my eyes as I saw him fight, as I saw him scavenge the hut looking for me. He never meant to leave me in Lux. I wasn't mad at the decision Kallon had made, even though I could feel Tezya still was.

Then, I saw Sie compelling him, forcing him to not go after me alone. He tried. The first week I was gone, it was all he did. He tried over and over again to leave the camp and fight through Sie's compulsion. It broke me, watching how much it destroyed him.

I knew Tezya saw everything I went through too. He knew what happened to Miles, what was currently happening to Vallie. I was thankful I didn't have to voice it. Tezya's rage heightened when he saw the King take me to the lower level of the dungeons. From his reaction, I knew it was his first time seeing it. He had no idea the King was keeping Advenians chained down there.

They still have Vallie, I said into his mind, still unable to speak even though I had my voice back.

Tezya pulled me into his chest, his hand meeting the back of my head as he stroked my hair rhythmically. *I'll fix it,* he said back to me. *I promise, I'll fix everything.*

I didn't have the energy to figure out what he meant or if they were just empty words of comfort. Everything felt heavy, and I was tired. I wanted to, just for a moment, soak in the moment with him. I wanted to feel safe and protected in his arms and block out everything else.

Sie shifted on the bed, bringing me back to the present and drifted my thoughts away from this morning. Tezya was gone. He was in Lux now. When he told me earlier that he would fix everything, I didn't realize he was going to go into Lux without me. Tears pulled in my eyes as anxiety worked me so thoroughly. I'd never felt so scared in my life.

"It's okay," Sie said, but it seemed like he was reassuring himself more than me. "They'll all be okay."

FORTY-SIX
TEZYA

I only slightly regretted not bringing Scotlind and Sie with us. Besides the fact that they would both be pissed at me for it, we could have used his telepathy and her enhancement.

I hadn't planned on leaving Sie behind, but I knew if we waited, Scotlind would have used her enhancement and attached herself to Kallon's portal again. I couldn't risk it.

She wasn't fully recovered and was still suffering the effects of Rainer's ability. Even if she didn't realize it or refused to believe it, it would take her a couple of days to rebuild her reserves after what happened. There was a reason electric users were so rare and sought after, their power was terrifying.

I knew Sie hadn't seen a healer. His hands were marred up to his elbows, leaving white scars from where he pulled Scottie off of Kole. But where Sie's were confined, Scotlind had scars all over her body. It broke me every time I looked at her. Over and over again, I attempted to convince myself it was necessary, that it was the only option we had to get her back, but I couldn't shake the feeling that I caused her more pain, one that would forever leave a mark on her. I was the one who came up with the logistics on how to overthrow Arcane's shield. I was the one who told Rainer to use his ability.

I swore to myself I would never be the cause of another scar on her body. When I first saw her in the dungeons in Lux, she was enveloped in them. The only scar I was okay with leaving on her was our blood bond. But now, I covered her in thousands of new scars. The lightning went over her zero brands, scattered onto her face, covered her forearms where she tallied twenty-seven cuts to mark how long she'd been in the Luxian dungeons. They were everywhere.

Except for her stomach and right forearm, it was flush to her skin, almost translucent compared to the thick, jagged lines that marred Kole and Arcane. The more transduction to Rainer's power, the more watered down it became. Not that it mattered. She was still hurt, still covered in them. I felt her pain the moment Rainer hit Kole with it.

I hurt her.

She'd been through so much already, too much for one person. A living kind of inferno took over my rage once I saw the full extent of what happened to her. I wanted to murder the King after he dragged her down to the lower levels of the dungeons. The fact that it even existed without any of us knowing was beyond me. I knew powerful people in Lux were disappearing, I just hadn't realized to what point until I saw her memories.

I couldn't stop wondering if my mom knew about it. Her blood magic was used to barricade the door. I knew it was hers immediately. It had her powers written all over it. The only other way to keep people out was to create protective shields, and I knew he wouldn't. Anything that involved him sacrificing a piece of his magic was out of the question. But my mother's abilities could be manipulated to keep anyone out who didn't have the right blood she infused into it. It was why no one knew about it until now. How he was able to keep something like this hidden for so long.

I shook my head, trying to push my white hair out of my eyes so I could see better. I hadn't had the time to cut it in Brighta and the top was getting too long to be functional. I ran my fingers through the longer pieces, slicking it back with sweat to keep it out of my face. I had to get Rumor out of my mind while I was in Lux. I had to focus or this wouldn't work. I made a lot of promises I intended to keep and something of my own I needed to do.

Kallon's portal transported the four of us to the outskirts of the castle. Dovelyn already had her invisibility over us by the time we landed. Our biggest concern would be if Athler approached us, because even with our concealment, he'd be able to detect our pheromones. Dovelyn couldn't maintain a shield and keep us invisible at the same time. It would use too much of her reserves.

"We need to make sure we all stay within Dovelyn's radius," I said. "But in order to do everything we need to do, we need to act fast and split up."

"And what is *everything* you plan on doing?" Dovelyn whispered-yelled.

"Peter, you're going to rescue Vallie and Sie's family. Dove will go with you since she'll need to add them all under her invisibility. You'll use the hidden entrance to get in. Dovelyn knows the way, but be quick. Kallon and I are going to the lab and then the dungeons. Meet us there after you get everyone. We're going to portal out at the furthest point down."

"Be careful, Tezya, even though Arcane's not here, the King still has access to his serums," Dovelyn said. I could tell she wanted to question me, but we didn't have time. She knew me too well, knew that when I had my mind set to something I wasn't going to stop until it was done.

"We will," I said. "If Sie's family isn't in the room with Vallie, check the dungeons on your way down. We're not leaving until we have *all* of them. We're bringing everyone back with us."

I assumed Dovelyn nodded and left because she didn't respond. I knew she'd be able to keep Kallon and me invisible as we made our way down the dungeons, but there was going to be a time when her powers stopped. I just prayed we were far enough along for this plan to work by the time that happened.

———

"WHAT ARE YOU PLANNING, Tez? If Peter and Dovelyn are getting Vallie and Sie's family, what are *we* doing?" Kallon asked me.

I couldn't see her, but we were holding hands so we wouldn't get separated as we snuck our way toward my brother's lab. To our luck, it was located next to the dungeons since his father often had him work on the prisoners there and didn't want them escorted through the halls of the castle. "Why are we risking going into the lab and then the dungeons?"

"We're going to recruit a lot more Advenians to our side."

"With criminals?"

I could tell Kal was arching a thin brow under her bangs without actually seeing her.

"Just trust me, and be quiet. Someone is coming."

We didn't talk after that. It took us a while to make our way to Arcane's lab and even longer to find what I needed once we got there. I finally pocketed the vial of blood I came for and was about to leave and head to the dungeons when I saw vials on vials all labeled *Vapor Alluse.*

I felt Kallon come up next to me, knowing exactly why I hesitated, she whispered, "If you do this, Tezya, the King will be notified. We will have seconds to leave Lux."

Anger rose in me. It felt wrong letting this go and not destroying the vapor with my flames. I wanted to blow it up and completely destroy Ar's lab. I knew anything I left intact would be used against us, but Kallon was right.

If I wanted to free the Advenians locked below, I'd need more time. They were suffering and probably had been for centuries. I owed them this.

We also needed time in case I had to find Sie's family. I promised him I'd get them. I sent a prayer to Pylemo that they were with Vallie and Dove and Peter already had them. But if they weren't, I'd need to search the dungeons, maybe even the entire castle until I found them. I swallowed hard, trying not to think about how Greyland was also my brother.

If we succeeded, the King wouldn't be able to make any more Alluse. He'd only have what was in this lab and eventually it'd run out. But looking at all the vials, it could last a long fucking time. So many Advenians from our camp could die.

I grunted in frustration, making up my mind. I had to leave it. I had to make sure I had time to pull off what I wanted. If I could do that, I'd be saving thousands of lives, while also dwindling the King's powers. He'd have to scramble to find more Advenians' blood to consume. And I knew the ones locked below were some of the strongest of our kind. They deserved to live. They deserved freedom.

I patted the vial in my pocket and prayed I was making the right choice. Kallon grabbed my hand again as we silently made our way through the dungeons. We walked further and further down, careful to avoid any of the puddles scattered along the path. As soon as we couldn't go any further and reached the dead end, I turned to Kallon.

"Make a portal here."

She released my hand and immediately got to work. This would drain all of her reserves, and I didn't know if she'd be able to manage it.

I took one deep breath, knowing that once I crossed this point, Dove's invisibility would vanish. She wasn't aware of this part of the castle, so she wouldn't be able to cast it over me once I went in. I pulled out the vial from my pocket and added a drop of the blood labeled King Arcane Xandrin the Seventh onto the wall. I didn't wait for it to fully open before I made my way down the pristine alabaster steps.

"Prince Tezya," a healer stammered, alarm crossing his face. I knew I couldn't compel them, there was no way the King didn't feed them Alluse, and it wasn't worth the risk of them telling him I had compulsion, so I tried another tactic.

"Give me the keys for the cells or I'll burn you alive." I called to my powers, pulling fire into both of my hands.

The healer's eyes widened in fear. I knew my reputation from being the commander of the Luxian army preceded me. Anyone who didn't know me believed the rumors of how vicious I was in battle, of showing no mercy before I burned everything in my wake to ash, and sometimes the reputation came in handy.

The healer took a tentative step back, raising his arms slightly in defense. The Advenians chained to the wall closest to me stirred and it took everything in me not to give them my attention, because once I did, I'd lose it. I was disgusted something like this existed, that the King was using them for vessels of power and not treating them as people. The healers weren't any better. They were gifted with the power to *help*, but instead they were using their abilities to suck the life from the people chained, only keeping them breathing enough to function for the King's liking. And the King threatened to bring Rumor here—

When he didn't answer right away, I sent my flames out toward him and burned the skin at his feet.

He screeched, his voice rippled in agony, "I will, I will." I kept my flames superficial, burning his flesh off while still keeping the bones. "I'll get you the keys," he half sobbed, half wailed.

"Now," I ordered, sending my fire up to his knees. I was half a second away from fully burning his feet off. I didn't feel bad, he'd just be able to heal himself later, and he deserved the pain for how he was treating the thousands of Advenians in this room. The healing ability was always believed to be a gift from the twelve lesser Goddesses and any healer working down here was a disgrace to their names.

The healer reached into his robes and pulled out a set of three keys dangling on a large circular loop. I stalked toward him once I cleared the stairs and ripped them out of his hands.

I heard a few chained Advenians chuckle and risked tilting my head to the side to see some of them grinning. My stomach turned as I wondered how long they'd been trapped down here. It was probably the first time they smiled in centuries, and I planned on changing that today.

"Get out of my sight." I gestured toward the long stretch of lined cells. I figured there might be another exit at the end, but I didn't want him running past Kallon. He half ran, half dragged his burned feet as he limped away from me.

I didn't wait as I called to the fire in my veins and focused everything I could on the shackles holding the Advenians to the walls. The other healers in the room panicked as they saw the room bursting in flames and started running in the opposite direction. I pushed my fire into every chain that existed down here, burning them off. It took all of my control not to hit the flesh that met with each shackle.

Once I burned through them, most of the Advenians collapsed to the ground, unable to keep themselves upright without the metal holding them in place. But there was a surprising number still standing.

Kallon came flooding down the stairs, her body materializing as Dovelyn's invisibility vanished the moment she crossed the threshold. She gasped as she looked around the room, her yellow eyes widening in shock. "What is this place?"

I quickly glanced at her, not bothering to answer her question. We didn't have the luxury of time. "Did you create the portal?"

She nodded before answering, her eyes kept scanning the prisoners. "Yes, it's just up the stairs. Peter and Dove are already through and back at the camp. They got Vallie and Sie's brother out."

"Not his mother?"

She shook her head. "She didn't make it. There were guards in the room with them..." Her voice trailed off as I nodded.

I couldn't think about it right now. If she was dead, there was nothing I could do about it. "Can you portal all these people out?"

"I'll manage." I knew she couldn't. There were too many to get out at once, but we both knew what her answer really meant. We'd keep going until we failed. Her pale skin was already ashen. She'd used too much of her reserves to create the portal, but Kal always pushed herself to her breaking point, not stopping until her body gave out. We'd done this numerous times before, bringing the rebels into Brighta. The only difference now was she didn't have a day or two to rest after creating the portal. We had minutes before this place would be flooded with soldiers.

"Good," I said, then turned toward the Advenians that were still managing to stand. They were hesitant, unsure what to do as they stared at me in shock. "Grab as many as you can around you," I called out as I stepped up to the bars and unlocked the cell door to my left. "Up the stairs, there's a portal to get you all somewhere safe."

Relief, confusion, and agony were flooding into my senses. I tried to block out my ability, but the amount of people around me suffering was too much. Everyone immediately fled into action. The strongest in the group, who probably weren't held captive as long, were helping hold the weaker ones. Some half carrying the ones who collapsed up the stairs. Others were being dragged.

I made my way toward the right side of the cells, unlocking the other half of the room. I saw in Scottie's memories how many people were trapped down here, but to see it in person was something else. Not everyone was going to make it to the portal. Some of us were going to be left behind.

Kallon seemed to know it too. Her weak smile was proof of that. "Tezya, I'll get as many out as I can, but Peter and Dove tripped an alarm. The King knows we're here. We have minutes, if that." She scanned the room, biting her lip. "I know I can't convince you to leave right now, but come up after a minute, and let me portal you back before—"

I nodded. I knew the odds when I decided to do this.

Everyone was moving too slowly, they were all too weak. I didn't think about it, about what would happen when the King got here. I knew he wouldn't kill me. He still didn't know I was Tennebrisian... I shoved the punishment room far out of my mind. I'd deal with whatever happened to me later.

For now, I returned Scotlind's best friend to her, and if Kallon and I succeeded, we'd be getting rid of the Lux King's powers in the process. After today, he wouldn't be able to drink the blood of the most powerful Advenians the Golden City had. He'd be scrambling. He'd lose all his powers. This could win them the war.

My mind was made up the moment I saw what had happened to Scotlind. I didn't want this place to exist for a second longer, and I planned on doing everything it took to give Brighta the advantage. "Get as many of them through the portal as you can. I'm going to help the ones who can't walk."

Kallon immediately fled into action, shouting orders at the Advenians who were closest to her as they all rushed toward the stairs. I let my eyes linger for a moment, taking in my friend as she portaled the first group through.

Soldiers flooded into the dungeons not long after. It confirmed there were multiple exits and entrances as they came at us from all angles. I didn't think about who I was fighting as I cleared a path to the stairs. I didn't want to recognize any of the men I fought with over the past century. Some hesitated. Others came at me willingly, some with savage smiles.

I did my best not to kill anyone, to only make a clear path for the Advenians trying to run out of this hell hole, but as time stretched and more and more soldiers flooded in, it became harder to do.

It was a mix of blood, metal, and magic. Swords, daggers, and axes were cutting into the Advenians that were too weak and too drained to fight back, and when the soldiers were too far to strike with a physical blow, they used their elemental powers to make the kill. Air was pushing everyone back down the stairs. Ground magic was wrapping around legs and yanking people backwards. Water was drowning, fire was burning. Death and gore were everywhere.

I could only use a little bit of my own abilities. If I used too much I'd risk burning everyone down in the dungeons if an air user decided to redirect the path, killing innocents along with the soldiers.

Some of the chained Advenians stood with me, mixing whatever they could from their powers with mine, but it wasn't enough.

Kallon returned. Our eyes locked for a moment before she saw the bloodlust below and vanished through the portal again. I didn't have time to think about how it might have been the last time I saw her.

Slowly, more Advenians were leaving the dungeons. Either leaving through Kallon's portal, if she returned, or they were just making it to the upper levels of the dungeons, I couldn't tell. I half hoped she went back to the camp for her own safety.

A knife sliced into my forearm as another dagger was thrown at my head. The Advenian next to me threw an air shield up, protecting me at the last second. The dagger bounced off the shield he'd erected and clattered to the ground.

I barely mumbled a quick thanks as a wave of water rushed past me, forcing me to take a step back.

"We need to make it up the stairs, Prince Tezya," he shouted over the chaos. I looked around, following the flow of water. It was thigh-deep and winding through the cells like rapids of a river, only it was following an invisible bank. I watched as it wiped out soldier after soldier—the current so strong, it knocked over everyone in its path.

Then I heard people shouting my name. Kallon's voice came through above the screams, but my heart stopped when I heard *her*.

Scotlind came. She was here, in Lux, and so was Sie. The Dark Prince was teleporting the remaining Advenians up toward the open portal, so they bypassed the stairs altogether, and Scotlind had one hand stretched toward Kallon and was working to enhance her portal. But her other hand... *holy shit*. She was using both of her powers at once. She was pulling the water from the room, shaping and redirecting it herself.

She was the reason the stairs were clear, the reason Sie was able to get so many out, the reason I didn't have a Luxian attacking me right now.

I stared at her in fucking awe, at the arduously amount of power she was putting into both of her abilities. I gave myself ten seconds to soak her in, ten seconds to be mesmerized by how fucking serene she was, before I took in the rest of the room.

Dovelyn was back creating an air shield, pushing the few soldiers back that were out of reach from Scotlind and preventing them from getting too close, and what I assumed was Peter in a bear form, was ripping into any soldiers who managed to get by. Lavender hair flashed in my vision, and Savannah was standing close to the portal, throwing star-like daggers at the soldiers, never missing her mark.

I looked toward the older Advenian who had stayed by my side. His auburn hair and coral eyes were something I'd never forget. A smile crept over my face because for the first time I truly believed that together we could win. I raced up the stairs as Sie teleported the coral-eyed Advenian next to me through the portal.

I grabbed Scotlind by the waist, pulling her into me, right as I saw silver eyes.

The Lux King made it into the dungeons.

FORTY-SEVEN
SCOTLIND

My vision was consumed by purple and black mist as we landed onto the grass in Brighta. I was two seconds away from falling flat on my face before strong arms caught me.

Tezya turned me around, pulling me into a deep hug. "Scotlind Rumor, you are so fucking amazing, but don't ever do that again," he breathed into my hair.

"What? Go head first into Lux like you just did? *You* left *me*."

He reeled back, and I couldn't tell if he was more impressed or worried. My body was shaking slightly from using too much of my power at once, but it also felt exhilarating.

"I couldn't lose you again," he said, his voice lowering. "I only just got you back. If you were caught—"

"I wasn't," I cut him off. "I'm right here. We're all here." I hugged him back, still furious he left me behind, but I'd yell at him later. Right now, I was just relieved he was okay.

Rainer came sprinting toward us. "What the heck guys? I didn't even know you were going somewhere. Wells just relieved me from my shift, and I only found out because of the boat load of people who showed up. Stop going on missions without me."

Kallon smirked at him. "Don't pretend you would have wanted to go. You're terrified of fighting."

"Just because I *hate* fighting—not terrified of it—ya dick, doesn't mean I wouldn't have helped." He looked taken aback. His normally large smile was gone as he crossed his arms over his chest. My gaze drifted toward his hands, toward the lightning he wielded. Tezya noticed and pulled me tighter against him.

"I'm just joking, Rain. We didn't tell you because we didn't have time. It was kind of a last minute thing." Kallon pulled Rainer in for a hug, which he willingly accepted, but his head kept scanning the camp, taking in the sheer amount of people we brought back with us.

"Where did you get all these people, and why are they all so bloody and naked?"

"It's a long story," Tezya said as he reluctantly pulled out of my grip. "For now, we need to get them all medically evaluated. They'll need clothes, food, water, and rest. Sav, can you send word to the healer's tent so they can prepare?"

"Yup." Her lavender hair was whipping behind her as she sprinted away.

I scanned the group around us, looking for red hair. "Where is she?" I asked, my voice breathless.

"She's already with the healers. Peter took her there as soon as they came back. She's okay," Kallon said, knowing exactly who I was asking about. "She's with Sie's brother."

"Okay," I said more to myself than anyone else. I was so relieved. She was safe. Everyone was safe. I couldn't believe it. We actually did it. And more than that, Tezya freed everyone from the dungeons.

Tezya leaned down to whisper to me, "You can go and visit her. I'll come find you after."

I shook my head. "No. I'll help."

Tezya eyed me for a moment, then nodded. "Okay. We'll get everyone settled, and then we'll go see her together."

———

IT TOOK us three hours to settle everyone. Then another thirty minutes of explaining everything to a pissed off Dravenburg. Many of the Advenians were too weak to even walk to the healer's tent. We had to prioritize who to tend to first. Anyone who was able to walk waited with warm blankets and food. We didn't have enough room at the camp anymore, and when Tezya told me he'd have to discuss things further with Dravenburg about food and shelter, I wondered how much we had before we would run out. I didn't even know how a camp like this survived. We potentially could have gained a lot more people to fight in the rebellion with us. I was positive that everyone we rescued hated the King, but they were all too weak, too malnourished. I didn't even know if everyone would make it past tomorrow.

I hadn't stopped shaking. At first, it was from using all my reserves to open Kallon's portal. But now my hands trembled for entirely different reasons. Tezya was waiting for me outside the healer's tent. Everyone was off doing different tasks. Sie was with his family. Dovelyn went to check on Brock. Rainer and Kallon were helping those who were already healed find a place to rest, and Savannah was passing out food and water.

But now, I was about to see Vallie. I hadn't seen her since I was taken for the broadcast. Since she told me she wanted to die. I was terrified. Terrified of the state I'd find her in, terrified the King tortured her more after Arcane and I left…

"We don't have to see her yet. We can let her rest some more. You probably need some too," Tezya started, noticing my hesitancy.

"No. I want to see her." There was no way I'd be able to wait any longer. Helping everyone earlier gave me a job to do. It was enough of a distraction to keep my mind from her, but now that things were settling down, I couldn't wait any longer.

I took a deep breath, then walked into the healer's tent. Agony washed into me, settling in my core. I felt like I was hit by a brick wall. So many different emotions were flipping through me—pain, fear, relief. I stopped in the middle of the tent, unable to breathe.

I briefly noticed Tezya move in front of me. He was holding my face in his hands, staring into my eyes. He was saying something over and over again. I saw his lips move, his face frantic, but I couldn't hear his words. All I could hear were moans and cries and sobbing. So much sobbing.

Scotlind. Scotlind. Focus. Look at me. Tezya's voice was in my head now. I looked up, meeting his gaze. *That's it. Keep looking at me. Block everyone else out. Only me.*

"What's happening to me?" I asked. I wasn't sure if I said it out loud or in my head, but I knew he heard me.

"I'm not sure yet," he admitted, his brows furrowed. "I think you might be picking up on everyone's emotions like I do with my ability, but I think it's magnified with your enhancement."

I stared at him in shock. Agony was still washing through me like it was my own. I tried to block it out, but it was impossible. "We'll look into it," Tezya said. "We'll figure it all out, I promise." He paused for a moment, still holding my cheeks in his hands. "Do you need to leave? I can tell Vallie you came."

"No," I snapped. I had to see her. "I'm fine."

I was pretty sure Tezya knew I was lying, but he didn't stop me. He gently released my face and the lack of his hands left me feeling cold. Before I could process it, he grabbed my hand in his. "Okay," he said as he started guiding me through the tent. "We'll be quick then."

I nodded, unable to speak. I kept focusing on the contact of his hand in mine and on the fact that I was about to see Vallie.

"She's in here," Tezya said gently. His hand moved from mine to the small of my back. I rounded the corner and stopped abruptly.

My eyes flared as I took in my best friend. Alive. Alive. Alive. She was lying in the cot with a scratchy blanket pulled up to her chest. Peter was standing off to the side not visible to her but still present.

I took a step toward her. I wanted to wrap her in a hug, to run to her side and never let go, but the expression on her face halted me. She looked haunted, and she definitely didn't look relieved to see me.

"Vallie, I—" I suddenly didn't know what to say. It was like being trapped in the King's room all over again. Nothing I could say would take back what happened. "I'm glad you're alive." I finally settled on, and she winced. Her eyes scrunched shut as she took an unsteady breath. I knew immediately I said the wrong thing. Why did I use that word? Why did I say *alive* when Miles was *dead*?

I could have picked any other word. *Here. Safe. Free.* Any other word...

"What happened?" she asked softly, still not opening her eyes. "Tell me everything." She swallowed. "From the beginning."

I told her what I knew, what I never told her before. From coming to Tennebris, to getting caught, right up until the broadcast and rescuing her. She listened intently. The only way I knew she was taking everything in was from the brief nods she'd make here and there. She kept her eyes mostly closed, and if she did open them, she didn't look at me. Peter and Tezya kept quiet, neither of them leaving our sides. Tezya's hand on my back was the only thing getting me through this. The only thing I could focus on to drown out the sheer agony radiating from the entire tent so I could concentrate on my friend.

"I want to see him," Vallie said as soon as I finished. We all turned to look at her. There were bruises around her throat that weren't there the last time I saw her, and she was so weak from the weeks of being starved and tortured that she could barely stand up straight. I didn't know if the healer's had even given her anything to eat yet with how overwhelmed they were. I saw a half drunk glass of water by the nightstand, but that was it.

She was wearing a long shirt now, and from Peter's lack of one, I wondered if he'd wrapped her in his own when he found her. It dawned on me then that he never left her side, not even to grab a new shirt. While it took me nearly four hours to check on her—

The last time I saw her, she was naked and chained to the King's floor. I pushed the image of her aside, forced myself not to think of how she was dragged into his bed at night.

Old blood still coated her skin, a mixture of her own, her twin's and the dead servant's, but fresh blood stained her too, brighter in color, from whatever she went through when Peter rescued her.

I'd never seen him so determined, so angry, so terrifying... Peter was always light-hearted. He could turn any tension-filled conversation around, but this was different. Something about seeing what happened to Vallie changed him. He was standing still, barely moving, with a new kind of livid mask donned.

No one answered her.

"*Who* do you want to see, Vallie?" Tezya asked gently. He had told me Vallie begged Peter and Dovelyn to bring Miles' body back with them, but they couldn't risk it. If that was who she wanted to see—

Her hands clenched into the sheets. "Kole."

Everything stilled. It was the last person I expected her to say.

"Do you want to try to sleep first? Maybe eat something?" I suggested, trying to mask my own shock at her request. My eyes flicked up to meet Peter's. His were narrowed, his fists clenched at his side as his jaw ground against his teeth, but he didn't say anything.

"No." Her voice was firm, demanding. Her eyes finally snapped open and met mine. "I want to see him *now*."

I turned to look at Tezya who nodded once before guiding my battered friend toward the makeshift prison at the camp. She was walking slowly, a limp taking over her gait. I looked down and saw she had a twisted ankle. I inhaled sharply, but quickly cast it down. If Vallie wanted to pretend she was fine, I wasn't about to ruin that for her. Whatever she needed to do to get through this, I'd help her.

"He's in there," Tezya said as he halted in front of a tent. Now that Dravenburg knew everything, he'd assigned multiple people to watch over Arcane and Kole. Four guards now stood in front of the one Kole was in.

Vallie turned on her good foot. "I want a knife." No one moved. No one spoke. "I said I want a knife." Her voice was breathless, but it still managed to raise an octave. Peter pulled one out and gently placed it into her waiting palm. His hand brushed against hers, and she flinched. Peter's jaw worked as he noticed, before he took a step back, giving her space.

Vallie's hand was shaking as she readjusted the blade before finally stepping through the tent flaps. I followed her after a second, staying out of sight toward the side of the tent, along with the guards.

Kole shifted on the ground once he saw her. He was leaning

against the bars of the cage that was positioned in the center of the room. His head was resting back, his legs spread wide. One bent at the knee, the other stretched out on the grass.

Two Alluse users were standing on either side of the bars to keep his abilities at bay. Brighta didn't believe in the use of Alluse objects, so they took shifts rotating within the tent. I was told Arcane had his own in the one next door. I had no idea what Dravenburg did with the Alluse shackles Tezya and Sie originally put on them, and half of me wondered if they were safer in the chains, even though I knew the process of making the objects were inhumane.

"Leave us," Vallie ordered, not looking at either guard, but directly at Kole instead. To my surprise, Kole's brown gaze held hers, but his face was unreadable.

"Miss, we can't. We need to keep casting Alluse on him—"

"Do it from outside the tent. I know enough about your abilities to understand the radius in which you can cast it."

They still didn't move.

Tezya stepped into the tent a second later. He didn't need to say anything before the guards looked at one another and followed him out. I turned to watch them go and saw Peter hovering at the entrance of the tent, watching the interaction.

Kole rose from the ground, his eyes intent on Vallie. He had ample room and was able to walk ten paces on either side before he was met with the metal bars of the cage. I half wished he was kept in one the size I was in at Lux.

Vallie limped toward the bars, gripping the rusty metal with one hand as she leaned into the cage. Kole didn't say anything, just waited and watched Vallie come to him. His eyes flicked to her ankle once before he met her gaze again and held it. With the jagged lightning scars covering his entire body, he looked more menacing than before.

"How could you?" she sneered. Tears pooled in her amber eyes, but she managed to keep them down.

"Vallie, I had no idea what he was going to do to you and Miles—"

"Don't you dare say his name," she screamed, and Kole flinched.

She was gripping the metal bar so tight that her pale hand was even more ashen.

Kole took a step toward her, closing the space between them until only the bars separated them. His eyes flicked to the blade she was holding before meeting her gaze again. My breath left me as I watched. It took everything in me to not interrupt, to not snatch the blade from Vallie's hand from fear that Kole would grab it and turn it on her. But I had to let her do this, whatever it was she wanted from this interaction, I had to give it to her.

"I'm sorry for what happened to your twin," he said gently. "But I didn't kill him. I wasn't the one who murdered him."

"Not doing anything to help is just as guilty as the act itself. You have his blood on your hands."

Vallie angled the blade toward him. She was shaking profusely, all her weight supported on her right while maintaining her grip on the cage with her free hand. Kole remained still as she passed the blade through the bars, the tip of the dagger digging into his chest. He met her gaze steadily, and I realized he was going to let her kill him. The dread that filled his usually hard, menacing face was gone.

They stood like that, connected only by the sharp end of the blade, for what seemed like minutes, their eyes never leaving each other's. Vallie's filled with anger and hurt, while Kole's held… grief. For some reason I could feel him. Feel that he hated what happened to her, that he was hurting because of what she went through, that he wanted to escape this prison just so he could go back to Lux and murder them all, which made no sense.

But nothing happened.

Vallie stilled. The only thing moving was her hand from trembling. Kole leaned forward, the tip finally piercing his chest and blood pooled down over his stomach. Her breath hitched once she saw the red pooling. She backed up like she'd been burned, the dagger clattering to the ground just outside Kole's reach.

"One day, when I find the strength to do it, I will kill you, Kole Sanders. I will kill you just like you let my brother die."

Kole's eyes never left hers. There was something he wanted to say, but he kept his mouth shut, and I couldn't read him anymore. The weird feelings I got from him earlier were gone.

I waited until Vallie cleared the tent before I walked toward the fallen dagger. I wasn't about to leave it with him.

He watched me, his eyes narrowing, but didn't say anything as I scooped up the blade and left.

Peter followed me outside the tent, and I finally turned to look at him for the first time since we got back—really look at him. He was in rough shape. His abdomen was still bare, with blood and gore covering every inch of him. A long gash ran from his left nipple to his flank, and I realized he was still actively bleeding. I scanned him with a newfound scrutiny. He was lucky to be alive. If the cut was made any deeper, his bowels would have been on the outside.

"You need a healer," I said to him. "You both do."

Peter didn't answer, only looked to Vallie, waiting to see what she wanted to do. No doubt, if she said no, the stubbornness in him prob-ably wouldn't see one either. But he was slowly bleeding out. We'd been back in Brighta for over four hours now, and he hadn't been looked at.

I held back a sigh of relief when Vallie nodded her head. It was so subtle that I barely noticed it. I wondered if she knew the condition Peter was in and realized he needed help too.

We walked back to the healer's tent in silence. Once we arrived, a male healer leapt toward us. "Ey, you boy," he shrieked as he spotted Peter. "You're getting blood all over the furs. Get in the tent before I decide to let you bleed out." His golden eyes flicked over to Vallie. "And you—" he said as he reached for her.

She jumped back. The healer's hand was still outstretched, ready to grab her. Vallie stared at the ground, avoiding all eye contact. Her chest was rapidly moving, her breath was coming out in ragged pants. "Please... don't... touch me," she whispered softly, her eyes still downcast. The healer glanced from her to me to Peter to Tezya, before he nodded, his brows furrowed as he moved to let her enter.

HOURS PASSED. I stayed inside the tent while Peter and Vallie were both looked at. Tezya left a little while ago to go check on everyone else, but not before he made sure I was okay about twenty times.

This time, I welcomed the agony and pain radiating toward me. I embraced it, needing a distraction from my own thoughts, hating that I was fine. I was fine, and my friend was broken.

I couldn't think about it.

Everyone in the tent was careful to not touch Vallie. She was in a chair now. The tent seemed to be divided off into sections based on critical injuries. They gave her proper clothes and warm food, which she barely touched. Her amber eyes kept locking with Peter's green ones. The two of them were unable to *not* look at each other from across the room.

"He's gonna be fine," a female healer said as she offered Vallie a cup of steaming water.

"Th-thank you," she replied, her voice shaky as she tore her gaze away from Peter. I wanted to say something to her. There was a hole growing in me with each passing moment of our silence, but I didn't know what to say.

Are you alright?—I knew the answer was no.

Do you want to rest?—she probably didn't, probably saw her twin's dead body every time she closed her eyes like I did.

Hungry?—she wasn't eating even though it was probably the first time she'd been offered food in the past month or longer. I didn't know when the King had captured her originally, but we had spent weeks together in that room.

I'm sorry—the words wouldn't bring back Miles. It wouldn't reverse all the suffering she endured from simply knowing me.

"You should try to get some rest," Peter said as he made his way toward us. I noticed the way his eyes scanned her uneaten plate. "You can have my tent," he added. "Sie and I will sleep somewhere else, so it'll be yours if that's what you want. You don't have to share it with anyone."

She nodded and silently rose from the chair she'd been sitting on. They fixed her ankle and healed any open wounds she had until there weren't any scars left on her body, but I knew hers were deeper than the surface of her skin, and those couldn't be healed.

"I'll show you where it is," he added gently.

I stood, deciding to awkwardly follow the two of them toward Peter's tent. I didn't know what else to do. Did she want me to follow? Did she want to be alone? Was being alone worse? I didn't know how to help her, and I hated myself for that.

Vallie turned to face me once we were inside Peter's tent. "Please, can you leave me alone…"

I winced. Her words were worse than anything that was ever done to me. Far worse than rotting in the dungeons, than the Luxian soldier's daily torture, than Kole drowning me.

"I'm sorry, Scotlind. I just…" she hesitated. "I just need space for a little bit."

"Val," I started, but she cut me off.

"Every time I look at you, I see my brother's face right before the King reduced it to ash." Her breath shuddered. "When I look at you, I'm reminded of being dragged into his room every night, forcing me to… to do things to him, forcing me to *enjoy* it." Sobs tore at her now. "I just can't stand to see you right now."

"Vallie, I…" I didn't know what to say. Nothing could change what happened.

Peter took a tentative step toward me, positioning himself in front of her. His eyes were soft as he looked at me. "I think you should leave, Scottie."

I nodded, twisting on my heel and ran out of the tent, not wanting to break down in front of Vallie. I didn't want to add a layer of guilt on top of everything else she was feeling, because for her to say that, to admit that she felt that way about me, probably took everything left out of her.

I made my way back to Tezya's tent. He was already waiting for me, standing as soon as I pushed the flaps open. He scanned my face, was by my side in one long stride, and pulled me into a tight hug.

"I'm sorry," he said. I didn't know if he already knew everything that just happened through our bond or if he just guessed it by my face.

"She hates me," I sobbed.

Shh. His soothing tone cooed into my mind as he patted my hair, his fingers lightly curling over my ear. *It's alright. It's going to be alright. She just needs time to grieve and process everything. She's been through a lot. You both have.*

I knew he was just trying to comfort me, telling me what I wanted to hear. Because Vallie would never forget what was done to her and Miles…

And I didn't think any amount of time would ever be enough for her to forgive me for it.

FORTY-EIGHT
SIE

I HADN'T LEFT Greyland's side since they brought him back. Peter stayed with me long enough to tell me what happened before he went to check on Vallie.

I didn't mind. I wanted to be alone.

Greyland was unconscious when they found him in the King's room, and he hasn't woken up since.

He looked so much worse than he had been at the broadcast—and it already killed me to see how badly he was beaten then. I curled my fists, hating myself. Peter was right, I should have gotten them out sooner. I shouldn't have waited until we had a clear plan. The abuse he went through after the airing—

I'd spent every damn minute pleading with the Goddesses to not take my little brother.

Peter told me the King had over a dozen guards watching them, and that Greyland would have died if our mother hadn't jumped in front of the blade.

I tried not to think about it. Both of my parents were now dead, and the only family I had left—the only one I ever truly cared about—was fighting for his life.

I looked down at Greyland lying on the cot in front of me. He wasn't dressed—it was easier for the healers to mend his injuries without constantly having to remove his clothes—but he had a thin blanket pulled up to his chest.

After his initial inspection, I was told he had at least five broken ribs, a fractured leg, three stab wounds through his stomach, and nearly every inch of him was covered in bruises. During his second inspection, they found even more damage.

It was all my fault. I should have protected him more, should have been more adamant and sent him away before my coronation. I knew Synder was going to try something, and I never should have let Greyland come.

I had no idea what happened to him, no way of knowing when they captured him and my mother, but I knew they were both coming to Palm the night I was imprisoned. And judging from his weight, my best guess was that it was then.

He was starved—for weeks, maybe months. I was losing my sense of how much time had passed since everything happened.

I had to constantly remind myself Greyland wasn't a little kid anymore. He was nearly as tall as me and almost as muscular. But looking at him now, I couldn't help but think just how fragile he was.

Greyland coughed, then sucked down a wince as he placed a hand over his ribs.

I stood, jumping to my feet faster than my teleportation could have taken me. It had only been a couple of hours since we were back, and the healers had no idea when he'd wake up...

"You're awake," I breathed.

I watched as Greyland's one eye blinked open. His other eye was so swollen and bloody, I couldn't tell if he still had it.

"Sie." His voice was husky, and his breathing instantly turned ragged as he tried to inhale through his ribs.

"Shh." I bent down, cupping his hand. "It's okay, Grey, you're safe."

"Where... are..." he inhaled sharply, "we?"

"We're in a refuge. You're out of Lux."

His one eye blinked rapidly as he took in my words. Then, all of a sudden, he snapped. He sprang up in bed, wincing and cursing from the pain, but it didn't slow him down.

"Where... is... she?"

"Grey, sit back down." He tried to stand again. "Shit. Greyland, stop." He was going to reinjure his ribs and any work the healers and menders did would have been for nothing.

He kept scanning the tent. "Is she here?"

"Is *who* here?" I asked, trying to push him back down. A few healers saw the commotion and started sprinting toward us.

If he was looking for our mother—if I had to break the news to him that she died...

"Lilia—" he breathed. "I couldn't get their parents, but I left Lilia in the woods—" His voice faded as a mender injected him with a tranquilizer, and he passed out again.

Fuck.

I'd completely forgotten about Peter's family, and I knew he was preoccupied with Vallie. He probably didn't even have time to register what happened to them.

I called to my powers, working through the camp until I found the mind I wanted. *I need your help,* I said.

Sie? the voice was puzzled.

Yes, meet me outside the healer's tent.

I turned toward the nearest healer. "Don't let him wake up. Keep him sedated until I get back."

I waited for her to nod before I reluctantly left my brother.

———

KALLON WAS WAITING with Rainer outside the tent. I scanned the latter. He looked so at odds with the damage he could do with his abilities.

My body tensed as it remembered what it felt like to have a flicker of his power pulse through me. I'd never experienced pain like that before. His power was so strong, so debilitating that I was glad electric users were super rare.

And I only felt the remnants of his ability tapered down through Scotlind, who was feeling it through Kole. I didn't want to know first hand what the full capability of it felt like. The little bit I did feel left my hands scarred. Seeing him now, he didn't seem capable of having such destruction living under his skin. Before that day, I had never seen him fight. I knew he was in the Luxian army, and by default, he had to be strong, but I underestimated him.

Kallon had her arms crossed and one thin brow arched beneath her bangs. "What do you want, Sie?"

"Do you have a portal set up anywhere near Tennebris or any mortal territory that can get me close enough to it?"

"Why?"

"Just answer the question."

She scoffed. "I don't think you're able to make the demands. Seeing as you want something I have, and you're bothering me when the camp is super busy. So answer my question first, why do you want to know?"

"We'll eventually need a portal close enough if we're going into a war with them," I lied. I didn't want to tell her what I planned unless she could deliver. If she couldn't, I'd have to think of something else. I thought about telling Peter, he'd be able to help, but I didn't want to get his hopes up.

"You're so daft. What is so important that you need to know in the middle of all of this?" She gestured around us. She wasn't wrong. I'd never seen Brighta so hectic. There were Advenians everywhere, some still naked, some bleeding on the grass. I was certain there were a few dead bodies not yet dealt with. "And no more lies."

"I need to rescue Peter's little sister," I answered honestly because clearly avoiding the topic wasn't working, and I was hoping I could manipulate her with sympathy. "She's a defenseless rank zero. Her family is tied to mine, and if the Council captures her, they'll kill her on the spot."

"And what makes you think she's not in their hands now?" Kallon asked.

"I know she's not. My brother got her to a safe house in the woods. She's been hiding there. I just need to get close enough to the continent so I can get to it." I hoped it was true. I needed the healers to have waited ten more seconds before they injected Grey, but I assumed that's what he meant. I told him if things went bad, to bring our families to the cabin, and I just had to pray it was where Lilia was now.

"What woods?" she asked, her yellow eyes widening a fraction of an inch.

I half wondered why it mattered. She probably knew nothing about Tennebris, probably couldn't even name the six villages that made up the kingdom, let alone know where the woods were, but I answered anyway. "There's a forest in between Palm and Kitlarn—"

She interrupted me with a wide grin, her arms uncrossing. "I have a portal there. In Tennebris. In those very woods."

I stilled, then shook my head, not believing I heard her right. "What?" I was trying to find my words. It was too good to be true. I half expected to have to teleport on my own, which would have taken days. I never imagined her actually having a portal inside Tennebris. "How?"

Rainer was idly standing next to her, taking everything in, and didn't seem the least bit surprised by our conversation.

The girl shrugged. "Dove figured at some point we'd need an entry point into the Dark Kingdom. She snuck me in when we went to collect your wife—I mean ex-wife, sorry—" I tried to hold back my sneer at the comment because I knew it was fucking intentional.

She continued with a sly smirk on her lips. "Anyway, I picked the woods there because it was a central location and close to where the castle was if we ever needed to attack. Plus the area has plenty of coverage."

"Fuck," I breathed, and I wasn't sure if I said the curse out loud. "Take me there."

"Sure," she agreed like we were discussing the weather instead of breaking into Tennebris.

"Really?" I asked, my eyes narrowing. I couldn't help but wonder if she had an ulterior motive. Like she'd leave me there once she portaled me in. I honestly never imagined she'd say yes. I thought I'd have to beg and grovel—

"Four reasons," she drawled as she took a step closer to me, and I realized that she was going to take me there *now*. "First, I know those woods, and if what you're saying is true, we can get her out without anyone noticing. They're deserted, and the trip should be harmless enough. Second, I think it would be beneficial to have you owe me a favor. Third, I have a soft spot for rank zeroes. And fourth, I could use another girl friend around here. There's entirely too much masculine energy."

A thick smoke of purple and black swallowed us up, and we were gone before I could even answer.

FORTY-NINE

SIE

Greyland was still unconscious when I came back to the healer's tent with a delirious Lilia.

I need you here. I found Peter's mind the moment I came back. A fly flew past my head before it transformed into my friend.

"What's wrong? Is everything okay—" His voice stopped as soon as he saw Lilia standing beside the cot. She'd been staring down at Greyland like she saw a ghost from the moment I brought her in here.

"Lilia." Peter pulled his sister into a hug, forcing her to look away from my brother.

She tensed before she realized it was Peter, then hugged him back just as tightly. She started sobbing the next second, and I think Peter might have been as well.

I always found it strange whenever I saw them together. Grey and I were close but from a distance. We grew up without love and affection, and if a family hug lasted more than two seconds, we were reprimanded.

But the Fervics were the complete opposite of the Norens. They were the warmest, most affectionate Advenians I'd ever encountered.

I wasn't sure how long it was before the two of them pulled away again, both smiling, shaking, and sobbing. They were speaking to each other, but I didn't give it any attention until Peter turned toward me.

"How did you get her?" he asked, wiping a tear away, before wrapping his arm around his sister.

Lilia was fine, minus dark circles under her eyes, she was unharmed. Somehow my brother managed to get her to the cabin before he got himself caught.

I looked down at Greyland. He wasn't much better from when I first left him, and I still wasn't sure if he was going to make it.

"I had Kallon portal me to Tennebris to get her." I noticed Lilia staring down at my brother again.

Peter tugged his ear with his free hand.

What? I asked.

Why didn't you get me?

I didn't know the state she was going to be in, I admitted. **All Greyland said was her name. I had no idea if he actually saved her.**

Peter nodded, and I knew it was something we'd be discussing later.

"Is he okay?" Lilia asked, biting her lip.

"Grey said something about not getting to your parents," I diverted. "I don't think they made it."

Lilia gasped, but she didn't look surprised. She just kept staring at my brother with tears streaming down her face.

I knew Peter was fighting off tears of his own.

———

PETER FOUND me in the healer's tent later that night. Greyland had been sleeping for the past two hours, but I still couldn't find it in myself to leave him.

How is he? Peter asked once I entered his mind. I didn't want to risk waking him. Ever since he'd first woken up, he's only managed to stay conscious for a couple hours at a time, and even though the healers reiterated that he was going to be okay, I was having a hard time believing it. I wouldn't until he was able to walk out of this tent without any pain.

As good as he can be, I replied. I hadn't told him about our mother yet. I was terrified because whenever Greyland did wake up, I knew beyond any physical pain, finding out our mother died would hit him the hardest. He loved her. He was always so much closer to her than I was, and I had no idea how I was going to break the news to him. There was no way in hell I was telling him she died saving him. He didn't need the guilt. I just hadn't figured out what I was going to tell him yet.

How's Vallie? I asked, not wanting to think about my brother right now because anytime I did, I was seconds away from crumbling.

Freaking horrible. She's... his words died on his lips.

She's going to be okay, I said, trying to sound encouraging. Even if she'd never be the same again, at least she was alive, something I couldn't say for half of either of our families.

I know, he sighed and slumped further into his chair. The healer's tent was still full, but at least there were empty seats now. *I'm also worried about Lilia.*

How's she holding up? I asked.

Peter shrugged. *She's been crying a lot. I brought her into a communal tent to sleep, but she's really shaken up. She keeps talking about how our parents' death are her fault. How she should have turned back for them, but when I ask her to elaborate, she doesn't.*

I nodded. Greyland wouldn't talk either. I had asked him during one of his bouts of consciousness how he got captured, but he wouldn't tell me. I couldn't blame him. I hated opening up and talking about things, but I knew it was unusual for Peter. They told each other everything.

She's been asking about him too. Peter gestured toward Greyland who was still sleeping on the cot in front of us. *I've been telling her he's fine. I'm not lying to her, am I?*

I sucked in a breath. *No,* I answered, even if I didn't believe it myself.

Good, Peter said, and I saw him nod in my periphery, before he placed his head between his hands. *I feel like the world's shittiest brother,* he admitted.

I didn't comment right away. I didn't know how because Peter just voiced exactly what I'd been thinking all day. Greyland was beaten and tortured because of me. I should have thought about them. I should have told Peter about the cabin, and we could have checked it. We could have gotten Lilia out sooner, and I would have realized the King had my brother before the broadcast even started. Maybe it could have changed things, maybe my parents would still be alive.

You're not, Peter, I finally said, because it was my guilt to bear, not his.

I didn't think about her once, Sie—

Peter, we had a lot going on, I cut him off, knowing exactly where this was headed.

I know, but it still doesn't change what happened. He blew out a breath. *There's a zero on her wrist, but she won't talk to me about it…*

I nodded, already knowing Lilia was branded and Greyland wasn't. It was one of the last orders Synder made before I was sentenced to the prison. He forced all zeroes to become servants, even if they were still in school. *She's safe, Peter, that's all that matters now.*

We sat in silence after that, both watching Greyland as he slept. It wasn't until hours later that he finally stirred.

"Peter," he murmured, his voice laced with sleep. His left eye was still swollen shut, but now blood was starting to drip from it, and it was taking everything in me not to freak the fuck out about it. It wasn't like that before the broadcast—

"Good to see you, Little Noren." Peter smiled. Any speck of worry and grief washed off his face for my brother's sake, and I could have hugged him for it.

"I… Lilia—" He started to get up again, the blanket falling over his waist.

"I got her, Grey," I said, gently pushing him back down onto the mattress. "You need to stop moving or you'll puncture a lung. You have five broken ribs…"

I watched as my brother sagged into the cot. We'd had this same conversation three times now, but every time I told him Lilia was safe, he passed out again.

Now his gaze slid to me. "Where is she?" he asked, not caring that I just told him how severely messed up he was. His breathing was shallow, and I knew it hurt to inhale. I'd broken a rib before, but never five.

"She's fine. She's getting some sleep," Peter said.

"I couldn't get to your parents… They weren't home when everything happened… and then…"

"It's okay, Greyland. It's not your fault." Peter's smirk vanished, his fun-loving front gone, as tears threatened to pool in his eyes again. He leaned forward, resting his hand over my brother's. "Thank you for saving her, Grey."

FIFTY
SCOTLIND

"I NEED TO DO SOMETHING," I said to Tezya.

We'd been holed up in his tent for a couple of hours. He was silently holding me, letting me sob until my tears ran dry. My eyes were swollen and puffy, my head throbbed, and exhaustion was slowly taking over me, but I didn't want to rest. I wiped my eyes, smearing the remnants of tears down my cheeks.

"I don't want to think." I kept hearing Vallie's words, kept seeing Miles' face right before it burst into flames. I had cried enough, and now I just needed a distraction.

Tezya was silent for a minute, thinking it over. "Do you want to visit Brock?"

Yes, I said into his mind. I hadn't seen him since I made the trade with Arcane. Tezya grabbed my hand, intertwining our fingers before leading the way back to the healer's tent.

Everyone glared at me as we walked past. Did they all watch the broadcast? Did everyone here hate me now? I'd been so busy since we got back to the camp that I hadn't thought about it. But now, I couldn't ignore the sneers people made toward me. I got the feeling I wasn't welcome anymore.

Wells created a code to hack into Lux's system a long time ago. Anytime they mandate a broadcast, a lot of people gather in the dining tent to watch. I don't know how many saw it because we were watching from Dovelyn's tent, but I think word of what happened spread to everyone, Tezya answered my thoughts, and I wish he hadn't. *But don't worry about it. No one will give you a hard time. They know you're… important to me.*

The King's theory before the broadcast came back to me. *When I was gone, did you feel me?* I asked.

Not always. But every now and then I could. Only through your emotions though, never your thoughts.

I couldn't be compelled when I was there, I said and my arm pulled back as Tezya stopped in his tracks. He knew that. He saw what happened through my eyes, but we never talked about it. We never had the chance to. *Do you think… I wondered… maybe if Arcane did something to me or if…* I let my voice trail off, letting him fill in the gaps.

We'll talk to Arcane once everything settles, and we'll find out, he said, but his voice was clipped. We didn't talk the rest of the way to the tent.

Brock had a permanent cot in the healer's quarters. I was told he'd been here ever since they got him back. I tried not to think about what that meant, about how badly he was hurt to have been here the whole time I was gone. I hadn't noticed the section when Tezya first brought me in here to see Vallie. It was tucked away toward the back and was more quiet and secluded than the rest of the tent.

Brock sat up as soon as he saw Tezya, then his golden eyes widened as they flicked to me. "You're back," he breathed. It felt like forever since I last heard his voice. Even when I saw him in Lux, he'd been half unconscious. His eyebrows furrowed as he looked at me again. "You're in pain. What part of you is injured?"

"I'm fine," I said, surprised by his words. The only pain I was in was a mental war.

"I can take it away if you want," Brock said, eyeing me. I could feel his gaze taking in my scarred flesh. I still hadn't looked in a mirror. If I looked anything like Kole or Arcane, I knew it was terrible, but I didn't want to know.

I shook my head. "I'm fine." I deserved to feel like this, and I deserved to look however I did now.

"Are you… Can you see?" I held my breath waiting for his answer, not realizing until now how badly I needed to know. I knew he had to have some sort of sight back if he was able to see my scars, but I had to make sure there wasn't any permanent damage. I had to hear it for myself. From him.

Brock nodded. "Yes. My farsightedness is still a bit hazy, but I should be fully back to health in a week's time—"

"I'm sorry," I blurted before he could finish. I still had this immense amount of guilt that my ability caused him his blindness and whatever torture the King had put him through afterward. He was just another person to add to my long list of people I hurt.

"You have nothing to be sorry for, Scotlind."

I was going to protest when Dovelyn rose, standing from the edge of Brock's cot. I hadn't realized she was there, and I wondered if she had been using her invisibility to stay concealed before. She looked so tiny compared to him. I forgot how large Brock was, how he was a brute even compared to Tezya—who was by no means small.

My eyes widened as Dovelyn walked toward me, pulling me into a hug. "Thank you," she whispered into my ear. "For saving him, for running the other way so we had a chance to escape."

"You're… welcome," I replied tentatively. She took a step back from me, and I could tell she was uncomfortable. "Thank you for going with Peter to get her," I added, surprising myself too, but I was too tired right now to have hate left toward her, and I was grateful to everyone who helped get Vallie back.

She nodded, not meeting my gaze.

Tezya and I stayed in the healer's tent for a long time. I went around checking on the Advenians who were saved and helped Savannah pass out food and clothes to those who still needed it. It wasn't until the moon was high in the sky that I realized I never checked on Sie's family.

His mother and brother were brought into the camp along with Vallie, and I didn't even think about them until now. I was about to tell Tezya I was going to visit them, but he beat me to it, already knowing what I wanted. *Sie's mother didn't make it,* he said into my mind. *He asked for space.*

What? How?

She died during the rescue. Only Greyland came back from Lux. Tezya's voice was hard, even in my head.

I nodded, sucking in my breath, not wanting to ask any more right now. Greyland was his half brother, and I didn't think Tezya or Sie were ready to acknowledge that or what it meant.

How do you know he needs space? I asked instead. Sie didn't have many friends here, and I knew Peter was with Vallie right now.

Because I visited him earlier. Tezya swallowed. *I needed to apologize.*

How did he take it? I asked slowly. I knew it wasn't Tezya's fault, but I also knew Tezya wouldn't see it that way. He left Sie and I behind.

As good as he could.

Even though we got everything we wanted, even though Tezya freed all those Advenians, taking away the King's access to powers, and we saved Vallie, it still felt like we lost, like too much was taken from us in the process.

I held back my tears, terrified for what it meant in the future. Who else would we lose if this war barely began? Tezya grabbed my hand and started leading me toward his tent.

And as soon as he closed the tent flaps—as soon as we were alone —I fell onto the ground and shattered.

FIFTY-ONE
SIE

ANOTHER WEEK HAD PASSED before I finally let myself believe Greyland was going to be okay—okay was an exaggeration. He was never going to be the same again. When the swelling of his left eye went down, and I was finally able to look at the damage, I realized he fucking lost it.

But when I tried to talk to him about it, he shut me down. He wasn't surprised, which meant the bastards fucking ripped it out of him while he was awake.

I wanted to kill them all. I wanted to rip out every last Luxian soldier's eyes, only to shove them back in the socket so I could do it again.

But Grey was going to live. It was the only thing I could thank Pylemo for right now.

He was now able to maintain consciousness and could stand at the side of his cot for ten minutes at a time. It was an improvement. Two days ago, all he could manage was to sit propped up against the headboard.

I thought seeing Lilia would change things for him. He was so happy when I told him we got her out of the cabin. I wanted to bottle his expression the moment he found out—relief and something else I couldn't figure out came over him. It was the only time I'd seen him slightly happy since we got him out. But as soon as she stepped into the healer's tent he was in, it was washed off his face.

The first ten minutes, all he could do was stare at her, and after the initial shock of seeing her, he went right back to ignoring her like he used to whenever our mothers forced us all together.

It was strange.

Lilia and Greyland were both feigning that they were okay as Peter and I spent the next couple of days by their sides. We didn't know what to say or do to comfort them. We were all orphans now. They only had us to take care of them, and we were two fuck ups who didn't know how to speak to them about grief or even acknowledge our own.

By the third day we brought Lilia into the tent, she was fidgeting and decided she wanted to learn mortal healing and help out.

Greyland's face went stone cold, and as soon as she left, he turned to me. "Don't let her be assigned to me."

I grinned down at him, rustled his black hair and left without giving him my answer. I overheard a healer saying they were going to discharge him by the afternoon, but I decided to not tell him that.

At least it'd be a distraction from what really haunted him for a little while.

———

IT WAS DARK, hours before dawn, when I was dragged out of my communal bed by Peter. *Bed.* We went from sharing a tent together to now having to sleep in the same bed. It wasn't nearly large enough for the two of us, and he somehow always gravitated toward cuddling me by the morning.

We were crammed into a tent with Tennebrisians and Luxians since Peter gave up our used-to-be-private-two-bed-tent for Vallie. I didn't blame him, but now I was regretting my friendship with him as he forced me to go to the training rings in the middle of the night.

It wasn't like I was sleeping anyway. I hadn't been able to since

Greyland came back... I just couldn't sleep. Even after my brother was discharged and was starting to act like his old self again, I could barely relax.

I glanced over at Greyland before I followed Peter out, careful not to wake the six other people in here with us. Lilia was also in our tent, but she slept on the complete opposite side from us and as far away from Greyland and I as she could get.

Everyone was terrified of me ever since the broadcast came out. They looked at me like I was deadly, like if they stared too long, I'd lose my temper and kill them on the spot.

At first I didn't mind it because I wanted the space. I didn't want to talk to anyone but Peter or my brother anyway. But now it was getting under my skin when people literally ran in the opposite direction once they saw me coming.

Long black hair was blowing in the wind up ahead. I squinted closer and saw Vallie was already waiting for us. "You changed your hair," I commented instead of saying hi.

She nodded once. "Kallon helped me." I didn't ask her why she wanted to get rid of the red, and she didn't give up any more information than that. The dark color didn't suit her. It made her face look washed out, accentuating the dark circles under her eyes. But I wasn't about to tell her that. I knew I looked like shit too.

"What are we doing here?" I asked, putting my hands in my pockets, more out of habit than for warmth.

Peter looked toward Vallie who was staring down at her feet. "She wants to train," he answered.

I was surprised. The girl didn't have an ounce of muscle to her. She was all curves with feminine features. She wasn't built as a fighter.

"Okay," I said slowly. "Why are we out here in the middle of the night then? Training happens every day during normal hours." Technically, the rings didn't close, but no one ever stayed past midnight, and right now the five rings were completely deserted.

"I don't want to be in groups," she answered. I looked toward Peter, whose face said it all. She didn't want to train when there were hundreds of males crowded and crammed throughout the rings. Peter told me how she couldn't stand being touched, how she flinched anytime someone got too close. I could understand that, but what I didn't get was why *I* was here. If she didn't want to be around males, it didn't make sense why Peter asked me to help.

"I'm sure Scottie would be happy to help train you—"

"No," she cut me off.

"Okay…" I said slowly, trying to keep my expression neutral. "What do you want from me then?"

"Go through drills with me," my friend answered for her. "You're one of the best fighters, and I don't want to ask anyone else. She isn't going to be sparring for a while. We just want to go over the basics for now."

———

ANOTHER TWO WEEKS of waking up hours before dawn to train Vallie passed. I was getting used to the lack of sleep and was surprised to find Vallie still coming every day. I'd asked her once why she never seemed groggy waking up so early and she responded with, "I don't sleep anymore." I didn't bother making small talk with her after that, not wanting to risk saying the wrong thing. She was broken, beyond broken. I didn't know how to help her, and I knew Peter was struggling with the same.

After the first week, Peter started to drag Lilia along. Having another girl around Vallie was the right move, and I knew Peter wanted his sister to train, but Lilia was the worst person he could have picked for Vallie. She was goddess-damned awful. I'd never met anyone with worse hand-eye-coordination than her.

The only positive was that we could demonstrate the maneuvers on Lilia, who would then show Vallie. But Lilia was so bad, it was honestly more time consuming.

Peter was getting stressed. While Vallie was improving, she still needed someone to spar, and Lilia just needed a shit ton of help.

After training today, I entered the communal dining tent actually needing one of those drinks the mortal consumed every day. The coffee was helping me get through the mornings, and I was discovering I loved the bitter taste of it.

The little bit we did sleep every night, Peter took up most of the bed, so I usually just found myself staring up at the fabric that made up the ceiling, trying not to think about how I lost both of my parents.

Lavender hair flashed in front of me as Savannah made her way toward the table with her brother.

I followed her.

She looked up and noticed me standing there. "Can I help you?"

"Yes."

"With?" She arched a brow.

I gritted my teeth, looked around the room, and braced myself for what I had to ask her. "Can we talk in private?"

She looked down at her uneaten breakfast, then at her brother. "Don't touch my bacon. I'll be right back."

Wells shrugged as he kept eating from his own plate. I watched her grab hold of her coffee before following me out of the large tent. I didn't start talking until we were long out of earshot from anyone.

"How did you learn to fight?"

"What kind of question is that?" she asked, blowing on the steamy liquid in her hand. I tried not to focus on her lips as she took a slow sip.

"A serious one. Who taught you?"

"Years of doing gymnastics, then everyone taught me once they started visiting," she answered, taking another sip. I assumed by *everyone*, she meant Tezya and his friends. I knew she was close with them.

"I don't know what gymnastics means, but can you teach someone who has no experience?"

"I could," she said. Her gray, opal eyes met mine. I honestly couldn't decide what color they were as so many different shades swirled inside her irises and it seemed to change based off the lighting. It was unsettling for a human and so at odds with her brother's solid brown coloring. I also hated that I was fascinated by them. That I kept staring at them whenever we talked. I didn't gawk at

Luxian eye coloring, but for some reason hers kept drawing my attention.

I shook my head. Who cares what color they were or the fact that when the sun was high in the sky I swore there were specks of lavender in them that seemed to reflect off her hair.

As much as I didn't like her cockiness, she would be great for Vallie and Lilia. She was a human, a far cry from the Advenians that haunted Vallie, and if Lilia could learn her footwork, she could work on agility next, which was probably her only saving grace at this point. "Great—"

"I said I *could*, not I *would*." My smile faltered at her words. "Who do you want me to train?" she asked, draining the last drop of her coffee. I regretted not grabbing a cup myself because I desperately needed the fuel to get through this conversation.

"Vallie and Lilia."

"Vallie," she repeated the name. "The redhead your friend rescued that day?"

I nodded.

"Why are you helping her? You didn't even want to rescue her."

I ran my fingers through my hair in frustration. Why I thought she would help was beyond me. "I never said I didn't want her rescued. I just didn't want it to be at the expense of my friend's life."

"Uh-huh, and who else?"

"Lilia. Peter's sister."

"Hmm," she huffed. "So you want me, a *human*, to help train two *Advenians*?"

I ground my teeth together at her mocking smirk. I didn't say anything, my jaw kept working as she stared up at me triumphantly.

"Why do you need *me*?" she added into the silence.

"We need a girl to help," I said because it was the obvious truth. Lilia technically was learning from Peter, just at a regressed rate, but Vallie was the real reason I was standing here right now. She was ready to start sparring, but would flinch anytime either of us got too close.

But her story wasn't mine to tell so I wasn't going to elaborate further, even though everyone in the camp knew what happened anyway. She was naked when Peter carried her through the portal. Bruises marred her throat, her arms, her wrists... And before Peter ripped off his own shirt to try to cover her body, everyone saw the bruises that marred her hips, inner thighs and everywhere in between. Everyone saw the way she flinched from every male in the camp. Everyone fucking knew.

"Okay, so why do you need *me*?" she asked again. I didn't miss the glint in her eyes. Why was I asking a human over an Advenian for help? A human who was supposed to be so weak they died as fast as the leaves changed colors.

I honestly had no idea. I didn't have an answer for her. I couldn't comprehend why she was the first person I thought of. I knew Scotlind was out of the question, but I could have gone to Kallon. She would have agreed to help in an instant, saving me the headache.

"Because we need someone weak, someone Vallie won't perceive as a threat." It was a lie.

"No." The glare she held was murderous as she stepped into my line of view. She crept into my space, her nose just barely brushing against mine. She was a fucking human. I could break her so easily, but the way she wasn't scared of me, the way she didn't run in the opposite direction, ignited me. Advenians fifty times stronger than her shook in my presence. Ever since the broadcast everyone was terrified of me. Everyone *but* her. The girl was anything but weak, and I fucking hated her for it.

She started walking away. Her hair whipped me across the face and a scent of lavender and citrus invaded my senses. Why did she have to smell like the color of her hair? Why did it bother me? Why the fuck did I even notice?

"Wait," I ground out, sucking in my pride for Peter. "Please help train her."

"Okay." She shrugged nonchalantly, taking a bite from an apple she must have kept hidden in her sweatshirt. "Since you asked so nicely." She was always consuming some sort of food or drink and it irritated the hell out of me. I kept staring at her mouth as she twisted the apple in her hand, inspecting it, before biting down again. A splash of juice ran down her lips before her tongue darted out to catch it. "Say I help you, what's in it for me?"

I groaned. "What do you want?"

She took her time swallowing the bite of apple as she slowly started walking toward me again. She was an inch from my face, pouting her lips and bringing a finger to the corner of her mouth before tapping it. It was like she knew I'd been staring at them this whole conversation… "Hmmm. What do I want?" she paused, taking her damn, sweet time. "I don't know yet."

"You don't know yet?" I growled. "You made a fuss about wanting something and you don't even know what you want?"

"It can be an 'I owe you' kind of thing," she suggested. "Since I don't know what I want from you, I'll be allowed to think of it at any point, and you'll have to agree."

"You want me to say yes to something without having any idea what it is yet?" I narrowed my eyes at her. Humans were more conniving than I thought. I was half tempted to tell her to forget it. I didn't think Vallie's training was worth the trouble. I highly doubted she'd want to fight when the time came, but I knew I had to. Peter wouldn't have hesitated to make the bargain for anyone if it meant he was helping Scottie or someone I cared about.

"Fine," I said through my teeth. "It can be an 'I owe you' thing, but you have to wake up before dawn."

I smiled as her brows furrowed. She stared at her empty cup of coffee. "Ugh. I'm going to need a gallon of this stuff."

FIFTY-TWO
SIE

I TOLD Savannah to meet us at the training rings the next morning. I half wondered if she wasn't going to show, but then I saw lavender hair swaying in the wind. She shrugged out of a gray sweatshirt, revealing a loose top that was too flimsy to be training in and tight black pants that exposed the exact shape of her legs... and ass.

I forced my gaze away from her body and turned to Peter. He kept hounding me relentlessly on how I managed to convince the girl who hated my guts to train with us. I ignored every taunt and told him to shut up unless he wanted me to stop helping.

Savannah frowned slightly as she approached Vallie. "How come you keep dyeing your hair black? You look better as a redhead."

"I hate the color red."

"Why?" Savannah pushed, and I wondered if bringing her was the wrong call. She had no filter. She didn't hold back, and her curiosity got the better of her, regardless of what it caused others. Her mouth was too big for her own good.

"Because it reminds me of fire and because it reminds me of my brother."

I entered Savannah's mind, half terrified she was stupid enough to ask Vallie what happened to him.

Everyone knew Vallie was tortured by the King. Her grief didn't have the mercy of being kept quiet, which I assumed was partly why she wanted to train in the middle of the night while everyone else was sleeping. I rarely saw her leave her tent during the day. But no one knew exactly what went down between her, Scotlind, and the King. A lot of it was assumed, but not everyone knew about her twin.

The King killed her brother, I said to Savannah, hoping she would drop it.

If she was surprised I entered her mind, she didn't show it. She completely ignored me, instead saying out loud to Vallie, "I'm sorry."

Vallie just nodded.

"Alright." Savannah clapped her hands together after tossing her sweatshirt onto the ground. "Show me what you got."

———

PRINCESS DOVELYN FOUND me later that night in the dining tent. I was exhausted and was only just sitting down to eat something for the first time today.

I never left the rings and trained the remainder of the day, trying not to think about Savannah and how her white shirt became drenched with sweat despite the cool draft. We started by running through the drills Peter and I had been teaching them. Savannah nodded, taking everything in, then went right into maneuvers of her own, showing Vallie and Lilia how to move their bodies in a way I didn't think was possible. She ran through different exercises for them to do every day. It was a mix of stretches, core work, and body weight maneuvers.

"What do you want?" I snapped at Dovelyn, bringing myself back to the moment and shrugging off all thoughts of training.

She sat down next to me. Peter wasn't around so I was at a table by myself. "I wanted to check up on you. How are you?"

I scoffed, nearly choking on my food. "We aren't friends, so you can cut the act."

A prolonged silence stretched between us as I kept eating. I waited for her to admit what she really wanted because there was no way she came over just to ask me how I was doing.

"You know you could be a little nicer and you might actually have more friends."

That got me to look up. She was staring at me with a narrowed expression.

"I think the same can be said for you."

"I risked my life to save not only you, but your brother too, the least you can do is not be a dick."

"Do you want a thank you?" I snapped and regretted it as soon as I said it. I *should* say thank you.

She rolled her eyes before finally rising from the table. "Meet me by the fields when you're finished eating. We can talk without anyone overhearing us. I *do* expect you to come."

She left without another word. I watched her go. My fork halted halfway to my mouth as I stared after her silver hair.

I took my time finishing my food, even though my curiosity was eating at me. But there was no way in hell I'd let that show. The girl could create shields. We could have talked in the tent without anyone overhearing us, but she wanted full privacy, didn't even want wandering eyes on us, and I had no idea why.

When I finally made it to the fields, Dovelyn was already waiting. "Alright. I'm here. What do you want?" I asked.

"I want to talk to you about your father—"

Oh hell no. I started walking away. There was no way I was about to talk to her about that, even if I owed her my brother's life. I'd been actively avoiding thinking about everyone I lost. I tried to block out my mother and Moli. They didn't deserve to die. The feeling of guilt and sadness and grief washed into me whenever I did and it was all too much.

And my father was even worse. The emotions I had about losing him were confusing as hell, and I didn't feel like figuring them out. The only time I'd willingly open those doors was if Greyland wanted to. He was the only person I would uncover that grave for. *The only person.* And he was just as stubborn as I was.

"I knew him…" she said, her voice was soft, but I heard every word perfectly. I stopped walking. "Before you were even alive. I met him over a century ago."

I slowly turned to face her, forcing myself to keep my expression blank, forcing all my emotions down. "So what?"

"So I wanted to tell you about him."

I scoffed. "No, thanks. I know who my father was."

"No, you didn't, Sie. My father and Athler, they… they…" she let out a breath. "They changed him. The person you knew and grew up with wasn't your father."

"I don't care," I started. I didn't want to hear this. I didn't want to know…

"Well you're going to listen to me whether you want to or not."

"Why?" I snapped.

"Because I can tell it's eating away at you. I can tell his death bothers you. You feel guilty about missing him. I can see what you're doing. You're spiraling, and as much as I don't particularly like you, we need you in this war, and we need you to be mentally sane."

"I'm fine," I snapped, and I realized I wasn't coming off remotely close to fine. My fists were clenched at my side, and I hadn't realized I'd taken a step toward her. I was leaning down, practically spitting the words in her face.

She didn't move. She just tilted her head up and met my gaze with her own piercing look of defiance. "Just hear me out once. Only once and then I'll leave you alone."

"I don't need to hear you out at all. I'm leaving."

I started to walk away when she said, "I'm either going to tell you in private now where you don't need to worry about anyone else over-hearing, or I'll tell everyone at the next meeting, and you'll be forced to mask your emotions while everyone stares at you. Your brother will most likely be there too. I'm sure you don't want him hearing this in front of an audience. If you do this now, you can decide if you want him to know."

"Fine," I seethed. If she wasn't a fucking air ability user who possessed shields, I'd compel her to never speak of it. But of course she was one of the few people who I couldn't naturally compel—assuming she had a shield over her now, which coming into this conversation with me there was no way she didn't. "You have three minutes of my time and know that I'll kill you if you tell Greyland anything."

"Five minutes."

I ran my fingers through my long locks, then turned to face her, waiting for her to start, trying to put up my walls high enough so I could stomach to hear this.

"He used to visit a lot, making up excuses to get a work visa in Lux, and then he would spend every single free second he had with my mother. We had our own quarters away from the King, so no one ever noticed. It was just Arcane and I at the time. Tezya wasn't born for another twenty years..."

I let out a breath, trying not to think about the fact that he also fathered the Fire Prince.

"I knew him from the time I was born. He was kind. He looked after Ar and I. He even brought us gifts every time he visited. I watched them together a lot—my mom and him." She swallowed. "My father was never kind to her, and as all rank five marriages in Lux are arranged, I'd never seen it before. I never saw what it looked like for two people to be in love. It was intoxicating. I always spied on them under my invisibility, imagining if I'd ever find what they had someday. I saw them holding each other well into the night. I saw the tears shed every time he was forced to go. I saw his rage when my father called on my mother in public, and he was forced to sit back and do nothing. But as I got older, I also heard them talking. It was rushed whispers when they thought they were alone. Your father... he... he didn't agree with the way things were. He wanted to get rid of the ranks altogether. He wanted a world where both Tennebrisians and Luxians could live together, and he could love my mother freely. Whatever the King said about him during the broadcast was a lie—"

"Dovelyn, I grew up with him. I know what he was like. He hated rank zeroes..."

"Let me finish, Sie. My mother didn't die until Tezya was thirty-one. I was fifty. That means I've known your father personally for fifty years. I knew him. The *real* him, and he was more of a father to me than mine ever was." She closed her eyes for a second before looking back up.

"I think you have the wrong person…"

"I watched him die during that broadcast, Sie. I don't have the wrong person." She blew out a breath before continuing. "When Tezya was born, they were more careful. My mother was terrified of what would happen if Tezya was ever discovered. When my brother turned four and the King's punishments started, she wouldn't let your father see us anymore. Ar and I were hurt, but Tezya was too young. He doesn't remember him. They still saw each other, but it was stolen moments. He only came to my mother when we were asleep. They tried to hide it from us, from Tezya."

Her breath hitched. "When my mother died, your father was distraught. He came to Lux without a work visa. My father and Athler found him before he even made it to our quarters. They thought he was there to overthrow them. Your father's views were the start of the rebellion, Sie. He and my mother—they started it all back then. People were only just starting to act upon their anger for how our society was being governed and how our citizens were being treated.

"I saw them drag your dad down to the dungeons. I was under my invisibility and too much of a coward back then to come out of it and do something." Her voice choked. "I didn't see him for an entire decade after that. I thought… I thought they killed him. But when I saw him again, he changed. He was a different person. I think Athler used his abilities to change his way of thinking while torturing him. I think the effects of it over a decade were starting to seep into his being. I think he was brainwashed so thoroughly until there was nothing left of the person I used to know. When he finally returned to Tennebris, he hated rank zeroes. He got servants for the first time in his life. He worked his way up the Dark Council. I stopped following his life after that. It hurt too much. I had no idea he went on to start a family until I saw the 'N' on my mother's grave. I didn't realize the connection. The person you grew up with was a remnant of my own father, Sie. Anything you suffered was because of what the King and Athler did to him."

There was a long moment of silence.

"I just wanted you to know it's okay to grieve him and hate him at the same time. It's okay to miss him even if he was a monster. I understand he wasn't kind to you or your brother. I understand your life was difficult. But I owed it to him, to the man who used to raise me, to let his son know he wasn't the kind of person you thought he was." Her breath hitched, like she was gearing up for what she was going to say next. "I think your dad would be proud of you fighting in the rebellion, would be proud to see you working with Tezya—"

"I have to go," was all I said as I teleported to the opposite end of the camp. I couldn't stomach hearing any more. People whipped their heads in my direction, their eyes bulging as they took me in. The pure, undiluted rage was palpating from me in hot waves, as I cursed, "GET THE FUCK AWAY FROM ME!"

I started hyperventilating. I couldn't breathe properly. I didn't want to know that. I didn't want to know that he was good. That the Lux King took away yet another thing from me.

I screamed, but I couldn't hear it as it echoed throughout the camp. My ears were ringing, and my vision was blurring, but even through the haze, through the unshed tears that I refused to let fall, I could see Advenians squirming. They were running away in different directions to get as far away from me as they could. Good. They needed to run. They all needed to leave me the fuck alone.

Memories came back to me in hot flashes. I couldn't shake them away. Him hitting Greyland. Him pressing hot iron against my stomach before having Moli heal it only to do it over and over again. His abuse of zero servants at our estate. Him belittling my mother. We didn't have a voice in that household. We were all caught in his choke-hold. But what we lived through, what we saw through him... Was it really just parts of the Lux King and Athler? Was the man who raised me really the same person who started the rebellion? He couldn't be. There was no way...

The people around me weren't leaving fast enough. I couldn't stand to look at them as they sprinted away. As they looked at me for what I truly was—a monster. For how I used to view my dad...

I needed to be alone. I needed everyone to fucking leave because I didn't trust myself not to rip apart whoever was in my sight until they were nothing more than fucking limbs pulled from bodies, until they were as lifeless and as dead as I felt—as dead as my father now was.

I curled my fists together and teleported to the border. I didn't stop as I walked through the protective shield, even as I heard someone scream after me, my name dying on their lips as I entered the mortal territory on the other side. Light fingers grazed over my skin, almost clamping down around my bicep, but I teleported before their grip could take route.

I teleported, and I didn't stop. Jump after jump after jump. A thrill ran over me at the use of my powers, humming deep in my bones. My abilities were the only thing in this world that wouldn't betray me. The only thing I knew for certain.

I halted, my breath caught in my throat, once I saw where I ended up. I was at the dead river Savannah took me to. I hadn't even realized I was heading here, didn't know I had the jumps memorized, that I now knew the way on my own.

My eyes scanned the snowy river bank before I beelined into the trees, following the same path Savannah showed me.

I didn't teleport. I walked this time. I wanted to feel my feet move one step in front of the other. I wanted to feel the dirt beneath me as I made my way toward oblivion. I didn't stop until my feet no longer had purchase, and I was plummeting toward the rapids below.

I didn't feel the sensations running through my stomach this time, didn't feel the drop.

It was too fucking close. I hadn't leapt as I fell into the water, only just missing a ragged rock protruding from the waterfall.

Too bad.

I let myself sink—down and down and down. At some point, I started screaming. Water rushed into me, burning me from the inside out. But it didn't numb the pain. It didn't take away my agony, only amplified it.

My brother's face flashed in my mind just as my lungs burned to the point of constriction. I couldn't leave him. I couldn't let him lose another person he loved. I had to suck it up. Fuck. I had to bite down my own pain because it would be nothing compared to what losing me would do to Greyland.

I started swimming toward the surface, taking my damn fucking time as I did and savoring in the last drags of agony.

When I finally took a gasp, a lungful of air filling me, I promised myself that the King would pay for this.

I would get my vengeance.

FIFTY-THREE
SCOTLIND

I'D BEEN BACK in the camp for four weeks now, and I spent every single night in Tezya's tent.

The first week, we helped out in the healer's tent all day and night that we barely slept. More Advenians Tezya rescued had died, most were in worse shape than we thought, but a lot survived too. Many were getting stronger and being discharged.

Some people recognized me from when the King brought me down to their cages. Many thanked me endlessly, and I had to constantly repeat myself—it was Tezya who saved them, not me.

They were the only Advenians who hadn't seen the broadcast, who hadn't seen me standing up on that stage. And being thanked when I did nothing felt wrong.

I could feel people staring at me everywhere I went now. I knew it was probably a mix of disgust from what they watched, but another part of me knew it was because of what I now looked like. I knew I had scars everywhere. I could see them on my hands and arms whenever I dressed in the morning. I tried not to look too long and had been wearing long sleeve shirts and pants to hide as much of my skin as I could. But my hands... I couldn't *not* see them. It was like I outwardly became how everyone perceived me.

I tried not to think about it. I tried to put all my focus into helping others so I didn't have a spare moment to think about myself. It worked until it didn't. Slowly, the healer's tent was emptying, and I needed to find something else to do.

By the second week, I started training with Kallon. I was working on my enhancement with her every day, seeing how long we could open her portal. Since I never disclosed the location of the first camp when the King held me captive, we'd been practicing portaling large groups of people between the two areas, testing out how many times we could do it before we were spent.

It also served to get anyone who never experienced it used to the aftereffects of portaling. The crippling nausea was no joke, and aside from Tezya first bringing everyone here, most never portaled in their life.

We knew we'd eventually have to portal everyone to both Lux and Tennebris. It would take too long to travel by foot. We just had no idea when things would happen.

I was surprised at how much I was improving, although it took a lot out of my reserves to widen her portals. I was constantly sweating and developed tremors four days in. Now, three weeks later, it was only getting worse. Tezya told me I wouldn't be able to fight with my enhancement because of it. I'd have to rely on my combat skills only. But it was working. Every day we were able to portal more and more people.

It also led to more complaints. The more people we portaled, the more who started to question why we didn't move back to the original Brighta. It was larger and more comfortable, but half the camp was too badly injured to transfer. We were waiting for the Advenians to fully recover from the dungeons before we planned our next move, and once everyone was healed—providing we could figure out the prophecy, and Kallon and I could successfully portal everyone for it to work—we wanted to attack right away. We couldn't afford the days it would take to move everything. We were stuck where we were, for now. But it gave us the privacy we needed. After Kallon returned everyone who had volunteered to help us that day, Tezya and I always stayed behind to train.

I knew he was working with Wells nearly every day. After the mayhem of the first week, Tezya told me about the ring they found at the bottom of the *Ex Cinere Renasci* when I was caught. We couldn't officially attack Lux until Tezya learned how to use it, so figuring out the ring and working on Kallon's portals became our focus while we waited for everyone to recover.

We stopped going to the communal training rings—or at least I did. I knew Tezya still went to spar Sie in the mornings while I was with Kallon. But by the afternoon, he'd always meet up with me, and his training was relentless. Ten times worse than when he was forced to discover my powers back in Lux.

Week two was also when Dravenburg started mandating meetings to discuss our goals for after the war. We'd talk for hours trying to sort through what we'd want at the end of this.

Even though we all wanted the same thing, we couldn't agree on the small details. We knew we wanted to ban the ranking system and eliminate the Luxian law of having to marry within your own rank, but other than that, nothing was unanimous.

Dovelyn was the hardest to please. She fought us at every corner, which left most of our discussions unresolved. It was horrendous.

Then, after endless hours of bickering, Tezya and I would walk back to his tent together, and I'd pass out from exhaustion.

It was how I liked it. On the nights I didn't train hard enough or the meetings ended too early, I'd stay awake, crying in his arms. I hadn't seen Vallie since she came back, and I tried to keep myself busy so I wouldn't think about her or Miles. But when I was alone with Tezya, it seemed like everything would hit me, and the guilt of that was even worse. Who was I to cry when I wasn't the one who lost so much? Sie lost his parents and his friend. Vallie lost her twin. Many Advenians from the King's dungeons had been separated from their loved ones for decades, centuries even, and most of their families were still in Lux... And here I was crying in Tezya's arms every night while I was fine. All I had were more scars and friends who resented me.

———

I JOLTED AWAKE, unable to catch my breath. My throat ran dry as images played in my head.

I was thrown face first onto the bed, my head slamming into a pillow. Rough hands pulled my ass up by my hips.

"What do you want, Rumor?" Tezya asked, his voice husky.

I whimpered, feeling him press against me. "I want... I want..." I was breathless, unable to properly form words.

His hands left my backside and ran up my spine until he fisted a handful of my hair, pulling my head back and turning it to the side. I could feel his breath against my cheek. His chest rumbled against me as he purred into my ear, "Say it, Rumor."

"I want—" I didn't know how to articulate what I wanted. I didn't know what word to use. Cock. Dick. Penis. It all felt wrong on my tongue. "You," I finally settled on.

That seemed to satisfy him because the next second he plunged inside of me. His one hand still fisted my hair as his other gripped my hip, manipulating my body to allow him in deeper.

The image shifted.

I was on my knees before him, trailing featherlight kisses down his abdomen. My tongue lingering over the small bit of hair that led downward. His eyes were feral as he looked down at me. A brief smile twisted my lips before I took him into my mouth...

I couldn't stop the ragged pants leaving me. My mind was hazy as I tried to make sense of everything. I shook my head, forcing myself to see what was in front of me. The tent. I squinted. It was still dark, only lit by glimpses of moonlight coming through the cracks of the fabric. Last night came back to me in a blur. That wasn't real, was it? I felt emotions from whatever I just watched... But I was certain it didn't actually happen.

I looked down at Tezya. He was stretched out on the bed beside me. His legs were too long for the cot that his ankles and feet were hanging off the low mattress, almost touching the furs laid out on the grass. Our shared blanket had fallen to his hips. He was shirtless, sleeping in just his boxers like he did every night since I'd been staying with him. *I sleep naked, Rumor*—his words from the first time we went to the mortal territory crashed into me. He hadn't completely undressed in the weeks we'd been back together, but he always got close.

I usually fell asleep in the clothes I was wearing from the day, too emotional and drained to change out of them. We'd wake up in a tangle of arms and limbs before we'd start our day again. Over and over on repeat. Our simple routine to stay busy while everyone was still healing.

Tezya twitched, and I watched his muscles pull taut. He was still asleep, one hand clutching mine while the other was bunched into the sheets, his veins bulging. I stared blankly down at our joined hands, blinking a few times, before I pieced it together.

He was dreaming. He was dreaming of doing that with me…

I swallowed, hard. Then gently pulled my hand out of his, not wanting to wake him.

My conversation with Sie at the lake came flooding back to me… How everyone in Tennebris believed we went on a sex spree after our wedding. They believed it because it was rumored that a bonded couple couldn't keep their hands off each other…

I kept staring at my palm. At the two scars there. Was Tezya feeling that way? Had he been fighting the urge to have sex with me? I'd been such a mess since I got back that I hadn't thought about it. We only had one day together before everything went horribly wrong. It wasn't even a whole day, just hours before Sie told us Dovelyn was awake, and besides cuddling every night, we hadn't done anything. Just stolen kisses he'd place on my forehead or cheek.

I looked down at him again, staring at his muscles bunching beneath him as he slept. This time it was my own brain that kept playing images of us together. I saw him pinning me down against the war maps. Then pulling me onto his lap as I straddled him on one of the chairs.

I tried to steady my breathing, but I couldn't shake the feeling of how he felt as he pressed inside me, filling me completely. Butterflies dropped in my stomach, leading deeper as a need for him was starting to wash over me. My heart accelerated, and I felt flushed all of a sudden. I pushed the little bit of blanket that was still covering me off.

Tezya stirred gently. He turned on his side, his hand reaching out and grabbing onto my thigh. His eyes snapped open, glancing up at me, realizing I was rigid in bed.

He sat up too, running his hand over his face, trying to focus. Then he grunted and shifted the covers over his crotch to block himself. "Could you not sleep? Were you having another nightmare?" His voice had a mix of lust and sleep on his tongue, and I could tell he was trying to shake both feelings off.

I shook my head, unable to find the words to tell him. My throat was still so dry, and my tongue felt heavy. I pulled my knees to my chest, hugging them around myself.

I wanted him.

"What is it? What's wrong?" He tried to tug me toward him, but halted as soon as his hand met mine. His eyes glazed over, and I knew he was seeing what I just had for the past five minutes.

He immediately dropped his hold on me and moved across the bed, putting distance between us.

"Fuck. I'm so sorry. I didn't mean to wake you, or for you to see that." He stared at me for a moment.

I still couldn't find my voice. I had to say something—*say anything*—but when I tried to open my mouth, nothing came out so I just closed it again.

He let out more of a frustrated sigh, ran his fingers through his white hair at the top of his head, then flung out of bed. Bending over, he picked up his fallen pants, keeping his back turned to me. He started stepping into them...

"Tezya, I—"

"Go back to bed, Rumor."

"Where are you going?"

He turned around slowly, I caught a glimpse of his bulge just before he buttoned up his pants. He didn't answer right away, his eyes pleading with mine. "I'm sorry I woke you. You weren't meant to see that."

"Are you struggling?" I started, then stopped, having no idea how to phrase what I thought was happening. "With the bond, I mean. Is it hard not to…" I let my voice trail off as I looked down at the sheets. We'd been apart for weeks and weeks and then when we were finally back together I tried so hard to shut everything off, to focus on one task at a time. I hated that I was nervous, that I was making this uncomfortable.

"I'm fine, Rumor. Just go back to sleep. You need rest."

"Where are you going?" I asked again, this time finally managing to look up.

"I'm going for a walk to… cool off." His eyes were gentler. "Just go back to bed. I'll be back soon."

He picked his shirt off the furs and started walking toward the tent opening before even putting it on.

"Tezya—please, don't go." He halted, his back turned to me with his hand frozen over the flaps. "Please, stay." I slowly dragged myself from the bed and started walking toward him. His breath hitched, but he didn't pull his hand away, didn't turn around yet. "I want… I want you to stay," I whispered as I closed the gap between us, wrapping my hands over his exposed abdomen from behind. His muscles moved beneath my fingers, his hands fisting the shirt he was holding. "Why didn't you tell me you were struggling with this?"

He huffed, frustration radiating from him as he finally turned around to face me. My hands grazed over him as he moved. "Because I'm not. I'm fine, Rumor. I know how to control myself. I just haven't slept much since you came back, and my subconscious took over when I finally closed my eyes. I didn't mean to send my thoughts to you while you were sleeping, but I'm fine."

I stared up at him. Was he purposely blocking me out during the day?

"Do you—do you not want to?" I hated the pathetic tone that came out of my voice, how this one question caused me to panic. My hands dropped at my sides as I diverted my eyes, staring at my feet, waiting for his answer. Did he regret the bond? Did he not want me in that way anymore, but now his body couldn't help it? Maybe it was how I looked now, maybe he wasn't attracted to me anymore—

His fingers gently tipped my chin up so I was forced to look at him. "Of course I want to, Rumor. Fuck. You're all I think about. You're all I want."

"Then why…" Why haven't you tried to touch me? Why are you purposely pushing those thoughts from your mind when you're awake? Why are you trying to leave right now? I couldn't get myself to finish any of the questions.

"Because I only just got you back, and you've been through a lot. I'm prepared to wait as long as you need."

"I want to—"

He shook his head. "Rumor, no. Please don't say that just because you know it's what I want. You need to rest. You need to get better…"

"It's not just what you want." I could tell he was going to shut me out again. He was still planning on leaving, so I brought my hand to his, our scars connecting. "See," I whispered, my voice breathless again. "I want it… I want… you. *Please.*"

I let him see everything, not keeping anything from him. Something snapped in me when I saw his dreams. It woke me up from just surviving each day. It was like I just learned that I wanted to feel—not just breathe and exist, but *live*.

I gulped, my throat bobbing, as I watched his pupils flare and chest heave.

Slowly, I walked backwards, my eyes never leaving his, scared he'd run if I let go. When my knees hit the cot, I pulled him toward me, twisting us around and moving to stand in front of him, blocking the exit. I let go of his hand only to press mine against the tops of his shoulders. I was on my tip toes, trying to usher him to sit down on the edge of the bed. "Please, Tezya… I want this."

At my words, he sank onto the mattress. It groaned beneath his weight. I dropped to my knees onto the furs, unsure what I was doing, but I kept thinking about the image from his dream.

Tezya was completely still, unmoving, as I reached for him. I didn't think he was breathing.

I fumbled over the fabric of his pants, trying to get the button loose, but it wouldn't budge. He let out a breathy laugh, smirking at my poor attempt to undress him, but didn't offer to help. Instead he just leaned back and watched me with a glint in his eyes. I knew how to unbutton freaking pants... It was just the way he was sitting. I couldn't get the angle right, and my hands kept shaking. Finally, I let out a frustrated sigh. "I need... help."

He arched a brow, amused. "I'll take them off," he murmured. "But you first."

My lips parted before I quickly snapped them shut. He didn't think I would. He was challenging me. Slowly, I stood on shaky legs, my toes digging into the soft furs over the grass. I was still in my clothes from yesterday, having fallen asleep in his arms again. My boots were off and neatly stacked by the edge of the tent. Tezya must have removed them before falling asleep himself.

I pulled my shirt over my head, tossing it on the ground. My pants came next, and I half tripped out of them before I tugged them down my legs. If Tezya was trying to get me to strip for him, this was definitely not how it was supposed to be done. I was messing everything up, but when I looked up to meet his gaze, he didn't seem to mind. He was transfixed, his eyes sweeping over my body, taking in every inch of me. His breath stilled again. I was down to my bra and underwear, feeling my own chest moving frantically under his assessment.

"Y-your... turn," I said breathily. I tried to have my words come off as sexy, but it was raspy and anything but. Tezya stood suddenly, his height looming over me. We were only a couple of inches apart, forcing me to tilt my head up to look at him, but I didn't take a step back.

I watched as he reached for the button and unhooked it with one hand—using only two freaking fingers while I struggled with both hands—then shrugged them down and off his legs. He never put his shirt on, so his boxers came next, and my breath hitched as I looked down. The first time we had sex, I barely got to take him in before he pressed himself inside me, and the rest of the day we'd spent so tangled into each other, I hadn't noticed what he looked like, only what he *felt* like.

I bit my lip, then dragged my eyes back up to his. "Sit... sit down," I stuttered.

He listened.

I let out a shaky breath before I sank back onto my knees. My fingers reached out as I ran them down his abs, feeling him shudder at my touch. I moved them lower and lower until I finally wrapped my hands around the length of him.

His body convulsed once, before he went rigid, completely unmoving. I started shifting my hand slowly up and down his shaft, trying to pay attention to his reaction, not sure if I was doing it right. I leaned forward, pressing a kiss below his belly button, then lower.

He groaned, his chest rumbling under my lips, giving me the confidence to keep going.

I glanced up to meet his gaze, not removing my lips from his stomach. He was already staring down at me, his pupils fully dilated. I kissed lower, then lower, my hand moving slowly up and down as I went.

"I—I want to but—I don't..." my lips stopped just above where my hands were. "I need you to... show me what to do."

He nodded, his chest rasping, but he didn't say anything. He just watched me between his legs. I removed my hands, then replaced them with my lips, taking him inside my mouth like the version of me had done in his dream.

I gagged immediately, having pushed him too far back. "It's okay," he half grunted, half moaned. "You don't have to fit it all. Just—fuck. Yeah, just do that."

I started moving my mouth slowly up and down him, savoring the reaction I was causing. He swore again when I started moving my tongue in circles while bobbing my head against him.

He fisted my hair, holding me toward him. I didn't stop this time as I half gagged on him. I kept going, kept taking more and more of him in, listening to him moan and curse above me. I could feel some of my drool drip down my chin, but I didn't care, didn't stop.

He moved further onto the bed, dragging me by my hair, my mouth never coming off as he readjusted us. Then he pulled my hips and twisted me so that I was sucking him from the side instead of between his legs. I was on all fours, my elbows straddling his hips to keep myself upright. One of his hands was on my neck, urging me to take more of him while his other unhooked my bra and started palming and teasing my breasts. I moaned as he swiped his thumb across my nipple. I kept sucking and licking him until—

His hand hooked under my knee, pushing my legs apart. I gasped, having to force myself to focus and keep moving my own mouth as he pushed my underwear to the side and found my clit. His fingers moved in rhythmic circles that had me moaning onto him.

"Your mouth feels so fucking good," Tezya groaned as his fingers shifted toward my opening. I couldn't control the sounds escaping me, my moans were so loud that I should have been worried that we were in a camp with tents too close to one another, only separated by fabric. But I didn't care. All I could focus on was what he was doing with his hands. His finger pushed inside of me, working in and out in a tantalizingly slow motion, before he added another. I gasped, the sensation so different at this angle.

"You're so wet," Tezya groaned. "Fuck." He fisted my hair again, pulling me up and dragged me on top of him.

"Why did you stop?" I panted.

"I don't want to come yet."

"What do you want—" He didn't let me finish, consuming my mouth and stopping my words with his lips. He flipped me onto my back as he hovered over me.

Holding my gaze, he pushed my legs apart with his knee. Then he ripped my underwear off, the last thing that was separating us before he thrusted inside me. My head snapped forward at the pressure, my forehead hitting his chest.

His fingers weaved into my hair, but this time it was gentle. His other hand found my cheek. "You okay?"

I nodded, tilting my head up as our lips crashed together again.

"Yes," I breathed as he made another deep thrust inside me. "Yes," I said again as my eyes fluttered close, and for some reason, I couldn't stop saying the word. It was like a plea, an acceptance, and a resignation. I was okay. For the first time since I came back, I let myself believe I was going to be okay.

FIFTY-FOUR
SCOTLIND

IT WAS another four weeks before Dravenburg called the first official war meeting. I was already in the tent and couldn't sit still. Almost everyone was healed from Tezya's rescue, and it was the first time Dravenburg was opening up the meeting to the entire camp.

I was restless after seeing how many Advenians showed up, how many were ready to fight. We moved the meeting to the dining tent so we could accommodate the sheer number of people. Wells brought out a monitor screen where the buffet tables usually stood, and the rest of the tables were cleared so we could fit more chairs. The tent was completely crammed.

Tezya was by my side, his brow arched at my fidgeting, but he didn't say anything.

After everyone filed in, Dravenburg finally started. "To anyone who is new, welcome to Brighta. This camp was originally created as a refuge. You're all welcome to stay and call Brighta your home. No one is under any obligation other than to live peacefully as that has always been our intention. That being said, we are now officially on the brink of a war." A murmur rang out across the tent. Most Advenians were locked up for Goddess knows how long and had no idea what had been happening on the outside world. Dravenburg explained everything quickly and efficiently. Then he gestured for his son to come forward.

Wells cleared his throat, pushed his glasses up to the bridge of his nose, bent each finger mindlessly like he couldn't stop fidgeting, before turning toward the monitor he'd brought in. "Right. Well, I'm Wells," he said, his voice squeaked. He turned his back to the crowd and then began talking a mile a minute facing the wall. But after Dravenburg's speech everyone was so eerily quiet that I could hear him as well as if he was standing directly in front of me.

"It took me some time to fix and rewire our connection to both kingdoms' broadcasts. After the original broadcast was, um..." He paused, narrowly avoiding Sie's gaze, then started again, "Well, after that, our original thread was cut off, severing our connection. I was able to break through it again, and I've watched all the broadcasts that have been airing over the past eight weeks. There's um... a lot," he added. "They started mandating them daily."

I held my breath. That correlated to when Tezya broke in and freed everyone.

"I'm going to show you them now, but if anyone has a weak stomach, I would, um, take this opportunity to leave." He waited a good minute, allowing anyone to do so, but no one moved. "Okay," he murmured, more to himself than the restless crowd at his back. He hit play and the screen came to life.

I watched in horror as I saw what unfolded. At some point, Tezya gripped my thigh, his thumb started mindlessly moving up and down my leg, but I barely felt it. I knew the kings wouldn't let what we did stand. I knew they would retaliate, but I wasn't prepared for this amount of brutality...

They aired so many dead bodies, all completely mutilated in different ways. The only similarities they all shared was the zero branded onto their wrists and the letter 'S' carved into their flesh.

'S' for Sie.

They were making him out to be a serial killer, framing him for the deaths of all rank zeroes.

I gasped as the screen showed over a hundred dead bodies, all robbed of their clothes as they hung in the wind. A large 'S' was carved onto their stomachs by a blade. Blood was still dripping from their wounds, running down their legs and turning the dirt beneath their feet red.

Then another scene was displayed and there were ten bodies now, all with their eyes and tongues cut out. An 'S' was carved over their faces, distorting who they were. Their tongues were thrown limp on the ground next to them, the same letter marked into them. In another scene, only the torsos and their wrists for their brand were left. A different one, the victims were drowned. The next video had only three deaths—the smallest number yet. Their foreheads had the signature 'S' carved onto them, but their chests each contained a different letter spelling out *nix*.

After each horrendous murder scene, one of the two kings would speak. They would explain how Sie attacked again, how he was becoming more brutal and even more dangerous by the day. They were provoking fear into everyone.

Then, they reassured them, saying something about protection as they used the mass murders as an excuse to further gain control.

Two weeks in, they announced how guards would be stationed outside of everyone's homes. They mandated that every male who bore a rank three or higher would now be required to join their armies, regardless of what their Trial outcomes were. The curfew limit kept growing shorter and shorter as the kings slowly chipped at their leashes.

When the broadcasts finally finished playing, and we were caught up to the present day, everyone was silent. There was a broadcast for every single day for the past eight weeks.

Every. Single. Day.

For the past fifty-six days, the kings were using Sie as a scapegoat, murdering rank zeroes in unimaginable, grotesque ways. They were slowly trying to rid the kingdoms of zeroes, and by framing Sie, they could do it without consequences while having a valid excuse for their new *rules* in order to keep them *safe*.

I glanced over at him. He was fuming, his eyes were wholly dark and his body was shaking as he held back untamed rage. He looked like a ticking bomb, ready to detonate at any given notice.

Just when things couldn't get any more tense, Dravenburg started talking again. "It's obvious that we need to do something. We plan to make our first attack in a week's time. Over the next two days, I want everyone to decide whether or not you want to join. No one is required to fight," Dravenburg reiterated, scanning the crowd. "But we need to know where our numbers stand. There will be a sign-up sheet outside the dining tent. You have two days to decide. Write your name down if you choose to join. We will meet on day three to discuss our plan of attack once we have our numbers. There will also be a secondary sign-up sheet for those who want to help, but don't want to be on the front line fighting."

I couldn't hear the rest of what he was saying. My ears were ringing as all I could think about was one more week. So much could happen in one week. So many more deaths would result from us wait-ing. The Lux King killed over a hundred people in a single day, if he kept up that brutality, how many zeroes would be left before we decided to take a stand?

Tezya's squeeze on my thigh was the only indication that the meeting had ended. I watched as everyone filed out around us. I tried to steady my breathing, but all I could focus on was Sie. He remained in his seat. He was unmoving, so still, I would have thought he was one of the dead bodies he was blamed for.

Once everyone left, Dovelyn placed a shield over us. I briefly heard her answer Peter's question confirming it was a silencing bubble. Dravenburg told us he wanted to discuss things privately after the open meeting.

My breath hitched as I realized Vallie had stayed too. It was the first time I'd seen her since she was brought here. Brock was also present. He was now able to leave the healer's tent, and I wondered if he was helping tamper down Sie's rage right now.

"Right. Thank you all for staying," Dravenburg said. "I want to pick up where we left off from our last meeting. We were discussing if we should merge the kingdoms together."

"What?" Kallon asked, just as shocked as I was. Of all the things I thought he'd say, it wasn't that. The knowledge seemed trivial compared to what was just shared with us. We shouldn't be sitting here discussing what would happen after the war when it'd only barely begun, when rank zeroes were most likely getting murdered and mauled as we spoke.

We'd been meeting every night, discussing our goals for what we wanted after the war. Besides abolishing rank, Brighta didn't have a structure in place that would work for both kingdoms, and if we wanted to change Tennebris and Lux, we had to figure it out.

I understood the need for the meetings before. I knew they were important, but to sit here and talk about it now after everything we just saw...

"You can't be serious?" I spat. Dravenburg glared at me. I knew he never cared for me, and at the moment, I'd be dead if looks could kill. I realized it was where Savannah got her scowl from. But I didn't hold back, leveling a stare of my own. "You want to sit here and continue to talk about our goals? You want to wait a week and do nothing when people are dying right now? We need to attack *now*. We can't wait a week for—"

"Miss Rumor, I highly suggest you learn to hold your tongue on matters you clearly do not understand." His voice sent chills down my spine. His words felt like a dagger in my back. How could he be so heartless? "This is a *war*," he spat the word in my face. "It needs to be calculated. We need to act on facts and clearly devised plans. We cannot make decisions based on emotions alone. We need time to formulate a calculated move so that we have no surprises. The Lux King is murdering these people as bait. He knows once we witness what has been happening, we'll walk into his perfectly constructed trap. So forgive me if I do not want to risk the lives of everyone in this camp because you can't wrap your head around the fact that people die in a war."

I was fuming. Tezya's hand found its way back to my thigh. I could faintly hear him enter my mind, *Relax, Rumor. Breathe. You need to breathe.*

But Dravenburg didn't stop his speech, his eyes didn't leave mine either as he continued on. "You've been discussing governing options for weeks now, but are nowhere closer to finding a solution. You cannot expect anyone to want to join you if they don't even know what they're fighting for. Obviously, you want to stop the death and maltreatment of the lower ranks. That has been the premise of Brighta since it started as a refuge, but what are you going to suggest in the interim? What will you offer those who might be willing to risk their lives and assist you? You will find that many people will not be willing to die for half-ass plans, and what has been working here will not work in Tennebris and Lux.

"If you don't know exactly what you're fighting for—if you don't know exactly what your end goals are—you're only setting yourselves up for failure. You can't wait until after a war to decide next steps. You're at your weakest once the fighting ends. It's the perfect time for people to crawl out of their shadows and attack, and then sooner or later, you'll be right back to where you started, and anyone who lost their lives would have died for nothing. So I'll tell you again, you must figure out your goals *before* starting this war. You have a week. You can't keep pushing off topics because not everyone agrees. Take votes and start making the hard decisions. You will not please everyone."

A long stretch of silence ran through us. I was fuming, forcing myself to take slow breaths and trying to stop picturing all the vile deaths I just witnessed, trying not to picture Miles among them.

Dovelyn finally spoke, "It's clear we should only have one kingdom after the war. This camp is proof we can coexist, and Tezya is proof our kind can mix."

"Okay, that's a start," Dravenburg said before moving onto the next question.

Two hours later, the thing we struggled the most with was what governing system we would use. We couldn't decide if we should still have a king and a queen. Dravenburg strongly recommended that we keep rulers and the Council the same, suggesting the more radical changes we implemented, the more likely people might not agree with us. That we should start slow and not change everything at once. We also had no idea what to do about the Trials.

Dravenburg finally sighed and said, "What kingdom will you take over? Will you live in Lux or Tennebris?"

A strange silence swept over us. If we only wanted one kingdom after this, if we wanted everyone to live together, we had to pick. But which one?

It was Sie who finally spoke, "Neither." Everyone turned to look at him. He had been quiet the entire meeting, not uttering a single word during the last couple of hours until now. He just sat there deathly still, taking everything in. And for some reason it made me question what would happen to him after everything was over. Was he quiet because he didn't think he'd still be here? Did he think he'd die fighting because of the target on his back? And then something else clicked in my mind—if we won, would we be able to set his record straight? Would we be able to convince everyone it wasn't him who had been killing their loved ones? Or would they demand his blood in retribution?

"I don't like the idea of your kind taking over another area on Earth. You have two places you already claim. Three if you count your prison, surely you can decide between the two kingdoms—"

Sie cut him off. "You should start over on Allium."

Everyone stilled, all shocked by his statement to go back to our old planet, but all I could think about was how he said *you* and not *we*.

It was Savannah who finally asked, "How?"

Sie swallowed, his jaw ticked, as he met my gaze for one millisecond before turning his attention back to the mortal leader. "The AASP is in Tennebris, located in Backerly—"

Rainer interrupted. "The AAA-what?"

Sie narrowed his eyes, but it was Peter who answered. "It's the Allium Advenian Space Program."

Rainer nodded, but Sie didn't bother to look before he continued. "When I was the prince, I visited their facilities. They have a means to go back, and their research discovered the planet *should* be habitable again."

I lost my breath. My mind whirling back to when we went on our tour. When Sie first met Miles, he had said, *"I would like to check out your research."*

I hadn't realized he actually went. I hadn't realized he took Miles up on his offer. And the fact that he'd done it. The fact that Miles succeeded. Tears welled in my eyes that I couldn't hold back. I tried to focus my vision, but all I saw was black hair with bright red roots and shaking hands. I watched Vallie sprint out of the tent.

The conversation I had with Miles the night I was leaving for the Tennebrisian castle haunted me.

"Maybe you could fulfill our childhood fantasy of finding us a planet to live on," I had said to him as I hugged him goodbye.

"Anything for you," he replied.

My heart stopped because he actually did it, but he wouldn't be able to come with us. It wouldn't be him, Vallie, and me like we had always planned, like we promised each other as little kids.

I zoned out the rest of the meeting. I couldn't focus. I knew they decided on looking into the AASP's research, but I wasn't sure what else was said.

All I could think about was how I lost the only family I had ever known.

FIFTY-FIVE
SCOTLIND

"Hi."

I froze. That voice. She was in my tent. I turned around slowly, nervous I would scare her away.

"Hi," I said back to Vallie. It had been an hour since the meeting ended with Dravenburg. We were going to keep meeting every night until we worked everything out, and I was already so emotionally drained. Everything felt so raw. Even though Sie didn't mention Miles' name, Vallie and I both knew, but I hadn't expected to see her here. I hadn't expected her to ever want to speak to me again.

My heart was thundering, and I felt sick. I missed my best friend. I prayed to the Goddesses every day that she would heal, even if it meant without me. Nothing could ever fix what had happened to her or take away the pain from losing her twin, but I couldn't stomach seeing her so broken. She used to be the life of the party. She used to be able to make anyone smile. She used to light up every room she walked into. Now she barely made eye contact with anyone, and I rarely saw her leave her own tent. She was a shell of who she used to be.

I looked at her, really looked at her. Her once bright red hair was now black. Her signature gloriously red lips were a dull shade of pink, and they were dry and cracked around the edges. She hadn't filled out her curves. She was still too skinny for her frame, and it made me wonder if she was eating anything since we came back.

"I heard you were training," I said to her. I was just happy she found some way to spend her time. I asked Peter about her every day. He told me about the first time she had asked for his help, how now Sie, Lilia and Savannah were helping too. And for some reason, hearing that Savannah was training her made me jealous. The fact that she picked someone else to spend her time with destroyed something in me, but I understood it. And if Savannah was able to give her the slightest bit of happiness, I'd suck up my own feelings about it.

"I am."

"I'm happy to hear that—"

She cut me off. "Why did you lie to us? Why didn't you tell us you were Luxian?"

I opened my mouth, then promptly shut it again. I wasn't expecting the question. I had told her everything that had happened the day I first saw her in the healer's tent, but I tried to keep it short with minimal details. There was too much to tell to go into the specifics of things. I only told her big events that happened, figuring we'd catch up later once she was healed, and I'd be able to fill in the gaps when it was just the two of us. Like it used to always be when we stayed up late talking in our dorm for hours when we should have been sleeping. When we opted to share a bed so we could whisper our secrets to each other in the middle of the night...

"I didn't want to keep it from you. I wanted to tell you every day we were in LakeWood, but I was scared." I sighed, trying to regroup my thoughts, to stop my hands from shaking. "Dovelyn told me I was compelled not to say anything by my counselor, but I don't know if I would have told you even if I could have. I didn't want to drag you into this mess. I didn't want to risk you getting caught up in it if you knew my secret. I was trying to protect you."

She half laughed before her breath caught on a sob. "It's a little too late for that."

"I..." I started. "Vallie, I'm so sorry, for everything. For lying, for what happened to you, for… Miles." My breath hitched saying his name, but I forced it out. I think it might have been the first time I'd said it since his death. But he deserved that, he deserved to be spoken about. Vallie deserved it too. I didn't get to wallow in my feelings if she was willing to face hers. I owed her that.

"Do you know why Miles and I even got captured?"

I shook my head and waited as a sinking feeling of dread washed over me and rooted in my bones.

"We went to rescue you. When Synder became king, he gave this whole speech about how you were in the Tennebrisian dungeons. We watched as they annulled your marriage to Sie. We thought you were trapped in the castle. He told everyone you were a rank zero who made all these plans to seek power, and we knew that wasn't you. We knew it was a lie. Miles and I thought you were in trouble."

She laughed softly, but tears were now spilling down her cheeks. "Miles found me at the school. He had this whole plan to save you. We wanted to get you out. We were going to run away to the mortal territory together. We had everything set and then… we were caught almost immediately. They threw us both in the dungeons, and we soon realized you weren't there. I don't know how long we were there until Synder made a deal with the Lux King. Then we were transferred to the Luxian dungeons instead.

"If I had known you weren't in the Tennebrisian dungeons. If I had known you were really from Lux…" Her sobs cut off whatever else she wanted to say. "I could have stopped Miles and told him you weren't there. We wouldn't have gone to try and save you…"

"Vallie, I'm so sorry." I stepped forward. I wanted to hug her. I wanted to pull her into my arms and comfort her, but she shook her head.

"I know you didn't mean for any of this to happen, Scottie. I know you're a good person. I don't regret being your friend for one second. I want you to know that. But nothing either of us can do will bring Miles back. I can't stop seeing him die, him lying on the floor between us…" She shook her head forcefully as if trying to clear the image. "I just can't be around you right now, but I wanted—I needed—you to know why. I need you to know that it's not your fault, but I can't... I can't look at you and not see his dead body. I'm sorry... I'm sorry I can't be your... *friend* anymore."

My heart broke, just completely shattered and broke as it fell onto the floor in crumbling waves. I felt like I was bleeding out, like I'd die from the numbness as everything I ever loved left me. But Vallie didn't look, she didn't see me bleeding.

She left the tent without another word.

FIFTY-SIX
LILIA

I GLARED at Greyland as he approached me outside the dining tent. I'd been in Brighta for over eight weeks now, but ever since he was discharged, I'd barely seen him.

I'd been spending my days with the healers, trying to keep busy, but it wasn't helping. He was all I could think about. I kept wondering if he was healing. But it wasn't like I could just ask him. Greyland and I were far from friends.

The only time I saw him was at night because our brothers were forcing us to stay in the same communal tent. But even then he tried to avoid me. He usually came into the tent hours after I was already there. I would try to stay awake just so I could see him. It was the only time I got a glimpse at how he was recovering.

He slept on the opposite end of the tent, the furthest he could get from me. I swore I felt his gaze on me on the days I pretended to be asleep. But most days, I actually was asleep.

It wasn't new. My brother always joked that I would sleep my life away if I could. But he didn't know I had a different life in my dreams, a life that was now dead. No matter how much I slept, I hadn't dreamt of Greyland Noren since he took me to the cabin.

And I tried. A lot.

I missed him, missed that version of him.

It made me question everything.

Neither of us brought up what happened in Tennebris, and I kept wondering if I made it all up. Maybe it wasn't true. Maybe I imagined everything between us. Maybe I'd been so crazy trapped inside the cabin that I started making up false realities as a coping mechanism for being alone.

He wasn't helping my conflicting emotions because he acted like nothing changed between us. Any chance he got, Greyland avoided me. If I was already in the dining tent, he'd take his food and leave. If he saw me with Sie or Peter, he'd walk away. He was even refusing his check-ups with the menders. I knew because I looked. He was supposed to come back daily to make sure his rib fractures were healing properly. But he never came.

But now he was walking right toward me, and I realized it was the first time I was getting a good look at his face. I knew he lost an eye—I read the healer's notes about ten times before I finally let it register, but this was the first time I was actually seeing it—well, kind of seeing it. He had a patch taped over it until the stitches closed, which they should have fully healed by now, but he kept reopening them. Or at least that's what I gathered from Peter. I overheard him talking to Sie about it, about how Greyland refused to stop training, how his healing was slowed because of it.

I was surprised he still looked just like he had in school. Intimidating. Mean. Dark. *Attractive*—

If losing his eye was affecting him, he wasn't showing it. As far as I knew, he refused to talk about what happened.

"Are you writing your name down for the menders?" he asked. He nodded toward the second sign-up sheet. The one listed for *non-front-line-fighting*.

I was so shocked for a moment, all I could do was stare at him. I hadn't spoken to Greyland in months, and now he was just casually asking me if I was signing up for the non-fighting sheet?

It infuriated me.

"No," I snapped, turning toward him.

I actually *had* thought about signing up to be a mender... a lot. It was constantly on my mind.

All I knew was that I didn't want to get left behind. I told Peter whenever the time came, I was going to Lux and Tennebris. I didn't want to be stuck here, waiting while everyone else was off doing things.

I already did that. Months of it, trapped inside the cabin alone. Waiting. Thinking. Going insane.

So wherever the crowds were going, I was going too.

Lately, I *hated* being alone. It had a visceral effect on me now. Just the idea of it... of being trapped in a camp that was completely deserted... I shuddered. When Grey left me in the cabin, I thought he was coming back. He promised me he was coming back... I knew he saved me. I knew I should be grateful. I would have suffered the same fate as my parents if he hadn't. And what he went through to get me there...

"Then what are you doing with the pen?" His one eye trailed down to my hand, bringing me back to the moment.

"I'm signing up to fight," I said.

He laughed. It was soft and gentle, unlike when he used to tease me in school, but it still had me seeing red. He stopped as soon as he saw the scowl on my face. "You're serious?"

"Yes," I mumbled as heat rushed to my cheeks. I diverted my eyes and stared down at the grass instead. "I've been training with my brother and..."

The next second the pen was ripped out of my hand, and he looked —pissed.

"What the hell, Greyland? I was going to—"

"You aren't fighting," he cut me off.

"Yes, I am."

"No, you aren't."

My eyes flared as rage sputtered through me. I knew it wasn't smart. The most logical thing for me to do was to mend, and it wasn't that I hated healing. I actually loved it, and I planned on continuing to help out while we were in Brighta. I found a weird sort of comfort from working in their tent these past couple of weeks. I was fascinated with the mix of Advenian and mortal medicine and how they seemed to combine both. It was what I wanted to Trial in, what I would have done if I had any powers—not that it mattered anymore. I was declared a servant before Greyland dragged me into those woods. I knew if I was still back in Tennebris, I wouldn't have been allowed to mend.

So his comment shouldn't have bothered me, but it did. It pissed me off that he didn't think I was capable. "I'm fighting," I said between gritted teeth.

"I've seen you fight Lander, Lilia. You're not fighting."

"He had compulsion—"

"And you think the Advenians we're going up against won't?"

I didn't answer right away. Memories from the last couple of weeks at Kitlarn Academia flashed in my mind. Of Lander ripping my clothes off, of him using compulsion and forcing me into the bath… of Greyland watching it all…

"Look at me," he said, and I realized I'd been avoiding his face. "They ripped my fucking eye out of my head, Lilia. Do you want that to happen to—"

"Stop," I cut him off. I knew what he was trying to do. He was trying to scare me so I wouldn't write my name down. But why did he even care? He acted like I didn't exist ever since Sie brought me here. "I liked you better when you were ignoring me," I said and watched as his jaw set.

He stepped toward me, close enough that I could smell the mint on his breath as he bent his head down to look at me.

"Sign your name up for the healers, Lilia, or don't sign up at all." His voice was lethal, set, hard.

I should listen to him. Despite the fact that I was sick of people telling me what I could and couldn't do, what he was saying was smart, even if it pissed me off.

The idea of fighting terrified me and it didn't help that I wasn't getting better at it. Peter told me I had to train if I was even considering it, but I was awful. He tried to mask his frustration, but I could see it. Vallie was moving strides past me while I was still stuck on the basics. I *should* sign up for mending, but I *wanted* to fight.

Ever since I watched the broadcasts where they were murdering all those zeroes, my mind was officially made up.

It should have terrified me even more, and honestly it did. Luxians were brutal. I'd be lying if I said I wasn't scared, but I *was* fighting. For all the zeroes who were killed, for how they treated us in school, for my parents…

I was going to fight for them.

I wasn't going to just sit back and let things happen to me anymore. I was going to make a difference…

"You can't fight," he said again when I didn't respond. "You don't have—" He cut himself off, but it was too late. I knew what he was going to say. *You don't have any abilities.*

I stared at the zero brand and my scar down my forearm. I instinctively pulled my sleeve down to cover it. Greyland noticed. Of course he noticed. He went to open his mouth to say something, probably another crude remark, but then closed it.

My wrist was burned, while his was still blank. I couldn't take it anymore. Not after what happened.

It felt too raw.

I wanted powers so badly. I wanted to be strong like Peter, but I wasn't. I had nothing but my two hands—my two powerless hands.

"I didn't mean that," he said softly, but I barely heard him. For some stupid reason my brain started to replay the day in school when they came to brand everyone that was a zero. All the students were forced into the Kitlarn auditorium. Then one by one, they made us walk onto the stage, passed us a knife, and had Alec compel us to cut our forearms.

Then they separated us into two groups. The ones who were forced to cut their own skin and the ones who could refuse.

If we were compelled, it was a telltale sign that we were a zero. A compulsion user couldn't compel a ranked Tennebrisian. And although I knew I was a zero, I knew there was no magic in my bones,

I'd still held onto hope all these years. Maybe I was wrong. Maybe my powers were simple. Maybe it just hadn't manifested yet.

But when Alec placed the dagger in my hand, and when the cold tip of it felt like it was burning a hole through me, I heard his compulsion sing through my body. My hands shook as I dragged it from my elbow to wrist, carving the blade deeper than I'd intended. I watched in horror as blood poured out of me, as I gasped in pain, and tried to drown out the sinking sensation that came with the realization of what just happened.

It was my first time I was ever compelled.

I didn't even get a second to process it before I was thrown toward the back of the stage. They branded us, marked us before our Trials, then sold us as slaves to our classmates.

It was meant to humiliate us, and by doing it in front of everyone… it worked. They didn't want us to wait, didn't want any of us walking around without the entire world knowing we were nothing to them… that we were all nixes.

I tried not to cry as the poker clamped down around my wrist and the zero was sealed into me. I tried to not dwell on the fact that this was final.

I'd been so scared they'd pull us all out of school and wouldn't let us take our Trials at the end of the year. But thinking back to my last weeks there, it would have been a mercy if they took us out that day. They forced us to finish the year, but the way our classmates were allowed to treat us afterward…

I huffed. How trivial it all was now. My parents were dead. Greyland's parents were dead. We only had each other and our older brothers, and Greyland could barely stand to be around me.

Did I make everything up?

He never liked me in school. I knew that. He ignored me like I was the human plague.

I ground my teeth together because he confused me. Why did he put so much effort into saving me?

I have to get you safe first. It was what he said before he promised me he'd go back for my parents. He told me he'd bring them to the cabin and to wait for him. Only he never came back, at least, not in the same way I thought. I couldn't decipher between what was real and what was a dream anymore.

Everything was a nightmare, and I was losing my mind.

It wasn't until Sie and the strange girl rescued me that I knew for certain what happened.

Greyland was caught. He saved me, and then he was caught for it. And now he lost his eye. I wasn't even sure how he was coping with it.

Seeing him in the healer's cot when I first arrived was seared into my memory. Seeing how badly he was beaten, what he went through. We all lost our parents, but Greyland was forced to watch their deaths firsthand. How many more deaths would we see as a result of this war? What else would we have to go through? I thought things couldn't get any worse. I thought being sold to our classmates was the lowest we'd be treated, but I was wrong. Now they were murdering us, trying to kill every rank zero in existence.

"What are you two doing?" My brother's voice snapped me back to reality. He pulled me into a hug before I could squeeze out of it. A large grin was smacked across his face, exposing his dimples as he looked between Grey and I.

Sie, on the other hand, wasn't smiling. His gaze was settled on his younger brother, on the pen Grey was now holding.

"What are you doing with that?" Sie seethed.

"What it looks like I'm doing. I'm signing up." Greyland straightened.

"No. You. Aren't."

"To hell I'm not. You don't get to tell me what to do—"

"Yes, I do. I'm your older brother, and you aren't fighting."

Grey turned his back to Sie and finally brought the pen to paper. He managed to write out the letter "G" before Sie grabbed it from him.

"What are you doing, Sie? Give that back."

"Not until you tell me you won't write your name on that paper."

Greyland ground his teeth together before he started to turn around to walk away. "Whatever, I'll just sign it later when you aren't around."

I was pretty sure Grey only meant to say it under his breath. He didn't mean for his brother to hear, but Sie didn't miss a single word of it. His body flared with golden markings as he let his compulsion wash over him. "You will not write your name on that paper."

Greyland stilled, turning around slowly to face us, then rolled his shoulders, the only indication that the compulsion went through him. "You promised…" he started, ground his teeth some more, then forced himself to unclench his jaw. "You promised you wouldn't use your total mind control on me."

"That promise was made before we were in the middle of a war. You aren't fighting." His voice softened as he added, "You're still recovering, Grey."

Greyland stared at Sie in shock, anger radiating off of him as he clamped and unclamped his fists. A part of me was happy to see Greyland compelled. Sie was the only person who could do it—he was the only person in our kingdom who could compel a ranked Tennebrisian —and I loved that Greyland now knew how it felt.

I smirked. The Noren boys were too eerily similar and both hotheaded. Most people claimed that Grey was the gentler, softer one, but they didn't go to school with him. They weren't on the laughing end of his amusement. They weren't bought by his friends and forced to serve them—

I gently stepped in front of Sie and pried the pen from his fingers. Greyland watched every second of it. I felt his gaze on me as I signed my name on the *fighting* paper.

"You can always sign that one," I gestured toward the one he told me to sign. The one that said *non-frontline-fighting*.

Then, I sweetly smiled at him before I walked away, knowing I was leaving him seething behind me.

FIFTY-SEVEN
SIE

Savannah was true to her word and trained with us every morning. And even though she always complained about needing coffee nonstop or groaned about how the sun wasn't up yet, she always showed up.

I couldn't stop thinking about what she'd want, what she'd ask me for that I wouldn't be able to refuse. I tried to ignore it, but a small pang in my stomach told me I made a huge mistake, a big fucking mistake, and that she wasn't worth the trouble. I'd regret it as soon as I found out what she'd demand.

But she was helping Vallie. She ran through all the drills we had already taught her, adjusting her form and shifting her positioning in a way Peter and I couldn't with words alone. And with Savannah helping Vallie, Peter could focus more on Lilia. They were both improving, and Peter was so fucking elated for it that it took some of my edge off.

I doubted I still needed to be here, but I found myself coming anyway.

Today was the first day Savannah was sparring Vallie, and with Lilia working through maneuvers and drills we showed her earlier, Peter and I found ourselves doing the same. But I kept watching them, watching *her*, instead of my own fight with Peter. I couldn't fucking tear my eyes away from the onslaught.

"Tighten your core here," Savannah said as she stood behind Vallie, her arm wrapped around her abdomen as she pressed a hand to her stomach. Vallie flinched, but she didn't pull away. She never pulled away from Savannah's touch, and I seemed to not be able to pull my gaze away either.

Savannah's eyes slid to mine when she found me already staring. "When you engage your core muscles, you can add more strength to your punches." Why wasn't *she* looking away? She was holding my gaze, her eyes never leaving mine as she kept instructing Vallie on what to do, as her hands kept moving over her body and repositioning her... Fuck. I swallowed.

She had a glint in her eyes like she knew she held power over me. I gritted my teeth as I forced myself to meet Peter's green-eyed gaze instead. He smirked, seeming amused as fuck, as we wordlessly went back to our own sparring.

He threw a kick, just narrowly missing my ribs, before he subtly tugged his ear.

I entered his mind, our signal when he had something to say. *What?* I snapped, furious even in my own head.

I told you she wants to murder you, he taunted. I threw a punch to his jaw. He rubbed it as he spoke out loud, "Ouch. That freaking hurt."

I didn't care. I kept fighting him, trying to ignore the purple hair to my left. Because while I kept looking at Savannah more and more out of curiosity, she looked at me like I was an ant to be squashed. I couldn't tell if I loved that she wasn't terrified of me or if I hated that she wasn't even the slightest bit intimated.

Maybe it was a little of both.

You need to get laid, Peter said as I just narrowly missed his leg slamming into my head.

Fuck off, I spat, this time landing my own hit, but he countered with the same. I ground my teeth as I rubbed my hip where his foot just connected.

He shrugged, then spoke in my mind. *I'm just saying, a good shag never hurt anyone.*

Worry about yourself, I seethed. **When was the last time you even touched a girl?**

Peter's eyes gleamed. *I can transform into one whenever I need a good boob grabbing.*

That's completely fucked. I don't even want to know if you're serious or not.

My eyes—my traitorous fucking eyes—flicked to Savannah again. She let out a hiss as she fell into her own sparring match with Vallie, who just landed a punch to her gut. The slight noise that came out of her had me wondering what sounds she'd make if I fucked her. If I slammed her body against a wall, grabbed her by her throat, and... shit. I was so completely and utterly fucked if this was what my mind was coming up with... with a *human*.

Maybe Peter was right. Maybe I needed to find a random Tennebrisian girl to screw for the night. I hadn't had sex with anyone since I met Scotlind, which I didn't even want to wrap my head around how long ago that was.

But at least the thought calmed my nerves. I didn't actually like Savannah. Not even the slightest. I just needed to put my dick somewhere and then I'd stop thinking about her.

Peter gave me a smirk, knowing exactly where my gaze had landed. I exited his mind, not wanting to hear whatever taunts he'd throw my way, and went full force into beating the living shit out of him.

———

SAPPHIRE EYES SEEPED into me as I picked up my pack from the grass. I had spent all day at the training rings, blowing off steam and fighting whoever was willing. It was all I did lately. Wake up early to train Vallie and Lilia, then grab a cup of coffee—which was a habit I was quickly becoming addicted to—even though I refused to go at the same time as Savannah.

I'd wait fifteen minutes after our early training session before heading into the dining tent, knowing full well she'd already drained her own cup of poison. Then, after I drank the bitter liquid, I'd forced myself to eat something before heading back to the rings. I would fight until I only had a few spare minutes left to shower before the nightly meetings with Dravenburg would start.

My days were simple. Mindless. And I tried my damn best to keep them that way. Most days, the Fire Prince still sparred me, which I hated to admit that I loved. It was the only real challenge I felt, and now that I was exercising every day and was no longer consuming poison, my body was growing exponentially. I could feel myself coming into my strength again, probably stronger than I was before.

I rubbed my rib. Tezya landed a hard kick to the area minutes earlier, and I was pretty certain he fractured it. I was supposed to get it mended. Dravenburg made it clear that everyone should continue to train, but we had to see a healer afterward so we were in top-notch shape for whenever the real fighting would start. But I refused to go. The healer's tent only reminded me of the one healer I'd never see again.

Besides, I wanted to feel the pain. It was something to think about. Physical injury was better than the mental war that was destroying me from the inside out.

I was surprised to see it was Scotlind who came up to me, though, and not the prince I despised. She hadn't been coming to the rings for weeks now. I knew she was training with Kallon, working on her enhancement.

I tensed, unsure what to make of it. I wanted this so fucking badly. Every damn day I prayed that she would have picked me, that she would've chosen me instead of him. But I also wasn't naive enough to think that's what was happening now. She already picked Tezya. Every person in the entire camp knew it.

"Hi," she said sweetly.

"Hey," I replied, not bothering to stop to talk. I started making my way toward the communal bath house with my pack over my shoulder and stifled the wince it caused when it landed on my ribs.

"Sie, I..." I could hear her voice growing louder as she followed me. "I want to talk to you."

I sighed. I didn't have the energy for more conversations that I knew were only going to leave me fucking hurting. I could barely stomach the conversation I had with Dovelyn when she said the same thing to me. I had no idea what Scottie wanted to talk about, and I had even less desire to find out. I spent my entire damn day building my walls up and blocking everyone out. I wasn't about to let her destroy them right now.

"Please," she added—and her voice, her tone, the way her eyes were pleading with me—I gave in and turned around to face her.

"Fine," I grumbled, pissed that I still had no control around her. "You can talk while I walk."

"Where are you going?"

"The bath house." I needed to bathe, and while most days I didn't mind the communal showers that everyone had to use—after I figured out how they worked, I found them to be more efficient and sanitary— but today I really wanted nothing more than to soak in a tub, purely for the fact at how stiff my muscles were.

"Okay." She nodded her head as she came up beside me, and we started walking up the grassy hill together. Everyone gave us a wide berth. No one came within a ten foot radius of me unless they were forced to in the dining tent or if they were crazy enough to spar me while training. Even after Dravenburg set the record straight about all the broadcasts, it didn't change anything.

"Um, I wanted to see how you're doing?" she asked, biting her lip.

I smirked. It was only a slight incline, more from annoyance and shock that she had actually asked me that. "Really, Scotlind? If this is what you want to talk about, then forget it."

"Okay, fine. We don't have to talk about *that*." She twirled her hair around her finger while she continued to bite into her lip. My heart lurched. She was fidgeting. I used to love watching her squirm when she was uncomfortable. I loved being the one who caused it. But now...

"I wanted to tell you I'm really sorry. For everything..." She stopped twirling her hair and met my gaze. I hadn't even realized we stopped walking and instead were turned to face each other. "I wanted to do something when… when everything happened… I didn't want to just stand there—"

"I know," I cut her off. I didn't need to hear it. It didn't stop the fucking hurt it caused me when I saw her standing on the stage, and she did nothing as my world shattered, but I knew now she didn't have a choice. She was being controlled.

It felt symbolic almost, in a sick sort of way. She'd been used her whole damn life, forced into doing things she never wanted to do. Growing up as a Luxian in Tennebris, she'd been compelled more times than I'd care to admit, some because of me. There wasn't much that Scotlind got to choose for herself. The only thing she did pick was *not* picking me. The only real decision she ever made was bonding with Tezya…

"I don't want to talk about it," I said. I couldn't bring down that wall. I just couldn't. I tried so hard to not think about the slight possibility that maybe my father wasn't a complete asshole, and that I never got to meet the *real* him. I didn't want to think about how my mother and Moli were now gone. That Greyland and Lilia were orphans with only two fucked-up older brothers to protect them. Or that my brother now had to live the rest of his life missing a fucking eyeball because I didn't think to check on him sooner. If I had known the King had him…

I shook my head. I didn't want to think about anything. I just wanted to take a hot shower before I'd be forced into another meeting that didn't pertain to me.

"Okay," she said softly, her voice barely audible. "I also want you to know that after this war, I'm going to clear your name. I'm going to set everything straight and make sure everyone knows you're a good person, that you aren't the one killing those zeroes. I'll make sure everyone knows what was aired on the broadcast was fabricated and—"

I closed my eyes, pinching the bridge of my nose. "Scotlind, most of it was real. I *did* hurt my family's servants growing up. I let my friends compel you for their own entertainment. I annulled our marriage. I gave you up and sent you to the Lux King. I caused you pain. I can see that now."

"No, no. *You* don't get it." She had tears in her eyes. "Because *I* get it now. I understand why you did it now. I know what it's like to have to make decisions like that, and I'm sorry I was mad at you for it. I'm sorry I blamed you..."

I knew this was stemming from something that happened between her and Vallie. No one knew the full extent of what went down when they were captive, but I could see it in her eyes, whatever she had to do, she regretted. Maybe she was cornered like I was with no real options. But now she was apologizing to me? There was nothing for me to forgive. Her anger toward me, her hurt—it was all fucking warranted.

"It's okay, Scotlind."

Tears poured down her cheeks. "I'm also sorry that... that I hurt you because I love him. I'm just... ugh," she swiped at her tears, "I'm so sorry for everything."

"Scotlind," I said, and her gaze snapped to mine. "Even though it fucking kills me to see you with him, I want you to be happy." I sucked in a breath. "I'm going to be fine, and so is your friend." She finally nodded, her tears slowing. "And you will be too."

It was a lie, and she knew it. None of us were fine. Not even fucking close.

FIFTY-EIGHT
SCOTLIND

"How did your talk with Sie go?"

I had told Tezya I needed to talk with him and get some things off my chest. Ever since I came to Brighta, I couldn't stop comparing what happened in Lux to what Sie did when he sent me there. I held onto so much resentment, and I realized, once Vallie viewed me in the same light, I finally understood why he did it.

"About as good as I look," I attempted to joke as I entered our shared tent. I honestly wasn't sure which tent I was originally assigned to, but when I asked Tezya how to find out, he made it clear that I was sleeping with him every night.

He scanned my face now, seeing my dried tears. "Did he hurt you?" His voice went from gentle to deadly in a millisecond.

"No, no. Tez, I'm fine. He didn't. The talk was fine."

"What's wrong then?"

I walked over to him, shrugging out of my boots before I straddled him over the edge of the bed. "I'm just tired," I answered honestly. "I feel so mentally drained and it scares me because this war hasn't even started. We've barely done any fighting and yet I feel so exhausted."

He tucked my hair behind my ears before cupping my face. "This war has been happening for the past century. It's just been in secret and only now is coming to light. And," his thumb started stroking my cheek, "don't feel guilty about being tired. You've been through a lot, Rumor. You've been fighting your entire life—"

I stopped his words as I pressed my lips to his. "Thank you for trying to comfort me," I murmured between kisses. "But I don't want to be coddled right now."

If we kept talking, if I kept opening up, I'd break down, and I'd admit he was what had me so anxious. I was terrified this war would mean I'd lose him. I was so scared of the prophecy, and I thought about it every day, going over the riddle Dovelyn chanted, trying to make sense of it.

Without a sacrifice from Light and blood spilled from Dark, the chosen one will lose his spark.

I didn't want to think about it now. I didn't want to know what we'd have to sacrifice or whose blood we'd have to spill in order to keep him alive. Right now, I just wanted to get lost in him, to embrace the feeling of being alive for as long as I could.

He bit into my lip, causing me to hiss. "What do you want then?" He teased, tugging on my lip before letting go.

I ground my hips forward, pressing into him as my nails raked down his back. A warmth settled around my body as I looked down to see Tezya burning our clothes off.

"I liked the shirt I was wearing today," I murmured as he flipped me around so my back hit the cot.

"Too bad," he said as he kissed my neck, then my collarbone. "I like you better without it." His hand cupped my breast as I arched into him. He pushed my legs apart, widening my hips, and lined himself up, about to fill me entirely—

A loud cough echoed from outside of our tent. "Tezya. Scotlind. Get dressed."

"Fuck," Tezya groaned. "Go away, Kallon. Whatever you need can wait until later." He bent down, applying another kiss to the tender part of my neck.

"No, it can't," she said, "it has to be now."

Tezya looked down at me, meeting my gaze, then covered my

mouth with his hand as he plunged into me the next second. His eyes glinted as he watched me struggle to not make a sound.

"I'm busy," was all he responded with as his hips started to move. His hand never left my mouth as he tauntingly pulled in and out of me.

We should... stop. My voice was breathless in his head. I kept gasping out loud between the gaps in his fingers, unable to control it.

There's nothing more important than this right now, Tezya groaned as he thrusted deeper, hitting the back of me.

"Please don't tell me that getting your dick wet is more important than this war?"

Tezya's free hand tightened into a fist around the sheets. He stilled his movements, but he didn't pull out of me.

"What do you want?" he spat.

"Dravenburg called a meeting," she said, then to my embarrassment, seemed to be addressing me, "come on, babes, I know you can hear me in there."

"Dravenburg can wait," Tezya growled. I still couldn't speak with Tezya's hand clamped over my mouth. I didn't trust my voice even if I could.

"No, he can't. I don't know how long the meeting right now will take, but Scottie and I still need to train today before the bigger one starts tonight. Unless you want her to not practice and be completely vulnerable when it's time to fight because she didn't learn the drop in her reserves, and she used all of her abilities to help me portal, and then someone's going to kill her when..."

Tezya half growled, half shouted at her. "Okay. Okay—we'll be there in five."

"It's starting now—" she insisted.

"Five minutes," he yelled, his voice left nothing to be questioned. Then he turned to me, his hand unclenched around the sheet before it found purchase at my hip, driving himself deeper inside me. *You have five minutes to come all over me.*

———

Everyone was already in the tent by the time Tezya and I entered. Since the big meeting with the entire camp was tonight, we were having our *goals* meeting now. We were making progress—we agreed on more things this week than we had in all the previous weeks combined—but it still felt too slow.

"What should we do about Sie?" Dravenburg asked.

"What do you mean *what should we do about him*?" Peter seethed, his smile disappearing as he set down the croissant he brought with him.

"I don't think he should fight," Dravenburg said.

Sie's fists clenched, his jaw clicked, but he didn't move.

"Why?" Rainer asked.

"Because he's going to die the second he steps into one of the kingdoms. We can't ignore the fact that he's been made into a villain. The broadcasts are atrocious." We'd been watching them daily now. At the same time they aired to the kingdoms, we also witnessed the horrors. The killing of rank zeroes didn't stop and somehow their deaths kept getting more and more grotesque. I had to force myself not to pull my gaze from the screens. And each person, each rank zero, had an 'S' carved onto their body somewhere.

It was '*Sie's*' signature move.

It was vile. I tried not to wonder if it was carved into them before or after they died, because knowing the Lux King, my gut told me it was while they were still breathing.

"Everyone from both kingdoms hates him. He'll be killed—"

Kallon interrupted Dravenburg. "That's not true."

"What's not true?"

"That everyone hates Sie. There are some people that actually support him. Not everyone believes the Lux King."

"We're watching the same broadcasts, right, Kal?" Dovelyn asked. "No one likes him." She turned to meet his cold stare. "There's no denying it. We shouldn't assume otherwise. It's not like he had an amazing reputation to start with."

"What I said isn't an assumption, Dove. It's a fact." Her voice was firm as she tucked a green piece of hair behind her ear.

"How do you know it's a fact?"

"From a source…" She bit her lip.

"Who?" Dovelyn's eyes narrowed.

Kallon didn't answer.

"Who Kal?" Brock asked, gentler than the princess had. Rainer was next to Kallon and was the only one who didn't seem shocked by what she was saying. He didn't say anything. He just stared at her, and I felt like an unspoken conversation was going on between them. He knew whoever Kallon was referring to, but he wouldn't say. He'd keep quiet for her. The two of them were closer than anyone else out of their friend group. Since coming to Brighta, I caught glimpses of it whenever I saw them together. I glanced at Tezya to see if he knew what was going on, but from the expression on his face, I could tell it was news to him too.

"Does it matter who?" Kallon asked as a slight blush crept over her pale cheeks. "If I say it's true, then you guys should believe me."

"I am not your friend," Dravenburg stated. "You may ask the others to trust you from blind faith, but if you're going to start making decisions that will dictate this war, I need facts." When Kallon didn't say anything, he added, "Right, well if you won't tell us your source, then Sie's not fighting."

"The fuck I'm not," Sie spat, and I shuddered. Every time I heard his voice now, it was more and more menacing. Probably because he rarely talked, but whenever he did, it was dripping in rage and disdain. "You don't get to order me around. If I decide I want to fight, then I'm fighting."

"You'll die," Dravenburg deadpanned.

"Then I'll die. It's *my* choice."

"I have a girlfriend," Kallon said abruptly, and the words seemed so random that everyone stared at her in bewilderment. "That's who my source is. I won't tell you her name, but she can be trusted." Kallon took an unsteady breath. "She told me there are groups of people who support Sie. He's the face of the rebellion just as much as he's been made into the face of the enemy."

"How do you know this?" Brock asked.

"Because I still see her." Kallon cracked her knuckles as she let out a shaky breath. "She won't come to the camp. She won't leave her family, but I have a portal in her home and I... visit her sometimes. She's been telling me what's been going on."

"Why is this the first we're hearing of this, Kal?" Tezya asked.

"Because I know what you're going to ask of me. She won't spy for us. I refuse to put her life in danger. If she happens to come across some knowledge then great, but I will not ask her to do anything that puts her at risk."

There was a long silence before Dravenburg said, "How many people? Do you have numbers for who supports Sie? And is this in Lux or Tennebris?"

Kallon shook her head. "I don't have numbers, but she lives in Lux. I don't know anything about what's been happening in Tennebris, but there's... enough. Many people aren't happy with the guards in their homes, many hate the new curfew, and most have already hated the Lux King before all the broadcasts. There's a lot of people who are seeing through what he's doing and realize it's all a farce so he can control them. I think we could use it to our advantage."

"I'm fighting," Sie said again, his voice lethal. "That's final."

"Fine," Dravenburg scoffed. "But it won't be my fault if your blood is spilled." He sighed then moved on. "Who has the ring that was obtained?"

"I do," Wells answered as he grabbed it out of his pocket. It was the first time I was able to look at it. Tezya mentioned it to me a few weeks ago, saying that he was working with Wells to figure it out, but I never actually saw it in person before.

It was beautiful. The width was wide, made to fit a male's fingers. It was a perfect mix of gold and black. The colors spiraled and swirled up the band of the ring, blending and mixing seamlessly together. It reminded me of the colors of our markings. I couldn't deny the symbolism of it.

"Have you figured out what it does yet?" Dravenburg asked.

"No," Wells said, his voice lowering. "Not fully."

"Have you had any visions of it?" Brock asked Dovelyn.

She shook her head. "I haven't. I don't know its significance yet, but I think Arcane might."

Dravenburg sighed as he pinched the bridge of his nose. "Why?"

"Because he's always been fascinated with artifacts. He hates all other aspects of Advenian history, but if there's a chance any magic is infused with it, he'll be able to tell us."

"No," Wells snapped. "I can do it alone. I don't need him. I already figured out there isn't any Alluse infused in it. Tezya can still use his powers when he wears it. All I need is more time to figure out the rest."

Tezya ran his hand over his face. "I agree," he said slowly, "with Dovelyn." A penetrating silence filled the air. The meetings seemed to be getting more and more tense, and I half wondered if we really were fit to rule over everyone if we came out on top after the war. We rarely agreed on anything. The anger and angst amongst us was palpable on a good day and a living breathing entity of its own on a bad one.

"Why?" Wells' voice held a glimmer of hurt, but he tried to hide it.

"We would be stupid not to utilize everything in our arsenal. My brother can help."

"It's settled then," Dravenburg said. "Arcane will assist with the ring. He'll be let out of his cell, but he must be kept in chains. I want at least five Alluse users surrounding him at all times while he's out. I want—"

He was cut off by Savannah sprinting into the war tent. Her cheeks were flushed, her breathing ragged, her eyes wild. She held clippings of gray and black paper in her hand that Dravenburg narrowed his eyes on.

"I think the King is taking mortals into Lux," she panted.

FIFTY-NINE
TEZYA

"Why do you say that?" Dovelyn asked, her voice cracking. Savannah ran toward the table, spreading the papers she held across the wood for us to see.

"There are weird phenomenons happening in the mortal world that aren't adding up," she said in between breathless pants. "See look here, this island was hit by a hurricane, and it destroyed everything. Three hundred humans went missing."

"So?" Dovelyn pressed. "We all know the planet is unrelenting. It's not abnormal for—"

"It *is* abnormal," Savannah breathed, her eyes wide and pleading for us to grasp what she was seeing. "One, we still have a couple months before hurricane season starts. Two, most people don't just go missing during one, nonetheless hundreds. And three, there wasn't much of a warning. This storm came out of the blue. Normally, we have days before we know one is coming. The meteorologist tracks it and states whether it has picked up speed and what category it is. But this one came fast. There wasn't a warning."

"You think it was because of Advenians? That air and water users mimicked one to take humans?" I asked, scanning the papers. She had ten of them. All unexplained weather related events with hundreds of people missing.

"Where did you get these newspapers from?" Dravenburg asked.

"From Ichi—"

"I told you not to visit him anymore. It's not safe."

"Well, it's a good thing I did because we wouldn't have known this was happening," she snapped.

"Do you even know how far his restaurant is from here? We aren't at our old camp anymore, Sav. His place is not a short walk…"

"I'm aware," she replied, not looking up from the papers. "It took me two hours and thirteen minutes to get there."

"Why on earth did you walk that far?"

She finally met her father's gaze, shrugged, then looked back down at the papers. "I was bored and craving ramen."

"Things are changing. This state could be crawling with Luxian soldiers hunting for Tezya, Sie, and Dovelyn. If they found you… if you had run into one of them…"

"Well it's a good thing I'm just a human then," she snapped. "They want nothing to do with me. They aren't going to just randomly kill me because—"

"They could though!" he roared. "They could kill you in an instant, and you wouldn't stand a chance. They'd kill you just like they had your mother for being in the wrong place at the wrong time."

Savannah straightened, her back going rigid. "That's hardly the point."

Brock added gently, "Regardless if you aren't a target, Sav. If what you're saying is true… if the King is capturing humans, they could have taken you too if they found you."

Savannah rolled her eyes. "Guys, I'm fine. I made it back in one piece, didn't I? Can we stop talking about your lack of confidence in me defending myself and instead focus on what I'm trying to show you?"

My jaw tightened as I scanned the newspapers Savannah stole, and I couldn't shake the feeling it had Athler and the King written all over it. "We should question Arcane," I replied slowly.

"Why?" Dovelyn asked.

"Because if what he said during the trade was true…" I shook my head.

Wells' eyes flared. "You think he already made the mass compulsion serum?"

"I don't know, but the only reason the King would want humans would be to experiment and run tests on them, so if he really is the one stealing them, then we're fucked."

———

WE HAD a few hours before the big meeting would begin so Dravenburg thought it would be pertinent to start with Arcane.

Scotlind, Wells, and I were standing outside his tent—makeshift-turned-prison—when the guards went to fetch him.

Arcane arched a silver brow as he exited. Chains were loosely clamped over his wrists, but otherwise he was free to walk. "Here I thought you all forgot about me."

Wells didn't say anything, but I could see him fidgeting with his fingers.

"We need your help," I said, knowing Wells was planning on not speaking for as long as possible.

"Oh," Arcane mocked. "With what?"

"We want you to examine a ring we found."

He tsked. "Is that all?"

"No," I said, gritting my teeth, bracing for what he'd ask in return. "We also want to know your progress on the mass compulsion serum."

He huffed a laugh. "Why would I help you with *any* of that?"

"Because I know you hate the King as much as we do, so you will."

Arcane smiled. "The *King*…" he let the word roll off his tongue slowly. "You know, I've been waiting for you to trust me, Tezya."

"What's that supposed to mean, Ar?"

"It means you've always called him the King or *my* dad or *Dove's* dad, but you never once referred to him as *your* dad."

I stilled. He knew. With all the commotion that happened, I hadn't thought about it. When I told the camp I was half Tennebrisian, Arcane wasn't here, and growing up, after our mother died, Dovelyn and I thought the less people that knew the better, so I never told him.

"How did you find out?"

"You mean besides the fact that I've been stuck in this tent and that gossip around here has been mildly easy to come by?" He met my stare, and even though he was smiling, I could tell there was some hurt behind it. "I've always known, Tezya."

"How?"

"You forget I'm the oldest. That I was around a lot longer than Dove, and I knew your father too. I was around when mom and him had their affair. I knew things changed the moment you were born." He shrugged. "It was easy to put two and two together."

"I..." I didn't know what to say. "I'm sorry you didn't find out from me."

"Me too."

"I didn't mean to keep it from you, Ar."

He was silent for a minute, then exhaled heavily. "I want something for my cooperation."

I waited, knowing this was coming. Arcane was predictable to a fault. I also knew my brother wasn't one to linger. He rarely ever opened up, and if he wanted to keep talking about why I kept it from him, he would.

Guilt coursed through me. I should have known. He was meticulous with details and missed nothing. Of course, he would have put it together.

And then more guilt ran through me. Arcane had a relationship with him, and then was forced to watch him die on the stage during the broadcast.

"What do you want?" I asked, letting him change the subject. We didn't have the luxury of time to dwell on family drama. And knowing my brother, he wasn't going to open up any more than that.

"Firstly, I want these off." He rattled his chains. "And I want a bed instead of having to sleep on the ground. And books. And it would be nice to not have people outside my tent at all hours of the night. They don't know how to keep quiet."

"The chains can go," I said. They weren't infused with Alluse anyway. It was the reason for the Advenians outside his tent. Ever since Dravenburg found out, he removed the magical ones and had Alluse users rotating on a schedule, keeping his and Kole's powers down. "The guards are staying, but I can get you any book you want and a bed."

"Fine. I want decent food and wine too. The stuff they've been feeding me is horrendous. And it better be good wine. I won't drink anything less. I'll also take a daily shower to clean myself and will require fresh clothes every morning."

"Are you done yet?" I asked. My brother was more of a pampered princess than Dovelyn, and I was prepared for him to list off about fifty more demands. When he wanted to, he knew how to negotiate.

His silver eyes slid from the three of us as he shrugged. "I guess."

"Great. Then let's go."

SIXTY
SCOTLIND

We had exactly twenty minutes to eat dinner before the meeting with Dravenburg and the entire camp was going to be there. Wells, Tezya, and I had been working with Arcane over the past hour. Well, that wasn't true. The three of us stared at him as he studied the ring in silence for the entire hour. At one point, he announced he needed access to his powers, but beyond that, he worked in complete silence. It was infuriating.

Wells wouldn't stop fidgeting, and I swore he was going to break one of his fingers. The only time Arcane spoke was to tell us to bring him to the meeting. He said he'd only disclose what he discovered in front of everyone. He also refused to admit if he was successful in creating the compulsion serum, so basically we weren't any closer to getting answers.

He was using it as leverage. We all knew it. He wanted in on the meeting tonight, and if that was the only way we'd get him to talk, he knew he held the power. He was back in his tent—for now—with the promise that we'd come get him before the meeting started.

"Let's skip dinner," I said to Tezya. "I'm not hungry." There was no way I'd be able to eat with the nerves racking through my body right now, and twenty minutes was more than enough time to—

"You don't want to miss dinner tonight. Trust me."

"Why?" I asked.

He smiled. "Because I might have told the cooks what to make tonight and it's not something that's normally on the menu."

My intrigue had me walking to the dining tent with him. The smell hit me way before I saw it.

"This is what we had when…" I inhaled deeply, at a loss for words, not remembering what the food was called, but I remembered loving it. Tezya had ordered two of them from a mortal food truck when he took me to his condo for the first time.

"Tacos," he finished for me. I dropped his hand and rushed into the tent. My mouth was already salivating thinking about them. Everyone else had the same idea as me because the dining tent was completely packed.

We found our usual seats. Besides Wells and Vallie, Tezya and I were the last to join. I had no idea where the mortal boy went after we dropped Arcane off, and I already knew Vallie wouldn't show up until dinner was officially over and the dining tent was transformed for the meeting. I was slightly disappointed because Vallie would have absolutely loved tacos. Freaking loved them, but I knew from Peter she was still barely eating. I tried not to think about it, tried to not let it stop me from enjoying them, because I was pretty certain tacos were my new favorite food.

I moaned loudly as I took my first bite. I stuffed mine with avocado, salsa, beans, beef, cheese—literally as much as I could pack into the small tortilla thing as I could.

Kallon laughed. "Slow down, babes. The food isn't going anywhere." I barely paid attention and just kept shoveling bite after bite of the taco into my mouth.

"Oh, that reminds me." Kallon smirked. "I totally forgot I found something out earlier today." That got everyone's attention. Whatever side conversations anyone was having at the dinner table ceased. Even Sie looked away from Peter to give Kallon his attention. She grinned broadly, satisfied that everyone was listening. "I found out that the noises Scottie makes when she's eating food is actually nothing, and I mean *nothing*, compared to what she sounds like when she's having sex."

The taco dropped from my hand and all the contents spilled out onto my plate. I had a bite still in my mouth, half chewed, that I just completely forgot about. "Kallon, what the—" I started, trying to think of every curse imaginable for what she just admitted to everyone.

Peter was the first to break the silence with a belly churning laugh. "I was curious," he started, but I shot my gaze at him, and he rightfully shut up.

Kallon just shrugged. Took a leisurely sip of her ale before saying, "If you don't want people to hear you, maybe don't continue to fuck when someone shows up at your tent."

Savannah looked between Tezya and I, biting her lip to mask a smirk. I glared at Tezya who tried to grip my thigh under the table to calm me down. I swatted his hand away, pissed that we were in this situation because of him, but another part of me kept replaying what happened. How he covered my mouth and thrusted into me... I really, really tried to not think about it because it was sending butterflies down my stomach, making me want him to take me again and again and not care who overhears. But I was equally mortified, and I couldn't decide which feeling was trumping the other at the moment.

Kallon was about to add something else when I cut her off. "Don't you dare say another word. You will shut up right now if you still want to be my friend."

Kallon just grinned, passed me a full glass of her ale, and smirked. "We'll always be friends, babes. You love me."

I didn't know what else to say so I chugged the entire ale she passed me. It was disgusting and burned the entire way down my throat. I half remembered Brock telling me how strong it was, but at the moment, I didn't care.

———

D ravenburg started the meeting after the tacos were cleared from dinner. I was pleasantly surprised by how many people stayed and wanted to fight. It seemed like almost all the Advenians that Tezya saved from the King's dungeons were eager for vengeance. I knew it was them, because even though they'd seen the healers numerous times, there were remnants of their maltreatment that would probably take months to properly heal. The ones that were kept there the longest, that the King was drinking from for centuries, had permanent scars from all the nicks made on them.

It made me happy to see so many people willing to fight for a change, to know how many others agreed with me and wanted a better life. But it was also unsettling. Ability wise, they were some of the strongest Advenians in Lux, but physically, they were nowhere near ready to fight. Their bodies were too malnourished even afters weeks of healing. I was scared we were setting them up to die when they clearly weren't ready.

Dravenburg was rambling on about the exact date we would attack as he ran through the numbers of everyone that signed up on the paper. As much as I wasn't a huge fan of him, he did think of everything. He told the saved Advenians—the ones from the dungeons— they'd be paired with someone from the camp. The people in Brighta had been training daily, and it was a smart tactic to implement.

After the meeting ended, Arcane stalked to the front of the tent, his posture at ease, regardless of the Alluse users trailing behind him, and I caught a glimpse of who he would have been as a ruler. Calm, poised, tranquil.

"What did you find out about the ring?" Dravenburg asked, not wanting to bring the prince out until after everyone left.

"Tezya needs to wear it when he goes up against my father," he said, and my heart stopped beating. "The ring will allow him to use his powers past his reserves."

"Going past his reserves will kill him," Dovelyn screeched. "Our reserves are the limits gifted to us by the Goddesses. It's their way of protecting us from having our abilities consume us."

"I know," Arcane replied, and this time he turned to look at his younger brother. "But if he wants to win, I think it's going to take everything he has. I think the ring was made specifically for him for this reason alone."

I was holding Tezya's hand, gripping it so tight that my knuckles were white, and from the contact, I could sense him. Tezya would. I knew he would. He would use everything he had. He would go past his reserves if it meant saving everyone.

"I tested it out on my own powers, and it still stops at my reserves. It doesn't work for me, but I can tell it's there. There's magic in it. If Tezya wears it, it'll work."

There was a stilled silence that followed. I wondered why Arcane needed access to his powers when we were with Wells, and now that I knew…

"There's more," Arcane said as his gaze shifted to me. "The bond has opened up a permanent link between you two. Tezya and Scotlind can powershare. From the blood bond, she technically has my brother's blood inside of her now, his Tennebrisian blood. It's the reason she can't be compelled anymore. I'm not sure if it means Scotlind could go up against the King using my brother's ability instead of—"

"That is out of the question," Tezya spat, his hand still in mine. "The prophecy was clear on who had to be the one to do it, and we only have one chance. We're not using Scotlind so don't ever fucking suggest it again."

I knew then Tezya wouldn't help me with his abilities. He wouldn't risk me learning how to wield fire until long after this war ended, and that was only if he survived.

———

"SCOTLIND, WAIT UP," Savannah called after me once the meeting ended. She was the last person I expected to want to talk to me.

"Um, hi," I said as she jogged to my side.

"Hi," she answered, then looked at Tezya. "Go away. We need to have some girl talk." Tezya was about to open his mouth to protest, but she cut him off. "I'll return her to you in a few minutes."

He gave me a once over before heading back to our tent. Savannah didn't start talking until he was well out of ear shot. Knowing his abilities, I was pretty certain that he'd be listening to our conversation anyway.

She pressed a cylinder vial attached to a long needle into my palm. The inside looked like clumpy milk. I looked up at her in confusion, having no idea what I was holding.

"You don't have to inject it," she said quickly. "I was just thinking about what Kallon said at dinner, how you and Tezya are... well you know what you're doing. Anyway, I just wanted to give you some options in case you didn't want to..." She paused. "I know Advenians have a hard time conceiving so you'd probably be fine, but just in case..."

"What is this?" I asked, not following her train of thought and completely confused as to why Tezya and I having sex would have anything to do with the conversation we were having now.

"It's birth control, Scotlind. It'll stop you from getting pregnant." There was a long moment of silence before she added, "I had some healers look into it, and they're fairly certain it would also work on an Advenian's reproductive system. You don't have to take it. I know you might want that with him, but with the war, I just wanted to give you the option, in case you didn't."

I didn't know what to say. The fact that she even cared enough to think about this was beyond me. "Thank you," I whispered a little breathlessly. I hadn't thought about it. I'd been so consumed by having sex, about how it felt with Tezya, that I hadn't even considered getting pregnant was a possible outcome. What Savannah was giving me was completely forbidden. With how rare it was, it was illegal to do anything to prevent bearing children. "I don't really know what to say, but thank you, Savannah."

"You're welcome," she said. "If you decide to take it, you have to inject the entire thing into your muscle either here or here." She tapped the very top of my arm and then the outer edge of my butt. "It's a hormone shot. It lasts three months for humans, but the healers think it might last closer to a year for you since your reproductive system works slower."

"Thank you," I said again, not sure what to make of it.

She nodded once before leaving.

I walked back to the tent clutching the injection like a lifeline. Tezya was standing when I arrived. His eyes flicked to the vial, then up at me. He didn't say anything. I knew he wouldn't. He'd heard everything Savannah said, and he was letting me decide.

Pylemo could curse me for taking it—

I took a steadying breath, then uncapped the needle and put the tip into my upper arm like she said. My finger was on the plunger, but I paused.

I couldn't do it. I couldn't push the liquid in.

Tezya was purposely trying to keep his face blank, but it felt like he had ten thousand emotions coursing through him as he watched me.

I withdrew the needle and tossed it before I second guessed myself.

If he didn't survive, if I got pregnant and his baby was all I had—

No. I wasn't going there. Goddess, please let there be an *after the war* with him. Please, please, please, let Tezya live. Tears pricked my eyes. I'd been trying so hard not to think about it, even though my brain recited Dovelyn's chant so many times, I had longed since memorized it.

"Are you okay?" Tezya asked cautiously.

I shook my head. Please, please, let him live. He has to live because now that I let my mind think about it, I wanted it. I wanted kids with him. I wanted a future. But I needed *him* to be with me for it.

Tezya didn't ask me what was wrong. He didn't need to. He pulled me into a hug and it just felt so right, so perfect. Nothing had ever been this perfect before. Nothing ever would again if he died…

No.

He'd live. He'd live. He'd live.

He had to live.

I recited my own chant over and over in my head, desperately trying to fight off Dovelyn's voice and the three words that haunted me.

He will die.

That night, we didn't have sex. We didn't do anything.

I wasn't aware of when he guided me to the bed, but at some point he had, and I'd spent the entire night wrapped in his arms, reciting my own chant until I started to believe it, but sleep never found me.

SIXTY-ONE
TEZYA

KALLON WAS PANTING, her yellow eyes wide, as she burst into my tent.

"What's wrong?"

"Scottie, she—" My heart stopped at those two words. Everything stilled. "—she's okay," Kallon added quickly. "She was showering in the communal showers, and well… she saw herself for the first time… since Rainer…"

I started running toward the bath house, not bothering to hear what else Kal was going to say. I'd heard enough.

I knew Scotlind hadn't looked at herself since she came back. She was afraid and had been purposely avoiding it. Hell, I fucking hated looking at her scars. I forced my expression to not change as my hands ran over her stomach, as I felt the raised ridges from where Kole had his hands on her. I forced myself not to show that it was destroying me.

Not that she didn't look Goddess damn beautiful with her scars. Not that I didn't love her any less because of it. It took absolutely nothing away from her. *Nothing.* She was still the most breathtaking fucking person I ever saw. And she always would be no matter what happened.

I hated her new scars for entirely different reasons. I hated them because I felt guilty. Because it was my fault she had them. My fault she went through that pain. Her screams still echoed in my head every single day. I could still feel the agony that rippled through her as his power collided into her flesh. I still saw her body convulsing on the grass. And every night afterward, every time she cried herself to sleep, I felt responsible.

My heart was pounding by the time I made it to the bath house. I sprinted into the girls' section of the communal showers, not giving one fuck who I'd offend.

"Get out," I spat venom at the two girls who were finishing up. I didn't look at them as they yelped and threw towels over themselves. I didn't even know who it was I was yelling at. All I could see was her.

She was dripping wet, her towel abandoned on the floor, soaking up water. Her long hair was plastered around her face, some strands covering her eyes, but she didn't seem to notice. She had her hands stretched out in front of her, and although she could probably see better by just looking down, she was staring at them through the reflection of the mirror.

She knew I was there even though her eyes never left her body. I slowly walked toward her. Pressed my chest against her back and pulled her into me. My fingers wrapped around her wrists. Her sapphire eyes just kept staring, blankly. She didn't react to my touch. She didn't make a fucking sound until I pulled her arm above her shoulder and brought her fingers to my lips and starting kissing them. Every single one of them. It wasn't until I put one fully inside my mouth, sucking and licking as I went that her eyes finally —*finally*—met mine. She gasped a little, seeming to come back to herself. I tried to get her to focus on the sensation I was causing, tried to veer her mind from whatever negative thought she was having.

"You're beautiful," I said as I brought a different finger into my mouth. "So fucking beautiful, Scotlind Rumor."

She was quiet for a long time. Her eyes now staring at mine through the mirror. I met her gaze, taking my time pulling each finger into my mouth. Then, I gently set her arm down and grabbed the next, starting with kissing each knuckle.

"I love you, Rumor. I love every fucking inch of you. You're so perfect, do you hear me? You're perfect." I shifted my hold on her wrist and held her hand instead.

"I—" she started and stopped. "I'm okay with it. It was just a shock. I hadn't realized they were on my face too. I think… I think I knew. I knew it was bad. I'd seen Arcane and Kole afterward." Her eyes drifted back to herself in the mirror. "I knew I had them all over my legs and arms and stomach. I saw glimpses of them whenever I got dressed. I just wasn't expecting it to be on my face, that's all." She paused, and I saw her gaze drift to my scar. "Did you feel this way?"

With our hands connected, I could see into her mind. I could see what she was really asking. Was my scar all people saw?

"In the beginning, yes. Everyone stared at me. Whenever I walked into a room, it was all anyone would talk about. They thought I couldn't hear them, but I always did. It took a while to get used to. Dovelyn and Arcane are meticulous in their appearances. None of their scars, if they have any at all, are visible. I think it was why it was picked for my punishment that day, why they did it to my face. But it doesn't bother me anymore because it means I survived. I might have had to fight to get to where I am, but I'm still here."

She took a deep breath as she looked at her reflection again. "I just… sometimes I think Vallie would have been better off if it was me instead of Miles."

"—fuck that." I cut her off as her gaze jumped to mine. "Don't ever think like that."

She opened her mouth, then closed it again, before looking back at the mirror.

"Rumor," I said carefully. "I'm so fucking sorry you have more scars and it's because of me, but don't for one second think your life is any less valuable."

"I don't. It's just she's struggling, Tezya, and I can't even help her."

"But she's alive and so are you. Just because she needs time to heal from what happened to her and her twin, does not for one second take away the worth of your life. *I wouldn't survive without you, Scotlind. I need you.*" I squeezed her hand. "Can't you see that?"

Her gaze met mine. She nodded but didn't say anything.

I gently brushed her hair away from her face and out of her eyes, tucking strands behind her ear in rhythmic circles. My entire frontside was slowly becoming drenched, but I didn't care. She was shivering, and it killed me to think how long she'd been standing here in the cold, staring at herself before Kallon got me. I called to my abilities and added flames around us for warmth and privacy, blocking everything out except for us. My hands started tracing her body, willing warmth into her. She watched me from the mirror.

"I love you, Scotlind," I murmured into her ear as my one hand grazed down her arm. My other was still cradling her head, tucking her hair behind her ear.

I love you too, Tezya, she replied in my mind before turning away from the mirror to face me.

My hands cupped her cheeks. "I think you are the most beautiful person I've ever seen in my entire life, inside and out." I needed her to believe it. "Nothing will ever change that."

She half laughed, but it died on her lips. "I think my looks are hardly important anymore," she admitted softly. "So many people have died, so many lost worse—"

"Other people's hardships don't negate your own," I said as my hands tightened around her cheeks, and I tilted her head up to look at me. I knew her, she'd push her own struggles down for the benefit of others. "It doesn't make yours any less."

She smiled softly. "The scars don't bother me, Tezya. I'm serious. I'm fine with it."

She leaned into me, and I wrapped her in a hug. I wasn't sure how long we stayed like that, just holding each other, before I realized I didn't even believe my own words.

Not all lives were held to the same value because she was my fucking everything—*she was my reason for just existing*—and I had no idea what the hell I'd do if I lost her.

SIXTY-TWO
SCOTLIND

"THE QUESTION IS where do we attack first?" Dravenburg asked.

Another three days had passed—making it six days since we found out about the King murdering rank zeroes—which meant tomorrow we'd finally be fighting back. I'd been restless to do something. The idea of war was terrifying—and I had no idea what to expect from a battle—but I didn't want to sit back any longer.

Kallon and I had been practicing with our powers for weeks now, and we were as ready as we could be. Everyone in the camp had gone through her portal at least once, so they'd know what to expect from the aftereffects of jumping, and Wells and Arcane developed a nausea serum to counter it.

Tezya and I had been training privately every day too, and I knew others were doing the same.

And despite me asking Tezya to teach me his abilities, to see if we could test Arcane's theory, he refused. He claimed there wasn't enough time to even try, which I knew some part of what he said was true. I was still learning and mastering my water and enhancement. And even though I was getting better at them, especially my enhancement, trying to learn his abilities—which took him decades to master —would be near impossible to do, and now we only had one day left.

But I also knew his reason for saying no was more than just our limited time. He wanted to be the one to go up against the Lux King. He didn't want to risk me trying, and anytime I tried talking to him about it, he'd brushed it off, telling me he was going to be fine.

He had the ring now. Ever since Arcane told Tezya how to use it, Wells didn't need to keep it in his lab anymore. Tezya wore it around his neck on a chain, but I knew he'd been sneaking off in the middle of the night to train with it when he thought I was asleep.

I hated it. I hated that as much as I wanted to go up against the King, it also meant we were one step closer to Tezya completing the prophecy. I knew it had to happen. Too many rank zeroes were being murdered every day. The daily broadcasts weren't stopping, and the death tolls were adding up to nauseating numbers. We had to act before he eradicated them completely.

"I think we should attack Tennebris first," Rainer said. "Lux is too powerful, and if we can conquer the Tennebrisian guards, they can help us when it comes time to fight Lux."

"I disagree," Tezya countered. "We need to do this once. We need to split up and attack both kingdoms at the same time. It'll be our only element of surprise, and if we blow it on Tennebris first, that'll give Lux more time to prepare."

"Asking us to split up is dangerous." Kallon glanced at Tezya. "It won't give us enough numbers."

"If we attack Tennebris first, we could lose a lot of people in the process," Brock interjected. "It'd leave us with the same numbers when attacking Lux."

"No." Dovelyn's eyes were the same eerily milky consistency. Her pupils were completely gone before she blinked back the silver into them.

"Did you have a vision?" Dravenburg asked, his back straightening.

Dovelyn nodded. "We attack Tennebris first. The Luxian army is too strong and lethal. We need Tennebris' soldiers in order to win against them."

"What happens if the Lux King brings his army to Tennebris?" Tezya asked.

"He won't. My vision was of him. I saw his reaction to us attacking the Dark Kingdom. He won't risk his own city for Tennebris. He's too selfish to leave himself unprotected, but he will grow his defenses. Tezya is right. We'll lose our element of surprise, but it wouldn't be enough to defeat Lux anyway. We need numbers and at this point the King will already be expecting some from the Advenians who got out of the dungeons."

"And you're certain Lux won't make a counter attack?" Tezya asked. I could tell he didn't like the plan.

"Not from what I could see. We'll have time to regroup before we go to Lux, and if we attack Lux from Tennebris, Kallon and Scotlind will have time to rebuild their reserves."

I could sense Tezya visibly relaxing at that. He hated the idea of me using all my reserves to help Kallon portal everyone. I'd have nothing left of my powers for the actual fight, and I'd be forced to rely on my fighting skills. Not that it was new to me. I'd been doing it my whole life, but now that I had my abilities, that I was getting better at fighting, I didn't want to go without them. But if we did it this way, I might have a small amount of my powers left when we attack Lux. I'd only have to get through the battle in Tennebris without my abilities.

"Alright. We attack Tennebris first. We'll leave at first light."

"We should leave tonight," Sie said, surprising everyone. "Tennebris is now in their dark season, so there's no point in waiting until the morning."

"You want to kill everyone while they're sleeping?" Tezya asked.

"No. I want to murder Synder while he's awake, but the only portal Kallon has there is in the woods in between Palm and Kitlarn. If we're traveling by foot, it'll take us half a day to get to the castle, and we don't want to attract their attention while we're doing it."

Dravenburg clapped his hands together. "Alright. We leave after dinner. I'll gather the camp and make sure everyone is ready." He turned toward Sie and Tezya. "Go with Savannah to go over the maps. We need to know the weak points inside the castle."

Vallie stood, her chair clattering to the ground, and it was so abrupt that everyone turned to look at her. "I can help with that. My ability is knowledge absorption, and I already have the entire kingdom memorized."

"Good." Dravenburg nodded. "Go plan out exactly where you want to attack."

SIXTY-THREE
GREYLAND

"Peter, wait up." I caught up to him as soon as he left the dining tent. I snuck into the meeting when Sie wasn't looking and heard everything Dravenburg had said.

"What's up, Little Noren?" my brother's best friend asked as he turned around. He looked conflicted as he watched the girl he'd been spending all his time with walk off. I knew he wanted to follow, but if we were going to portal into Tennebris tonight, I had to talk with him now. It couldn't wait.

"I want to fight."

"You're asking the wrong person. You need to talk with your brother."

"That's bullshit. You and I both know Sie's too stubborn to let me go. He's always been like that, but I can fight, Peter. I'm good. I took guard classes in Kitlarn."

Peter was quiet for a minute, but his gaze snagged on my eye—or what was left of it. I knew it was one of the reasons Sie didn't want me to fight, and judging from Peter's reaction, he told him. "I've trained with my ability," I added, pissed off about the whole situation. I still had my two feet, my hands... I could still hold a blade and knew how to use it, even if my peripheral vision was completely shit now.

"Why do you want to fight so badly, Little Noren?"

"Does it matter?"

Peter arched a brow like it very much did matter, but I ignored it.

"I'll make a deal with you." He crossed his arms over his chest, but he didn't flat out say no, so I continued, "You're going to be busy with Sie and Vallie, and we both know my brother is going to go after the Council—"

"What's your point, Grey?"

"My point is you won't be able to look out for your sister. And whatever training you've given her over the past couple of weeks isn't enough." Lilia wasn't a fighter. Hell, half the time she could barely walk straight without tripping over her own two feet. She was just too stubborn to realize it, and unlike my brother, Peter wasn't the type to tell someone they couldn't do something, especially her. If Lilia wanted to fight, she was fighting.

"So let me fight," I said. "Distract Sie so I can slip through the portal, and I promise I'll protect her."

"Sie compelled you not to fight."

"No. My brother compelled me to not sign my name on the paper. He never said anything about not fighting."

Peter groaned. "Sie's going to murder me when he finds out."

"I know." I smiled, knowing I won him over. Peter was worried about Lilia. He'd been training her every day since she came to Brighta. I knew because I was keeping tabs on her, but it wouldn't be enough. Lilia was the most uncoordinated person I'd ever met. It wouldn't surprise me if she accidentally tripped and fell right onto someone's sword. She needed me. She needed someone watching over her.

"So don't let Sie find out." I grinned.

"WHAT ARE YOU DOING HERE?" Lilia asked as she caught the apple I threw at her. Dinner was questionable as Dravenburg didn't want us throwing our guts up from Kallon's portal, and even with the nausea serums Wells handed out, we were only served bread and porridge.

"Your brother asked me to watch over you."

She was about to bite into the apple, but stopped with the green core halfway to her lips. I forced my gaze away as they curled. "No, he didn't."

"He did. Like it or not, we're fighting together." I was relieved when Peter agreed to tell Lilia it was his idea. "I know he told you earlier today about the arrangement. If you want to fight, you have to fight with me."

She narrowed her eyes, dropping the apple onto the grass in the process. Her blonde hair was tied back into tight braids, but she still had pieces falling out onto her cheek, and I had to fight the urge to tuck the loose strands behind her ear.

I bent down to pick up the apple, then did a slow job of wiping it off with the ends of my shirt.

I took a step toward her, then smirked as I bit into it. She did her best not to watch me, but I could feel her eyes on my throat as I swallowed. I honestly had no idea how to act in front of her anymore. My mind kept yelling at me to stop being a dick and admit everything was real, but some inner part of me kept crumbling at the idea.

So here I was, falling right back into my usual habits.

"I am capable of taking care of myself." Her voice lost its edge, and I noticed her tugging at the sleeve of her shirt, trying to hide her zero brand from me.

I tried not to think about that day, about how helpless I felt as I watched her on the stage, and how everything got so much worse in the weeks that followed.

Dravenburg gave us all leathers to wear, and since Tennebris was in their dark season now, it would automatically feel thirty degrees colder. I stared at her arm, knowing there was a scar running from the tip of her elbow stopping at her wrist, where she was compelled to cut herself. The leather blocked most of it from view.

I gritted my teeth. "It's not about being capable, Lilia. It's about being smart. Everyone should have a fighting partner, someone that has their back."

"Right," she huffed. "And I'm supposed to believe you'll have mine?"

"Yes," I said, then thought better of it. "Like it or not, besides your brother, I'm the only person who knows you here. I'm the only one who cares."

I knew she wouldn't believe me if I told her the truth. Besides bringing her to the cabin, I'd never been nice to her before. She still thought everything was in her head. And I couldn't blame her. I made her life hell. Why would she think any differently? My so-called friends were the sole reason she was treated so badly at school, and I did nothing to stop it.

Half of me wanted to scream at her, to tell her what my second ability was until she realized it had been me the whole time. I wanted to kiss her. I wanted to throw her down onto the grass and fucking crumble in her arms.

No—I wanted to pick her up and take her back to our communal tent. I wanted her as far away as she could possibly get from the fighting, and I wanted to make her mine.

I'd never been pissed at Peter before, but I was getting close to it now. I knew he didn't like to put limits on Lilia. He never wanted to make her feel inferior because she didn't have any powers. But fucking hell, I couldn't understand why he was letting her fight tonight.

I was forced to watch Lilia go up against Lander in school, forced to witness her complete inability to hold her own in the ring.

But this wasn't Abilities Class. This was real life shit and there would be no teachers to protect her now.

She pushed me aside and walked over to the group of Advenians waiting for Kallon.

I followed her through the crowd, keeping enough distance between us without taking my gaze off of her. I wasn't about to let her run away from me the moment we got there.

My brother and Peter had already left in the first wave. Everyone that would be fighting directly inside the castle was already in

Tennebris, starting the long trek through the woods. Lilia and I were in the fifth and final wave. We were the backup fighters. Normally I'd be pissed about it, but with Lilia here, I didn't mind. Because even if I wasn't ready to admit it to her, I wanted to protect her for more reasons than just because she was my ticket into Tennebris.

I *needed* her to be safe.

———

IT TOOK an hour before Scottie and the dual-color-haired girl finally showed up to portal our wave. The latter looked even paler than she normally did, and her bright hair was dyed a navy blue today, probably an attempt to blend in, even though it was impossible. She was one of the tallest females I'd ever seen.

I looked over at Scottie. I liked her, but some part of me was mad at her for not picking my brother. He could be an asshole at times—I guess it was the Noren specialty—but I could still see how much he cared for her, how hard he tried to hide the fact that he was still madly in love with her even now. Her sapphire eyes found mine, and she gave me a hesitant smile.

Her body was shaking, and she had sweat dripping down her forehead. This was taxing for them.

Scottie stayed on Brighta's side as she cast her enhancement for the tall one and together they brought twenty to thirty people over at a time. I pulled Lilia's braid, not able to find any purchase on the tight leather outfit she was in. But I realized my mistake as more of her silky strands immediately fell loose.

"Not so fast, *Little*," I said into her ear, knowing how she hated the nickname. *There was another one I could use, one she actually liked and wouldn't scowl at me for.* "You're going with me."

I drank the nausea serum half an hour ago, but even with its effects coursing through me, the jostling of the portal still hit me hard. I couldn't stomach my brother's teleportation on a good day, but portaling—it was so much worse. It felt like it lasted an eternity, and I swore I was going to vomit ten times over as we were pulled through the endless purple and black smoke. When we finally landed on firm ground, it took me a minute of deep breathing before I could even walk.

It was weird being back in Tennebris. I found it oddly calming. I loved the winter months here and was one of the few Advenians who actually liked the dark season. I found the stars and moon comforting, but it was also freezing as hell. Even with our thick layers, I could tell Lilia was shivering next to me. She was armed with knives, not being able to use any abilities, and I planned to not let her use her blades either.

Everyone was eerily quiet as we started our long trek through the woods, the only sound was our boots crunching on the frost-tipped grass. I tried not to think about the last time I was here, dragging Lilia away before I got caught.

Scottie and Kallon were leading the group, having no one else to portal, and I could tell they were both anxious that all their friends had already reached the castle.

I started silently praying to Pylemo on the walk over. I was worried for my brother. I saw the broadcasts they were airing each day, and as much as I feared for Lilia being caught, that she'd be one of the zeroes murdered, I was just as terrified for Sie.

I didn't know how the Tennebrisians would react to seeing him again, and I prayed they wouldn't heed the two kings' instructions and try to kill him on the spot. My brother wasn't known for his pleasantries, no one from my family was, and it scared me that the airings were so believable. Hell, if Sie wasn't my own flesh and blood, I would have had a hard time finding the lies in what the kings showed.

I was so caught up in my thoughts that I wasn't paying attention to the woods around us. I hadn't realized as the trees became less dense and the forest sounds were replaced by screams and metal clashing against metal.

We were here.

We made it to the castle and all my hopes of Lilia not needing her blades went out the window.

SIXTY-FOUR
SIE

Things were worse than we anticipated. The entire Tennebrisian guard was waiting for us, and I couldn't make my way through them fast enough to get to Synder. I wanted his death. I needed it, and I had to make sure I was the one to do it.

Frustration coursed through me as I took out guard after guard after guard. I didn't have any qualms fighting them, except that it kept me occupied while Synder was still breathing somewhere else inside the castle. He was the reason I was in that prison, the reason Scotlind was sent to Lux and was no longer mine. He was responsible for capturing Greyland. He was the one who brought my family and Moli to the Lux King. He was the reason they were now dead, and I wanted him to join them. I *needed* it just like I needed the blood in my veins.

I fucking hated him.

I cursed as more guards fled into the hall. Peter was at my side, shifted into a bear, dislocating limbs. He was trying to leave the guards unable to fight without actually killing them. I didn't do the same. I didn't really care who died right now as long as I could add Synder to the list.

Peter awkwardly tugged his hairy ear with his claw. I knew his shapeshifting didn't affect his voice, but whenever he transformed into an animal, he could only speak mind to mind. **What?** I shot into his head, opening mine to him.

There's too many of them. We aren't going to win.

We aren't if you keep fighting only to temporarily take them out. I think we're past trying to not kill them.

I know, he grumbled, then weird gurgling sounds entered my mind as he bit off a foot of the nearest guard. *Goddess, that was freaking disgusting. I love being a bear, but I hate the taste of—*

Then stop eating people, I said. **You have claws, use them, or shift into literally anything else that doesn't involve using your mouth to fight.**

I saw Peter pause briefly at my side. He was staring at his large black claws. *Oh yeah, I keep forgetting about these,* then he started slashing at everyone around us. I couldn't suppress my smile when the guards started fumbling away from my friend.

Peter, I said once I realized he was still only going for nonlethal parts. **I'm serious about killing. We won't make it out of here alive at this rate.**

Peter sighed. I knew he didn't want to.

You need to warn the others. You're the only one who can clear the hall and make it back in one piece. Tell them the guard is out for blood and to not hold back.

I can't—

I'll watch over her while you're gone. I knew where his mind went. Vallie was on this level with us. Not because she should have been in wave one, but because Peter refused to leave her side. And even though she didn't possess fighting abilities, she was an asset. Peter and I knew the castle well from frequently visiting as children, but Scottie's friend somehow knew it better. Her knowledge absorption was impressive. She was privy to all the ins and outs of every nook and cranny. And besides that, I was surprised her physical fighting skills weren't *that* bad. She was holding her own. I was worried she'd regret coming in the first wave, that she wouldn't actually be able to go through with using blades against Advenians, but she surprised the hell out of me. While Peter was holding back, she wasn't. The girl killed more people than most of our group. Not that her skills were amazing—average at best, but impressive for the fact that she only just learned to hold a blade for the first time a few weeks ago—but she was tenacious. She seemed more like a beast than Peter was in his bear form. She was taking all her anger out with her blades, and I couldn't help but see a similarity in her as I did myself. We were both left with barely anyone in our lives, leaving us with nothing but rage and revenge.

Peter, go, I said again because he needed to hear it. ***I promise I'll watch over her until you get back. She'll be fine.***

He sent a couple curses into my mind before he shifted into a fly and flew toward the ceiling, out of range from anyone. I watched his little form until he exited the hall, then slowly made my way toward Vallie in case she needed back up. The girl let out a savage scream as she hacked into the nearest guard.

I found myself smiling as I fought next to her, flowing into a rhythmic pattern, but the more people we took out, the more that kept flooding in. We were still far too outnumbered. Coming in waves was necessary for the distance we had to portal, but it was to our own disadvantage now until the rest of the camp showed up.

Peter flew back into the room at some point. He nodded his head as he shifted back into a bear, my only indication that he was successful. It also meant all of the waves were here, but it still wasn't enough. We weren't enough, and Tennebris was supposed to be the easier kingdom to conquer...

My breath hitched as a guard almost killed Peter. He was seconds away from losing his head when someone stepped in front of the blade. No, not just someone—it was a Tennebrisian guard. I looked around, only now noticing the guards were fighting each other.

I found myself face to face with Abherham—Scotlind's old guard from when she lived here with me. I hadn't realized he survived the night Kole captured her. I ran out of her room so fast, leaving him bleeding on the floor.

Guilt washed through me. I'd never even given him a second thought. At the time, all I cared about was her. I was so stupidly and selfishly blinded to everyone else around me. But he was very much alive, and he was fighting *with* us.

"Prince Noren." Abherham paused long enough to give a quick bow and hearing the title stumped me. It had been a while since I thought of myself in that way and even longer since someone acknowledged me as the prince. Everyone was either appalled or terrified of me. Respect was far out the window, and I found myself not really missing it, but then again, I was numb to everything that used to be important to me.

I didn't know what to say for several long seconds. I wiped the sweat off my brow, finding that no one was attacking me for the first time since we arrived. I scanned the hall and it was flooded with Tennebrisian guards with their moon symbols ripped off. But it couldn't be true. What I was seeing... What I thought was happening... It was too good to be true and lately my luck was absolute shit.

"We are at your service," he said.

"How?" I finally managed.

"There's a lot of us that want the same thing as you," he replied as he took out a guard that came barreling toward us. "I knew the broadcasts weren't real. I knew it wasn't you murdering rank zeroes. So I left the castle and started recruiting anyone who would listen, anyone that wanted to fight with us when the time came."

"How did you know it wasn't real?" I asked as I started fighting again as more Tennebrisians slipped past Abherham's men.

"Because you love her, and she's a zero. I watched you when I used to guard her, and I knew then just as I know now."

Scotlind. He was talking about Scotlind. Fuck, the thought made me feel like I was being impaled by a blade.

"We're happy to have you," was all I responded with because I didn't know what else to say.

———

"WHAT THE FUCK are you doing here?" I snapped once I saw lavender hair. I almost killed her. Fuck. If I had...

"I came to have a picnic," the human smirked as she killed two guards without hesitation.

I rolled my eyes, then shoved her out of the way as a guard with energy weaponry threw an axe at her.

"This isn't a joke," I pressed as I came up beside her, my voice more of a growled whisper. "You know that anyone with compulsion can make you kill yourself, or tell you to jump out the window, or have you turn against us."

"You think I don't know what your kind is capable of after living with them my entire life? Save it for someone who cares."

She turned down a hall, running so fucking fast I almost lost her. I cursed before I decided to follow, but by the time I got to her, three more guards were dead. We were nearing the top of the castle where the royal quarters were. Judging by the fewer guards stationed here, I knew we were close to the Council. They never thought anyone would make it this far with all their forces stationed below, and if it weren't for Abherham's men showing up, we wouldn't have been able to. They were the only reason I was able to break away from the group and get past the guards blocking this part of the castle.

"Following me?" she quipped over her shoulder.

We were the only two people up here, save for the dead guards she just killed. I closed the distance between us with my teleportation. She didn't falter, didn't retreat even as my nose brushed hers. "Be quiet," I whispered. "The Council is here."

We were at a dead end with only one door separating us. I tested the knob and found it locked. I turned to Savannah. "Stay here, but if anything happens, run like hell."

I didn't wait to hear her protest as I teleported past the door and found myself in a room with the entire Tennebrisian Council. I smiled as my eyes met dark ones—Synder.

I twirled my sword in my hand. Once. Twice.

Finally.

SIXTY-FIVE
GREYLAND

THE MOMENT we arrived outside the castle gates, all hell broke loose. Lilia and I were toward the front of the group, and I immediately lost sight of Kallon and Scottie.

I unsheathed my own blade from my back, testing the weight of it in my hands. I knew how to use it, and I was good at it too. But I'd never gone up against someone like this before. All my fights were strictly set within regulated rules in guard classes. Even when I competed in school for the Six Battles, there were rules. We were never allowed to make a killing blow.

But this... this would be different. There were no rules here. There would be no one to yell at us to pull back. And even though Dravenburg made it clear we didn't want to go straight to killing, he warned us all that it could quickly escalate to death. Our goal was to only take out the High Council, which was exactly what my brother and the first wave of Advenians planned to do.

We didn't want to kill any civilians, but as far as the Tennebrisian guard went, we had no idea what would happen. We didn't know who they would be loyal to, which was the purpose of our wave, the fifth wave. We were the backup in case a full-fledged battle took place, and judging by the sounds, I already knew where this day was heading.

I turned toward Lilia, whose hazel eyes flared as she took in the blood already soaking the ground before us. "Stay by my side, *Lil*, I mean it."

She nodded, silently reaching for the daggers strapped to her thighs. Her hands were shaking, and all I wanted to do was get her as far away from here as I could. If I had my brother's powers, if I could teleport, I would have.

I swatted at a fly that wouldn't stop buzzing around my face before it—*he*—shifted into Peter.

I cursed, taking a step back. "What the hell are you doing being a fly in the middle of a fucking war?" I swore at Lilia's brother. "Do you know how easy it would have been to squash you?"

He grinned, his dimples sinking far into his cheeks. His sister had the same ones, but hers were shallow, harder to see unless you were paying attention to them—which I always was. "Awe, that's cute you think you can kill me that easily, Little Noren, but I can *fly* pretty fast, get it? Fly," he gestured toward himself, "cause I was a fly."

I shook my head, fighting off my own smile. Only Peter would shift into the weakest creature imaginable and not be worried about himself.

His tone changed as he took in his little sister, then at the blades she was holding in each of her hands. His smile immediately vanished. "You two shouldn't go inside."

"Why?" My head snapped toward his.

"Things are bad," he started. "Sie sent me out here to warn everyone we're fighting to kill. The guards aren't backing down."

"Shit." I blew out a breath.

"We're fighting, Peter," Lilia said as she gripped the daggers tighter, determination written all over her face. "We didn't come here just to sit back and watch."

Peter's green eyes slid to mine, his were so vibrant, one solid color of bright green compared to Lilia's hazel. I found myself getting lost in the mix of her gold and brown hues with the edges of green bordering her irises.

I nodded at him. I knew what to do. Lilia would fucking hate me for it, but at least she would be alive.

"We'll fight," I said to both of them, "but we'll stay on the perimeter of the castle."

Lilia whipped her head to me about to protest, but I cut her off. "We can still help from out here, Lilia."

"Fine," she grumbled, and the look Peter gave me—such relief—made me know I was doing the right thing. It was why he agreed to sneak me in without Sie knowing.

As soon as he left—shifting back into a fly—I gestured for Lilia to follow me. If I was going to do this, I had to make it believable.

I was thankful for the thick leather uniform we were wearing and that my markings only spanned across my chest and stomach as I called to my abilities. Because Lilia didn't notice my skin changing colors, as golden swirls spanned across me, the Tennebrisian telltale sign I was actively using my powers.

I entered her mind easily with my illusion, making it seem like she was fighting guards, but in reality, and to everyone else, she was attacking nothing—just air.

Yeah, she was going to fucking murder me once she found out.

I kept half my mind focused on her, on making her imaginary battles believable and keeping her occupied at the border of the tree line, while I actually fought off whoever came our way.

There was no way I was letting anyone get within a foot radius of her.

SIXTY-SIX
SCOTLIND

WHAT ARE YOU DOING HERE? Tezya seethed into my mind. He was down the hall fighting his way through four guards. I saw Peter for a split second on my way up here. He shifted back into himself to tell me not to hold back. The guards were loyal to Synder.

Apparently, during the two hours it took Kallon and I to portal all five groups into the snow-laden territory, wave one tried to reason with them. Sie said that his brother mentioned people might not be loyal to Synder, that not everyone was happy about the drastic changes they'd been making in Tennebris after they sent me to Lux. But after too many of our own men and women were killed, they resorted to plan B.

I tried not to think about how many of us were already dead, tried not to dwell on whether I knew any of them. All Peter said was that Vallie was okay before he shifted into his now-new-favorite bear form and went back into the throes of fighting.

Vallie was fine. I knew Kallon was okay because I just left her. But who wasn't? I sagged the first moment I saw Tezya. He was fighting alongside a few people I recognized from the camp, but I didn't know their names. Tennebrisian guards were falling to the floor beside him like moths trapped in fire. One moment, they were fine, then the next, they were gurgling as their throats were slit. I knew immediately it was Dovelyn fighting under her invisibility. Even if I couldn't use my enhancement to feel her powers, I knew she'd never leave her brother alone.

She, like me, was terrified for Tezya. It was stupid. Her visions showed her the King staying in Lux. He was safe, for now, but seeing him fight, seeing blood splattered across his chest and onto his face and over his scar... I knew I made the right decision to come inside and fight.

I'm helping, I shot back as I dodged a sword to my chest.

You were supposed to stay with Kallon outside the castle, Tezya said a moment later. A quick glance up, and I saw he was slowly making his way toward me. *She needs to create a portal because we can't risk the time it'd take to walk back through the woods if we need to retreat.*

I know. She already created the portal.

Scotlind, creating portals are more taxing for her than transporting people through them, and you're both already tapped out. You need to focus on refueling your reserves, not using more of your powers.

No, what I'm supposed to be doing is helping. I stayed outside with Kallon and the rest of the fifth wave for ten minutes before I couldn't take it anymore. I had to help. I couldn't stand around while the people I loved were fighting inside. I couldn't listen to the screams and not know if it was someone I knew.

You aren't helping us if your reserves stay depleted.

They won't. I hissed as a blade nicked my arm.

Do not tell me you're fighting without abilities. I could hear the menace in his voice through my head.

I shrugged even though neither of us were looking at the other. *I've been doing it my whole life.*

I had two short swords in either hand—I used one to take out a guard in front of me as I blocked with the other. Tezya was still across the hall, trying to make his way to me, but there were too many guards.

Fire exploded in a circle as two more guards charged me. It took me a second to realize what was happening. *Tezya, drop the fire. I can handle myself.*

I know you can handle yourself, he said, but he still wasn't dropping the fire. *I realize I can't talk you out of fighting inside the castle, but if you're staying, you're fighting with me.*

I looked around, still protected by Tezya's flames and saw too many lifeless bodies in piles on the floor. The Tennebrisian twin pink moons were embedded onto their chests—they were all guards.

Where's the High Council? I asked him.

They're hiding like cowards. Sie went to find them.

Sie. My chest ached thinking about him. Anyone that saw him would be out to get him, but we were spread too thin to do anything about it now.

Dovelyn's scream brought me back to the battle. I couldn't focus on him right now. Sie would have to protect himself. I had to stay in the moment. I had to force myself not to get distracted, to stop thinking about everything at once and only focus on this.

I trained my whole life for it. I spent years fighting, hoping to become a real guard, and now I was finally ready.

I looked up and saw the two men who'd been fighting alongside Tezya were now dead. That left just me, him, and Dovelyn with too many Tennebrisian guards to count.

Tezya, drop your fire.

Seconds passed where I was still protected—trapped—by Tezya's wall of fire. I could hear him and Dovelyn fighting too many. I could sense he was hesitating. He didn't want to leave me vulnerable, but I could hold my own. He knew that.

Just wait until I can get to you—he started to say.

"Tezya, drop the fire!" This time I screamed the words out loud, but he wasn't listening. He couldn't—four soldiers were attacking him at once. He was outnumbered...

It took me one millisecond before I realized I wasn't going to just watch Tezya fight while he kept me protected by his flames. Even if it was only until he could get to my side.

I called to the remnants of my powers. I knew my reserves we low, despite feeling ready to fight, my body was trembling, and I was sweating out of every orifice imaginable. I focused on the call of water, pulling it out of the four guards that were attacking Tezya. I didn't stop until all of them collapsed in front of him with a resounding thud.

Tezya's gaze snapped to me. I was still trapped in the circle of fire he created, but I didn't wait. I moved the water from the now-dead bodies and doused the flames surrounding me.

Remind me to tell you how fucking amazing you are, Scotlind Rumor, Tezya smirked before he turned to block the next guard that attacked him.

Don't worry. I'll make you tell me every night before we go to bed, I teased as I made my way toward him. *And I told you I can fight.*

Tezya didn't respond. We didn't have time to talk even if we wanted to as more and more guards came at us. We made our way to each other, fighting back to back now, with Dovelyn floating in and out between us.

I didn't think about who I was killing in the process. I refused to look into their eyes, and it took every ounce of my control to not let my mind wonder if they were brainwashed and forced into fighting. Did they even know why they were risking their lives? Why they were now losing them?

The longer we fought, one thought kept coming to my mind—how was I going to be okay with all of this if I survived?

SIXTY-SEVEN
SIE

SYNDER'S oily skin had a thick layer of sheen to it as sweat coated every inch of him. His hair had fallen over his face and was plastered across his forehead and down his cheek. It wasn't like that when I first entered the room. Part of me rejoiced in seeing it—proof that he was fucking terrified—but the majority of me was just downright pissed. I wanted to soak in his features, the way his eyes widened as he took me in, the way his fingers trembled and his knees quivered as he took a noticeable step back.

"S-sie..." he half stuttered, his eyes finally landing on me after sweeping over what was left of the room.

I smiled, and for the first time since the broadcast, I was fucking elated. I could feel blood dripping from my lip and staining my teeth, but I embraced it. Every ache and cut and bruise across my body felt like it was lit on fire, but instead of feeling the heat from the flames, it gave me energy. It ignited me from the inside out. This feeling, this vengeance, *this* was what I needed, what I craved.

As soon as I teleported in, I went rampage. I didn't give anyone a second to collect themselves as I murdered them. All twenty-eight members of the Council were now dead. Twenty-nine including my father, and I was about to make it an even thirty. I killed them all. I lost it, lost myself to it as I used everything I possessed to tear into them.

I twirled the blade in my hand as I took a step toward Synder. I knew blood was dripping from the tip, but it wasn't nearly enough, wouldn't be enough until I had his. The room around us was a blur. Bodies were limp and scattered, making it an obstacle to move through, but I didn't care.

Synder and the Council had been hiding like cowards. They locked themselves in here, thinking we wouldn't get past their guard.

"Let's talk about this," he said, his hands raising in the air.

"Sure. Let's talk." I flashed a bloody smile. "You are the reason Scotlind was sent to Lux," I drawled slowly, my eyes never leaving his dark ones. It was the first time I spoke since I teleported in. I wanted Synder to be last. I wanted him to watch as I killed everyone else first, knowing he'd be next. "You're the reason my father is dead. The reason Moli is gone." I pointed the tip of my blade at him. "You took my mother and brother to Lux. They were beaten and tortured because of it. My mother didn't make it. My brother lost his eye." Synder kept retreating, slowly backing himself against the wall as I spoke, half tripping over body parts and corpses. I let him, holding my ground and letting my voice carry, not following him… not yet. "*You are the reason everything I ever fucking loved is now gone.*"

"Th-this is just a misunderstanding. Let me explain. We can come to an agreement and work together—"

"No," I spat, cutting him off. "You aren't walking out of this room alive." Distantly, I could hear banging on the door at my back and knew Savannah was pounding on the wood, trying to get in. I didn't want to think about her right now, about what she must think of me. I was living up to my reputation. I was a murderer, but for once, I was glad.

"Sie. I mean, *Prince Noren*, you don't understand. We were all forced by the Lux King. Everything that happened was because of him. I didn't want to do any of it, but I didn't have a choice. We can establish a new Council, we can work everything out, and together we can over-throw the Lux King. I'll help you…"

I teleported to his side in a heartbeat, digging my free hand into his mouth and pulling out his tongue. My blade ran through the thick, slimy muscle as I cut it from his throat. He wailed, the sound distorted and more of a grunt now that the appendage was on the floor by his feet. "I don't want to hear another lie from your mouth."

I pointed my blood-soaked blade in his face and spoke my next words slowly, letting each syllable sink in, knowing full well that with his ability, he'd know I was telling the truth. "You will die today. By me. Right here. Right now. And I plan to make it slow and painful."

Tears were pouring down his slimy face, mixing with the sweat that was spilling out of every orifice of his skin. The smell of urine filled my nostrils as his pants became drenched, and my only regret was that the entire world wasn't privy to witness how much of a coward Synder truly was.

———

My hands were shaking, my adrenaline going haywire as I tried to collect myself. That should have made me feel better. I was glad he was gone, glad he was a pile of limbs on the floor, but I also felt like it wasn't enough. I savored every moment of tearing him apart, but now that it was over, I came back to myself. The wound in my heart wasn't healed like I thought it would be. I still felt hollow. I was still broken.

I had no idea how much time had passed before he took his last breath, but I was pretty certain I kept chopping into him long after he was dead. I inhaled, taking a moment for myself, before I got the courage to unlock the door.

Savannah stumbled forward, her fist fell into my chest instead of the wood as she pounded against it. She straightened, and I couldn't help but notice her eyes bulge as she took in the room behind me.

I was drenched in blood. But the room was worse. I could already smell the stench of death taking over. I could still hear the screams coming from each of the men I just killed. I expected her to run away from me. I expected her to finally have the same fear that everyone in Brighta seemed to share.

Her hazel, lavender—whatever color they were—eyes finally landed on me. "Are you okay?"

I didn't respond because who the fuck asks that after witnessing the horror behind me. I knew she heard everything. I knew she was aware of exactly what happened in this room because I heard her just as easily. I couldn't block her out, not fully. Her pounding on the door and screaming my name was just as ingrained in my ears as their death wails were.

"Sie, are you hurt?"

"No." I finally found my voice. I knew I was. I was covered in bruises. The blood coating me was just as much my own and every member of the Council. I just couldn't feel the physical pain, not yet anyway, but I knew it would come.

"The fight is over," she said softly. "Tezya... he came up to help you, but I told him..." She stopped abruptly. "When Tezya told the guards the Council was dead, most stopped fighting. The ones who didn't are being escorted to the dungeons right now." I nodded, only half paying attention to her words as she continued, "You should see a healer."

"No," I snapped before pushing her aside and walking down the hall. I wanted to be alone, and I didn't need her getting into my head.

No matter how badly I was injured I wasn't planning on seeing a healer. There was only one I cared about anyway, and she was dead.

SIXTY-EIGHT
TEZYA

A DAY HAD PASSED, and I was finally starting to accept that staying in Tennebris wasn't a death sentence. I understood the logic. It was easier to bring the healers here than portal everyone back to the too-cramped camp. It was also strategic to stay with the Tennebrisians, to make sure no one had the opportunity to spew more lies, and if we were lucky, more would want to fight with us when the time came to go to Lux.

I met with Rumor's old guard yesterday after the fighting ended. His men would be joining us, and so far that alone was worth coming here first. We wouldn't have won in Tennebris if it weren't for them. I was so thankful for my sister's visions. I couldn't stomach thinking about what would have happened if we spread ourselves thin and attacked both kingdoms at once. There would have been a lot more deaths and bodies to burn...

Besides not particularly liking the constant cold and darkness of the place, I was worried we were leaving everyone vulnerable, but Dovelyn was right, the Lux King wouldn't leave his city unprotected. When it came down to it, he'd sacrifice Tennebris again and again. We were safe here, *for now*, while utilizing the kingdom's resources and still able to hide Brighta's location as a safe haven if needed.

Wells was able to disconnect the kingdom's broadcast from Lux's so we could make our own announcement. One that wasn't filled with lies and deception, and I was surprised by how well it went. There were a few hiccups, a few groups that fought back—mostly people from Palm and Kitlarn—but everyone that did was brought into the dungeons—just until we could figure out what to do with them. We didn't want any more blood spilled, but we couldn't risk them turning against us and fighting with Lux.

The new laws Synder had implemented in the past couple of months helped us. The people were mad. Most were more than ready for things to change.

All in all, it was a success. The healers were tending to the wounded and everyone was taking a much deserved rest. Everyone but us.

We were leaving Palm today to check out the spacecraft. Sie told us Miles' research was valid, and that we'd be able to go back to Allium, but everyone wanted to see it for themselves.

Backerly was a half day's travel by the monorail, and Kallon was slowly setting up portals throughout the kingdom. We stopped seven times already, but it didn't take more than fifteen minutes at each one. Sie would teleport Kallon to a new location, she'd create a portal, and then we'd be moving again.

Rumor and I were in a compartment by ourselves, and I tried to soak in the moment, holding her while we watched the snow drift by the darkened window.

"Are you ready?" I asked as I kissed the top of her head. She was nestled between my legs, both of us opting to sit on the floor with a bunch of blankets laid out before us.

She nodded but didn't speak. I knew her mind was drifting toward her friends. Vallie was somewhere on the monorail, apparently sitting with Peter and Savannah.

I hated how much it was affecting her. I understood the redhead. I knew firsthand that trauma takes time to heal from and the girl went through a lot. I just hated how it was seeping into Scotlind. She tried desperately to hide it from everyone. But it was moments like this, when we were alone, that her mind wandered, and I knew it still hurt her.

"I'm scared that Sie will be right," she finally admitted.

"You don't want to return to Allium?" I asked, genuinely curious. We'd been having more and more meetings about what to do if—*when* —we won, and everyone was onboard with returning, pending Miles' research. It was the right thing to do for both Advenians and mortals. We deserved a fresh start, one without the tainted world the current kingdoms created. We would no longer need to be confined to small territories. We could expand, live anywhere we wanted within Allium.

And the mortals deserved to live without us. They shouldn't be dragged into a war and forced to accept changes because of our mistakes.

I just prayed it wasn't too late. The newspapers Savannah had been collecting were unsettling as more and more *disasters* kept occurring. I was starting to believe that the Lux King really was collecting humans.

Arcane admitted to creating a compulsion serum, although he said it wasn't finished yet. It was only ninety percent done and never tested, but I didn't put it past the King to use it anyway.

"No, I do," Rumor said softly. The blanket was pulled up to her chin, and she was mumbling into the fabric. "I think we should leave if we can, and I would love to see Allium. I used to read books about our old planet. It's always fascinated me. I fell in love with the diverse climate and changes throughout the land. Not that we'll know if any of it still exists today, but when I was stranded here growing up, I craved something warmer, something different."

"Then why are you scared it's possible?"

"I'm scared it's going to hurt more," she admitted. "It was our dream growing up. Vallie and Miles," she paused on his name. "It's our childhood dream coming true, and the fact that he isn't here to witness it… it just sucks."

"I'm sorry," I said as I kissed the top of her head again and pulled her tighter into my chest. "I never knew him, and I know this doesn't make losing someone any easier, but he'd want you and Vallie to be happy."

"I know," she sighed.

The monorail came to a halt, but this time it wasn't one of Kallon's stops to set up a portal. We were here. I'd never been to Backerly, but I was aware the land was mountainous, even more than LakeWood. We'd been traveling at an incline for the past hour, and the town was built into the peaks themselves.

Rumor stood first, shrugging off the blankets. She went to open the compartment, but I grabbed her arm before she could slide the door open and pulled her into a hug. She exhaled as she pressed her forehead into the crook of my neck.

I love you, I said into her mind.

I love you too, Tezya.

———

BACKERLY WAS the most tech-heavy town out of the six villages in Tennebris, and I found I liked it the most. It was colder, being at a naturally higher elevation than the rest of the kingdom, making it closer to the top of the shield. But the mixture of electric heat and warmth from the fireplaces made it more cozy than dreary.

Each building was built into a different mountain with interconnected bridges linking them, and the rooms themselves were designed on a vertical incline with the top floor circling the peak. It made the need for stairs everywhere. I couldn't stop smiling at Rumor's complete dread. I knew her legs were killing her. Despite the obvious shake she had to them, she had told me multiple times now how she never planned to come back here after today and kept condemning the stairs with each new flight she saw.

The AASP was located on one of the peaks. Floor-to-ceiling windows, similar to the monorail, took up the length of the room, and the view was breathtaking. It overlooked everything.

Several Tennebrisians greeted us when we arrived, all eager to show off their work. Everyone was silent during their tour. By the time we finished, the day had passed, even though the darkness remained the same.

"So you guys are really going to go then?" Savannah asked later that night. We made it back to the castle in Palm well past midnight, but everyone was too anxious to sleep.

"Yeah," Peter replied. "I can't believe it."

"We still have to win the war first," Dovelyn deadpanned. "And we just barely survived this battle."

I loved my sister, but she was a realist to a fault. No one wanted to think about the next fight in Lux. I especially didn't. Not that I was personally dreading it. I was ready and knew the Lux King needed to die. But whenever it was brought up, Rumor went further into her desolation. She didn't believe I was going to survive it.

"Right," Wells said as he pushed his glasses back up his nose after wiping the lenses on his shirt. "You guys should make another broadcast with the information about the spacecraft and going to Allium. It might help sway some of the Tennebrisians to want to fight, and you need all the numbers you can get. We lost—"

"Let's not focus on that," I cut him off. The first day after the battle we went through all the names lost. They deserved the acknowledgement. It was something I did after every fight when I was forced to attack the rebels. To the Luxian soldiers, I would list all the names of our own military, and then later at night, when it was just Rainer, Brock, and Kallon, I would list all the rebels who died. I sent the list to Dravenburg, knowing he'd share it with the new recruits at the camp when the time was right.

But tonight, right now, I didn't want to focus on death. "We'll make another broadcast tomorrow morning. We can see if anyone else wants to join, but I want to make sure it's clear it's not mandatory. No one is required to fight." It was something I hated about our society. If you were strong within Lux, you were forced into the army. I'd watch countless men, who had no stomach for bloodshed, change.

Everyone was silent after that. Savannah made us coffee—which she claimed was decaf, but I didn't believe her—and we all sat around a fire, holding the warm beverage, and letting our final night sink in.

We were attacking Lux in two days, and similar to when we came here, Kallon and Rumor were going to start portaling everyone in waves tomorrow night. Which meant this was our last night of peace. Our last night of waking up without having to go into war. It might be our last night all together. We might not all survive past the next battle, and I didn't want to think about my chances of making it were even less.

But I knew what I had to do, what I would do.

"Let's go to bed," I whispered to Rumor as I helped her up. Our coffees were now cold. I'd been reheating them over the past hour we'd been sitting here, but I wanted to leave now.

If tonight might be my last night alive, I wanted to enjoy her *alone* and planned to make the most of it.

SIXTY-NINE
SCOTLIND

I woke up with a sense of dread. In a few hours, we were going to start portaling everyone into Lux. It didn't seem real. Tezya and I barely slept. When we got to our room last night, we practically attacked each other. After we had sex, we just held each other for hours.

It was only after he drifted off to sleep that I snuck out to meet Dovelyn at the library. We read through as many texts as we could, trying desperately to figure out what the prophecy meant and how to save Tezya before we had to go to the broadcast. We found nothing. Absolutely nothing indicating what a sacrifice from Light and blood from Dark meant.

Dovelyn and I spent hours scouring all the books in the royal library, but still came nowhere closer to answers than when we started. I even sucked up my pride and knocked on Vallie's door half way through the night.

"Scottie." Her amber eyes were red-rimmed and wide as she took me in. A large fireplace was roaring to life behind her and a thick, wool blanket was pulled up to her chin.

"I hope I didn't wake you," I said slowly.

"You didn't." Her voice was soft and gentle, compared to her usual teasing and bickering. "What's wrong?"

"I need your help," I started to say and tried my best to choke back my tears. "I'm so sorry to ask anything of you, but we only have tonight and I can't..."

"Scottie, what do you need?"

"I need you to help me save him. Dove and I are in the library, trying to figure out the prophecy. We're reading every book we possibly can, but we aren't finding anything. There's no reference to a sacrifice of Light or what blood from the Dark means, and now we're running out of time. I just thought, maybe with your ability, you could—"

"Sure," she cut me off, and I was startled.

"Really?" I asked.

"Of course, Scottie. I'd do anything for you." My heart swelled before she added, "I just can't..." She sucked in a breath. "It doesn't change anything though... I'm sorry."

"I know. Thank you, Vallie."

And even with her help, we still found nothing. Absolutely nothing on Pylemo, or prophecies, or magical rings, or going past your reserves. It wasn't meant to be possible.

And now Tezya was going to do it, and we had no way of saving him.

We were back in our room, dressing in silence. He was giving me space on purpose, but I couldn't stop the panic stirring inside me.

"Tez," I started, watching him lace his armor up.

"Hmm?" He looked up, meeting my gaze.

"Promise me you won't die." My own eyes drifted to the necklace peeking through his shirt. I knew the ring was attached, dangling across his chest. "Promise me if you start to go past your reserves, you'll stop."

"Scotlind, I promise that I'll do everything I can to stay alive," he replied as he rose from his chair and started making his way toward me, pulling me into a hug. He kissed my forehead, and I tried to hide the tears threatening to spill. Because it wasn't enough. I knew him. I knew he would kill himself in order to save everyone, in order to save me...

———

EVERYONE WHO WASN'T an air or Alluse user was given a clear mask to wear. It was brilliant and would protect us from whatever supplies of vapor Alluse the Lux King still possessed. Even though we had Arcane now, and he couldn't make any more, he admitted the current stock was astronomical. The Lux King had enough to make a difference in the war.

The first wave we were portaling into Lux was being led by Dovelyn and Tezya. They were going to destroy the lab and hopefully what was left of the vapor.

Sie, Brock, and Rainer went in the second wave and their job was to overtake the underwater monorail that spanned between both kingdoms.

By the time we were portaling the third wave, I was shaking. The amount of Tennebrisians who came to help us fight was overwhelming. It was mostly because of Abherham, and I was so thankful that I was able to see my old guard. I hadn't realized how much I missed him until I saw him again. I could barely stop crying when I hugged him.

I was growing impatient knowing that Tezya was already on Luxian soil while I was stuck portaling between the two kingdoms. I knew he wasn't planning on going up against the King until the very end, but it still didn't sit well with me, knowing that at any point, he could run into him.

"What are you doing?" Kallon asked, breaking my train of thought. I looked up and saw she was talking to Savannah.

"I'm fighting, obviously," she responded. She was dressed in fighting leathers—they were less thick than the ones we wore in Tennebris, but still provided full coverage—and if it wasn't for her purple hair, she would have blended in with everyone else.

"Dravenburg said you couldn't fight."

"Since when do you take orders from my dad?"

"Okay, good point, I don't, but I happen to agree with him on this. It's too dangerous, and it's not your battle to fight."

"Kal, this life, all of you, it's all I've ever known. I was freaking homeschooled for crying out loud. My world has been surrounded by more Advenians than humans, so it's not fair for you to say it's not my fight. It is. Brighta is my home. You guys are my home. I want to fight for you as much as I want to fight to make sure that humans never have to know what's happening. If we lose, if the Lux King wins, he's going to take over Earth, so it *is* my fight. It's always been."

Kallon sighed. "I know, I'm sorry, Sav. I just don't know what I'd do if something happened to you."

"You won't have to find out." Savannah winked as she pulled a black hood over her hair and positioned her mask in place. "I'm not going to die."

"Your dad is going to kill me."

Savannah grinned. "Lucky for you, it'll be too late by the time he realizes I left Tennebris."

Savannah snuck into the fourth wave with us. It was the last wave Kallon and I were portaling. If Sie, Rainer, and Brock were successful, the fifth wave should be boarding the underwater monorail by now. If everything went to plan, everyone would be in Lux by dawn. And judging from the light smearing the horizon, it was soon.

I had my mask pulled over my face, making the air stifling. Lux was hot and sticky, such a contrast to Tennebris, that I kept having to use my water powers to manipulate the steam off it.

We portaled the fourth wave to the middle of the jungle by the waterfall. It was equal distance between the hut Tezya brought me to and the castle.

The third wave was already brought to the bayside. They were made up of water and air users so they could hide under the surface until it was time, while our wave slowly made our way through the jungle. Our only job right now was to be ready for whenever Tezya and

Dovelyn blew up the lab, and now that we were close to the castle, I could sense him through the bond.

How's it going? I asked into his mind.

Good. We're in the lab now. It took us a while to navigate through the castle. The King has every single guard on patrol. He knew we were coming.

I nodded even though there was no way he could see me—no one could see me right now. Multiple air users were stationed in each wave so they could cast invisibility over everyone, and even though we should still have the cover from the trees, we didn't want to take any chances.

We should be done in about five minutes, but wait until you see the explosion before you guys blow your cover, Tezya said.

Okay, be safe.

"Tez and Dove made it to the lab," I whispered out loud, knowing Kallon and Savannah were close by. "He said they'll need another five minutes before we can go and to wait for the explosion."

"Okay," Kallon replied. "Have you heard from Sie yet?"

"Not yet." He was supposed to locate me and enter my mind once they overtook the monorail. Only Brock and Rainer were going to ride it back to Tennebris, so Sie should be nearing the castle by now. Everyone else in the second wave should be positioning themselves around the castle like we were, waiting for our signal. Unless something happened to them...

"We need to stop here," Kallon ordered, and I heard numerous feet behind us come to a halt. We were close to the castle now, but if we went any further, we'd be putting ourselves at risk for being discovered too soon.

I nodded at Kallon, constantly forgetting that no one could see me. "I'm going to take a quick look."

I left the group and started making my way toward the tree line. We were on the furthest side from the gardens toward the training grounds. I expected to see the miles of open fields that surrounded the castle—which technically I did—but they weren't vacant. Hundreds and hundreds of people were standing on the field, but something was off about them.

They weren't wearing the sun-symboled uniform of the Luxian army. In fact, they didn't have on any uniform at all. Most of them were standing awkwardly, barely able to hold up the weapons in their hands. I squinted, trying to get a better look. All of them were different sizes—and *ages*.

I gulped, realizing what I was seeing at the same time Savannah came up next to me, and gasped, "They're humans."

SEVENTY
SCOTLIND

SCOTLIND? Sie's voice came through my head at the same time the explosion went off.

Yeah, I'm here.

Good. Brock and Rainer just took the monorail back to Tennebris. There were more soldiers than we anticipated, so the last wave will take longer to get here.

"What should we do?" Savannah whispered.

"I don't know," I admitted to her, but it also must have gone to Sie.

What don't you know? he asked.

Sorry, I was talking to Savannah, I shot back. *We're at the border of the jungle and—*

The mortal is with you? he snapped.

Yeah, but that's not the point. Sie, the King has…

That girl has a fucking death wish.

Sie, I stopped him, *the King has humans surrounding the castle, and they're all armed.*

Fuck. I'm coming back now. Don't attack yet.

See if you can tell any of the other waves with your telepathy. Try to warn them about the humans, I said to Sie.

We're done, Rumor. Tezya's voice came through. *All the serums are destroyed. The King will only have whatever he has on hand.*

Tezya, we have a bigger problem. Savannah was right. The King was stealing humans. He has them surrounding the castle.

Shit. Tezya's voice sounded. I was starting to feel his emotions through our bond. Worry and frustration were coursing through me.

What do we do? I asked.

Can you get past them without conflict?

I scanned the miles of open fields in front of us. The humans were crammed against one another so tightly there was no way of getting through them without a fight.

No. There's too many of them. They're completely surrounding the castle.

Okay. Have an air user create a shield to—

I cut him off. *Tezya, the air users aren't wearing masks since we didn't have enough supplies for everyone. Once we attack, they're suppose to stop their shields to make ones for themselves. If they keep us covered, most won't have any reserves left to protect themselves against any vapor Alluse.*

"What's going on?" Kallon asked as she placed a warm hand on my back.

I turned away from the massive crowd before us to look back at the jungle and was surprised to see a full head of purple hair and another with half black, half aqua. We weren't invisible anymore.

"I told the air users to let down their shields," Kallon said, noting my shock at seeing them. "But I told everyone to wait to attack until you guys came back. I wanted to see what was taking so long." Kallon looked past me, and her face crumbled the moment she saw what we did. "Are they—"

"Humans," Savannah replied, then half screamed as Sie teleported next to us.

He placed his hand over her mouth. "Shut up or all your humans are going to start attacking us."

She bristled as she nudged out of his grip. He withdrew his hand immediately then turned to me. "I could only warn my wave. Apparently the third one already started attacking. The humans are fighting to kill."

"We can't kill them," Savannah seethed. "They're innocent."

"I know," Sie gritted his teeth. "I tried to compel a few of them to stop fighting, but it didn't work."

"It's the mass compulsion serum," I breathed. "It worked."

"Well, I guess Arcane's serum just went from ninety percent effective to one hundred," Kallon attempted to joke.

"Shit," Savannah cursed. "What can we do?"

"I can portal everyone to another point," Kallon started.

"They're surrounding the castle from all sides," Sie interjected.

"Then I'll portal everyone inside like I did for Tezya and Dove. I have portals throughout the castle."

"Portaling this many people is going to kill both of your reserves," he countered, meeting my gaze. "Plus with the amount of times you'll have to go back and forth, the King will catch on and send soldiers to stop you both. It's not smart."

I sucked in a breath at a loss for what to do. I didn't want to drain myself. I needed to still have access to my abilities in case Tezya needed me, but to do nothing would mean we'd have to fight our way through the humans. I was already starting to hear screams coming from the other side of the castle...

Portal the humans, Tezya's voice sounded in my head again. He must have been listening to our conversation through my thoughts.

Tez, they aren't going to willingly go with us.

I know, Rumor. Have Kallon open a portal and then use your enhancement to widen it. You don't have to portal all of them. Just enough to make a path for everyone to run through. Have the air users put up shields, making an archway so the remaining humans can't get past it and fight you as you make your way across the field. It's the only way I can see you guys getting into the castle without spilling their blood or yours. If you do it fast enough, the air users shouldn't use up too much of their reserves.

And where are we sending the humans? I asked. *We can't put them back in mortal territory while they're compelled and all holding weapons.*

Send them to the hut. Kal has a portal there and it's far enough that they won't be able to find their way back to the castle in time. Let the serum run out of their systems, and we'll help them once this is all over.

I quickly told them all Tezya's plan.

"It might work," Kallon said, "and it would use less of our reserves than portaling everyone inside. I'll check with the air users to see if they can make an arch."

Once Kallon left, Sie turned toward Savannah. "I thought Dravenburg gave you orders to not fight."

"He also tried to stop you from fighting today, but here you are. You have more of a target on your back than me."

Sie shrugged just as Kallon came back with five air users. "Okay, Scottie. You ready?"

I nodded then turned to look at the humans.

"Make us invisible," Kallon ordered. "We need to get inside the crowd. Sav, go get the rest of the group and make sure they're ready to run on my command."

Kallon grabbed my hand just as we both turned invisible.

We were slowly making our way to the middle of the clearing, but it was hard to navigate without accidentally touching anyone.

I felt her squeeze my hand once before she dropped it, indicating that she was going to make her portal. My enhancement so familiar with her now, it felt like second nature. I was getting better at connecting to all different kinds of powers, learning the telltale signs of each ability.

Once Kallon was done, she tapped my forearm, and I widened it, consuming and expanding the portal to make a long pathway from here to the castle.

We didn't have time to process the human's reaction as we forced them through the portal, because the moment our feet sank into the sand, Kallon grabbed me and took us back to the clearing. We were no longer invisible. The air users couldn't maintain their connection inside her portal.

For one long moment, Kallon and I were standing in the middle of the field. The remaining humans looked at us in a daze for a split second before they started charging.

"Now," Kallon screamed at the same time the air users put up their shields, forming a tunnel around us. Savannah must have said something to our wave because everyone immediately started sprinting toward the castle.

I stood in shock, staring at the humans charging into the invisible shield. Most had expressions of abhorrence, and I knew the feeling. They had no idea why they were doing what they were doing. No idea why the weapons were glued to their hands, why they kept running into an invisible wall with thoughts of murder.

I saw some of them collapse, some bleeding from the carelessness of their blades, some with broken bones from the force at which they were throwing themselves into the shield. It was barbaric.

Kallon wrapped her hand around my arm. "Come on, Scottie. We have to go. They can't keep the shield up long."

I nodded, trying to push my thoughts away from the helpless humans, and followed Kallon and the others as we ran toward the castle.

All I could think about was how much I hated the King. I hated what he was doing and how he used people as nothing more than objects at his disposal.

I wanted him dead.

I just prayed it wouldn't be at the cost of Tezya's life.

SEVENTY-ONE
SCOTLIND

It was a bloodbath.

I thought the battle in Tennebris was bad, but it was child's play compared to this. The Lux King was prepared. More than prepared. We were lucky Wells and Arcane made us masks. The amount of vapor Alluse, and potentially mass compulsion serum, he still had was overwhelming. Whatever Dovelyn and Tezya managed to blow up barely made a dent in the King's supplies.

Any chance the soldiers got, they'd try to swipe our masks off. Some Luxians even burned them, some went too far and burned our faces in the process, and I hoped Vallie didn't see what was happening. I prayed she was safe, that everyone was still alive, but people were dying left and right.

There was a thick fog in the city forming from all the vapor, and with both sides wearing masks, it was nearly impossible to know who was fighting who.

Blood was splattered everywhere. Screams were piercing my ears on repeat that I thought it'd never end. If I made it out alive after today, I knew I'd continue to hear them.

I turned to Sie who was fighting next to me. "How long until Rainer and Brock come back with everyone else?" I asked.

"Probably an hour if we're lucky."

"We need them *now*," Kallon chimed in next to us. "There's too many Luxians."

Agony ran through my body but it wasn't my own. *Are you okay?* I shot into Tezya's mind as panic started to consume me. I needed to get to wherever he was. There was no way I was going to let him challenge the King by himself.

I'm fine, Rumor. Just a scratch, he replied a second later, but I wasn't stupid. Whatever injury he just got wasn't a scratch.

Where are you?

Stay with Sie, he said instead of answering.

That's not what I asked you, I seethed. Rage coursed through me as he kept avoiding my question. *Where are you, Tezya?*

I'm with Dove.

Are you going after him, NOW? I wasn't sure if I also shouted the words out loud because everyone turned to look at me.

Just stay with Sie, was all he said.

Tezya, stop. Don't do this. You can't do this alone.

I didn't get a reply back, even though I knew he heard me. I could still feel him, but he was shutting me out.

I whipped my head toward Sie. "He asked you to keep me away from him, didn't he?" I spat.

Sie's sword swiped into a soldier at my left, just barely missing my abdomen. Everything was starting to click into place. Tezya was the one who came up with the locations for the different waves, and he put me in the furthest one from him. He made sure I'd be far away from him when he planned to challenge the King. He didn't want me in the crossfire, but he couldn't do this alone. If he did, he would...

"He asked me to keep you safe," Sie responded.

"I'm going to find him," I yelled. "Don't think about trying to stop me."

Sie cursed, running his hands through his thick black hair, and leaving blood splattering across his face in the process. "Fine, but I'm coming with you."

"A little help before you all up and leave us," Kallon shouted as three soldiers swarmed her. Before Sie and I could move, Savannah had them knocked down in seconds.

"You guys need to wait until Rainer and Brock show up," Kallon gritted as another soldier attacked her. "If you all go now, you're leaving our wave unprotected."

Kallon was right. My feelings aside, until the fifth wave came, the Luxians outnumbered us three to one.

"Can you locate Dovelyn with your telepathy?" I asked Sie.

"I can try," he said. "Why?"

"Just make sure Tezya isn't going after the King right now. Tell her to do whatever she can to stall him."

He nodded, and I knew he was focusing on pinpointing her throughout the castle. I covered for Sie while he worked, praying he could do it. If he could talk to the princess, she was probably the only other person here who would understand. She wanted Tezya safe just as much as I did.

Sweat was beating down Sie's temple by the time he finished. "She said he's fine, and they haven't found the King yet. We have time."

"Okay, good. We need to—" I started to say, but was cut off by Kallon.

"What are you doing here?" she screeched as she grabbed a beautiful brunette by the waist and pulled her into her side. She was half the height of her, but whereas Kallon was lean with hard angles, the brunette had curves. Her eyes were bright blue, a couple of shades lighter than my own and looked striking against her dark complexion.

"I wasn't going to let you fight all by yourself." The girl winked, her voice was sing-songed and rhythmic.

"How did you even know it was going to be today?"

"Besides the fact that the King was going crazy and ordered everyone to stay in their homes, even though we all saw the mass herds of humans he had surrounding the castle, Rainer tipped me off."

"I'm going to kill him," Kallon spat.

"I'm not. At least he had the decency to let me know. I told you I wanted to fight, Kal."

"And I told you it was too dangerous, Raeya. You aren't used to fighting."

"Then it's a good thing my girlfriend is a badass who can protect me."

Kallon looked pissed and worried and relieved all in one single look. "Stay by my side, Rae. I mean it." Kallon scanned her girlfriend up and down before cursing. "Are you even armed?"

"I have my ability."

"That's not good enough." Kallon ripped off her mask and forcefully shoved it over her girlfriend's face so only her eyes were exposed. "Don't take this off. They have vapor Alluse that will leave you without your powers." She shoved a knife into her palm. "And take this too just in case."

Savannah took off her mask next.

"What do you think you're doing?" Sie snapped.

She handed her mask out to Kallon. "We might need her portals later. We can't risk her not having access to them, and I don't have any abilities, so it doesn't really matter if I wear one or not."

"You're wearing it so you don't run into the mass compulsion serum. Do you want to be manipulated like the other humans outside?"

Savannah shuddered but held her ground. "Then Kallon can portal me to the hut if that happens. We need her more than me."

I couldn't argue with the girl, and if I wasn't so worried about Tezya, I would have offered Kallon my mask too.

"You have a fucking death wish," Sie spat at her. "You're going to get yourself killed."

"I don't know why you care."

"I don't," he ground out at the same time he saved the girl from an oncoming blow.

Kallon smirked, noting Sie's frustration, before turning toward Savannah. "Thanks, Sav. I promise I'll make sure nothing happens to you."

I WASN'T sure how much time had passed before Rainer and Brock finally showed up, but I could see the sun shifting through the open windows of the castle. We finally cleared the first floor, and I tried not to think about how many bodies were left down below.

"It's about time you boys joined us," Kallon grinned as she hovered over her girlfriend. She never let Raeya out of her sight.

"We would have made it much sooner if it weren't for the mass amounts of humans surrounding the castle," Brock said as he went right into the thick of fighting.

"Did you kill—"

"No, Sav," he cut her off. "We just fought through enough to knock them out or leave them wounded. I ordered the group not to kill any of them. It's what took so long, because I had to convince the Tennebrisians the humans were being compelled."

The group from the monorail was meant to spread out between all the waves, and I prayed the extra help was enough.

Rainer smirked as he wielded his lightning into boxing gloves he donned. "Besides, we couldn't let you have all the glory," he teased with a smile, and the gesture and words reminded me of Raeya for some reason.

"Don't pretend you actually like fighting." Savannah laughed. "You'd be the first to run away from here if you could."

"I never said I *liked* it. I just want to make sure my name goes down as a hero from *The Battle of Good and Evil*." He punched a Luxian soldier in the face with his glove, sending his lightning out in pulsating waves from the contact. I shuddered as I glanced down at the unconscious soldier. He was still convulsing on the ground, foam seeping out of his mouth, as his eyes rolled in the back of his head.

"You made up a name for this?" Raeya balked. "You're so lame."

"Rae," he beamed as he spotted Kallon's girlfriend behind her. "You made it, and duh, every battle needs a name."

"Yeah, she's here, no thanks to *you*," Kallon hissed. "We're going to have a talk later, Rainer."

"Can you all do a little more fighting and a little less talking?" Sie snapped as he took out another two soldiers. "You're giving me a headache."

"I'm heading up," I said before anyone else could interject. "I'm going to find Tezya now that you have reinforcements."

I reached my hand out to Sie. "Do you still have a connection to Dove?"

"Yeah," he said. "I kept it locked on her so she could let me know once they found the King."

"Great. Teleport me to her now."

SEVENTY-TWO
SCOTLIND

"You promised me you'd keep her away," Tezya snapped at Sie as soon as he saw us.

He was covered in blood and a quick scan from head to toe showed me the "so-called scratch" I sensed from him earlier. A diagonal cut ran from his collarbone to hip with blood still pouring from it.

You need a healer, I immediately flooded Tezya's mind. *We need to get Brock.*

"No. I promised I'd keep her safe, and I'm still doing that," Sie shot back. "She was going to find you with or without me."

I'm fine, Rumor, Tezya answered in my head, then turned to Sie. "You knew exactly what I meant."

We didn't have time to talk as more Luxian soldiers rushed us. Even with Brock and Rainer's reinforcements fighting somewhere below us, the King had more and more men at his disposal.

An axe was about to split me in half before it disintegrated into ash along with the arm holding it. Wails of agony reached my ears as the Luxian soldier started burning alive in front of me. I looked up and saw Tezya staring before he turned back to his own fight.

Night had fallen by the time we got a semblance of a break, and we still hadn't seen Athler or the King. The rest of the group met up with us at some point, and we barricaded ourselves in a room long enough for us to heal our wounds. Dovelyn had a shield around the room so we could take our masks off to eat something, and Kallon already had a portal at her disposal in case we got trapped inside or someone from the army found us.

Peter must have stolen croissants from the kitchen at some point, and Vallie was sitting on the floor next to him silently eating one. They were covered in blood, but I was so happy that, for the most part, it wasn't their own.

Brock healed the large gash over Tezya's chest and abdomen until it scabbed over and stopped bleeding, but he refused to let his friend heal him fully, claiming he didn't want to waste all his reserves.

Tezya had pulled me into a hug the moment we locked the door. I was so relieved that we were all still alive—so relieved that Tezya was.

"Are you hurt?" he whispered into my hair.

I shook my head, refusing to move from his chest, though I was careful to only put pressure on the side that wasn't injured. My translucent mask was pulled down around my neck, and although it was lightweight, it felt so nice to be able to breathe without it pressed against my mouth.

"You should have Brock look at you, just in case."

"Tezya, I'm completely fine. I don't even think I have a scratch to show for the day because anyone who got within a foot radius of me, you burned alive."

He inhaled, but I knew he wasn't satisfied with my answer, so I grabbed his hand and let him feel me. My body was aching and bruised in a few spots, and my arms felt like jello, but other than that, I was fine.

Once he realized I was completely uninjured, I pulled away from him enough to scan the room we were in. Everyone was exhausted, but that was expected. What I didn't expect to see was Savannah curled up in a corner. Out of all of us she was probably the most excited to fight. I squinted to get a closer look and saw she was crying to herself.

Don't, Tezya said into my mind, stopping me from going to her. *She needs to be alone right now. She doesn't do well when people bombard her right away.*

What's wrong with her? Is she hurt? She didn't look injured, but she could've been hiding an injury beneath her clothes. I was amazed by how well she fought and half the time I found myself forgetting she was human. Even without a mask on, she managed to escape any vapor while still taking out a huge chunk of the army. She was skilled and it seemed to come naturally to her, so I didn't think it was the bloodshed affecting her.

Her father was killed, Tezya said a moment later, and I gasped out loud, causing a few glances my way.

Dravenburg? How? What happened? I thought he wasn't fighting? Questions were pouring out of me and into Tezya's mind. The camp commander had a knack for war and strategies, and I couldn't deny that he had helped us a lot, but I knew he was only planning on leading from the sidelines. He made it clear this was our war, and that he'd assist as much as possible without putting himself or his children in the direct line of fire. But I'd been so consumed in my own fight, I barely got to see how anyone else was fairing until now.

He wasn't supposed to. Wells is still in Tennebris, but when Dravenburg found out Savannah snuck into one of the waves and was fighting, he came with the group on the monorail. She blames herself for his death.

I'm so sorry, I said, knowing Tezya respected Dravenburg and that he was close to all three humans.

Me too, he said as he pulled me back against his chest, and I lost myself to the feeling of him.

"I know where my father is," Dovelyn said into the silence. I looked up at the princess. She'd kept her invisibility over herself while fighting, and I only knew she was by me when soldiers dropped dead for no reason.

Her eyes were fading back into her usual silver, and I could sense with my enhancement that her ability had just been used. She had another vision.

"Where?" Tezya asked, straightening his back.

"He's hiding at the Goddess Temples. He's hoping his men will take care of us."

"He's a coward for hiding behind the army," Kallon interrupted, her thin brows furrowed beneath her bangs.

"A strategic coward," Dove finished. "He knows his limits. He's scared that without Scotlind and all the Advenians he used to keep chained, he doesn't have as much power as he used to. He's spiraling."

"That's perfect. If he's weak, now is the time to attack," Rainer chimed in.

"He isn't weak, not in the slightest. He's still been drinking from Advenians and stealing an ungoddessly amount of powers. It's just not what he's used to consuming. He also has vapor completely surrounding him."

"I want to go," I said immediately, not wanting to wait to hear Tezya's excuse for why I shouldn't.

"No." Tezya moved across the room. "You aren't an air user. If the King has vapor you shouldn't—"

"I have a mask," I cut him off as I pointed to it dangling around my neck. I knew what he was trying to do, and it wasn't going to work.

"There's more," Dovelyn said, glancing down at Savannah. "I also saw Athler order the army to start murdering the humans surrounding the castle as a way to draw us out."

Savannah stood almost immediately. Aside from the redness around her eyes, I wouldn't have known she'd just been crying or that her father had died. "Those humans are innocent. We need to stop it—"

"I know, Sav."

"When?" Tezya asked. He started slowly pacing. "When does Athler make the orders?"

Dovelyn shook her head. "I don't know but soon."

Brock was watching Tezya pace. "You have any ideas on what to do?" he asked.

Tezya nodded. "Get every ground and air user you can and barricade the doors for as long as possible so the army can't get out.

Everyone needs to stay here and fight." Tezya said the last part looking right at me. "Kallon, I need you to portal me to the Goddess Temples, then I want you portaling yourself back to Tennebris—"

"You can't seriously think I'm going to leave you all and go…"

"Kal, I need you to portal back to Tennebris to bring Arcane here. Dovelyn and my brother have some of the strongest shields, and while Dove has been using her reserves all day, my brother hasn't."

I'm coming with you, Tezya, I said into his mind. *I don't care if you leave me behind, and I have to walk there myself, I'm not letting you face the King alone.*

He, of course, ignored me. "And Scottie needs to stay here so she can enhance your shields once your reserves start diminishing."

"Absolutely not. I'm going with you," I half screamed.

Dovelyn's silver eyes slid to mine. "I can handle the shields," she said. "Especially if I have Arcane with me, but you shouldn't go by yourself, Tezya. I'll only agree to this if you aren't alone."

"The prophecy says I'm the only one who can defeat him so why would I risk bringing anyone else? Besides, we need everyone here to protect the humans."

"I agree with Dove," Kallon said, and to my relief, everyone else slowly began chiming in and nodding in agreement.

"Fine," he half growled. "Someone can come with me, but Rumor stays here."

Brock rose slowly and started making his way toward us. "Tezya, you're like a brother to me, and you have to know I would never purposely go against your wishes, but I think Scotlind should go with you." I couldn't tell if Brock was only suggesting it to appease Dovelyn or if he meant what he was saying, but either way I wasn't going to question it. "Arcane said that she has access to your powers. In the event things go wrong, she's the only other person who can take on the King. This is about the safety of our entire people."

Tezya was silent for a while, letting his friend's words sink in, and I could feel the confliction radiating off of him. I knew it was the exact reason he didn't want me coming. He was scared I was going to interfere, and he wasn't wrong. All day I'd been holding my tongue and consciously blocking my thoughts from him.

"I'll go with the two of you," Brock added when Tezya still wasn't answering. "I promise I'll stay with her and heal her if she gets hurt."

"I'm also going," Sie said. "Since Kallon is leaving, I'm your next best thing. Peter told me the Temples are on the opposite side of the island."

Dovelyn glared openly at Peter who just smiled through eating his croissant. The fact that he was able to get the entire layout of Lux and managed to relay the information to Sie while he was my maid was beyond me, and it pissed Dovelyn off beyond belief. I honestly had no idea how he didn't get caught sooner.

"You'll need someone there if things go south. I can teleport anyone away who's in danger," Sie added, and I knew he meant me, but if Sie being there was the only way Tezya would agree to me coming, I wasn't about to say anything. There was no way I'd let Sie teleport me back to the castle, but neither of them had to know that.

Tezya's jaw clenched as moments passed.

Please, I added into his mind.

"Fine," he gritted out, then turned to glare at Sie. "The moment I say so, you teleport her and Brock back."

"Done."

Tezya flexed out his hand before he made his way toward me. My mouth parted at the confidence in his gait, the way his hair was slick with sweat, pushing the long strands off his forehead. Even covered in blood and grime, he was breathtaking. I hadn't been able to look at him for more than a few seconds while fighting today, and since we got into this room, I'd been trying to limit talking to him because I was too scared he'd read my thoughts.

"Rumor," he said gently once he reached me. I could feel everyone's eyes on us, but I looked up and focused on him. "Can we talk —*alone?*"

I scanned the room, and yup, everyone was watching. "Um... where?"

He grabbed my hand and started leading me toward the bathroom.

Dovelyn's abilities swirled around me as my enhancement picked up on it. She was casting a privacy shield over us.

Before the door fully closed, Tezya pulled me into an embrace, picking me up by my hips and slammed my back against the wall. His tongue was inside my mouth in seconds, and I willingly opened, letting him consume me. My fingers fisted his hair as I pulled him closer to my face, breathing him in. I couldn't get enough.

At some point, I started to taste salt and knew it was from my tears. I wanted this moment to last. I wanted to be kissing him with all the time in the world, instead of a rushed fleeting moment. We could both feel the weight of what was about to happen.

Tezya pulled back enough to look at me, his hands resting on either side of my cheeks, but he didn't put me down.

"Rumor…"

"Don't," I stopped him. "I don't want to hear it."

"Rumor, please. I need to—"

"No." I twisted out of his grasp, and he obliged, setting my feet back down on the floor. I turned away from him, making my way toward the door, but he grabbed my wrist.

"Rumor—"

I pushed back against his shoulder. I couldn't hear it. I didn't want him to say his goodbyes. If he was going to do that, it meant he didn't think he would make it.

His grip on me tightened, not enough to hurt, but enough to keep me there. Tears were pooling in my eyes at an alarming rate. This couldn't be it. This couldn't be my last moments with him.

I don't plan for it to be, he said gently, reading my thoughts. *Fuck, Rumor, I want forever with you, and I'm going to do everything in my power to make sure that happens. Do you hear me?* When I didn't answer, he let go of my wrist, only to cup my cheeks again, then said out loud. "Rumor, I need you to believe me. I don't plan on dying today. But please," his voice faltered, "please, let me say this."

I met his gaze. His perfect crystal blue eyes with specks of silver were already searching my face. I inhaled a sob, but nodded.

"I love you, Scotlind. I love you with all my being, and no matter what happens today nothing can change that. I will always love you, and I will always come back to you. I hope it's in this life. I fucking pray to the Goddesses that it is, but if it's not, I will find you in the next, and the one after that, and every fucking life we might get because I love you."

I was sobbing now. I couldn't muster a response out loud. *I love you too, Tezya.*

"I need you to promise me you won't interfere. Promise me you'll let me do this."

I shook my head. I couldn't. I couldn't promise that.

He sighed before leaning down to kiss my forehead, then whispered so softly I thought I imagined it. "Then forgive me."

He left me standing alone in the bathroom, crying uncontrollably, praying to Pylemo and all twelve lesser Goddesses that Tezya wouldn't die today.

"Sie," he called once he entered the main room, and I immediately felt Dovelyn's powers fading as her shield vanished. "I need your compulsion."

SEVENTY-THREE
TEZYA

COLD, pale eyes seeped into me. I could feel him long before I saw him. I wasn't sure if it was Rumor's enhancement or if I was just sensing his emotions, but I knew he was ready for a fight.

I made Sie compel Scottie before we left. She wouldn't be able to interfere until Sie teleported her. It was the only way I agreed to her coming. If he hadn't, she would have thrown herself in front of the King, and now that she has my Dark blood running through her veins, Sie's total mind control would be the only compulsion that works on her.

I just had to trust Sie to keep her in the compulsion until I was done.

The three of them were hidden a couple miles out, still within reach of Sie's teleportation. He could be by my side in the blink of an eye, while still being far enough away that the King wouldn't notice them.

I also knew it didn't matter where Rumor was, she was probably listening and feeling everything through our bond. Her emotions were so strong that it was taking everything in me to block her out and focus on what I had to do. I knew she was pissed at me. Pissed didn't even begin to cover it—I had never seen her so livid before.

She punched me a hundred times over with tears streaming down her face as she cursed me out. I let her anger run its course, taking it as her punches slowly lost their power and she collapsed in my arms sobbing.

I hated it. I hated that our last moment together before coming here was tainted and hostile. I hated that I was the one who caused her pain, that I had asked Sie to compel her, knowing her history with the ability.

But I'd rather her hate me for it and be alive, than dead, and if Sie hadn't compelled her, she would be reckless enough to put herself in harm's way. I knew she was blocking me out for a reason today.

I just prayed I'd get the opportunity to rectify things with her after this.

I focused on my surroundings instead, trying to push her out of my mind. I wasn't as familiar with the Temples as I should have been, and it was likely the reason the King chose the spot. No one frequented the area except Dovelyn. The only time the general public came to them was on Allium Day.

I hated the Temples. I always had. Even though I liked to pay tribute to Pylemo, I was never as devoted as Dovelyn was. I still worshiped and respected each Goddess. I just liked to do it from the comfort of my own room or the hut. But Dovelyn loved it here. She came nearly every day and would soar over the dense trees below before they opened up into the vast mountain range.

It was probably why I hated it. The hike on foot to the Temples was unbearable, and the further I walked, the thicker it became, drawing more insects to my sweat.

When I was little, I was envious of my siblings' wings. I sometimes wished I was the King's son just so I could possess air abilities like Dovelyn and Arcane. But as I grew older, I realized it was the opposite. I knew they would have given anything for a different father—would have each given up their wings for it—and being raised by the man too, I wanted nothing more than to give that to them.

And now I could. I was going to kill him.

Even if it cost me my life, the King would never hurt anyone else after today.

We were on Pylemo's peak. The mountain range had thirteen all together—twelve smaller slopes leading toward the tallest one dedicated to the High Goddess. It was located at the tip of the island, creating a large cliff drop into the ocean from the other side. It was the only part of the ocean around Lux that wasn't tame. Air users didn't put their efforts into the shields over here. You came here for one reason and one reason only—to worship the Goddesses—and you didn't go swimming.

Old ruins sat at the top of Mount Pylemo with balding desert-like rock covering the slope. It all felt dead to me. Besides the jungle before the range, there wasn't any vegetation. No color. No signs of life, which felt wrong for worshiping the Goddess who blessed our kind with fertility during Lakimi. Even the ruins were graying stone columns that sat empty. Nothing but different kinds of rock and rubble.

"You have a lot of nerve coming here," the King said as his eyes swept over me. He stood above me, blocking the entrance to the Temples. "All these years you've been disobeying me. All these years when I gave you orders to murder those rebels, you've been hiding them? Training them? For what? To overthrow me? I offered you the crown over your brother. I wanted you as my sole heir, not Arcane. *You said no.*"

"It wouldn't have been my rule. It would have been dictated by you, and I meant what I said then just as I do now. I don't care about the crown. There's only ever been one thing I cared about."

"And what's that?" he sneered, annoyance lacing his voice.

"My mother," I said into the silence and even though he didn't kill her—even though her death was technically on me—if he hadn't been so cruel, there wouldn't have been a prophecy to begin with. He was a poison seeping and killing all of us slowly, and I saw the damage that lingered in her while she was still alive.

I took a deep breath before I continued with the only other people that mattered to me growing up. "And my siblings... The only thing I cared about all these years was protecting them from you."

He smiled, lifting up only the left side of his mouth. "You did spare Dovelyn and Arcane from me most of the time." His eyes gleamed over my scar with a hint of amusement. "There was no saving your mother, though, she was too weak for this world." I knew he was trying to taunt me, to get a rise out of me, but I wasn't buying it. I'd had a century to settle into my grief.

"And once I'm finished with you, any ounce of sympathy left in your bones for her will be gone." He paused, looking down on me. "You and your sister are looking at centuries of retraining. I'll have you begging me to kill you. You'll regret everything you've tried to do here."

"You're wrong."

He scoffed. "I'm never wrong."

"We aren't leaving this mountain together. One of us is going to die, and I have every intention of it being you."

He started laughing. "What the fuck are you on about? I trained you myself. I taught you everything you know. Do you really think I would have let you live if you were stronger than me? You can't beat me, and I never thought you were stupid enough to think you could. Even if you're more powerful than your siblings, you're still weaker than me, son. I'm the strongest in our family by a landslide."

"You're wrong again." I said it calmly as I felt his anger radiate toward me, as I welcomed it. For my mother. For everyone he's ever hurt. "Our mother was the strongest in our family."

"You're mother was soft and—"

"She was strong enough to last in a marriage to you and even stronger for still finding love with someone else despite it." His crooked smile started to vanish. He never knew my mother had an affair, and I was going to fucking savor it.

"What did you just say?" His voice lowered.

"You heard me." I took a step toward him, then another and another, until I was standing next to him on the mountain. I let the words sink in. Let him figure out what I meant as I kept staring into his cold, dead eyes.

After a minute of stunned silence, I spoke again, letting my body flare in golden spirals as I slipped the ring over my finger. "I'm not your son," I said. "And you didn't teach me everything I know."

SEVENTY-FOUR
SCOTLIND

HOURS HAD PASSED, and I had no idea how either of them were continuing to fight. I could feel every power being wielded by the King. Despite not having his prisoners to steal from anymore, he was just as strong, still taking too much to be natural that my enhancement was repulsed by him.

But I could also feel Tezya. I could feel his flames. They were hotter than I had ever felt before. They were burning through everything, burning through whatever abilities the King threw at him. But they were also burning through him, through his very soul, dwindling his reserves as he began to take from an endless well.

"We need to get closer." I turned toward Brock and Sie. "Please. He's going to die."

"He told us to stay hidden until he needs us," Sie said while Brock stayed silent.

"But he does need us. He needs us now!"

"I left a connection open between us. Tezya will let me know if he wants backup, but he hasn't reached out, Scottie. He's fine—"

"Fine?" I spat. "He's dying, Sie. If you know Tezya at all, you'd know he won't ever tell you."

His dark eyes met mine before he turned back to stare at the mountain range. He ran his fingers through his long locks and continued to pace. I needed his compulsion off. I needed to be closer to Tezya. He didn't stop me from using my abilities, which was why I was subconsciously hearing everything through Tezya's heightened senses, but he compelled me not to leave the mountain I was on. The only problem was, we were five mountains away from Mount Pylemo. I couldn't do anything else from this distance but listen to Tezya struggle, and it was going to kill me along with him.

I turned to Brock instead. "Brock, please. Tezya is going to die if I don't do something. He's wearing the ring, and he's going through his reserves too fast. He won't last long enough for the King's powers to wear off."

The plan was for Tezya to distract the King until he was fighting without any stolen powers. We didn't delude ourselves into thinking that just because we freed everyone in the dungeons, he'd stop stealing abilities. We knew he most likely found other powerful Advenians by now. But we prayed if we timed it right, they could start their fight on the cusp of his twenty-four period. It was why he waited so long to find him, but it wasn't going to work. He wasn't going to last another hour at best with how much power he was exuding. And deep down, I knew the prophecy wouldn't let that be an option. Standing on the Temples, I could feel it, feel the Goddesses. Whatever the riddle meant was going to come true one way or another.

Tears were streaming down my face and blurring my vision. "You're going to have to release me from this compulsion sooner or later. This isn't about me being selfish. We're going to lose our only chance at killing the King. Tezya's going to die, which means I'll be the only person left alive to take him on, and that's only if I can manage to get the ring. And besides that, who's to say Tezya's fire won't die with him? And if by some miracle it doesn't and I can still access it, I don't even know how to harness it. I've never trained with his fire before. If you let Tezya die right now, that's it, we lose. But if you let me go, I can help. I can save Tezya. I know I can. He can't do this alone despite what he thinks." No one said anything, the only sounds were distant and coming from Tezya and the King... "Please, just trust me."

Sie ran his fingers through his hair again, but at my words he stopped pacing and turned to face me. "Trust you? The last time you said that you ran off and let yourself get caught."

"I did that to save you, Sie, and we all got out eventually."

He ignored me and went back to pacing.

I screamed as Tezya's agony shot through me. Pain unlike anything I'd ever felt was coursing through our bond.

"He's killing him." I fell to the ground, my knees slamming against the bare rock. "He's going to die." I looked up and saw a vision of blurry brown and gold and knew I was staring at Brock, but I couldn't make out his expression through my sobs. I couldn't focus on anything.

"Dovelyn won't forgive you," I begged and pleaded with him. "And I won't either. I won't forgive you—either of you. I won't ever forgive you for this."

Strong arms grabbed my forearms and pulled me up. Then rough fingers scraped against the underside of my eyes, wiping my tears away until I stared into onyx ones—Sie. "What's your plan then?"

———

Sie teleported me halfway down the slope of Mount Pylemo, then teleported Brock and himself to the top where Tezya and the King were fighting by the ruins.

He refused to get me any closer, claiming that if Tezya saw me, he'd lose his focus, which I couldn't deny. If Tezya knew what I planned on doing, he wouldn't allow it. He'd find a way to make me stop, but I was close enough now that I could manage it from here. With my heightened sense of sight from him, I could see everything perfectly, and as long as he didn't look down, he shouldn't notice me, and even if he did, I'd be too far away from him that he wouldn't be able to stop me.

Brock was instantly putting everything he had into healing the injuries Tezya had. He was covered in blood. His cut across his chest had reopened, soaking through his shirt as he was slowly bleeding out. There was another cut across his face and a dagger embedded into his calf.

Brock's healing powers couldn't keep up. The King kept attacking, kept coming after Tezya without a break for even a second to breathe.

My enhancement felt Brock use his other ability as he tried to take away the King's senses, but he had an air shield surrounding himself.

Nothing was breaking through it—the only ability that could penetrate the kind of power he was using was Tezya's fire through the ring. It was different than any elemental ability I'd felt before. It could burn through anything, so I focused on it until it was all I became, and I didn't stop until I felt like I was burning alive too.

I put everything I had into his fire, enhancing it with my own reserves. At some point, my hands started shaking. Then my legs gave out, and I could only manage to slowly crawl up the slope. Then came the sweats. I was drenched, making navigating upwards nearly impossible. There was nothing to hold onto, no boulders or rocks embedded into the mountain. It was all small pebbles and loose stones that sent me tumbling anytime I tried using them as leverage.

I was approaching the bottom of my reserves. I could feel it. I started crawling again, laying flat on my stomach and slowly inching higher using my elbows and toes for support.

I glanced up at the ruins. The King was using ground magic, sending hundreds of vines toward Tezya, trapping him to one spot. Tezya was burning through them instantly, one after another, after another, but it wasn't enough. He was stuck in place because the moment it all turned to ash, the King was making more.

Fire was everywhere—the stone ruins were starting to collapse, and the smoke was so heavy I could barely see through it. My own lungs were burning from the inhalation, and I was pretty sure it was so thick I wouldn't be able to speak if I tried.

I squinted, trying to get a better look. The King had over a dozen daggers strapped across his chest, and one by one, he was sending them flying toward him. Tezya burned through the metal each time, but whenever he did, more vines wrapped around him. They were at his throat now.

Another dagger came flying at Tezya. I could feel his fire start through my enhancement, but then he swore, and I felt the pain for myself.

The King sent electricity toward him at the same time, and I watched in complete horror as it debilitated him—as it debilitated me too, and all I could do was watch as the blade went straight for his heart.

The smoke was too thick and too high. It was blocking my view, but Tezya's pain had my adrenaline soaring. It was going to kill him—

I forced my legs to move, forced myself to stand on shaking limbs, finding the strength to run the rest of the way up the slope. I was closer now, somehow managing to make it to the top. I expected to see Tezya laying on the ground. I imagined our bond breaking abruptly, but he was still being held up by the King's vines. Alive, he was—

I screamed, but it died on my lips because all I saw was black and red.

Black hair in a pool of blood.

Sie was on the ground before Tezya with the dagger embedded inside of him.

SEVENTY-FIVE

TEZYA

I COULDN'T MOVE. I was still trapped by the vines. Distantly, I could feel more tighten around me, but I didn't care. I was numb.

Sie was face down in the rubble before me, bleeding to death. He jumped in front of the blade to… save me.

The world stilled, and all I could hear was his heartbeat. It was fading fast. From the angle and all the smoke, I couldn't tell where the dagger pierced him, but he was rapidly losing blood, and he wasn't moving…

Then everything came back to speed at once. The King was laughing. Brock ran toward Sie and started dragging him away, and Rumor… she was standing before me, screaming uncontrollably.

Rage consumed me.

I promised myself when I came to this mountain, my siblings would be spared from the King. Sie and I didn't exactly get along, but he was still technically my brother, and the idea of the King taking away another family member was paralyzing. He didn't get to do this. He didn't get to take anyone else from me.

It had to end now.

My eyes met Scotlind's for one moment, one moment long enough for me to open up our bond and say, *I love you*, before I blocked her out again. I didn't wait for her to respond.

I turned back toward the King and burned through the rest of the vines entrapping me until there was nothing left.

Distantly, I felt Brock trying—and failing—to heal Sie. Scottie was standing in front of them, screaming and completely drained, but I couldn't focus on her, not if I wanted her to live. So I burned everything down except for them. I kept pouring and pouring my power toward the King.

Abilities hit me like a brick before I burned through each of them too. Glimpses of agony came crashing into me as the King tried to fight off my flames. Wind would push me back a few steps, water hit my body with such force that it took my breath away, new vines and roots would appear from the rubble, attempting to hold me down. But I destroyed them all.

My fire turned from varying shades of orange to bright blue as it poured out of me.

I didn't feel it as I pushed past the bottom of my reserves. The pounding headaches that usually left me crippling weren't affecting me because of the ring. Pylemo was giving me this chance to use everything I had to kill him once and for all, and I didn't plan on wasting it.

I knew the moment my flames started burning his skin. It was like acid was raining over his face before it melted everything off. The fire no longer took the shape of flames but water as I must have subconsciously mixed Rumor's ability with my own, creating molten liquid. I didn't hesitate as I encapsulated him in it, trapping him just like he trapped my real father on that stage.

I kept it going, kept pushing more and more into the flaming, molten circle. I could barely see him through the smoke, but I *heard* him screaming, and I wanted to savor the sound. I wanted to bottle it and repeat it so I would never forget him dying.

But then it stopped. His screams faded until I heard nothing but silence, but *I* didn't stop. I burned through him until he was nothing but ash, but even that wasn't enough. I needed his ashes gone. I wanted nothing left of his existence, so I kept burning and burning and burning, knowing that Scotlind would get to live in a world without this monster.

I looked into the blue, molten liquid and smiled. The color was the same sapphire as Rumor's eyes, and I was happy with this being the last thing I ever saw—

Warm hands gripped my bicep, pulling me from my trance. My chest was heaving as I slowly let the fire sink back into my veins, not ready to fully believe he was gone. My brain kept telling me that if I didn't stop, he'd come back and kill everyone I ever loved.

Sapphire eyes melted into me, but they were sunken in, devoid of life. Scottie was drenched in sweat, her normally light brown hair was dark and slicked back and her clothes were clinging to her skin. Blood was dripping from her nose and ears, and her breathing was staggered.

Her fingers slackened around my arm as soon as I stopped casting my fire and that's when I noticed her trembling. She was shaking all over, almost convulsing.

I grabbed onto her, catching her in my arms as she collapsed. "Rumor, are you okay?"

Worry consumed me as I let our bond open back up again. Agony and exhaustion were seeping from her.

I... love... you, she choked on the words in my mind—outwardly she was coughing, struggling to breathe, sucking in air through sharp gasps that were too ragged to be normal.

No.

No...

NO!

This couldn't be real...

I fell to my knees, still cradling her.

"BROCK!" I was screaming his name over and over again, tears were spilling down my face at an alarming rate that it didn't matter if there was smoke covering the mountain or not, I couldn't see anything.

"BROCK!"

"I'm trying to save Sie right now!" he shouted back through fits of coughing. The smoke wasn't clearing. I could feel it slowly burning my own lungs, but I didn't care, barely noticed.

"I NEED YOU HERE!" I screamed. Distantly, Scottie's body went limp in my arms. Her breathing was getting softer and lighter.

Fuck.

"Stay with me, Rumor," I cried, even though she couldn't hear me. "Please fucking stay with me..."

"BROCK!" I screamed again, this time glancing up at my friend. He was covered in my half brother's blood. Sie wasn't moving in his arms, just like Scottie wasn't in mine.

Blood spilled from Dark.

I hopelessly looked down at Scotlind, my abilities running over her and searching for any sign of injuries. She wasn't hurt, nothing looked fatal from what I could tell. Besides blood pouring down her nose and out of her ears, she wasn't cut...

But her heart was slowing, mixing in with the sound of Sie's rapidly dropping beat. It was all I could hear. It felt like drums, the sound was deafening, even as it slowly grew more and more infrequent.

Our bond was still there, but it was dimming, slipping away from me, and she wasn't responding.

"Scotlind, please..." I sent a million prayers to all thirteen goddesses, then started cursing them out when they didn't answer. "Pylemo, don't take her from me... DON'T YOU DARE FUCKING TAKE HER!"

I might have been screaming.

"Stay with me, Scotlind. Stay fucking with me!" I tilted my head toward Brock. "BROCK!" I cried. "Save her! Please, fucking save *her...*"

Brock looked up at me now. I saw his golden eyes flicker to the girl I loved dying in my arms. The look he gave me... I wasn't ready to decipher it—wasn't ready to accept it.

Fuck. This couldn't be happening.

"Please," I begged. "Do something... Do fucking anything!"

I was lost in my own rage that I hadn't noticed what she was doing. I hadn't noticed her using her enhancement, harnessing onto the ring I was wearing through our bond.

She went past her reserves, while I still had mine. I wasn't at my limit because my heightened senses were still intact. But hers—

I hadn't noticed that the one person I loved more than anyone else —the one person I was trying so desperately to protect—was killing herself to save me.

Sacrifice from Light.

SEVENTY-SIX
GREYLAND

I HAD NEVER SEEN SO many people go down so easily. The soldiers were slaughtering the humans in one go, sometimes more than one dropped at a time. There was so much blood it felt like we were bathing in it.

They were hacking into them, cutting them to pieces. I had to fight my composure as I kept seeing flashes of Lilia's parents.

And the ones that weren't slaughtered were burned to ash. Others drowned. Some had the air taken from their lungs and were writhing on the ground until they collapsed.

They were compelled to not fight back. I knew they were because no one in their right mind would just stand there and wait for their end, but that's what was happening. They didn't do anything to stop it.

It was intentional, just another ploy to convince our kind that humans were weak.

The eldest Luxian Prince managed to shield out the army and trap them inside for a couple of hours. It worked… until it didn't.

Now the sun was up and reflecting against the bay. There was grass when we arrived yesterday morning, but it was all gone now.

Either stomped away from the thousands of boots that kept marching over the courtyard or buried beneath layers and layers of blood.

It was becoming difficult to navigate, to not trip over the bodies that were piling up. And the stench…

Lilia was with me, not by her choice. She was taking every opportunity she could to try to weave through the massive amounts of bodies to get away from me. And as much as it killed me, I couldn't blame her. She was pissed when she found out I was using my illusion on her.

I shouldn't have done it. It was cruel to make her believe she was fighting when in reality she was attacking nothing.

After the battle in Tennebris, someone had seen her "fighting" and made a comment that the air would be terrified to see her coming. I tried to deflect, telling her everyone just needed a laugh. A slap across the face later, and I knew that didn't go over well.

So now here we were, *actually fighting*, and it scared the living shit out of me. I didn't know where that left me.

Lilia glowered every time I cut in front of her. But I didn't care. I still took out whoever was coming before they got to her. At this point, I just wanted her alive. She could hate me for it all she wanted. She already hated me for everything that happened in school…

Kallon was trying to portal the humans to some hut, but without Scottie's powers, it was taking too long.

The rest of us were fighting throughout the courtyard. We were spread out, trying to do the same thing—protect the humans, take out the soldiers, and not die.

"Kallon!" A voice screamed over the chaos.

"KAL!" I faintly recognized it.

Again. "KALLON!"

It was echoing across the courtyard, and I looked up in time to see Tezya sprinting through the Luxian soldiers. He wasn't using his powers. But he was fighting through whatever poor soul came his way. Fighting wasn't the right word for it—he was slaughtering whoever came at him without even looking.

Dovelyn came running up to him, more flustered and out of breath than I'd ever seen her before. "What happened?"

I noticed a shimmer go up around us as the eldest prince erected a shield. I honestly was so impressed by his power. I knew air users made shields, but the strength of Arcane's were insane. No one could penetrate it.

I relaxed for the first time since coming outside. I hadn't realized how stiff my body was. All the areas that were throbbing suddenly felt all consuming.

But I didn't think the youngest Luxian Prince even noticed his brother's shield.

He was covered in blood. His entire abdomen was drenched in it. He had a burn going up his right arm, a dagger sticking out of his calf, and more bruises and cuts than I could count.

"I need your help," he panted to his sister. "I need you and Kal to come with me right now—"

"Is the King dead?" Arcane asked, his voice was quiet, but even with all the fighting still going on, we could hear him.

Tezya nodded his head a fraction, like he couldn't be bothered with answering, even though it was a big fucking deal if he actually killed the King of Lux or not. He didn't even turn his head to look at his brother. Just nodded like it was nothing. Maybe he was in shock.

I looked at him more closely and realized he was shaking. His eyes were red-rimmed and swollen—

"Brock?" the princess asked, but Tezya cut off her.

"He's fine. We need to leave now—" He was out of breath, and I half wondered if he ran all the way here. I had no idea where the Goddess Temples were, but judging from his appearance, it couldn't have been close. Tears welled in his eyes and dread spread through me as the prince's emotions clicked. "Help me. *Please!*" He turned to Kallon who hadn't spoken yet.

A sinking pit formed in my stomach. My brother wasn't here. He could have teleported the prince, but he didn't.

I took a step back. I knew Lilia placed her hand over my arm, but I didn't feel it. Peter stilled next to me as he shifted back into his

Advenian form. The guy had been smiling while fighting this whole time, but now his grin was wiped off his face.

"Who is it?" Peter asked, the color drained from his face. "Which one—"

Peter was friends with Scotlind and Sie, and neither of them were here.

"Both." He was shaking. I might have been too. "We have to leave right fucking *now*!"

"Tezya, slow down. What exactly do you need?" his sister asked.

"Fly us to them. They're too far away. Then, Kal, portal them to Tennebris." I could see the frustration on his face. He was speaking a mile a minute.

He needed them to go to Tennebris—where the healers from Brighta were.

"Have Brock heal them—"

"He fucking tried," he yelled, cutting her off. "But they're both dying. Their injuries are..." He paused, letting out a shaky breath. "Please. Brock is trying, but it's not enough. They won't make it unless we get them to the healers, and they needed them a fucking hour ago!"

"Are they still alive, Tezya?" Kallon's voice was soft, gentle, but I didn't miss what she was insinuating. She thought Tezya was delusional, trying desperately to save something that was too late. Maybe it was...

"Barely." His voice cracked. "Please... the more time we waste here, the less of a chance they have."

"Okay," Dovelyn said, and I could have hugged her. "I'll fly you back to them."

He turned toward Kallon. It wouldn't matter if Dove flew Sie and Scottie back. They needed the healers in Tennebris...

"Kallon," Tezya's voice broke and sobs wrecked him. "Please help me. I can't... I can't lose her... Please."

"Do it," I pleaded along with the prince. "Sie's the only family I have left..."

I didn't care how close to death he was, if there was any chance of my brother surviving, they had to do it. The Fire Prince's silver eyes slid to me. It was so quick, I couldn't read the expression on his face.

"Please," Tezya choked. "Please, Kal. They're dying."

"Raeya…" Kallon murmured, and I knew she was hesitating. I entered her mind, erasing the hundreds of soldiers from view. But in reality, even with the King dead, we were still fucked. The soldiers didn't stop fighting, but she didn't need to know that. I used my illusion to make it look like they were backing off, like news of the King's death was spreading.

"I'll be fine," Raeya said, squaring her shoulders. "Rainer is with me."

The curly-haired Luxian stepped forward, and I hadn't realized how similar he looked to Raeya until he put his arm around her shoulder. They had the same dark skin, the same smile and mannerisms. "I won't let anything happen to her, Kal."

"Okay." She was still hesitant, but she stepped up to Raeya and grabbed her face in her hands. "Stay with Rainer, I'll be right back." Then she bent down and kissed her.

SOMEONE PROJECTED a command across the courtyard ordering— no compelling—the humans to start using their weapons against themselves. The voice made my skin crawl.

I wished energy weaponry worked in reverse. That a Tennebrisian could vanish a weapon instead of create one because one by one the humans started slitting their own throats. Some turned their swords around and plunged it into their stomachs. The ones that were lucky enough to lose their weapons started searching through the dead bodies, looking for a fallen blade.

"We have to take out Athler," the eldest prince said. Tezya, Dovelyn and Kallon weren't even gone two minutes and all hell was breaking loose.

The Luxian soldiers, not having to split their time between the humans anymore, focused solely on us. I just barely took out the

Luxian who charged Lilia and almost killed her. We were getting overwhelmed.

She had sweat pouring down her forehead, her pale blonde hair was sticking to her cheek. I could feel blood running down my own. I lost my eye patch at some point during the fight, and my stitches ripped open—it hurt like hell.

"The serum I made, there's two parts to it. One's a drink. It gives the person compulsion. The other's a vapor," Arcane said as we watched more and more humans kill themselves. "Whoever takes the serum can control anyone exposed to the vapor. The only way to stop this is to stop him. Athler and my father were the only ones who had access to my research."

"How do you propose we do that?" the mortal with purple hair asked as she swiped her dagger across a Luxian's stomach.

"I never create anything without first making an antidote," Arcane said as an arrow slammed into a shield he erected. "I made a reversal for the mass compulsion in case this ever happened."

"Your lab was destroyed," Rainer called as he punched a Luxian in the gut, sending tendrils of lightning scattering around him. I felt heat at my back and knew someone else was using fire.

"What I need isn't in my lab. It's in my room."

"And how are you going to get close to him?" Rainer challenged, fighting back to back with Raeya.

"His powers can't get through my shields."

"So you get the serum close to him and the compulsion the humans are under will go away?" the mortal questioned.

"Essentially, yes. I'll leave my siblings to figure out what to do with Athler when they get back, but we need to stop the compulsion or all the humans are going to be dead."

If they get back… If Scotlind dies, the Fire Prince won't be functional anytime soon. Honestly, maybe never again.

I pushed thoughts of my brother out of my mind because if something happened to him, I didn't think I'd be either. I couldn't think about it, couldn't imagine losing him too.

"I'll go with you," the mortal girl said, and it was still shocking as hell that she was human. I couldn't believe it with how well she fought, how she wasn't scared of anything.

I didn't want Arcane to leave. Maybe this made me a selfish dick, but I didn't care about the humans. I only cared about one girl, and without the eldest prince's shields, it was going to get harder to protect her.

There were times when I couldn't, where my fucking lack of an eye left me blind on that side, and I didn't see a soldier charge Lilia. If it wasn't for Arcane's shields… I didn't want to think about it.

The guy wasn't a great offensive fighter, but defensively he was phenomenal. He seemed to pay attention to everything and everyone around him. Whenever my sight of vision lacked, one of his shields would be there, but now he was leaving the battlefield.

I couldn't shake the feeling that we were spreading ourselves too thin, and that maybe it was exactly what this guy Athler wanted.

SEVENTY-SEVEN
SAVANNAH

ARCANE and I moved in silence. I could feel his shield hovering around me, which I was thankful for since I still didn't have a mask.

The humans had to live. Seeing them kill themselves... It was ingrained in my head. I couldn't stomach it. I was barely keeping myself together.

All I kept seeing was my own dad die over and over again. I couldn't let that be anyone else. I couldn't let any more of them die. How many fathers were in the courtyard? How many human children were going to be left without parents because of Advenian greed?

Athler needed to die. And I needed to concentrate enough to do it. But all I kept thinking about was how I was going to face Wells after this. How was I going to tell my little brother our dad died because I was reckless and didn't listen to him...

We made it to Arcane's room, and I whistled as I took it in. It was the only part of the castle I'd seen so far that wasn't ruined by death and blood. I'd never been to Lux before. I was envious when I found out that Arcane had brought Wells in the past and not me.

I'd always wanted to know what the Advenian Kingdoms looked like. I heard countless stories from my friends, but seeing it in person was something else. It was eerily similar to the mortal world—well,

Lux was. Tennebris seemed more like a fancier version of the Middle Ages. But for the most part, everything was the same. The same but different. You couldn't distinguish between the Advenian electric user's lights versus ours. The buildings were similar. The furniture looked identical.

And Arcane's room—I felt like I was walking into the most luxurious hotel I'd ever seen. He had floor-to-ceiling windows encompassing the entire back wall overlooking the ocean. And his bed was so tempting, I wanted to surrender to it. I wanted to forget everything that happened today.

I should be dead, not my father…

"This is it," Arcane said as he grabbed a black swirling liquid off a test tube rack. Leave it to my brother's ex lover to have a mini lab set up in the corner of his room.

"It's liquid," I said, stating the obvious.

Arcane looked at me. "What did you expect?"

"I assumed it would be another vapor or something."

"Vapors are unpredictable and unstable. This is safer."

"Okay," I said slowly, walking over to him and inspecting it myself. "So what do we need to do? Get him to drink this?"

I didn't see how this was going to work if that was the case. It wasn't like we could ask this Athler person to have a drink with us, and I highly doubted either of us were going to get close enough to shove it down his throat.

"No," he scoffed. "It's transdermal. We just need it to touch his skin." He then poured the black liquid into another, larger vial that had a grayish tint to it.

"What are you doing?"

"Mixing it with Alluse," he said, not looking at me and concentrating on what he was doing. "We need to take him out. I came up with this a while ago. I figured we'd need a way to get rid of his powers. I originally planned to use it on my father…" His voice grew softer as he focused on the task.

The only word I heard was father…

It kept repeating over and over again in my head.

Father. Father. Father.

My father was only fighting because he found out I snuck into Lux. He wasn't even supposed to be here—

Arcane finished mixing the liquids and pocketed the vial. "Do you still keep those sedatives on you?"

I pulled out one of my needles, already filled with a dose heavy enough to knock out ten people. "You mean this?"

"Yes. Think you can stab him with it if I make you invisible?"

I grinned. "I could probably do it even if I wasn't invisible."

SEVENTY-EIGHT
GREYLAND

Peter shifted back into a bear, ripping into the soldiers who got too close to us, but without Arcane's powers, we were slowly becoming overwhelmed. He had been using his air ability to push the soldiers back so we weren't swarmed by them. But now that he was off with the mortal girl, we were slowly being surrounded. I could feel them closing in on us.

"Fuck," I growled as Lilia just managed to dodge an axe being thrown at her. I stormed to her side, gripping her bicep, and pulled her toward me. "Stop running away from me."

"Why? So you can use your powers on me again?" she snapped. Her chest heaved as she turned to face me, and her rage was undeniable.

"So I can keep you alive!"

Her hazel eyes narrowed. "You made me fight nothing. Everyone saw me—"

I was glaring down at her. "I don't fucking care if you become the laughing stock in both kingdoms. It's better than being dead. You can hate me for it all you want, but stop being so fucking stupid."

I entered the minds of twenty or so Luxian soldiers, changing their perception to make it look like Lilia and I weren't standing in the

508

middle of the courtyard having a verbal sparring match. I knew it was dumb to waste my reserves on this, but I didn't want to be interrupted, and I *needed* her to understand.

She stepped back, ripping her arm out of my grip. "Don't use your powers on me, Greyland."

I exhaled, twirling the blade in my hand before refocusing my attention on the fight around us. Lilia went right back into it, and I decided to keep using my illusion.

If she didn't want me to use my powers *on* her, I'd use them on everyone *around* her. Even if it gave me the worst fucking headache of my life.

I could feel blood start to drip down my nose, but I didn't stop. I kept moving my illusion, transferring it to everyone around her so that no one knew she was there as she moved across the courtyard. I was at her back, fighting whoever came at us too fast, whoever I couldn't put my illusion on.

I was finding it easy to kill the soldiers. I honestly didn't know where that left me. I knew Sie tried to protect me from this, from the guilt of taking a life, but I didn't feel any. At least not right now. I was scared shitless for my brother that it made killing anyone who came remotely close to Lilia and me as easy as if I was giving them a handshake.

I wanted them all dead. They were the reason my life was complete shit. My parents and I were shipped off to this kingdom and these soldiers beat the living shit out of us for weeks. They ripped my fucking eye out and laughed—and my mother... she died from one of these pieces of shits.

So yeah, I went to town on them, and envisioning any of them doing the same thing to Lilia, made me happy to see them die.

Three Luxians charged Raeya next to us. Rainer and her—who I found out were cousins—were fighting side by side. We all naturally paired off in twos. Peter was with Vallie, but every so often, I saw his eyes drift toward his sister. To Lilia's dread, I stayed with her. And Rainer never took his gaze off his cousin.

Rainer swiped off his boxing glove and spewed lightning into two of the soldiers who came after her, but the third sidestepped, just missing the brutal bolt of energy. My eyes drifted toward the two that were lying on their backs. Their faces were glazed over with foam spilling from their mouths. Their bodies were covered in thick jagged scars. The same scars covering my brother's hands.

The guy's power was sick, and I wished I had something more tangible to fight with. Only one of my abilities was helpful right now —my second power was useless for this kind of stuff—not that anyone even knew I had a second ability. Lilia was the only person I told, and she refuses to believe it...

The third soldier drove his weapon into Raeya's chest before Vallie used her own sword to cut through his neck.

We all watched for a moment as the soldier's head flopped and rolled onto the wet ground. It was as if time stilled for one prolonged second. One second before Raeya's screams echoed through us.

She fell to her knees, clutching her chest as her shirt instantly reddened. Rainer threw his other boxing glove off, tossing them both on the ground.

"Rae, no—no, no, no," he cursed as he sank down next to his cousin.

"Rainer..." she groaned, her small hand trembled as she cupped his cheek.

"You're okay," he crooned. "You're going to be okay."

But tears were pouring from his eyes while blood was pouring out of the girl's mouth. There was so much of it she started choking on it. Her hand dropped from his cheek leaving a trail of red in its place.

I grabbed Lilia, pulling her into my chest as I pushed my illusion into everyone I could around us. They needed a fucking minute because the girl was *not* okay. Lilia tensed under me. I could tell she was about to protest before she realized what had happened.

I couldn't watch over her while I used this much of my power. I felt Lilia still in my arms, and I knew without looking that her eyes drifted toward the girl on the ground.

"Kallon," Raeya choked through coughing fits.

"Yes, wait for Kallon," Rainer cried. "Hold out, Rae. Kallon is coming. Brock will heal you, and Kallon will be here, and everything will be alright. Just hold on." The last word broke him as he cradled the girl closer in his arms, the sword still awkwardly piercing her chest.

But they weren't coming. Kallon wasn't going to make it in time.

I used my remaining reserves of power to enter Raeya's mind. No one should die alone.

"Kal," Raeya smiled through the blood. To everyone else, it looked like she was talking to herself, like she was seeing things, which I guess she technically was.

Rainer let out a sob.

I tried recalling every interaction I saw of Kallon and Raeya together. The little bit I did see, I knew she was obsessed with her.

"I'm here, Raeya," I said as Kallon. "I love you. I'm right here."

Raeya relaxed. Her eyes fluttered closed as she continued to smile. "I love you too, Kal. And yes, my answer is yes. It was always yes."

I had no idea what she was talking about, but I had my illusion of Kallon tuck the girl's curly hair behind her ears and continued to whisper, "You're safe. It's okay. Sleep." I could feel my reserves depleting, could feel myself on the brink of passing out, but the Luxian deserved this. She deserved to die in the arms of the girl she loved.

Guilt was slowly working its way through me. Would she still be alive if Kallon didn't leave to help Tezya? I altered Kallon's perception. I made it look like the battle was dwindling down instead of worsening. Was she dying because I needed Sie saved more? If Sie could even be saved...

I didn't stop my illusion. I let it run out, trying to find words to comfort the girl as she slowly bled out. I waited until her eyes rolled back, and she was limp in her cousin's arms.

My vision swirled as my illusion died with the girl. Rainer was sobbing now, rocking her dead body back and forth, and screaming at the top of his lungs.

SEVENTY-NINE
SCOTLIND

My body ached, and my head was screaming when I finally came back to myself. The last thing I remembered was Tezya holding me, and I was okay with dying in his arms.

I slowly blinked my eyes open and was blinded by bright lights.

Crystal blue and silver eyes were staring into me. "Tezya?" My voice cracked, unsure if I was imagining things.

He leaned forward, his bone-white hair covering his forehead. "I'm right here." His calloused hand cupped my cheek too gently, and I couldn't decipher the expression on his face.

I looked down and saw I was lying on a cot. A scratchy, cream blanket was folded neatly over me, and Tezya was perched on the side of the mattress. He looked so tired, so exhausted.

"What happened?" My throat felt like sandpaper, making it difficult to get any words out. Tezya leaned forward, grabbing a glass of water from the table next to me, then helped me sit up with his other hand.

"Here, drink first." He tilted my chin as he guided the water down my throat, and I gulped greedily. He refilled the glass from a pitcher, then brought it to my lips again, before pressing a tiny white circular pebble into my mouth. Why he wanted me to eat a rock—

He laughed gently, reading my thoughts. "It's not a rock. It's a pill. It's mortal medicine. Savannah said it will help ease the pain. Too many were injured that the healers are only tending to vital wounds… for now."

I nodded, then swallowed the tiny rock—pill—before meeting Tezya's gaze again.

How am I alive? I asked into his mind. I knew what I was doing on that mountain. I knew I went past my reserves.

Tezya hesitated for a moment. *You need to rest*—he started.

Show me, I said, grabbing his hand. I needed to know what I missed. I needed to know what happened and who was still alive.

Tezya hesitated for a second, before he obliged, and I started seeing everything through his eyes. I soaked it all in as if I lived through it myself. I'd been out for days apparently. After the King died, Brock healed Sie enough to make him conscious. Tezya fought him over it, but they needed a way to get back to the castle. Tezya kept holding me —screaming, and crying, and begging Brock to heal me. Then, he was pleading with the goddesses. I'd never seen him so distraught, so out of himself.

I was terrified I was going to lose you, he said into my mind before continuing with what happened.

Sie teleported us until he collapsed a mile out. He shouldn't have been able to teleport at all, let alone, teleport all of us. He was pale and sickly and covered in too much of his own blood to even be standing.

We didn't have a choice, Tezya commented. *If we did nothing, you both would have died on that mountain.*

Is he—I couldn't finish my thought, but Tezya knew where I was going.

He's alive. I sprinted the rest of the way to the castle, and Dovelyn flew Kallon to where Brock was waiting with you and Sie. Kal portaled you both to the medical ward in Tennebris.

I nodded as I watched what else happened through Tezya's memories. Some of it he witnessed himself and others were from what everyone else told him.

The battle ended shortly after that, but it was brutal. There were some soldiers who didn't stop fighting, regardless of the news that the King had died. They wanted the ranking system and believed in what they were fighting for. Tezya said a lot of the army had been brain-washed into brutality and that half of them were dead by the time they finally surrendered. Most of the remaining Luxians cooperated, although the high ranks didn't take the news as easily as the Tennebrisians.

Arcane and Savannah managed to stop the mass compulsion serum. The humans who were still alive were healed, fed, and then compelled to forget everything that had happened. But out of the thousands of humans who were captured, not many were still breathing.

Kallon and Savannah brought them all back to their home territory. The two of them were purposely staying busy and went head first into any task that needed to be done. I could feel Tezya's worry for them. I knew the mortal lost her father, but Kallon's girlfriend died too. Raeya. I'd been so consumed by losing Tezya that I never anticipated anyone else losing the person they loved.

How did it happen? I asked.

Three Luxian soldiers charged her at once. Rainer took out two of them with his lightning, but the third got to Raeya before he could.

I could sense he wanted to keep the rest from me, but it was too late, I already saw it through our bond. She died because of me. Kallon left to help me and now...

It's not your fault, Tezya said. *I was the one who asked Kallon to leave, not you.*

It still doesn't change that you and I have each other, and she can't say the same. Kallon left her girlfriend to help me, and while I survived, she didn't.

I talked to Kal, he said after a moment. *She doesn't think it's anyone's fault. Everyone that was fighting knew the risks, and even if Kallon stayed with Raeya, the outcome could have been the same.*

Tezya's words hit me, but I saw it for what it was. He didn't even believe it himself. The guilt was eating away at him too.

Is she okay? I asked.

No, but she has Savannah, for now, and Rainer. His words "for now" had my mind racing. Did that mean we were leaving? That we were going back to Allium?

Yes, he answered, knowing exactly where my thoughts drifted. *We're leaving in a couple of weeks to go back.*

What about everyone else? Peter and Vallie instantly flooded my mind next.

All okay. Everyone else is okay. Peter was badly injured at the end, but he'll live.

And Greyland? I started, but stopped, knowing it was Tezya's little brother too.

Alive.

I nodded, relief flooding me because I couldn't stomach any more death. But in reality so many lives were lost because of this. How many families were suffering now? How many lost their parents, siblings, significant others? I prayed it would all be worth it.

I hope so too, Tezya said gently. *The fighting stopped, but there's still a large number of people that aren't happy with the changes. Everyone has agreed to return to Allium, but once we're there it's going to be difficult. We'll have to implement our new plan for governing immediately and pray more wars don't break out because of it.*

I nodded, now understanding this was what Dravenburg meant when he said we needed to be prepared before we fought. The Advenians were split down the middle. Most agreed with us, having lived through some of the suffrage, but the ones who benefited before—the ones who were high ranked and thrived from the old system—they'd be harder to convince. This was far from over.

Athler? I asked, realizing I hadn't seen the King's second during the battle.

He was the one controlling the humans while we were with the King. Savannah and Arcane were able to capture him.

Capture? I repeated. *So he's alive?*

Tezya nodded. *Everyone agreed there were too many deaths to add more right now. He's in the dungeons with five Alluse users and two air users. Plus,*

Sav has been giving him heavy sedatives so he doesn't wake up. Once we get to Allium, we'll figure out what to do with him and everyone else.

What about your brother? I asked.

He's also someone we will have to figure out what to do with.

You mean you're keeping him locked up? Shock coursed through me. I knew Arcane was technically a prisoner prior to everything starting, but he helped us, he fought with us… I saw it through Tezya's memories. All the humans would have died if he hadn't agreed to come back with Kallon to help.

I know, Tezya said. *I don't like it either. But he's not in the dungeons at least. He's being confined to his room with an insane amount of luxury and endless wine so he's fine for now.*

I shifted on the bed, sitting up even higher before slowly removing the itchy bedding. I wanted to see everyone. I had to see they were alive with my own eyes.

"Rumor, wait—" Tezya started, and I jumped, shocked at him speaking out loud after being inside my head. "There's more."

"What?" I asked, slumping back down onto the cot, mentally preparing myself as I held my breath.

"You and Sie, you both saved me." I waited, terrified for where he was going with this. "You locked onto the ring through our bond, and you were using all your enhancement on me. I didn't realize what you were doing until it was too late. I thought I was going past my own reserves, but I wasn't…"

"But I did," I finished for him.

He nodded. "You used up all your reserves. You're lucky to be alive right now, but…" He paused.

"Tezya just spit it out and tell me," I said, hating the hesitancy.

"Your enhancement is gone."

His words settled into my core, but I couldn't fully comprehend them. Not yet anyway. I reached into my powers and immediately the call to water came. I could feel it in everyone's bodies behind the curtain that was pulled shut, in the pitcher of water next to me, I could sense the little bit of sweat down Tezya's forehead. But whenever I tried to access the powers around me—I came up blank. My enhancement was gone. It felt like I was searching my mind for a memory I couldn't remember.

The only other powers I could sense now were Tezya's fire and his *summa sensibus*. But everyone else around me... I felt nothing.

"I'm so sorry, Scotlind. I'm so fucking sorry... If I had known what was happening..."

"It's okay, Tezya," I interjected. "It was all worth it. *You* are worth it. I'm just happy you're alive."

Tezya's expression didn't relax. He didn't believe me, but I meant what I said. I would give everything I had in order to keep him alive, and if sacrificing my ability meant that, then I was fine with it. I'd learn to deal with the part of me that now felt hollow and empty. But for now, I was happy.

He leaned down and kissed my forehead. "I'm happy you're alive too. I don't know what I would have done if..." He didn't finish his sentence but kissed my forehead again. "You need to eat something, and then we can go see the others."

I smiled at Tezya and pulled at his shirt, tugging him down toward me, and I kissed him.

I kissed him simply because I could.

EIGHTY
GREYLAND

I STILLED as Lilia walked toward me. I found a small, deserted room off to the side of a lavish one.

I guessed it was some sort of chapel. It was filled with wooden benches with red velvet cushions. A statue of Pylemo was erected in the center of the room with the twelve lesser goddesses all bowing around her.

The ceiling consisted of stained-glass, like almost all of Tennebris, but because it was their dark season, the sun wasn't around to light the space. I could have lit the sconces that lined the walls, but I didn't care enough. It didn't matter anyway. I could make out enough.

"Hi," she said as she closed the door behind her.

I didn't turn around, but I knew it was her before she even spoke.

Her footsteps sounded as she came to sit next to me. I picked a bench directly in front of Pylemo and had been staring at her for the past hour.

I turned away from the Goddess to look at Lilia, and my heart nearly stopped. She was so damned beautiful I had to pinch myself. Her hazel eyes were more gold than brown today, and her pale hair was pushed behind her shoulders.

She was closer to me than I realized, and I had to fight the urge to want to pull her onto my lap.

I wasn't sure how to act anymore. I was too exhausted to keep up my facade, and honestly I didn't want to. I didn't care how vulnerable it made me or if she decided to laugh in my face and reject me, I wanted to tell her everything was real.

No—I *needed* her to know everything was real.

It was on the tip of my tongue. I was about to admit that every dream she ever had of me for the past four years, were all because of me, because of my second power.

But she spoke first. "You used your illusion on Raeya, didn't you?"

I opened my mouth, then closed it. It wasn't what I expected her to say. I figured she'd want to ask me about her parents, or about the cabin or anything about that day. Hell, maybe she'd even want to talk about school, about what Lander and my friends did to her.

"I did."

She nodded, her eyes filling with tears. "You gave her peace, Grey—"

"I only did it because I first used my illusion to make Kallon leave," I cut her off. I didn't want to be praised for something I originally caused.

"What do you mean?" Her eyes widened.

"I used my illusion on Kallon to make it look like the soldiers were backing down when they found out the Lux King died. I'm the reason she wasn't fighting with Raeya when she died."

Her lips parted before she collected herself. Whatever she thought of that, she didn't say.

She stood abruptly, about to walk away, when I grabbed her wrist. I hadn't realized which one it was until I felt her brand beneath my fingers. She flinched but didn't pull away.

I stood, towering over her.

"I think you're an asshole, Greyland." Her voice came out soft and without its usual edge of hardness whenever she spoke to me. "And it has nothing to do with Raeya."

"I know," I said. I still didn't let go of her wrist. Her back was to me, and I slowly turned her around, forcing her to look at me. "I'm sorry."

She started crying, so many people had been since the fighting ended, and weeks later, it didn't stop. There was so much death, so much loss, that I kept trying to find deserted places to escape it all. But hers—Lilia's grief—I didn't want to run away from it.

Her head tilted up to look at me. I abandoned her wrist, only to wipe at her tears.

"Sorry for what?" she asked, holding her breath.

"For everything. School. What happened with Lander. For not stopping it sooner. But I'm not sorry for using my illusion on you when we fought."

She tried pulling away, not liking what I said, but I cupped her face. "Lilia. I'm not sorry because I would do it again and again if it meant keeping you alive."

Her lips parted. Her breathing hitched.

Say it. Say it, Greyland. Admit to everything. Tell her about the dreams.

"I like you, Lilia."

Coward. I was a fucking coward.

I didn't give her time to think before I leaned forward and kissed her in real life.

And fucking Pylemo. It was divine. It was better than what I imagined in my dreams.

She tasted like heaven and wine and everything fucking blissful in the world.

And what had me fucking losing my mind, what had me cursing and moaning her name, was that Lilia Evalyn Fervic was kissing me back.

EIGHTY-ONE
SIE

I COULDN'T BELIEVE I was still alive. I expected this outcome, that we'd win, I just didn't think I'd be breathing long enough to be a part of it. I never imagined returning to Allium with everyone.

I only had snippets of memories from the mountain. I remember seeing Scotlind pass out. I remember Tezya screaming. I knew I teleported them, but only the Goddess fucking knows how I managed to pull that off. I was told I was out for two days. Scottie had been out for five.

A bandage was wrapped over my wrist and around my hand. The healers tried to save it. When I threw myself in front of Tezya, my arm was stretched and the dagger sliced through my wrist, hitting an artery. It left me with severe nerve damage, and I lost almost all feeling below my elbow.

I wiggled my fingers through the bandage, wondering if I would ever be as good of a fighter again. I didn't even know if I would be able to properly hold a utensil, nonetheless a blade. I would have to retrain myself on everything I knew with my left.

I had no idea why I did it. I hadn't expected or meant to. I didn't even realize I liked or cared for the guy. But once I saw the King use electricity on Tezya, I knew he wouldn't be able to function long enough to burn the dagger before it reached him. I felt enough of Rainer's power to know the ability was debilitating. It was going to kill him. I reacted without thinking and teleported in front of him in the split second it took the dagger to fly through the air.

I thought of Scotlind. After everything she'd been through, I didn't want to see her hurting anymore. There was a part of me that would always care for her.

But then there was another part of me, a much deeper part, that was starting to accept that he was family. He was my half brother, which made him Greyland's half brother, and even though Grey didn't know it yet, I hated the idea of him losing another family member. Our parents' deaths were already too much for him.

But here I was, alive, just not whole. Fighting had become my identity over the past couple of weeks at the camp, and now I couldn't even properly do that. Not that anyone was up for sparring or training anymore. Everyone was exhausted and beyond wounded. There weren't enough healers to go around.

I pushed down the heaviness I felt about losing Moli. I hated that I always thought of her. Anytime I was with the healers, I knew she would have been helping day in and out, healing anyone and everyone she could.

I couldn't grasp how I made it out alive when the entire world hated me, but Moli and my mother didn't. Moli was so pure and innocent. She wouldn't hurt a fly. And my mother's only fault was marrying my father. But now they were both gone, and I was here.

I knew my chances of survival were limited to begin with, especially with how I was painted during the broadcasts, and although they tried to set the record straight during our own broadcasts after the battles, there were many Advenians who didn't believe it. They needed someone to blame for the loss of their loved ones, and I was the easiest target. It was hard to forget the image of the fucking 'S's carved into all the dead bodies.

I still had to watch my back. I wasn't liked or welcomed. I was more feared than anything, but I didn't mind. The only people I needed in my life were still alive—Peter and Grey—so that was good enough for me. Everyone else could go to hell for all I cared.

"Hey," a soft voice called out. Everyone was now in Tennebris. It was larger than Lux and housed the spacecraft. It took about three weeks to convince the Luxians of our plans and another two to prepare for the journey.

I turned around toward the sound of the voice. I was outside of Palm, sitting by the edge of the woods. Savannah was dressed for the cold. Tennebris was still in their dark season, but I could make out her features from a mile away. Her lavender hair was tucked into a black hat and a matching scarf was so tightly wound around her neck that it covered the tip of her chin.

Her boots crunched in the frost-filled grass before she sat down next to me. I kept staring at her as I noticed the tip of her nose turning bright red. I knew the cold bothered her just as much as it did all humans. But it was easy to forget. Mainly because she was crazy enough to travel to the dead river in the human territory for fun, but it was weird seeing how fast the weather affected her now.

"Hi," I finally said, turning my gaze from her to stare back out at the woods. We were leaving for Allium tonight, and as much as I knew it was the right thing to do, I felt uneasy about leaving my home. "How are you doing?"

She shrugged, but I knew her real answer. She wasn't good and it was probably stupid of me to even ask. I definitely didn't want to talk after my father was killed, so why I expected her to do the same was beyond me. And she actually liked her father.

"I'm sorry," I managed to get out. "I know you probably don't want to talk about it, but I wanted you to know."

I kept replaying what happened during the battle. I kept hearing her scream as I teleported her away from Dravenburg. They were bickering and yelling at each other while they were fighting Luxian soldiers. Dravenburg was scolding her for coming, and Savannah kept saying it was all she's ever known and that she wanted to help her friends. I was fighting next to her, something I kept subconsciously doing without knowing why, so I overheard everything. Their last moment together was a fucking fight.

Savannah was distracted by something he said and was about to get sliced in half with a sword before her father stepped in front of the blade to save her. She stood frozen for a moment with his blood splashed over her nose, painting red freckles across her face. She didn't move, *wouldn't* move. She was in shock, and I knew she couldn't fight. So I teleported her away… away from her father. It wasn't until I brought her into the safe room that she flipped out and started screaming and hitting and yelling at me to take her back to Dravenburg.

"He's gone, Savannah. He's gone. You have to let him go."

"No," she sobbed as tears ran down her face. "No, he's not! Take me back to him." She kept hitting me over and over again until I finally grabbed her wrists and pulled her into me.

"I'm sorry," I whispered. I kept repeating the same phrase into her ear, not letting go of her arms, until she finally collapsed and started crying into my shoulder.

I wasn't sure how long we stayed like that before Tezya and the others found us. She took a step back from me once they did. Her glossy eyes and watery face met mine, before she walked toward the corner of the room and sat down.

But looking at her now, if I hadn't seen her grief from losing her father, I never would have known. She had her emotions in check. I wasn't sure if she was just strong-willed, hated breaking down in front of people, or if she pushed it so far out of her mind that she refused to think about it, and I found myself curious which one it was.

I knew her brother probably had something to do with it. She was the older of the two, and I kept watching her the past couple of weeks. The mortal boy broke down all the time, and Savannah was there for each one, comforting him in ways I knew were probably destroying her on the inside. Because unlike her brother, she had the added guilt of his death. Same as I did for my father. They both died because of us.

"I didn't come find you to talk about him," she said after several moments, and I couldn't hold back my shock at her admitting she sought me out.

I turned to face her and was mesmerized by her hazel, gray eyes and how her lavender hair seemed to reflect in them. She was sitting closer to me than I thought, and it was only now hitting me that this was the last time I was ever going to see her.

"I know what I want from my bargain with you," Savannah said, pulling me from my thoughts.

"Bargain?" I nearly forgot I made one with her. That I would have to say yes to one thing she demanded in exchange for her training Vallie and Lilia.

Of course she hadn't forgotten it. If this was my last time seeing her, she was going to use it. I was stupid for thinking she came for anything else. "What do you want?"

"I want to go with you. I want you to take me to Allium."

EIGHTY-TWO
SCOTLIND

I WOKE up to warmth surrounding me. I smiled before I even opened my eyes, knowing the cause behind it.

Tezya.

We'd been in *The Miles*—the name given to the spacecraft—for a month now. I could understand why our ancestors agreed to the Peace Treaty all those centuries ago—being in space sucked.

Without Tezya warming the air around me, I was pretty sure I would have been freezing twenty-four-seven. But I couldn't believe it —we actually did it. We were both alive and heading to Allium together. Everything felt so surreal.

"Good morning," he murmured onto the top of my hair. His hand wrapped around my back, pulling me closer to him.

"Morning." I kissed down his chest, something I hadn't been able to stop doing since we'd been in space. Every day felt like a dream, and I was too scared to wake up from it.

He's real, I kept telling myself. *He's alive. He's here with me.*

I felt guilty being this happy. Anytime I saw Kallon or Vallie, my heart sank a little.

Kallon was doing better than my best friend, or at least that's what she wanted everyone to think. She put a mask on her emotions and pretended like everything was okay, but I knew it wasn't—she wasn't okay. Whenever Tezya and I weren't in our shared pod, we tried to spend all our free time with her. Rainer was by her side whenever we couldn't be, but she tried to brush us off.

I had no idea how Vallie was managing. Peter said she'd been distancing herself more and more, and I knew it had to do with being in space. Miles should have been with us.

"I know what I want to do when we get to Allium," Tezya said after a moment. I opened my eyes and adjusted to the darkness. Neither of us had turned on the lights yet, and although our pod had a large window overlooking the stars, it only cast a slight glow over us.

"Hmmm," I mumbled, still trailing kisses down his belly. When he asked me the question two weeks ago, I told him that I wanted him to train me with his abilities. Since all I had were my water powers now, I wanted to explore our bond—something we couldn't do on the spacecraft because if I burned it down—well, we all agreed not to use our powers for the next six months. Air, electric, and Alluse users were the only ones that were allowed to. And although Tezya snuck some of his fire abilities when we were alone in our pod, he technically wasn't supposed to.

Air users helped with the pressure stabilization, electric users supplied the lights and mechanics, and Alluse users rotated watching over the prisoners in the belly of the craft. But that was it. No one else was allowed to use their abilities.

I tried to avoid thinking about it—how many Advenians were kept in cages down below. We decided to empty the prison, and that included everyone inside it—the prisoners in the cages and the ones thrown into the pit. Athler was also somewhere below us too... It made me uneasy, but we couldn't leave anyone on Earth. It wasn't fair to the humans. They needed a fresh start, just like we did.

We planned to have a trial for everyone, knowing that some of the prisoners were probably wrongly convicted just like Sie had been—but it was something else we were pushing off until we got to Allium, something we'd worry about later.

So for right now, I decided I just wanted to soak up these next six months—well five now. Five more months of no responsibilities. Five more months of recovery, of just enjoying Tezya. When we reached Allium, then we'd figure everything else out.

Tezya had kissed me and agreed to train me as long as I trained him with my water. The idea of training him felt weird, but I knew I was going to enjoy every second of it.

When I had asked Tezya the same question, *what he wanted to do when we got to Allium,* he said he needed time to think about it.

He pulled me up to his face, his hands instantly cupping my cheeks. "I want to get married."

I was speechless for a moment. One whole moment and then, *"What?"*

"Marry me, Scotlind." He was smiling down at me, his scar rising slightly across his face, and his hair was tousled from sleep.

"I thought you didn't want marriage—" I kept thinking about one of the first conversations we had at the hut, how he told me he didn't believe in them.

"With you, I want it. I want it all. I want you to be mine in every way." He kissed my lips softly, barely a touch. "I want you as my best friend, my bond mate, the love of my fucking life, *and* my wife." He kissed me again. "So will you marry me?"

"Yes." I smiled, tears rolling down my face because apparently I even cried when I was happy. My hands intertwined in his hair as my legs locked around his hips, and I rolled on top of him. "Yes." I grinned into his mouth, consuming his as I kissed him. "I want to be yours." I kissed him again, my tears falling onto his face. "I love you, Tezya."

"I love you, Scotlind."

I couldn't stop smiling. "Scotlind Xandrin, I could get used to the sound of that."

"I was thinking…" He pulled back just enough to look at me. "What if we changed our last name together? Xandrin was the King's name. It never belonged to me."

"What do you want to change it to?"

"What about Sirena?"

I gasped, thinking it over as more tears fell from my eyes.

"Only if you want to," he added quickly.

I shook my head, not able to form the words of how much I wanted to. *Sirena*—my real last name. I finally felt happy enough to deserve it. *Scotlind Sirena* seemed like the perfect mix of both—the perfect name to start over with.

"Yes," I finally managed to get out. "I would love that."

I was so happy, and I realized that it didn't matter where I was—abandoned in Tennebris, a prisoner in Lux, a refugee in a camp, or a girl on a spacecraft—because as long as I was with him, I would always be home.

Tezya Anthony Sirena was my home, and I finally found where I belonged.

EPILOGUE
PART ONE

Sie

"GET DRESSED." Tezya burst into my pod. We'd been on the spacecraft for months now.

"Ever heard of knocking?" I snapped at him as I grabbed onto the waistband of my towel. Not that the fabric was going to come undone, but more out of habit.

"I had my senses locked on your pod, and I knew you finished showering." He shrugged.

"What's so important that couldn't wait until I was dressed then?"

"We're about to land."

I whipped my head toward the circular window in my pod. To be honest, I hadn't paid attention to anything outside the craft. It all looked the same after the first month.

But now I could glimpse the planet. It was small, barely visible, and I couldn't make out anything but a blur of colors, but it was there.

I knew we were supposed to be landing soon, but I thought it'd take a couple more days.

"Shit," I blew out a breath, running my fingers through my wet hair as adrenaline coursed through me. I wanted nothing more than to get off the ship.

"So get dressed," Tezya repeated. "We should be landing in an hour, and there's a lot we have to do."

I was about to respond when Scotlind entered my pod the next second. Her cheeks instantly flushed as she took me in. "Sorry, Sie. I didn't know you were…"

"It's nothing you haven't seen before." I smirked as the Fire Prince momentarily frowned.

"Like I said, get dressed. Meet us outside your door in two minutes." His voice was calm, but his stance was anything but.

As soon as the door to my pod closed, purple hair flashed in my vision. I was seconds away from dropping my towel… "Shit, Savannah. I told you to stop doing that."

"Doing what?" She smiled as she plopped onto my bed. Well, I guess it was her bed. She made it part of her deal that she got access to my pod, which left me with the uncomfortable as shit floor. And if I thought Tennebris was cold, it was nothing compared to being in space in a craft made entirely of steel.

"You know this would be a perfect time to tell them I'm here," she said as she braided her hair down her back. It was starting to grow past her shoulders from the six months we'd been here.

"No, it's not. No one can know I brought you yet."

Her bottom lip puckered out. "Are we still on that? Tezya just said we're landing in an hour. I highly doubt we have enough fuel for him to turn around and take me back to Earth."

"This craft is run off of electric users like Rainer. We don't need fuel, so yeah, he could."

"Whatever. He wouldn't do that."

"You really want to risk it now?" I asked. "If Tezya decides to send you back, I don't care what deal you and I made, I won't stop him."

She slumped further onto my bed as she crossed her arms. "I'm sick of sneaking around. I wanted to explore the ship without having to hide for once."

Something told me she'd already explored every inch of it. I made it very clear that I wasn't catering to her, and she'd have to fend for herself, which she took seriously.

The fact that she even managed to wander the halls of this place without being seen was beyond me, and she was gone almost every day, only turning up at night to sleep or to piss me off like she was now. And since coming onto *The Miles*, it seemed we weren't going to shy away from technology now that we were attempting to merge both kingdoms, so there were cameras everywhere.

"Turn around," I snapped. "I'm changing."

She shrugged but kept staring, so I entered her mind, which was something I found myself doing often since she became my unwanted roommate. ***Fine, don't turn around.*** I dropped my towel before walking slowly over to my dresser to get a matching onyx set of sweatpants. She gave Tezya a bunch of mortal clothes from Brighta before we took off, and I was surprised by how much I fucking loved them.

I cursed as I went to open the drawer with my right hand out of habit, and the stupid thing wouldn't work. It was temperamental, and so far I could only manage touching my pointer finger to my thumb. Even with Brock's help there was little to no improvement in the stupid appendage. I spent hours doing pointless physical exercises every damn day, but nothing worked.

I grabbed the clothes with my left hand and forced the hoodie over my wet hair. "Stay here. I mean it," I snapped before I opened the door to my pod to meet Scotlind and Tezya outside.

Peter was with them, his green eyes blazing into mine. ***How's the no bread thing going?*** I teased as he bit into what we were told was beef jerky.

Freaking horrible. I'm dying inside, and I can't wait to get off this spacecraft so we can have real food again. I need a dozen warm croissants, no, make that hundreds. I'd eat hundreds of them right now.

I laughed.

"If we aren't landing for another hour, what's so important that you needed me now?"

"We need to make an announcement," Tezya said. "Let everyone know the process when we land. We don't want—"

"Fuck," I cursed as the circular door to my pod slid open, and I knew without looking that Savannah came out into the hall.

Everyone stilled like they were looking at a ghost, and I guess to them they were.

Peter smirked as he looked between me, Savannah, and the door she just came out of. ***Don't even think about fucking saying anything.***

"What is she doing here?" Tezya was fuming, looking directly at me.

"She wanted to come." I shrugged, trying to play it off, but I was going to murder the girl later.

"So you just *let* her?" he seethed.

"Wow. Nice to see you too, Tezya. I missed you so much." She crossed her arms over her chest, and the movement drew my attention to her. She had one of my sweatshirts on, and even though I yelled at her every time she stole my clothes, I was starting to like seeing her in them. I knew she only did it because it was cold as shit in the halls for an Advenian, so being mortal, I couldn't even fathom how she wasn't freezing from the inside out. The sleeves went well past her hands, which she had rolled four times so she could use them.

"Sav, do you realize what you just did by coming here? I told you to stay on Earth, not because I didn't want you to come, but because I wanted you to *live.*"

"What do you mean?" I asked, whipping my head to the Fire Prince.

"Allium was tested to be habitable for *Advenian* life, and while our anatomies are similar, they aren't the same. There's no way to know if she'll survive the moment she steps off the craft."

I turned to look at Savannah, wondering if she knew what she was risking by coming with us.

"Well, there's one way to find out, right?" She attempted to smile.

"Sav, you can die. This isn't just some hike to see something new, and now you're surrounded by Advenians forever. You can't just go back to Earth whenever you're homesick. You can't see Ichi or have ramen. It means no more coffee…"

I didn't bother adding that she snuck a boatload of instant coffee into my pod. She'd been rationing it, and I had no desire to be around her whenever she finally ran out. She already was putting up a hissy fit when she could only have one cup a day instead of her usual three.

"It's not like we aren't used to it, Tez," she said as the sleeve of my sweatshirt rolled down, making it hard to take her seriously. "We've grown up around more Advenians than humans our entire lives."

"*We*…" Tezya growled, and I stilled.

She bit her lip as my gaze turned toward her again. "I may have snuck Wells into the craft too. I couldn't just leave him, and he felt the same way I did."

"You WHAT?" Tezya snapped. "How could you be so stupid, Sav?"

"What did you want us to do? Go join a mortal college and try to blend in with our kind when we're so far from it? You guys are the only family we've ever known, and Wells and I didn't want to lose anyone else."

Tezya glared at me and somehow I knew what he wanted. **What?** I snapped as I opened my mind to him.

You're in charge of them. If she dies, it's on you, and she better not fucking die.

EPILOGUE
PART TWO

Vallie

I HAD no idea why I kept coming down here. Some part of me hated myself for it, another part of me didn't care. Maybe I just couldn't stand to be around everybody else. Maybe I was sick of pretending I was okay.

Kole was in a cell by himself—I was told all the prisoners had their own in the belly of the spacecraft, but I'd only ever visited him. He was leaning against his cage, his head resting against the back wall as he stared up at the ceiling. I was sitting crossed-legged—*outside his cage*—by the door.

"Why did you do it?" I asked him.

"I've done a lot of things, Vallie. You're going to have to be more specific."

I narrowed my eyes. Fine. "Why did you work for the Lux King?"

"That wasn't really my choice. I mean, don't get me wrong, I didn't protest when Synder suggested I was the one to go. But it was before I realized he was a sadistic asshole."

"You're an asshole too."

"Well aware, Valerina. I haven't done much in my life that was good."

I scoffed. At least he knew it. "Why were you so mean to Scottie?" I asked next.

"Why do *you* think?"

"I always thought you had a crush on her," I admitted softly. I looked down at my feet as I said it, not able to meet his gaze.

He started laughing then. "She's pretty, but no, I never liked her like that." I felt his eyes on me, but I refused to look up. I heard him exhale before he said, "I was mean to her simply because I could be mean. There isn't much more to it than that."

"I don't believe you."

"Don't do this, Vallie."

"Do what?"

"Search for things. Try to make connections and find reasons to convince yourself I'm a good person because I'm not. You should kill me."

"I know."

"Are you ever going to then?" he asked.

"I don't know," I admitted softly. When I first started coming down here, that was my intention. I kept telling myself I was working up the courage to kill him, but now I didn't even bring a dagger with me.

I came here today on my own accord.

I finally looked at him again. He was still staring at me, his brown eyes hardening. "You're running out of time."

"Yeah," I sighed, tilting my head up to look at the ceiling. We were supposed to be arriving on Allium any day now, and I couldn't even pretend to be excited about it. It felt wrong to live out my brother's dream, to see everything he worked so hard for come true when he couldn't be here to see it for himself.

Kole sighed, and I felt his gaze leave mine even as my own eyes were glued to the floor in front of me.

"I still hate you, though. Just because I'm not trying to murder you anymore doesn't mean I'm not thinking about it."

He scoffed. "I'm well fucking aware of that, Vallie. You remind me nearly every damn day."

"Good. I don't want you to forget it," I snapped a little too quickly, then I asked, "Why would you let me kill you?" I knew he would. Out of the past six months, I'd been coming down here for five of them. The first two were spent with a dagger in my hand as I stared at him, and I knew he would have let me. I was pretty sure he still would if I wanted to and that realization bothered me because I didn't. I realized month four that I didn't want Kole dead, and I hated myself for it. I couldn't even understand why I didn't want to kill him anymore.

"Even if you don't kill me, I don't have a life here anymore." He gestured to the cage surrounding him and then at the chains on his wrists. "You'd be saving me from misery."

"Well, if I have to be miserable, so do you."

He looked at me then. "You don't have to be miserable, Vallie. You can have a new life. Start over and be fucking happy."

I scoffed. It was what everyone kept telling me. Everyone except Kallon. *Move on*—it was what they all kept thinking, but I couldn't.

"Everything I ever wanted is gone. I can't even—" I stopped talking. I could feel the tears well in my eyes. What I was about to say, it was something I never admitted to anyone.

"You can't have kids," he finished for me. My eyes flared as I met his gaze. He was already staring at me, watching me. I wasn't sure if he ever looked away.

"How did you know?" I haven't been able to talk about it, especially not to Peter.

The only people I could stand to have a conversation with were Scottie and Kole, and it was only because they were both there. They saw everything. I didn't have to explain. But every time I looked at my best friend, I kept seeing my brother's face burn off. So Kole became my only option.

"Aside from seeing the two scars Semander gave you across your hips?" He shrugged. "I knew the King wouldn't have ra—*done anything* to you without eliminating all consequences, and I'm sorry, Vallie. I'm sorry for everything that happened to you. He never should have touched you."

I was crying now. "The worst part isn't that he haunts my *past*. It's that he took away my *future*... I wanted..." I couldn't finish as the sobs wrecked me. I wanted to be a mother so badly, and now I couldn't. He took everything from me. He took my twin, the family I already had, and now he took away any chances of me having more. I was alone. And I was empty.

Kole was silent as I kept crying and crying, and once I started, I couldn't stop. I wasn't sure how long I sobbed, but at some point my tears dried and my head ached, making it hard to think about anything but the pain.

"I think it's for the best," I finally said. I pulled my legs to my chest now, resting my head on my knees.

"Why?"

"Because if I had kids, even decades later, I'm not sure I'd be able to handle it if they had red hair... If they had *his* hair..."

"You might not see it now, but you're going to get through this, Vallie—"

"I can't even look in a mirror, Kole. I can't stand my own reflection." If I wasn't seeing the parts of Miles in me, I was seeing what the King did to my body... "How am I supposed to move on when I can't even do something as simple as that?"

"It doesn't matter if your hair is red or if you keep dyeing it black. Fuck mirrors. You don't need—"

I jolted as the door to the pod opened, cutting Kole off. I was on my feet in an instant, wiping my tears that were long gone.

My eyes met green ones—Peter. He looked between us, and I knew he was trying to mask a frown. He found out I'd been coming down here a month ago, and instead of talking to me about it, he ignored it. It was driving me insane.

"We're about to land," Peter said. His hand was still on the door, and I saw his knuckles turning white. I knew he hated this—hated that I kept coming down here. "I thought you'd want to be with everyone when we do."

I nodded. I didn't say goodbye to Kole or even acknowledge him as I followed Peter out.

I could feel Peter glancing at me as we walked up the steel stairs leading toward the rest of the ship. It wasn't until we were well out of earshot from the dungeons that Peter whispered, "You should stop visiting him."

I whirled on him. He didn't want to talk about it for the past month, but now all of a sudden he was going to demand I stop going? He didn't get to tell me what I could and couldn't do.

"You don't control me—" I started, but he cut me off.

"Vallie," he said gently, "he could be playing with you. He knows he messed up and is probably looking for a way out."

"He's not," I snapped before I even realized it. I wasn't even sure if I believed it myself. Kole probably *was* using me, and I was just too hurt to see it or even care.

He reached out, placing his hand on my shoulder, and I flinched.

My heart was beating erratically in my chest, and I couldn't calm my breathing... I was back in the King's bedroom, feeling things that weren't my own...

"Shit," Peter cursed, immediately pulling his hand away. "I'm so sorry, Vallie. I didn't mean to... I'm so freaking sorry."

"It's—okay." My voice was trembling, and I think my hands were shaking more.

Peter wasn't buying it.

He sighed. "If seeing him helps you, then fine. Even if I hate it, I'm not going to stop you. But you shouldn't do it alone anymore, Vallie. He's dangerous."

I didn't answer him. I didn't know how. I knew I was hurting Peter, but I couldn't help it.

He tried to smile, his voice softening. "Come on. Everyone is going to the back of the ship for landing. We need to hurry so we don't miss it."

I flexed my fingers at my sides. Breathing in and out slowly before I followed him again.

I glanced at Peter before he opened the door to the back. I wanted to say something to him, but before I could, voices hit me, and I was greeted by everyone.

There was a large window along the length of the wall and an even larger hatch door that I knew was going to open the second we landed.

I gasped, frozen in the doorway. For months and months anytime I looked out the windows all I saw was endless black and a splatter of stars...

But not anymore.

Allium was in view. It was a mix of green and blue and tan and some darker shades of brown toward the bottom. My hand clutched my chest as it ached for Miles.

He did this. He made this possible. He should be here, seeing this...

"I still can't believe you came," Kallon said to someone, interrupting my downward spiral. "I mean, I'm happy to see you, but jeez."

"I'm my own person, Kal," a female snapped back, and I recognized the voice—I'd trained with her back on Brighta for months.

"Savannah," I said in disbelief as I turned to look at her. Her lavender hair was pulled into a braid, and she was wearing sweatpants that were too big on her.

"Hey, Val." She smiled at me.

"What are you doing here?" I asked.

"Sie made a deal with me." She shrugged. "So he had to bring me." The latter rolled his eyes but didn't comment. Tezya looked half furious, half worried.

"A deal that's going to kill her," Dovelyn snapped. The princess had her arms crossed as she stared us down.

"What do you mean?"

Tezya answered for her. "We don't know if the atmosphere is adaptable to humans."

"Well, like I said, there's only one way to find out." The human grinned, and I couldn't help but smile back. Other than Kole, she was the only other person I liked being around. She didn't coddle me or treat me differently, and since everyone knew what I went through—

everyone looked at me like I was going to break, but Savannah would say things exactly as they were. I found it refreshing.

"I'm glad you're here," I said and meant it. With her here, I could train again. I could have someone else to talk to. I wouldn't have to sneak around in the dungeons anymore. I could forget about Kole and the past five months...

Savannah winked before turning toward the window. Clouds parted as the ship was starting to sink, and I felt my breath leave me. This was it. The area we were hovering over was mostly green as we sank lower and lower into the atmosphere, into our new home.

I looked at Savannah as soon as the hatch opened. She stepped forward before anyone could stop her.

I watched in disbelief as she stepped into Allium and took a deep breath.

Thank you so much for taking a chance on Lake of Sapphire and making it this far in the Allium Series. Scotlind's story is finished, but this is not the last book in the world!

Reading order for the Allium Series

Lake of Sapphire
Ocean of Silver
Illusion of Hazel
River of Lavender

————

Want more of my books? Check out Hunted by the Dead King—a dark Hercules retelling with dragons.

Hunted by the Dead King

————

The Allium Series in an all new format—check out the Advenian Omnibus—includes all four books in a new cover with interior color for the physical version. Available in paperback & ebook.

ACKNOWLEDGMENTS

To Rin. Many hours of editing this book consisted of you sitting on my lap while I wrote it with one hand, and I wouldn't have it any other way. I can't even begin to express how much you mean to me. I don't want to be in any world without you in it. I love you forever, Rin Manning. I love you. I love you more. I love you the most. You are my heart walking outside my body.

To Anthony. My love. My husband. My soulmate. My best friend. My everything. There are bits of you in Sie and Tezya. I am so happy and grateful that you are mine, and I am yours. I love the character you made in this story—Ichihana—and every time I wrote him, it made me smile. Thank you for always supporting and encouraging me with my writing. You have always embraced and celebrated every little moment throughout this journey and it means so much to me. Here's to always being dreamers together and going after what we want. *My home is wherever you are, for helping me find my strength, I will choose you in every lifetime.*

To Nari. My soul dog. You are my OG writing buddy, and even though you can't read, I just wanted to say that I love you so much! Thank you for always hanging out by my desk and keeping me company while I write. I love you.

To my mom. Thank you for always supporting me, for reading my books and helping me even 3,000 miles away. I will always cherish our proofreading trips together, and I appreciate you more than I can ever express. I love you so much, and I thank God every day that you are my mom.

To my dad. I love you so much. Thank you for reading all my books (even though I think there are a few chapters you should skip). Having amazing parents who encourage, support, and guide me has shaped who I am today. Your confidence and love has allowed me to take risks and pursue my dreams. Thank you for being my role model and the best dad a girl could ask for.

To my Nana. Thank you for always reading my books and all your help with editing them. I appreciate your feedback and cherish all of your support. Thank you for loving my story and characters. I love you with all my heart! Hugs n Kisses.

To my family—my immediate and extended. Thank you for always supporting me and helping spread my story with the world. To anyone who has listened to me ramble on and on about my book—thank you (and I'm sorry). I love you all so much, and I feel so fortunate to come from such an amazing and supportive background. To my family members who have given this book a shot and read it—even if it wasn't your genre—thank you! I can't begin to describe how grateful I am and how loved it makes me feel. I love you all so much!

To my sisters and brother. I feel like the luckiest girl in the world to have you three for siblings. Thank you all for supporting me on this journey and for all your help along the way. I love you.

To Cassie. I can't express how grateful I am to know you. I feel like we are so similar and that I found myself in a best friend. I'm a huge introvert, and you are one of the few people that refuel my well instead of drain it. Thank you for reading all my books and for all your feedback. You have helped shaped my books into what they are, and because of your input, they are so much better. Now I just need you to move across the country so we can go on mom bookish dates together with our daughters.

To Ashlynn. I am so happy I met you last year. It has been so amazing having you as a writing friend and critique partner. Thank you for all your support with Lake of Sapphire and for all your help with Ocean of Silver, Illusion of Hazel, and River of Lavender. I love our long—*rambling*—phone chats, and thanks for always answering my "odd" author texts.

To Lana. I cherish our friendship so much, and I love having you as a book bestie! I always trust your judgement on what to read and it means the world to me when you take the time to read my books. I can't thank you enough (and Cheese too). I always feel like my books aren't ready until after you read them. I don't know how I got so lucky to have met you!

To Hailey. I have been editing this book from the moment I met you. I am so happy we became friends, and I have a writing and reading bestie on the West Coast. I love and cherish all our writing days, and I'm so excited to finally work on something new when we hangout!

A special thanks to all my high school best friends, but especially Natalie, Katy, and Steph. You all have read every single thing I wrote before it was published and have helped me so much. I love you, and I feel like the luckiest girl ever to have met my best friends early in life.

To the bookclubs who have read my books. Thank you to the B.A.B. Bookclub and my Aunt Robin. You were the first to ever host me and it continues to mean so much to me that you do the same for each book I write. Thank you for all your support and love. Thank you to the Bayou Beer and Book Club and Kyle Schaeffer for reading my story and hosting me. It has been such a surreal experience and means so much that you included me. Thank you!

Thank you Brittany Uller from The Author Experience for proofreading my book! I can't thank you enough for everything you have done for Illusion of Hazel and River of Lavender.

To my beta readers. I could cry with how much you all mean to me. I feel so blessed to know each and every one of you. Thank you so much from the bottom of my heart for helping me with this entire series. I love you all. Cassie Stockwell, Lana Gooch, Ashlynn Caudle, Colleen Hill, Kelly Pepper, Kasey Benjamin, Natalie Hague, Katy Farrell, Corinne Staub, Mary Benjamin, Stephanie Berardi, Madison Obritz, Lisa Worthy, Carter Benjamin, Nancy Kohutka, Robin Benjamin, Michelle Bradham, Victoria A. Richardson, Sara A. Miller, and Sabrina Nunn.

To anyone who has read my books. If you made it this far, thank you so much! It brings me so much joy and makes everything worth-while whenever anyone loves one of my characters and/or story. Thank you for giving Lake of Sapphire and the entire series a chance.

Scotlind's story is finished, but this is not the last book in this world!

ALSO BY MALLORY

THE ALLIUM SERIES

Lake of Sapphire

Ocean of Silver

Illusion of Hazel

River of Lavender

ALLIUM COLLECTION

Advenian Omnibus

IMMORTAL HUNTERS

Hunted by the Dead King

ABOUT THE AUTHOR

Mallory graduated from Penn State with her bachelor's in nursing and spent eight years working as a nurse before becoming a full-time author and mama. You can usually find her drafting stories, chasing her toddler around the house, and surviving on energy drinks. When she isn't completely consumed by imaginary worlds and fictional characters, she's spending time with her family, capturing everyday moments through a camera lens, or treating herself to buffalo wings.